THE READYMADE THIEF

Augustus Rose is a novelist and screenwriter. He was born in the northern California coastal town of Bolinas, and grew up there and in San Francisco. He lives in Chicago with his wife, the novelist Nami Mun, and their son, and teaches fiction writing at the University of Chicago.

THE
READYMADE
THIEF

Augustus Rose

WILLIAM HEINEMANN: LONDON

1 3 5 7 9 10 8 6 4 2

William Heinemann
20 Vauxhall Bridge Road
London SW1V 2SA

William Heinemann is part of the Penguin Random House group of companies
whose addresses can be found at global.penguinrandomhouse.com.

Penguin
Random House
UK

First published in Great Britain by William Heinemann in 2017
First published in the United States by Viking in 2017

www.penguin.co.uk

Frontispiece: 'Typo / Topography of Marcel Duchamp's Large Glass,' 2003,
by Richard Hamilton (1922–2011). Purchased 2004. Artwork © R. Hamilton.
All rights reserved, DACS and ARS 2017. Photo © Tate, London 2016.

A CIP catalogue record for this book is available from the British Library.

ISBN 9781785150975 (Hardcover)
ISBN 9781785150982 (Trade paperback)

Interior design by Spring Hoteling

Printed and bound by Clays Ltd, St Ives plc

Penguin Random House is committed to a sustainable future
for our business, our readers and our planet. This book is made
from Forest Stewardship Council® certified paper.

MIX
Paper from
responsible sources
FSC
www.fsc.org   FSC® C018179

For Nami and Auggie, my illuminators

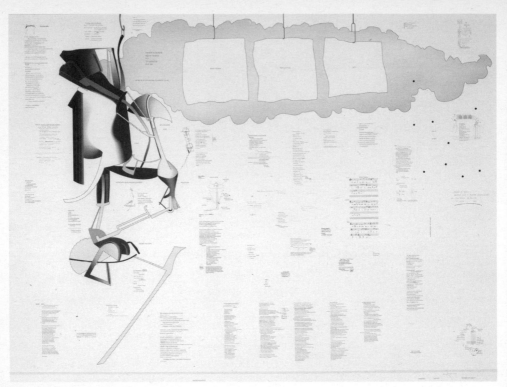

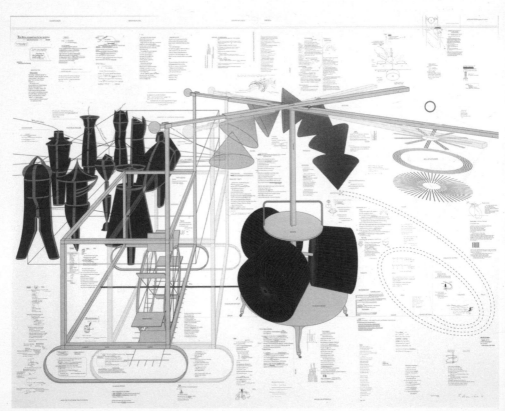

There is no solution, because there is no problem.

—MARCEL DUCHAMP

PROLOGUE

TO make your way to the DePaul Aquarium and Museum of Natural History, on Petty Island in the middle of the Delaware River, you can drive through New Jersey and over the only bridge. But then you'll be confronted by a CITGO guard and will either have to social-engineer your way in (and good luck with that) or be forced to turn around and go back. Better to temporarily liberate a small boat from one of the old piers on the Philly side and row the half mile across the river. Once on the island, you'll want to avoid the large shipping lot—busy with dockworkers in the daytime and prowled at night by a se-curity cruiser—and instead cut through the wetlands to the southern end of the island. The aquarium stands nearly solitary amid a village of bulldozed foundations, one of two preserved relics from an aborted 1960s attempt to turn the island into some sort of tourist attraction. The other is the Blizzard, a rusting megalith of a roller coaster that silhouettes the night sky. The aquarium—a long, low-slung, single-story building—hunkers in its shadow.

Entry to the unguarded aquarium is straightforward. Although the front gate and the doors are chained shut, climbing the stone wall on the eastern side is not hard, and there is a loading dock around back whose steel door has been pried open at the bottom. Inside you're free to shine your flashlight at will, letting it trail over the rows of empty tanks, some with bone-whitened coral and ersatz reef displays still intact. You can climb down into the alligator pit and crawl into old burrows or over rocks coated in a patina of dried algae. A row of life-sized plaster shark models still hangs above the entrance lobby, fins and tails cracked but otherwise complete. The fossils are gone from the Paleozoic Room, but one display remains intact: a Cambrian ocean diorama of faded plastic models—orange trilobites, green nautiluses, sea slugs, kelp, and anemones, a frozen, surreal arena of underwater plants and feverishly imagined bugs.

It is in this room that Lee has spent hours, losing herself in the diorama every time she visits the derelict aquarium. She imagines that this must be what scuba diving feels like: isolate in an alien seascape. Tomi, the other member of the Philadelphia Urbex Society (membership: two), is not with her tonight, because tonight she needs to be away from Tomi and his endless talk, his name-dropping arcane art movements—Fluxus and Lettrism, Pataphysics and Situationist Psychogeography—his insatiable craving for her attention.

Urban exploration is not the safest of recreations, especially not for a single female, especially a female as slight and—as Tomi once (but only once) put it—as *elfin* as Lee, but she feels safer here than at other sites. The sheer remoteness makes the aquarium uninhabitable by squatters, as testified by the dearth of graffiti or other vandalism. She supposes that one of the Petty Island guards could potentially come by, but it is unlikely: the aquarium is not part of CITGO property (the whole wetlands area of the island is under heavy dispute between environmentalists and local developers), and by nature security guards are incurious and lazy.

Now she sits on an old wooden office chair she's commandeered from behind the cashier's desk, staring past the pregnancy test stick in her hand at the little plastic seascape, the broken fronds and wilted arthropods, all now faded and cracked, and thinks about the tiny thing growing inside her. Lee knows who the father is, though she has no intention of telling him. The thing inhabits some subterranean cave of her body, floating in amniotic silence, just waiting to emerge and wreak havoc on Lee's life. All her hopes and plans—a life made by her own choices, even a chance at college—snuffed before that life can take in its first breath. Unless she snuffs the thing inside her first. That is the real question hovering before her right now, occupying space in the diorama tank, somewhere between the *Wiwaxia* and the *Hallucigenia*.

The thing is thirty-three days old—she knows the exact moment of its conception—and so she doesn't have long to decide what to do or the decision will be made for her. Lee stares into the glass tank a while longer, stares without seeing, until a single object begins to come into focus behind the field of molded prehistoric kelp: a rolled strip of paper, what can only be described as a tiny scroll, tied with a lock of what looks like human hair and propped up in the green plastic tentacles of a Cambrian anemone. Breaking one of the two cardinal rules of the Urbex Society—Take Nothing, Leave Nothing—Lee reaches in through the back of the tank and plucks out the scroll. The hair, black and long, snaps when she pulls on it, and the paper unfurls in her fingers. Lee flattens it with her palms onto the glass top of the tank and stares at it for several seconds, trying to comprehend its intent. Because she understands immediately upon seeing the photograph that it has been left for her. Which means the Station Master has found her.

She's seen the photograph before, hanging above the desk in his room, and Lee studies the woman in it closely now. The photo is very old; the brittle paper crumbles a bit in her hands. She brings it to the bathroom, holds it up beside her head as she stands in front of the cracked mirror, and shines her flashlight. It is like looking back in time to another version of herself, a visage that has changed only slightly as it echoed through the decades. She and the woman in the photo look nearly identical. Lee turns it over. Penciled along a top corner in a fluid European script is "A.T. Juli 1911." Below that is the now-familiar cryptogram, still unsolved after nearly a century. And below the cryptogram is a short note in the crabbed handwriting of the Station Master:

Return what you have taken.

· BOOK I ·

Dust Breeding

ONE

LEE was just six the first time she stole something. Deposited by her mother at a birthday party to socialize with kids she barely knew and hardly liked, she secreted herself in the bedroom closet of the birthday girl's parents during a game of hide-and-seek. Lee was a tiny child, mostly silent and near invisible anyway, so hiding was easy, and the game was a good chance to be alone. She stayed in the closet a very long time—lingering well after the other kids had moved on to other games—and, while there, she discovered a box covered in faded green velvet and tied with old twine. Something inside rattled when she shook the box. Lee didn't intend to open it, but then her finger caught in the loop of the bow and the twine just kind of fell loose.

Inside the box was a stack of yellowing letters held together by more twine, a painted iron toy steamship, an old wooden pipe, and the source of the rattling: a small glass bottle with something trapped inside. Lee crouched there, listening to the shrieks of the other kids and holding the bottle up to what dim shafts of light came in through the slats, trying to guess what was inside. When she heard her mother calling her name, she panicked—stuffing the bottle in her pocket, then pushing the box back below the pile of sweaters where she'd found it. As Lee followed her mother through the house and out to the car, she realized it was late, well after dark, and all the other kids' parents had come and gone. Her mother held the back door open as she climbed in, and Lee's father turned to her from the front seat and gave her one of his smiles, the smile he used when he'd screwed up, and handed her a partially eaten chocolate bar. "Did you have a nice time, honey?" he asked her, but Lee's answer was caught in the slam of her mother's door. They were silent the whole ride home. That night Lee tented herself beneath her covers with a flashlight, then took the object out and examined it again. The bottle was blue glass clouded with age. Lee felt a twang of guilt at having taken something that was not hers. But when it rattled in her hand, a surge of pleasure ran down her spine. She had to hold the bottle up to the light to see the tiny silver die inside.

When Lee would come home after school, her mother would be at work, but her father was usually there. Sometimes he'd be in the driveway, working on his old Dodge Dart, its hood up, and he'd let her sit up on the fender, her feet dangling into the engine compartment as she'd hold the carburetor or distributor in her hands and he'd explain what all the parts were. When it was running, he'd sometimes take her out for a drive and even let her sit in his lap and steer on the byroad straightaways.

Often when she'd come home, the house would be full of her father's friends, people from the local music scene and the occasional semifamous bassist or ex-drummer from this or that band passing through whom Lee was too young to recognize. Her father worked an irregular schedule, inspecting and repairing hospital x-ray machines, but really he was a singer-songwriter and musician. He put out a self-titled album with an indie label a year before Lee was born, and sometimes he was invited onstage to perform on a song during some band's show, but he never made a living off of any of it. His friends all said he could have been another Elliott Smith, if only his life had gone a little differently.

Her father had a disarming smile that softened any room he entered, and people naturally gravitated to him, the center of some subtle magnetic force. Lee loved coming home to a crowded living room, where she could sit in a corner unnoticed and listen to the stories. She loved watching her father especially, seated in his usual spot at the end of the sofa, staring down at his socks as someone would be telling some tale of loss or excess. And she loved watching others watch him, as her father would inevitably look up, smile from the corner of his mouth, and deadpan some line that Lee rarely understood beyond the fact that it would set everyone else in the room off laughing.

As though through some unspoken understanding, the visitors always left a good half hour before her mother, a nurse, returned home. By which time her father would (with Lee's help) have the errant glasses collected and washed and put away, and some semblance of dinner going. On one occasion they'd missed a few glasses that had been set down in a planter, and her mom had taken her aside and asked if anyone had been over. Seeing no reason to lie, Lee told her yes, a few of Dad's friends were here.

"What were they doing?"

"Just hanging out and drinking grapefruit juice and talking."

As soon as Lee said this, her mom's jaw set, and she walked to the kitchen and placed the two glasses on the counter above the dishwasher. Lee understood that it was for her father to find—a simple, direct message that her mom knew.

They argued that night, Lee could hear it from her room, and she never understood what could have been so bad about drinking juice with your friends or why her mom was always so wound up and angry. Her father wasn't around in the morning and didn't come back for several days, but this brief vanishing act was something he did all the time, and Lee was used to it.

Lee was seven when her father left for good, disappearing without a word. She simply came home from school one day to a house that felt different. Lee looked around without landing on anything until she went into her parents' bedroom and saw that all her father's stuff was gone, emptied from the drawers and the closet and the top of the dresser. The bathroom was clear of his things as well.

He'd taken more than he usually did, but Lee still expected him to return after a few days. When five days passed, then a week, she asked her mom.

Her mom looked down at her dispassionately. "He might come back tomorrow, or he might never come back. I can't tell you which. I think you'd better just get used to it."

"Where did he go this time?"

"I wish I knew."

Her mom said nothing more about it, though as the days, then weeks, and then months passed and it seemed finally clear that her father wasn't coming home or even sending a letter, Lee could see her mother crumble, bit by bit, from the inside. Some nights Lee could hear crying behind the closed door of their bedroom, until she didn't anymore; but by then her mother seemed emptied out entirely. Lee liked to listen to her father's CD sometimes when she came home from school, before her mother got off work. It was sad and funny at the same time, scratchy and full of longing, and Lee liked the way she felt when she listened to it. One day she came home to find it gone.

At eight she stole a glossy black paintbrush from the desk drawer of Mrs. Choi, her pretty English teacher, who used it to keep her hair bunned. At nine Lee slipped things from the backpacks of her peers: pencil cases and charm bracelets and sticker books. At ten she made a game of trying to steal one thing from each of the kids in her class:

pens and mittens and colored Nalgene drinking bottles, never any-thing of real value. She kept her swag in a box in her closet, and sometimes she would lay it all out on the floor of her room. It was the only way she used any of it. Lee didn't consider any of the kids friends. It wasn't that they teased her or ostracized her or thought her weird, but none of them seemed to see her, either. Holding these objects in her hands allowed her to imagine something like closeness.

Her mom became a palimpsest. She had erased herself a layer at a time, until only the dim outline of who she was remained. Every now and then the mom Lee knew would emerge to celebrate her daughter's birthday or Christmas, and she made sure the bills were paid and that food was on the table, but mostly she was gone. Lee hated her for her slow retreat into herself, for leaving Lee behind. Her mom's hours at the hospital kept Lee from seeing her much anyway, but even when she was around, Lee felt she could almost see through her.

So when she told Lee, now twelve, that she was bringing a friend home for dinner, Lee didn't know what to think. Steve was the opposite of her father. He wore a white linen tunic and crisp linen pants and white canvas slip-on shoes. Around his neck was a leather cord tied around a pale crystal. His hands were soft when he shook Lee's, and when he saw her looking at one of the half-dozen braided colored-leather bracelets he wore on his wrist, he took one off and gave it to her. Lee smiled thank you and put it in her pocket. Over dinner he asked her a few bland questions about school, wiping his hands and the corners of his mouth after every bite.

He came by more and more frequently and sometimes stayed over. Steve didn't talk much, and when he did, it was often in whispers to Lee's mom. He moved in so stealthily that Lee didn't realize he had until she noticed he'd set up a small meditation area in the corner of the living room, with a floor pillow, a mandala on the wall, and a small bowl of incense. Lee would often come home to the smell of that incense, Steve facing the wall with his back to her. He asked her to join him one time, and she did, but Lee didn't understand what he wanted her to do. How was she supposed to empty her mind when it was constantly filling back up?

At thirteen Lee stuffed a vintage Misfits T-shirt into her backpack because she had seen a girl in the store admiring it. When she wore it to school, a boy mumbled "Cool shirt" as he passed, which left a ringing in her ears. The next day she dropped the folded shirt on the cafeteria table in front of the boy. The gesture had taken every ounce of nerve she could muster, and she felt dizzy with it as she walked away. He never said another word to her, but the day after, another boy gave her ten bucks to get one for him, and a business was born.

Soon she was regularly taking orders from her classmates, anything from jeans to jewelry to CDs. She'd hit the boutiques and department stores on Walnut Street in downtown Philly, shop small and steal big, then sell the stuff for a third the price. The money—loose change and wadded bills—she pushed into a hole in her father's old guitar case. Lee's tastes were simple—jeans and hoodies and Chuck Taylors—and so she had little to spend the money on. It wasn't about the money. Stealing scratched a locationless, tingling itch in her.

At fourteen she stole a stack of blank birth certificates from the hospital where her mother worked, along with a stamp of the hospital's seal. She laid the sheets out on her roof, exposing them to several days of sunlight, and aged them with coffee grounds until they looked like they'd been sitting in a drawer for twenty years. Then she sold them to her classmates for a hundred dollars apiece so that they could use them to obtain fake IDs at the DMV. This earned her the attention of Edie Oswald. Pale and athletic, tall without being gawky, Edie had a face that looked as though it had been carved from marble by some Renaissance genius. She carried herself with the ease and insouciance bestowed by a life of privilege and was the only girl in school who could dress like a 1960s socialite one day, an early-'80s punk the next, and get away with it.

"Can I bum one?" Edie asked.

Lee was standing against the wall outside the gym where no one ever came, the remains of a sandwich on the ground by her feet. She fished a cigarette from her pack and handed it to Edie, then helped light it with her own.

"I've been looking all over school for you. For a while I thought you might be one of those gone kids."

Over the past few months seven teenagers from the Philadelphia area—two from their school—had simply disappeared without a trace. One of them showed up again a few weeks later, a fifteen-year-old boy from a foster home in the suburbs, but he was still gone. His eyes were engorged and depthless, and it was as though his consciousness had been scooped out—he'd lost the ability to communicate and responded only to simple commands. Lee hadn't known any of them, but she knew Edie did; one of them had run with her crowd.

"So this is your spot, huh?" Edie looked around the patch of dirty grass and wrappers and cigarette butts as though it were Lee's living room.

The buzz of Edie's recognition left Lee mute. To be seen by Edie Oswald was to suddenly exist.

Edie pointed to a bit of graffiti, a cartoon stick figure with a cock rammed through its mouth and out the back of its head. "That one of yours?"

Lee took this opportunity to stare into Edie's unblinking green eyes. Edie had a jagged black bob and a mouth that was always turned up at one corner as though perennially on the verge of amusement. Lee understood she was supposed to say something clever back, but the moment for that had passed, and now there was just awkwardness.

They stared out across the football field. Lee watched a kid arc out for a long pass and stretch his arms, only to have the ball drop through his hands. Edie wasn't the kind of girl who needed to go trawling for friends, so Lee knew the score: within a minute or so Edie would ask her for something. She began counting in her head: one, two, three, four, five . . .

"I hear you can get things," Edie said.

Five. The girl was to the point, Lee had to give her that. She looked down at her cigarette.

"So how's it work?" Edie flicked her cigarette away. "You take orders or what?"

Edie asked for a green cashmere sweater with abalone buttons from Bloomingdale's. She even had a picture, and Lee couldn't help but be a little thrilled when Edie texted it to her—they now had each other's numbers on their phones. Edie probably had hundreds of numbers on hers, but not Lee. Lee now had twelve.

What Lee didn't expect was that a few days later, after she had delivered the sweater, Edie would invite her over to her house after school. They ended up drinking from Edie's parents' liquor cabinet and gossiping about the kids in school Lee only ever watched from afar. Edie asked Lee things no one had ever thought to ask her— about what she wanted to do after high school, where in the world she most wanted to visit, what kind of man her father was—and Lee realized she didn't know how to answer these simple questions. She had never talked to anyone about her father and did not know how to start. She asked Edie about hers, and Edie lit up when she spoke of him: what an important man he was and all the places he took her. She talked about where she wanted to go to college, and when she asked Lee about it, it was as though Edie were asking what pro basketball team Lee wanted to play for. Lee was silent. Edie drunkenly put one finger to the mole above Lee's lip and seemed about to say something, then just giggled.

This is what it must be like, Lee thought as she walked home, drunk on Edie's attention even more than the booze, to have a friend.

They began hanging out more and more after that, and Edie was careful to ask Lee for things only occasionally, insisting on paying her even when Lee would refuse her money. Lee took notice of Edie's taste, and she couldn't help stealing for her the more-than-occasional gift. Her feelings for Edie were as formless as a weather pattern. All Lee knew was that she tingled under Edie's attention and sometimes placed herself in Edie's path after school in the hope that Edie would collect her. With this friendship came an acceptance into Edie's crowd, and before long Lee found herself invited to parties and out to clubs.

For the first time she went to a school dance. She gave Edie the combination to her locker, because it was near the gym and accessible, and Edie stashed a few booze-filled bottles of Coke there earlier in the day. Drunk and emboldened, Lee even danced, awkwardly bouncing around with the kids in Edie's crowd—her crowd now, too, Lee reminded herself—listening in as they gossiped and gave each other shit about who was fucking whom behind whose back and who'd pissed on whose toothbrush. But for Lee the highlight of the dance took place in the bathroom with Edie, as they sat up high by the windows and shared a joint. When she was with Edie, it was as if Lee were the only person on Earth; Edie focused in so totally, with such sincere interest, that Lee felt herself seen in a way she never had before.

"What do you think of Danny Poole?" Edie asked her.

She hadn't much noticed this boy from Edie's crowd, except that sometimes Lee would feel herself being stared at, though he always looked away when she turned. Lee tried to see him through Edie's virescent eyes.

"He likes you," Edie said.

"He told you that?"

"I can tell. You want to go out with me and Deke sometime? The four of us could have some fun."

Deke was Edie's boyfriend. He dressed like a headbanger and played guitar in a metal band but drove his parents' Infiniti and wore four-hundred-dollar boots. Lee felt as though she'd been chosen. "Sure," she said. Why not.

"Cool. I'll set it up." Then Edie reached into her purse and took out a folded Kleenex. She unwrapped it, revealing two powder-filled gel caps. Edie held them out until Lee took one. She waited for Edie to go first, then swallowed the one in her hand.

"What did we just take?"

"Molly-olly-oxen-free!" Edie trilled.

Lee had never taken Ecstasy before. "What's it feel like?"

"You're about to find out." Edie hopped down from the window, and Lee followed her back into the dance.

Lee didn't remember much about that first time; it just got swallowed up with all the other times. She did remember dancing in a way that felt as fluid as a river. She remembered a sensation of pure joy, and she remembered the people all having auras, trembling outlines that she kept trying to touch. Mostly she remembered going home with Edie that night, sharing Edie's bed and the feel of Edie's skin against hers, Edie's fingers tickling up and down her back, Edie's eyes on her own.

"Why'd you choose me?" Lee asked her, the drug making all questions suddenly possible. "You can have . . . you can hang out with anyone in school you want. Your friends, they wouldn't have anything to do with me if you hadn't taken me in."

Edie's eyes were softening with sleep, but when she opened them wide again, Lee thought she could see herself reflected in the pupils. "You want to know what's special about you."

It made her feel stupid to hear it phrased that way, but yes, Lee supposed that is what she wanted to know.

Edie was silent for a moment. "When I was nine, I found a little baby bird. It couldn't have been more than a week old, but it had all its feathers and it was walking around in drunken little circles on the sidewalk. So I bundled it up in my jacket and took it home, made a nest in a cardboard box, and fed it seeds and ladybugs and Cheerios. It was the first thing I woke up to every morning, and every day after school I rushed home to take care of it."

"You think I need rescuing?" Lee asked.

Edie looked at her with a mix of affection and pity. "The first time I saw you, I wanted to bundle you up and take you home with me. You're so pretty, a beautiful little bird, but you look so lost, Lee—anyone with a heart would want to do the same."

Lee thought about how to take this. She wanted to be seen, especially by Edie, as strong and capable of handling herself, but the drug was making her so velvety inside, it was hard not to smile. "What happened to the bird?" she asked.

But Edie was already asleep.

Lee was used to being invisible, she had been her whole life, so it wasn't easy to know what to do with the spotlight, even if she was only taking up the diffuse edge of the light shined on Edie. The drugs helped. White powders and blue pills and yellow pills, little red plasticky stars, mossy purplish weed laced with crystals, things snorted and smoked and ingested. Stimulants and sedatives and entactogens and dissociatives and psychotropics and hallucinogens. Things that made her at once open up into the world and sink so deeply inside herself that she grew scared she'd never find her way out. Meth made her jerk and flop on the inside like a windup mechanical toy. Ecstasy made her oozy with love. Ketamine made her float. Oxy wrapped her in a warm, steamy blanket. Soon enough she was trading stolen goods for drugs, and soon after that for drugs in bulk, which she sold to the kids in her crowd.

Danny Poole turned out to be a nice boy, shy but thoughtful. He played drums in Deke's band. Lee could tell that he mistook her disconnection for shyness like his own and saw an affinity where there wasn't one. But she liked having him around all the same, and for several months they went to movies together and got drunk together and had clumsy, gawky sex that turned sweet with time.

Lee honestly didn't know what to feel when he broke up with her, in a long handwritten letter, which he made sure to point out was blurry with his tears. The letter detailed how much he cared about her, how he even thought he might *love* her (at least that is what Lee thought she could read within the big blue smudge), but that they were just too similar—"too shy together and too silent together"—and that he felt as alone with her as he did by himself.

Lee couldn't bring herself to feel much of anything, though she missed those nights they would sit together in his room, wordlessly playing some drinking game until they were buzzed enough to fumble toward each other.

Life went on, and Lee remained the go-to girl for drugs and stolen merchandise. All the money she made she stuffed into the hole in the guitar case, until it became too full to squeeze in another wad. And so, for the first time in nearly four years, she opened it. The money fell out onto her bed in a big green pile of bills: crumpled bills, folded bills, rolled bills, wadded bills, a geological strata of bills—the smaller denominations, from when she'd just started out, at the bottom; the larger ones layering the top. The pile had an earthy, fungal smell. To get the money back into the case, she sorted the bills and flattened them and bundled them, counting as she did, feeling her hands grow a filmy layer of dry mold. By the end she had just over twenty thousand dollars, an amount of money Lee could hardly fathom. She began to feel like getting out was really possible; that she might actually make something of her life. College, maybe, something she and her mother had never even discussed.

Lee was apprehended for shoplifting at sixteen, pinched in a Nordstrom by an undercover security guard she'd marked but had taken for oblivious. He led her by the arm through the store, the evidence—one crumpled teal cashmere cardigan—draped casually over his shoulder. She felt the eyes of the shoppers on her in a way they never had been before, and burned with shame.

The store security called her mother and involved the police as well, and though they did not press charges, the police made her aware that the incident would remain on her record and that a second arrest would entail real consequences. Lee promised that she had never stolen before and would never do it again. Her mother didn't speak to her at all except to ask her, in the parking lot on the way to the car, what the hell she wanted with a sweater like that? Did Lee think they were country club people?

The second time she was caught came only a month later, and the police threatened to throw the book at her, chuck her into a juvenile detention center and see how she fared with a little structure in her life. Her mother had begged them to give Lee another chance, had described the disappearance of Lee's father and how tough the years had been on both of them.

Lee's mother wasn't happy to have to do the whole song and dance for the officers of the Philadelphia Police Department, and on the way home she made it clear just how long was the limb she had gone out on for her. Lee soon stopped listening, wondering if her mom had meant any of what she'd said about Lee's father.

Lee was curfewed for the rest of the semester, and she kept her hands clean. She stopped stealing, stopped doing drugs, stopped partying. She worried that Edie might no longer want to be her friend, but this wasn't the thing that cracked their friendship.

They were sharing a table at a café downtown, talking vaguely about college, when a tall young man wearing some sort of vintage military uniform, a few dull medals peppering his chest, sat with them and asked for a cigarette. He had short black hair, severe avian features, and intense, sunken eyes. He put the cigarette behind one ear and chatted easily with them, talking music mostly. He performed a little puppet dance on the table using two spoons and a napkin, his eyes on Lee the whole time. "You know, you remind me of some-one," he told her.

Lee pulled a cigarette out for herself before realizing she couldn't smoke here. "Oh, yeah? Who?"

"Someone very special. What did you say your name was?"

"I didn't."

"Her name's Lee. Lee Cuddy."

Lee gave Edie a dirty look, but Edie just grinned back.

"It's a pleasure to meet you, Lee." One of his spidery hands flipped open an old canvas shoulder bag and pulled out a stack of fliers. He handed them one each. "Why don't you two come to a little party we're throwing this Friday." He pulled a small black notebook from the bag and wrote something in it. "Go to this Web address on here and type in the code on the bottom. It will give you a time and a place to meet one of my associates. She'll take you there." When he turned to leave, Lee could see a large star shaved into the back of his head. She watched him hop onto an antique bicycle and ride off.

"Do you know what this is?" Edie said, gaping down at the flier in disbelief.

The flier was on thick card stock, about the size of a postcard, and it had an old black-and-white photo that looked like an aerial shot of some just-excavated ancient city. TO RAISE DUST was typed in, by manual typewriter, at the top, and SOCIÉTÉ ANONYME was printed at the bottom. Below that it read ADMIT ONE. There was a date, September 3—this coming Friday—but no street address. Only a Web address, followed by a different six-digit code on each flier.

"Isn't that your birthday?" Edie said.

It was. Lee was turning seventeen.

"Well, happy fucking birthday. This is an invitation to an S.A. party." Edie looked around the café and slid her flier quickly into her bag, as though someone might try to take it away from her.

"What's an essay party?"

"Dude. These things are legendary. They're thrown in an old missile silo somewhere outside the city. I've been trying to get into one for months, but they're totally underground. You can't just buy a ticket; you have to wait for one to come to you."

Lee handed Edie her flier. "Give it to someone else. You know I can't go."

"What are you talking about? That guy was totally into you."

"I'm grounded."

"So sneak out. Your mom doesn't even have to know you're gone."

It was true; she could probably get away with it. But Lee liked that she was no longer doing drugs or staying out nights drinking. She was thinking more clearly, and her grades were moving back up.

Edie seemed to take Lee's pause as answer enough. "Fine," she snapped, grabbing the flier from Lee's hand. "I'll ask Claire."

Edie really knew how to stick it where it hurt. Claire Faver had been Edie's best friend before Lee came along, and Claire's animosity toward Lee was barely concealed.

Lee spent her birthday at home, sharing a dishwater-colored cake that tasted of socks with her mom and Steve. "We noticed some links you left up on the computer." Steve took a bite of cake and closed his eyes with pleasure. "Looks like you've been researching colleges?"

Lee took a mouthful of cake and shrugged. She tried to get a view out the window, but Steve's face was in the way.

"College is expensive, you know. That means debt."

Lee forced the cake down. "I can get financial aid. Scholarships."

Steve nodded. "Financial aid is complicated. And scholarships take really good grades. Maybe if you had thought of that a year ago . . ."

Steve had no idea what Lee's grades were. She'd kept them up, despite everything. She felt like grabbing last year's report cards and shoving them into his smug face.

". . . but anyway, we think college is a fine idea."

Lee looked at her mother. "You do?"

"Sure we do," Steve said, waiting until she looked at him before continuing. "But we also think that a year or two of real life under your belt would do you some good. Most kids waste college because they're not mature enough to handle it yet. And after a year or so you might find that it's not really for you anyway. I never went to college. Did you know that?"

Lee looked down at her hands. She had bent the fork nearly in half.

"It's true. And look at me. I love what I do. My business is booming. And I could use a smart, energetic assistant soon."

Lee knew he was waiting for her to look up, but she wouldn't give him the satisfaction.

"Julia and I talked about this. She's on board, too." Steve looked at Lee's mom, who was trying to smile. "Anyway, just give it some thought. Oh, and happy birthday." He handed her a bright red box with a sheaf of loose papers inside. She didn't take it, and he set it down in front of her.

"It's for a Buddhist liturgy," he said. "These are sutras. You sit with them in the morning and chant them, aloud or silently. Like this." He opened the box and read aloud from the first page: "Shelter is the foundation for all you will set out to do. Shelter is the milk and honey of daily life. Shelter is the doorway to liberation." He cast a smile at her. "Happy birthday from your mother and me."

"I'm going for a walk," Lee said.

"Just be sure you're home by dinner." Steve carefully placed the paper back in the box and closed it. "Curfew doesn't go on hold for your birthday."

Lee left the house for Edie's. It was a long walk but still early. Edie wouldn't have left yet for the party. Fuck her curfew. When she got to the house, a medieval-looking two-story stone Tudor with elaborately manicured hedges, she made her way around to the back, to Edie's room on the first floor. Peering through the window, she could see Edie from behind, applying makeup in a mirror. Lee was about to tap on the glass when she spotted a pair of oxblood Doc Martens in the mirror, attached to a pair of stockinged legs on Edie's bed. Lee couldn't see the rest of the person, but she didn't need to to know it was Claire. When her eyes shifted back, she could see Edie staring at her in the mirror. Then Edie returned her attention to her own face, and Lee knew she'd been dismissed.

On her way home, hurting in a way she hadn't let herself feel in years, Lee began to notice a man following her. Edie often complained about unwanted advances from strange men—in cafés, on the subway, walking down the street—but Lee rarely had that problem. The man was heavyset and a little hulking and was not at all subtle about stalking her, especially considering his attire: an old-fashioned tailcoat with brass buttons over a tight black waistcoat, black trousers, and a black bow tie. He looked ridiculous, like an English butler lost in the city. Lee quickened her pace, ducked down into a subway station, walked through it, and came out at the other end. She thought she'd lost him, but then he was right in front of her, blocking her way. Lee felt frozen in place. "What do you want?" she said.

He said nothing. When she looked into his eyes, she could see that his irises were weirdly misshapen. He shuffled in place, smiling at her, and there was something childlike about him. Lee was suddenly more curious than afraid. Then she noticed a black box in his hand, about the size of a cigar case. He clumsily flipped it open, and a lens on a bellows popped out. He raised it to his chest and snapped a picture of her. Then he bowed slightly, turned, and walked away. Lee wanted to tell someone about the encounter, to confirm the weirdness of it, but there was no one to tell.

The following Monday at school Claire and Edie spent the day huddled together, whispering and laughing and sharing glances. A door had been shut in her face. The one time she found Edie without Claire, she asked her about the party, but Edie just shook her head and laughed, then went back to texting.

The prospect of college, and with it the prospect of reinventing herself, had become something more than a distant, formless hope. She began looking into programs, researching college towns. Edie had slowly opened the door to Lee again, and Lee spent every day after school at Edie's house, where they leaned against each other on Edie's bed and fantasized about disappearing. They began making plans, which were vague at first but solidified as they discussed which schools offered the brightest fields of hope and possibility and plain old American fun. Lee persuaded Edie to look out of state—New York or California or some small town where they could rent a house together and bicycle to class.

Edie wanted to study psychology, and Lee considered that as well, until she happened upon a photo in a *National Geographic* magazine. The article was about the discovery of a buried Assyrian city, which was being carefully unearthed, and in the photo a young woman in boots, khaki shorts, and a green cotton shirt squatted low as she brushed dirt from the head of a statue. The woman had a scarf wrapped around her black hair, and her clothes and tanned skin were dusted in red earth. She worked solo. Lee knew immediately that she wanted to be that woman. She tore the photo from the magazine, put it into her pocket, and brought it out again in the seclusion of her room that night. She tacked it to the wall above her bed and fell asleep wondering what it would take to become an archaeologist.

As she turned down requests from the kids at school and stopped dealing drugs, Lee found herself growing invisible again by degrees. Her new friends, the kids in Edie's crowd, had always found Lee to be a little off, too distant and inside herself to ever be one of them. They tolerated her when she was dealing and stealing for them, but she no longer sensed the eyes of the other kids on her as she'd walk the halls, no longer felt the twitchy anxiety of some boy nearby trying to get his nerve up to ask her for something.

Edie persuaded Lee to introduce her old dealer to Edie's boyfriend, Deke, and Deke became the new go-to guy. The itch to steal never went away—in fact, it got worse—but Lee refused to scratch it, and after a while it became like a phantom limb.

Claire seemed pleased with Lee's fall from favor with their crowd, and even warmed to her some, until one day Claire just didn't show up at school anymore. Poof, gone, just like those other kids. When Lee asked Edie about it, Edie looked around the quad as if she'd only now noticed. "Maybe she finally ran off with that skinny indie bassist dude," she said. "She was always threatening to."

Then two detectives came by the school one day to interview her friends, and Edie took Lee aside and made her promise not to tell them about the S.A. party she and Claire had gone to.

"Why?" asked Lee. "What does that have to do with anything?"

"It doesn't. It doesn't have anything to do with anything. But if my father finds out I went, he'll kill me. And if the police find out about it, you can bet my father will, too."

Lee promised, but it didn't matter. The detectives never asked her anything anyway.

Lee was seated by herself on the bleachers with a sandwich and a short list of colleges. She had narrowed it to four, and Edie was supposed to narrow hers to four, and together they were to agree to a first choice, then a second and a third. Lee had a 3.7 GPA and had scored a 2100 on a practice SAT test. Edie had money and connections. If they didn't shoot too high, they were sure to get into one of them together, and they had made a pact to choose only a school that accepted them both. Lee saw Edie approaching from across the field, hugging herself against the wind. Edie skulked up the bleachers, her big eyes moist and smeared in mascara. She snatched the cigarette from Lee's mouth and sat beside her.

"What's wrong?" Lee asked.

Edie took a drag and handed the cigarette back to Lee, sniffling as she gazed out across the empty football field. Despite the chilly October air Edie wore only a short skirt and a tight-fitting cardigan.

Lee pulled a sweatshirt from her bag and held it out, but Edie ignored it, taking the cigarette back. "I really fucked it up this time."

Edie Oswald. Golden girl. Touched by angels. Nothing ever went wrong for Edie. How bad could it be?

"I got scared. I panicked. I'm sorry, Lee."

Something in the distance spooked Edie, and she stood up and inhaled from the cigarette, then made her way down the bleachers. She turned. "My father will help you, I swear. I'm really sorry."

Lee leaned forward and squinted. An amorphous blob across the field resolved itself into three separate figures as they approached. Lee recognized Mrs. Bartlett, the school principal, followed by two uniforms of the Philadelphia Police Department.

TWO

SOLITARY in the Queensbrook Juvenile Detention Center was a concrete box measuring six paces by eight, with freshly painted pale walls, a stainless-steel toilet, and in the middle of the room a concrete slab with a vinyl pad on top to sleep on. They put Lee in and left her there, they told her, for her own protection. She stayed in the cell for twenty-two hours a day for thirty-three days with nothing but a Bible and the nonstop screaming of a girl two cells over for company. Lee had been alone all her life but never like this. The cell had no window, and the guards never talked to her and never turned out the light in the room, so each hour stretched out in meaningless succession until she lost sense of time completely. An hour was a day was a week was an hour.

To pass the time, she played out the events leading to her incarceration as though they were scenes from a movie, rewinding and replaying them again and again. She had to guess at a lot of it, determine what had happened based on what the prosecutor had laid out in court, what Edie had confessed to her in one short, tearful phone call, and what she knew to be the truth.

As far as she could piece it together, it had gone down like this: Deke, not long after taking over Lee's connections, had gotten greedy, expanding outside their closed circle, and his greed had turned to sloppiness. But the cops had been sloppy, too, and Deke spotted the two plainclothes officers following him on his way to school. He lost them, then called Edie, who met him in the school parking lot. He gave her his stash to hold, but Edie panicked. If they were watching him, they would be coming for her once they found nothing on him. So she stuffed the bag in Lee's locker. This anxious gambit might have worked out, except that Edie broke when they found a small bindle of cocaine at the bottom of her bag. Edie must have thought about her father's reaction and about expulsion from school and about her blown chances of getting into a good college, and Lee's name probably just sort of spilled out in a flood of remorse. When they went into Lee's locker, they found a butcher-paper-wrapped block of cocaine the size of a microwave burrito.

Lee's mother came to the police station in tears, with Steve consoling her. They sat across a table from Lee in the interview room, a bored-looking detective from the narcotics squad leaning against the wall behind them. When Lee asked about hiring a lawyer, her mother looked at Steve for a long time before answering.

"All our money's tied up in Steve's business," she said, still staring at Steve. "It's just getting off the ground." Steve ran his business—Amused Buddha! Tools for the Humorous Buddhist—from home, and the whole house was cluttered with boxes containing cheap goods imported from Nepal and Thailand and China: Buddha coffee mugs and bobbleheads and car fresheners, yin and yang bath towels, dharma whoopee cushions and nirvana beer cozies.

"It could be *our* business someday," Steve said to Lee. "I still believe in you. But your mother and I believe it's time you take some responsibility," Steve said.

"Then go into my room. In Dad's old guitar case. There's money there."

Steve turned to interrogate her mother with a stare, and her mother shook her head in ignorance. Whatever look was on his face passed when he turned back to Lee. "Remember what I told you about everything in life being a kind of opportunity? We think this might be one for you," he told her. "A chance to turn things around."

"They weren't mine," Lee said, her eyes still on her mother, refusing to look at Steve. "The drugs."

Her mother turned to the detective, who shifted his gaze and scratched his armpit as if to say he'd heard it all before. Steve pursed his lips. "Then whose were they?"

Lee wouldn't say. Her mother wasn't going to come through for her, but Edie would.

"You've been out of control for a long time," her mother said, turning back to Lee. "It's my fault. I should have done something about it earlier."

Steve put a hand on her mother's knee. "Julia. This is not yours to carry."

The image of her mother at that moment burned into Lee's memory: sitting as though frozen, staring at the welts that the cuffs had left on Lee's wrists. She looked hollowed out, filled with straw.

"Mom . . ."

"Look at me," Steve said, drawing Lee's eyes to him with his fingers. "You're a juvenile; it won't be too bad. And it will give you time to reflect and find your path. Remember what I taught you about using your Wise Mind? Do you think you were using your Wise Mind when you started dealing drugs?"

"I have money. I can do what I want with it. I want to hire a lawyer."

Steve got up and took her mother's hand. Then he led her out of the room. Her mother had never once looked Lee in the eyes.

Lee felt a quiet rage enveloping her. She ground her teeth so hard she was afraid she might crack one. But Edie had told her that her father, a powerful lawyer with powerful friends, would help her, and Lee knew he would do anything for Edie. And Edie owed her. So Lee kept quiet, knowing that Edie would come through.

In court, Lee sat beside the public defender, a man who smelled of corned beef and had orange Cheetos residue powdering his cuffs. Before the arraignment, he'd pressured her to agree to a plea deal, but Lee had refused. In the end, the truth would win out. A minute and a half into his opening statement, he realized he had the wrong case file and had to shuffle through a stack of folders until he found Lee's. Edie's father sat in the gallery, whispering sometimes into Edie's mother's ear. Lee stared at Edie as Edie testified against her, willing her to look at Lee just once as she answered questions from the prosecutor. If she could just get Edie to meet her eyes, she would stop. Edie never did.

Lee spent a lot of time thinking about Edie, her friend who had once told Lee that she wanted to save her. Lee hated that Edie had been right: she *had* been lost, and Edie had found her and rescued her before abandoning her again. For a while Lee had had direction in her life, plans for college and a friend to make them with, but now she felt untethered again, floating in space with nothing to orbit. Lee had taken the fall for her. Why? Because she felt she owed Edie something? Lee was pretty sure she knew now what had happened to the baby bird that Edie'd brought home with her. She'd probably just moved on, found some other project, and left the bird to die in her room.

Lee tried to hate Edie. She knew she had it in her—she found hatred for Steve and even for her mother—but Edie was just weak and scared, and Lee couldn't hate her for that. The scenes that kept running through her head—times with Edie—were all positive memories. For most of high school, Edie had given her everything she'd ever wanted. Lee felt so sick inside it hurt.

After a while—Lee couldn't tell how long (a day? a week?)—this film loop in her head began to make her crazy. There was nowhere to be comfortable in her cell. The bed was in the center of the room, and so she couldn't lean back while on it; the floors were cold; and the only other seat was a lidless toilet. Sometimes she lay awake on the bed staring up at the ceiling, feeling exposed, like something was there stalking her, just outside the periphery of her vision. The corner farthest from the door felt safest, and she curled up there for hours at a time, until she'd feel the cold begin to seep into her bones.

Lee didn't start out in solitary. She came in to the juvenile detention center—a squat encampment of long beige buildings that looked more like a community center than a jail—on a bus with twelve other girls, none of whom looked as scared as Lee felt. The JDC consisted of three cellblocks, each block holding thirty to fifty girls according to their assessed risk. Lee was assigned to Block Two, designated for nonviolent, low-risk offenders.

Block One was for girls convicted of violent crimes—assault or armed robbery—or repeat offenders, girls hardened by the system. Block Three, a long, windowless building set apart from the other blocks by the yard, was simply called, by both staff and inmates, Wonderland.

Though the inmates were separated otherwise, their daily hour in the yard—a mangy strip of grass surrounded by benches, with a half basketball court in one corner—and their meals were communal. The blocks tended to sit together, and the time was supervised, with a guard stationed at each corner of the cafeteria and two more roaming between the tables. Conversation was kept quiet.

Lee treated the JDC as she did her first months at high school: she kept her head down, stayed out of the way, and observed. But unlike in high school, invisibility wasn't possible here. Her attempts to remain unseen only made her a target. On Lee's third day inside she was sitting at an unoccupied corner of a table, keeping her head bent close to her tray as she shoveled food into her mouth, when she felt a presence behind her. She tightened the grip on her fork but kept her head down. A girl came around to her side slowly and drifted into the seat across from Lee. Lee saw a pair of hands with skin so pale they were nearly translucent. Lee allowed herself to look up.

The girl across from her had a matted bramble of short black hair over sharp cheeks and a wide mouth. She smiled thinly.

Lee understood enough not to make eye contact with anyone inside, which could always be construed as an invitation or a threat, but she couldn't help it now, and once she did, she couldn't look away. Within the whites of the girl's large eyes drifted electric-blue irises that were lumpy and misshapen. Twin cobalt jellies floating in bowls of milk.

Lee and the girl stared at each other across the table, Lee getting lost in those eyes, the girl placid and unblinking. The other inmates were watching them. The girl reached out and took Lee's hand. Her skin was dry but warm. She widened her smile and emitted a long, high-pitched whine from somewhere deep in her chest. Then a man who looked like some kind of doctor came and touched the girl's shoulder, and she let go and allowed herself to be led off to another table, where she sat and waited for the man to bring her food.

A girl at the end of the table scooted down across from Lee. "She say something to you?"

Lee shrugged into her food.

The girl was a chunky Latina with a name tattooed on her wrist in script too elaborate to make out. "Why aren't you wearing no shoes?"

Lee said nothing, didn't even look up. The day before, a girl, with two other girls on lookout, had tripped Lee in the bathroom, sat backward on her chest, and taken her shoes, then left without a word. Lee had felt relief that that was all the girl did, but she knew that giving in so easily, without a fight, meant she now had a target on her back. Not only was she quiet; she was easy prey. None of the staff had even noticed she'd spent the day walking around in socks.

"Don't worry, I'll hook you up."

Lee carved out a bite of tuna and cheese casserole, which had hardened into a solid block. She risked a look up. Not as far as the girl's eyes but to her mouth. Her lower lip had been split at the middle and was scabbed over.

"That girl? She from Wonderland." She pronounced the word without "d's." When Lee didn't respond, she added, "Three Block. She a Thrumm girl. They letting them dine with us now. It's an experiment."

Lee learned later that Wonderland was what they called the JDC's psych ward, which had been commissioned several years prior to contain what had become a rash of kids found drifting through the city, their eyes engorged and jellied, their agencies gone. Those whose parents could be found were sent home, but too many were runaways or throwaways who remained unclaimed, and no hospitals or foster centers were equipped to handle such a wave. They were like sleepwalkers, helpless, and such easy prey they needed to be separated from the rest of the detention center's population. Lee thought of Claire, how she had just vanished. No trace. Is this what had become of her? Lee didn't know what to believe, but for weeks as she would fall asleep she would see the Thrumm girl's jellyfish eyes floating in the dark field of her vision.

Lee still thought about Edie, though not as much as before. The montage had been cut down to a few brief scenes that Lee could not get out of her head: the first time Edie'd brought her home and they'd sat drinking in her bedroom; the time after Edie had shut Lee out in favor of Claire, then let Lee back in, by the simple gesture of falling asleep against Lee's shoulder one day at assembly; and the time she'd begged Lee not to tell the detectives about the S.A. party she'd gone to with Claire. What had happened there?

It was nearly January; Edie would be sending off her college applications. By the time Lee got out, Edie would be finishing her freshman year.

Lee's mother visited three times, finally giving up after Lee refused to see her each time. She wrote letters, but Lee read only the first one. Her mom used the pronoun "I" only once and relied on "we" for the rest, explaining that she and Steve had done a lot of soul-searching and had agreed that Lee had a lot of searching to do within herself, that this was Lee's journey to take, and that it was best for her to find her own path. They were sorry that Lee didn't want to see them, but they understood. They knew Lee would have trouble understanding this but knew, too, that in time she would come to realize the wisdom of it and would return home a fully realized woman. Lee wet the letter into a sopping ball and threw it at the ceiling, where it stuck among the wads of toilet paper thrown by the girls who had come before her.

Nights she lay awake, terrified. There were rumors of girls getting raped in the laundry room, girls getting cut just for being too pretty. She took a job in the library that allowed her to keep clear of most of the other inmates. It didn't escape the notice of the three girls who had stolen Lee's shoes that Maria, the girl who had hooked Lee up with a new pair, had taken Lee under her protection. Maria Velasquez was always talking—she was like a faucet that never turned off—and maybe that's why she took such a shine to Lee, who rarely talked but always seemed to be listening. Nearly all of Maria's stories involved her boyfriend, Javi, who ran with a gang and had killed people but was true to her. Maria had another year on her sentence, after which they were going to get married and start a family. She was determined that Javi was going to leave the gang life behind after that, even if he had to be beaten out. She would hook him up with her uncle, who fenced stolen goods from a pawn shop, or else her father, who ran a salvage yard, where she and Javi used to have sex in the back of old cars.

Maria had a reputation for crazy violence—she had once tried to gouge a girl's eye out with a spoon simply because the girl had looked at her wrong—and so the three girls who had been mounting a campaign of escalating harassment against Lee changed their strategy and began tormenting her more subtly. They blew her kisses as they passed her in the halls. They tripped her and spit on her when Maria was not around, and when she was, they winked at her with the implied promise of what was waiting. One of the girls worked in the cafeteria, and Lee often found things in her food: glass shards and insects and blobby viscous masses. They knew they could throw all their anger Lee's way and she would never fight back.

Maria had told Lee to come to her if anyone ever so much as looked at her funny. Lee was grateful and even touched—Maria never asked for a thing in exchange—but Lee knew better than to go to her with her problems; any problems she had were hers alone to handle. And so, after more than three months of trying to ignore them, of living in constant fear that she'd be cornered in some dark recess of the prison, of picking through her food so thoroughly that mealtime was over before she'd gotten more than a few bites in, she found a piece of what may or may not have been the tail of a rat in her spaghetti. Seeing the three of them laughing together at a table, Lee did the worst thing she could do in her situation. Something in her core that had been holding her together split, and before she realized it, Lee felt the tears on her face.

Lee could feel all the eyes in the room now trained on her. She snuck a peek at Maria, who had a look of disgust on her face. But then Maria got up, pulled a filed toothbrush from her sock, walked calmly over to Mel, one of Lee's harassers, and, before Mel could turn around, stabbed her in the shoulder.

Her scream caught in her throat, Mel just twisted her neck back and tried to make sense of the toothbrush emerging from her shoulder. The other girls got up and walked quickly away, as though Mel were the epicenter of an explosion and the girls shrapnel. All but Maria. It was as though she wanted Mel to look her in the eyes, to know who it was who had stabbed her. When Mel's scream finally emerged, two guards were on Maria, one pressing her hard against the concrete with his knee, the other zip-tying her hands behind her back. Lee stood there, just watching. Maria was smiling.

Mel was pressing herself against the table, crying for someone to take the thing out of her back, but no one wanted to get near her. Finally an orderly from the hospital ward led her away, the toothbrush still sticking out of her shoulder.

The guards had not seen Maria in the act, the video coverage was the wrong angle, and none of the girls were talking, not even Mel, but they took her in and charged her anyway. Lee knew what she had to do—both what was expected of her and what was right. What Edie had never done and never would do. When Lee asked to see the warden and confessed to stabbing Mel, it was clear he didn't believe her. But with her confession the case against Maria fell apart and they only had Lee to pin the charges on. So they did.

The overhead light in her cell in solitary was always on, and Lee would see its afterimage—a hovering orange globe—when she closed her eyes. It followed her around the room when she paced, and it floated above her when she tried to sleep. She couldn't get away from it. After twenty-eight days, she lost hope of ever being let out of her shrinking box. With nowhere to go but inward, Lee burrowed. She tunneled inside herself a little more each day, without direction or even a sense of what was up or down; there was only inward. One day she thought she heard a low vibration, like the sound of a cello being tuned, somewhere in the darkness that was herself. And so she followed the sound, digging down, or up, or in whatever direction, to try to locate it, to feel the vibration in her hands. But she never got closer; the more she burrowed, the farther the sound retreated, until she was so lost within herself that her physical body, the one that sat in the pale concrete room, stopped moving and stopped taking in food.

They brought her to the psych ward after that, the block known as Wonderland, and Lee spent a few days in a hospital bed, taking food in through a tube in her arm. They wrapped her hands in gauze because she'd bitten her nails bloody. She stopped hearing the vibration and stopped burrowing, and soon she was walking the ward in slow, aimless circuits. She still didn't talk, to the other inmates or to the guards, and they made little effort to talk to her. The inmates of Wonderland were different from those of Block Two. They passed each other in the hall like ghosts or sat smiling to themselves in their rooms, and a few of them were like the girl she had encountered in the cafeteria, with jellied eyes and faraway smiles directed at nothing and no one. The staff called them Thrumms, as Maria had. The guards shuffled these kids around like air hockey pucks, giving them a slight nudge that would send them wafting aimlessly in any given direction. They seemed harmless, but they gave Lee the creeps.

It wasn't horrible in Wonderland. Once she got to know them, the other girls were mostly okay. The food seemed uncontaminated by insects or phlegm. And there was a garden that Lee got to tend. Every day she gained a little more weight and added a bit of color to her skin. But Lee knew she wouldn't stay here for long. When they decided she was well enough, they would send her back—either to solitary or to gen pop—and she didn't know which she feared more.

When she thought about the future, she found herself unable to breathe, no matter how much air she sucked in. The doctor told her she was having panic attacks, and he gave her pills to calm them. Because the attacks were the only thing keeping her out of gen pop, Lee avoided swallowing the pills, spitting them out and hiding them in a tear in her mattress, but then the attacks started to subside on their own. The staff began allowing her responsibilities, filing and tidying up the Wonderland office, and Lee knew her days there were numbered.

Lee was alone in the office when she felt a blast of cool air prickle the back of her neck. She turned and stared up at the slats of a rectangular air vent. She took a moment, mentally measuring it against the width of her shoulders, then rifled around the office until she lit upon a strip of metal from a hanging file folder: it made a serviceable screwdriver. Lee climbed up on the desk, got the vent cover off, and just barely managed to squeeze herself into the shaft.

Using her shoulders and hips, she pushed forward by inches. It was too tight to turn around, and the light quickly went from gray to black until she was in total darkness. Lee hadn't thought through what would happen if she got stuck, and she began to imagine herself trapped there, what it would feel like to starve to death enclosed within this long tin box. Her breaths grew shorter and quicker until she began to labor to breathe at all. She was having another attack, and Lee knew that this time, trapped and sightless as a worm, she would die. The darkness pushed into her lungs until each breath was just a hiccup. She tried to wiggle back the way she had come, but her elbows and wrists were at the wrong angle and every movement just wedged her more firmly into the space. She managed to turn onto her side and pull herself forward a good six inches. She did it again, then again. When she saw the light ahead, her breath came back quickly. She tried to stifle her coughs, but coughing had never felt so good.

The vent let her out into a mechanical room, full of water heaters and furnaces and a series of fuse boxes. There was a door at one end. She stood listening for a while, trying to figure out what might be on the other side, but finally just turned the knob. Through the crack she could see a hallway, with a line of closed doors to one side. She could hear voices behind the doors as she passed, ducking below the slatted windows until she came to a large metal door at the end, which she could see, through its single square window, led outside.

· BOOK II ·

The Passage from Virgin to Bride

THREE

THE door closed behind her with a hard click, leaving Lee standing on a swath of dry grass, the sun warm on her face. It was mid-August. Eight months and a few days into her seventeen-month sentence, she was out. It was that easy. To her left was a parking lot, and behind her extended the long low wall of Wonderland, which from the outside looked like nothing more than a storage facility. It was just a makeshift trailer, she saw now, not unlike the temporary classrooms her school had put up one year during renovations. The detention center, made of painted brick and more formidable, stood behind it. In front of her, across a patch of yellowing weeds and wildflowers, a wooded area fanned out along the access road she'd come in on by bus 244 days ago.

Lee crouched when she heard voices followed by a beep. A car door slammed shut, and a gray SUV pulled out from the lot, passed through a security gate, and disappeared down the road. Across the field was a tall cyclone fence ringed with razor wire. Lee loped over to it and climbed it quickly; once at the top, she found that she could push apart the wire enough to squeeze through and drop to the other side. She had at most thirty minutes before lunchtime, when her absence would be noticed. Once she was into the woods, she started to run.

Lee was never an athlete, but her time inside, and especially the time spent in solitary, had left her feeling boneless and wormy. Quickly out of breath, she pushed through by concentrating on the soft crunch of her shoes against the fallen leaves. The world began to blur past her in a repeating loop of trees and flickering sunlight.

She stopped, suddenly dizzy, then put her hands on her knees, leaned forward, and coughed out a ropy mass of saliva and phlegm. The woods were dense here, and she couldn't see more than a dozen yards in any direction. Lee thought back to the ride in from the courthouse downtown. The bus had traveled north-ish from the courthouse for a good twenty to thirty minutes before turning off the freeway onto the access road. The woods had left as little of an impression on Lee as an unbroken wall.

She walked well past dark, walked until she was stumbling and tripping forward, and still there was nothing but woods. She could hear a river, which she was careful to keep to her left to avoid going in circles, and the moon was full, which was her other stroke of luck—without it she would have walked headfirst into a tree hours ago. She knew she didn't have much left in her and kept moving only because the idea of stopping, of sleeping in the middle of these woods, terrified her. So she kept going, falling into each step and keeping herself upright just enough not to fall forward.

Until the woods stopped so suddenly that Lee nearly ran off an embankment, a steady stream of freeway traffic thirty feet below. She skidded onto her butt and caught hold of a vine. Then she pulled herself to her feet and backtracked, cutting along the freeway until she spotted a set of concrete stairs, which took her to an empty lot beneath an overpass. There were no cars down here, no people, just the steady thump of traffic from above. Still she didn't stop. She didn't want to sleep here any more than she did in the woods.

But where could she go? Home would be the first place they'd look for her, and anyway, fuck her mom and fuck Steve. A teen shelter would be the second place they'd look. Her orange cotton uniform may as well have had FUGITIVE stenciled onto the back. She thought of the homeless kids she'd seen bumming change downtown and wondered where they slept. Was that who she was now?

Lee tried to remember where she'd seen them, those raggedy spare-changing kids she used to avoid eye contact with. She knew that by late morning they'd be spread out around the department stores in the shopping district, but there was no way she could go somewhere so public. Lee kept to the shadows of buildings and to alleys when she could, keeping her eyes out for cops, her head otherwise down, arms wrapped around herself as though she could hide the orange JDC uniform. She passed a Mexican bakery, its window lined with pillowy white bread loaves, and the whole area smelled like grilled meat. Lee hadn't eaten since breakfast the day before, and her hunger gnawed at her insides.

She could see the Delaware River a few blocks away, and she headed toward it. There she sat on a bench beneath a tree and watched three men night fishing from the rocks by the shore. By the time they had gathered their rods and pails, packed them into an old truck, and left, the moon was down and the sky and the water were nearly indistinguishable. They'd left some fast-food wrappers behind, and she picked through them but found just a few pieces of soft bread and half a slice of onion. Lee had no idea what to do. Trying to steal something in what she had on would be suicide, so she returned to the bench and stayed glued to it, because getting up meant she'd need a place to go.

A lone figure across the park was watching her. He was mostly a shadow, standing just out of the light, but she sensed him taking her in. Lee got up. When she began walking, she could feel him moving after her. She was out of breath before she even knew she'd been running, each inhale stabbing at her lungs. She slowed but didn't look back until she'd turned a dozen corners and begun dodging pedestrians. The streets were busy here. Lee recognized the area and kept walking, afraid to leave the anonymity of the downtown crowds but afraid to stop, too. Even as the crowds thinned and the streets emptied and the blisters tore on her feet and her ankles began to scream, she kept walking. A group of drunken men spilled out of a bar, and one of them asked, "How much, little kitty?" while two of them laughed and a fourth offered Lee an embarrassed shrug. She watched them hail a cab and speed off, and she continued walking. She walked until she was hobbling.

The man who'd been following her was gone, and Lee felt herself ease up, but with that came an almost overwhelming fatigue. With what little strength she had left, she limped to the edge of a small park, where people had laid out sheets of cardboard on the ground behind trees or bushes and were sleeping. Lee was too tired to look for a cardboard square of her own, but she found a copse of bushes with nothing occupying it but a ring of empty beer cans and a soiled magazine, and she crawled in. Shivering despite the late-night heat, feeling ants crawling across her back, the dirt against her cheek, Lee didn't think she would sleep, but then she did. Immediately she fell into a dream in which she was floating underwater while a school of electric-blue jellyfish floated all around her, their tentacles sending electrical jolts through her skin.

She awoke to a hand shaking her. She saw the insignia on the shoulder of his jacket first, and her body went limp, surrendering. That was it: already she'd been found and caught. She was going back. Back to solitary, probably. Then she looked up and saw that it wasn't a cop at all, just some guy, and that the jacket was old military surplus. Really old, like World War I or something.

"Can't sleep here," he said. He had a beard and dirt on his face, but he looked young, more like a guy who should be serving lattes than sleeping in a park.

"It looked free," she said. "I didn't know."

He pointed to the circle of cans. "My sign. Everyone knows."

"Where can I go, then?"

He spoke to the top of her head. "You got anything to drink?"

Lee said nothing.

"Any money?"

She shook her head.

He pursed his lips in disappointment. "Not here. Maybe you talk to the Station Master. He'll find you something."

"Who's the Station Master?"

"Know the old Willow Steam Plant? Out in Callowhill?"

Lee shook her head.

"Near there. If you're meant to find him, you'll find him. If not, you won't."

She got up, cast her eyes across the small park and its sleeping forms, and left.

Lee was digging through a Dumpster, pushing aside rotting vegetables and plastic bags bulging with discarded butchers' trimmings, looking for anything edible, anything sealed, when she felt a presence behind her. Then a man's arm wrapped around her front, and she felt the weight of him pressing her up against the Dumpster. His hand reached under her smock and began to squeeze her stomach, and her neck grew warm with his breath. When she tensed up, he tightened his grip and slowly shifted them both along until he had her up against a building, between two Dumpsters. Lee could feel his erection pushing into her back as he shifted and tried to work her pants down. She was paralyzed, too afraid to move. She tried to clench herself into something hard and impenetrable, but when she felt his finger rub up against her, something inside lost hold and she kicked back hard with her foot. He wrapped one leg around her, and she struggled, trying to squirm out from under him, suffocating under his weight, until she felt him tense up, shudder and gasp, then go limp. She hung there a moment as the man's thick breath in her ear slowed to a steady wheeze, and then she carefully took his hand and moved it away from her. She slid out from between him and the wall. Her pants were still on. His belt was open and his top button undone, but he had never managed to get his pants down, either. She couldn't bring herself to look at his face. Lee left, limping harder, and didn't stop walking even as the sun was up fully and warm on the back of her neck.

Her mouth felt swollen and dry, and the hunger turned to a stabbing pain in her stomach. Walking through Fishtown, she saw a woman leave her outdoor café table, a half-eaten breakfast sandwich still on her plate. Lee swooped it up without looking back and devoured the thing in three bites. The food was not enough and only made her feel her fatigue more strongly. She oriented herself south, toward Callowhill, because it was someplace to go.

The girl was dandelion thin, with curly brown hair and a pointy face that pulled all her features forward. She had a spot staked out by the 7-Eleven; a little cardboard sign beside her read FUCK YOU, PAY ME.

The area didn't have a lot of pedestrian traffic, and Lee wondered why the girl had set up here. A young man in a bowler hat, riding an antique bicycle with one huge wheel and one small one, rode past, winking at Lee as he did. The girl didn't even look up. Lee tried to work up the nerve to approach her half a dozen times, each time turning back before she could get a sentence out. When the girl spoke to her, Lee was so startled she didn't catch the words.

The girl was digging into a black industrial trash bag held together by duct tape and didn't look up. "I said, you can't shake here. This is my corner."

"I can't *what* here?" Lee understood what the girl meant, but something about the word made her want to hear the girl say it again.

"This is my corner. My sign, my 7-Eleven, my customers. You need to go and find your own."

"Where?"

The girl pulled down the bottom lid of one eye with her middle finger, laying naked a moist red crescent. The gesture was so unexpected Lee couldn't take it personally. "Do I look like a real estate agent?" the girl said.

When Lee sat down next to her, the girl looked at Lee like: what the fuck?

"So this is your view?" Lee tried to smile but felt her face contort into a kind of grimace instead.

"You look like puke," the girl said.

There were girls like this back in the detention center, girls sunken so far into themselves that trying to reach them was like talking down a well. When Lee looked into the girl's eyes, she saw only burning hatred. "I just need a place to sleep," she said.

"So long as it's not my corner, I don't give a shit where you sleep."

Desperate, Lee pressed on. "Where do *you* sleep?"

"Fuck off." The girl shivered inside her coat, though it had gotten swampy hot through the afternoon.

"I heard about someone called the Station Master. I heard he takes care of people."

"I don't know no station master." The girl glared hard at Lee. Lee was about to get up and let the girl be when the girl said, "What the fuck are you wearing?"

Lee looked down at the orange cotton uniform as though just noticing it. "This was my sister's," she said, the lie coming easily and out of nowhere. "She was gonna burn it after she got out, but I think it's cool."

"It's all right." The girl reached out to touch the sleeve, and Lee settled back down and brought her legs up under her.

"I'll bet you look good in orange," Lee said.

"I look all right."

"You want it?"

The girl looked at Lee suspiciously. "Give it to me."

"What am I going to wear?"

"I got a pair of jeans and a T-shirt I'll trade you, no charge. Never let it be said Lois left a homegirl hanging." The girl was already pulling the clothes from her bag, a dirty pair of jeans more holes than denim and a huge purple T-shirt from some sort of hospital program that said TOUGHER THAN CANCER in big orange letters across the front.

Lee could feel the eyes of the convenience store clerk on her as she pulled the smock up over her head and replaced it with the T-shirt, which smelled like old Tater Tots. She pulled the bottoms off and handed both pieces to the girl in a ball, then pulled on the jeans.

"I'm so tired," Lee said. "Isn't there someplace I could crash? Just for a night or whatever?"

Lois was holding the smock up, reading out the number stenciled over the left breast. Her mouth opened to answer, but then her eyes drifted to something over Lee's shoulder and she crumpled the smock into her lap and found sudden interest within her bag.

Lee turned to see another girl behind her, looking down at Lee with her head tilted to one side. When Lee met her eyes, the girl smiled brightly. "What's your name?" she asked. She had a swirl of blond hair pinned atop her head and silver eyes and carried herself with the erect ease of a dancer.

Lee didn't know why she told the girl her name, but she did.

"That's pretty," the girl said, but Lee cringed inside. It was a boy's name and not pretty at all. "Are you needing someplace to stay, Lee?"

"Go on," Lois said, not looking too happy about it. "Ester gonna take care of you now."

Ester's eyelashes were mascaraed into thick black points that gave her the look of a Russian starlet from an age gone by. She wore an old black knit dress stretched taut like a spiderweb over a gauzy red shirt and jeans. She was so pretty Lee had trouble not staring at her. She held her hand out. Lee turned back to Lois, but Lois was done with her.

Lee got up.

"You must be something special," said Ester, turning and waiting for Lee to catch up. "Lois doesn't talk to *anyone*. Most of us stay clear of her."

Lee knew she wasn't special, that the girl was just flattering her, though Lee couldn't figure why. But she liked it when Ester smiled. Ester had big, horsey teeth with a friendly gap in the front that only made her more beautiful. "She just wanted something from me."

They came to an old brick building with all its ground-floor windows boarded up. "Where are we going?"

Ester didn't answer but pulled on a sheet of plywood nailed over the front entrance, which opened on hidden hinges to reveal itself as a door. Ester held it open for Lee.

Lee could see only a dozen feet or so into a large, dark space.

"Coming?" said Ester.

"In there?"

"You prefer to sleep outside?"

Back up the street, some kids were trading dance moves, one of them gliding backward in his sneakers alongside a brown paper bag blowing down the sidewalk. In the distance beyond them, Lee could see the little lump that was Lois.

Ester frowned thoughtfully. "We've got beds and food and running water."

What was Lee waiting for? She'd been wandering, directionless, searching for a place to stay for over a day. She wasn't going to get another opportunity like this. She remembered a joke a pastor in the JDC had told her, something about a true believer who was drowning and kept passing up offers of help, telling them that God was going to come and save him. Lee took a step forward into the entranceway. The door shut behind her, taking most of the light with it. Ester flicked a switch, and a single bulb illuminated the space, a large lobby with a high ceiling that looked like cracked frosting on an old cake. What must have once been shopwindows were boarded up. It smelled of old hamburger grease.

Lee followed Ester up a set of stairs at the far end of the lobby. At the top of the landing Ester turned and headed down a hallway lined with rooms with their doors removed. Most of them were empty but for a mattress, maybe a few scattered books or magazines. There were teenagers in a few of the rooms, and they turned to watch as Lee passed.

"It used to be an office building—dentists, jewelers, shrinks, that sort of thing—before it got abandoned."

Lee met the eyes of a boy her age. He was lying on a bed and wearing headphones. When he smiled, his eyes were very far away. "What is this place?"

Ester stopped at the last room at the end of the hall, the only room with a door. She licked her thumb and wiped something from Lee's face, and Lee was aware and suddenly ashamed of what she must look like. "He's in here."

"Who?"

Ester knocked on the door. "The Station Master."

A man's voice answered from the other side, and Ester opened the door. The room was bigger than the others, and furnished. Several black caps hung from a wooden hat rack. A neatly made bed on an old iron frame stood in one corner, and on a table beside it was a chess set, the pieces in mid-play. A man sat at a small wooden desk facing the wall. He didn't turn to greet them but kept his face close to the page of a large black ledger, carefully writing in it with a fountain pen. He wore a thick brown wool suit, though it must have been eighty-some degrees in the room. In a corner was a stool with an upended bicycle wheel mounted on top. The man kept writing.

Eventually he raised his head, capped his pen, placed it on the desk beside the ledger, closed the book, and put it in a drawer. He removed his glasses and replaced them with another pair. Finally he turned toward Lee. His small, watery eyes met hers. He had short, thick brown hair slicked back from a delicately molded face. He must have been in his late thirties. He looked her over, saying nothing. Lee felt scrutinized, as if he were looking into some part of her even she couldn't see. The room smelled of garlic, and Lee saw a half-eaten bowl of noodles on his desk. Pangs of hunger worried at her insides, and she turned toward the window. She could see Lois on her corner at the end of the block.

The man nodded at Ester, who gave Lee an encouraging smile and then left her there.

"So," the man said after Ester had shut the door, "tell me a little about yourself."

The man had short, nicotine-yellow fingers, but his nails were manicured and glossy.

"What do you mean?"

"Okay. Let's just start with this: how did you make your way to us?"

He had a strange effect on her. She wanted to tell the man what he wanted to hear, though she didn't know what that was. Which put her off balance. He seemed very much aware of this effect, matching her unease with glassy tranquility.

Lee thought about how to answer. "That girl, Ester. She found me." Found me—why had she put it that way? It made her sound like some lost puppy.

The man put a hand on the bicycle wheel and gently spun it. "Perhaps that is how it seems. But our residents find us, always. Because they need to in some way, sometimes in ways they don't even know until they know."

Lee watched the spinning wheel. She didn't tell the man about the guy in the park who'd told her to come and find him. "I was looking for a place to sleep, is all."

When he got up, Lee saw he was not much taller than she was. He crossed the room to gaze out the window beside her. "Did the correctional facility not prove adequate to your needs?"

She looked past him to Lois, wearing the orange smock. He must have seen the whole exchange. "That was my sister's uniform."

"So if I were to call the juvenile detention center right now, they would tell me they don't know anything about an escaped girl?"

She mapped the man's face for some indication of his intent. Lee was good at lying when she needed to be, but sometimes it paid to tell the truth. She said nothing.

He was handsome until he smiled, displaying a clusterfuck of large, rabbity teeth. "Relax. We take in all kinds here. So long as you're willing to do your part." He took an old silver case from inside his jacket and offered her a cigarette from it, but she refused. If nothing else, the JDC had taught her never to accept anything until she could see the strings attached.

He lit the cigarette for himself, squeezing his eyes shut as he exhaled. "Shall we get you set up?"

Lee's room was diagonally across from the Station Master's. And like all the others but his, it was doorless, with only a mattress on the floor, a blanket, and a pillow. Lee lay down on the mattress and faced the wall. The Station Master had helped her get settled, and told her before he left that she could come to him at any time, for anything at all. She tried to sleep, but soon she smelled the garlic again, as if it was in the room with her. She sat up to find Ester standing over her, holding a plate of plain noodles, like she'd seen on the man's desk. Her hair was up, tied back with a handkerchief.

"You must be hungry," she said. "It isn't much, but it will fill you up. We'll get you a real meal at dinner."

Lee took the bowl without hesitation and stuffed a forkful of noodles into her mouth, not caring when the warm oil slid down her neck.

"Hold on." Ester pulled a packet of grated cheese from her pocket, opened it, and sprinkled it onto Lee's plate.

Lee stirred it around and continued eating, staring at Ester's bare feet until the girl sat down beside her.

"It's okay?"

Lee nodded, her mouth still full.

"I know you're in trouble," Ester said, "but you're safe here." Ester was sitting so close Lee could feel the heat of her. She kept herself from leaning into it. Something about the way her body responded to Ester reminded her of the way she was drawn to Edie, and she didn't trust it.

"I also want you to know that you don't have to tell me anything but that I'm always here if you want to talk. About anything at all." She undid the handkerchief from her hair and wiped upward along Lee's neck.

Ester shook her head, and her long blond hair fell around her shoulders. With her hair down she went from Russian starlet to '60s peacenik.

"What is this place?" Lee said.

Ester folded the handkerchief and handed it to Lee. She got up. "We call it the Crystal Castle. For now, just think of it as a safe place to stay. You'll get the lay of the land soon enough. Until then, feel free to roam around, introduce yourself to the others. Just don't go upstairs, okay?"

"What's upstairs?"

Ester smiled. "Put in a little time first. You'll see eventually. When you're ready."

Lee closed her eyes for what felt like a second, but when she opened them, Ester was gone. She was so exhausted her body felt evacuated, as if she were just old bones held together by stretched skin. She fell asleep immediately.

When she woke, it was dark, the room lit only by the faint glow of the streetlamp outside. Lee lay awake, watching shadows pass along the walls. Somewhere upstairs a door opened and closed. Once Ester passed Lee's room on her way to see the Station Master. Lee heard the low hush of their voices.

Lee wished Ester would come in to talk to her, but when the girl left the Station Master's room and saw Lee awake, she only offered up that gap-toothed smile. For so many months in the JDC, Lee had lain awake imagining what it would be like to walk freely through the city. To eat a meal at a restaurant, to go to a movie, to hear waves crashing and feel beach sand between her toes. Lee was out now, but she still couldn't do any of that. She had accepted the offer of these people, whoever they were. Was she now trapped in this place? Suddenly the room was shrinking, not much larger than her cell in solitary. She began to feel dizzy. Lee got out of bed. She took her shoes and carried them, stepping as quietly as she could down the hall and into the stairwell, expecting someone to lurch from the dark and grab her at any moment. But she made it to the ground floor. Lee put on her shoes. She crossed the lobby, expecting the building's front door to be locked, but it opened right onto the street.

A siren wailed in the distance, but otherwise the neighborhood was silent. Lee walked down the middle of the street, everything around her yellowed and wan from the streetlamps. She wondered what would happen if she went back home, stood pale and wasted in front of her mother, told her what it had been like in the detention center. What would her mother do? Steve would want to turn her in, but maybe her mom would stand up to him?

Lee reached the corner 7-Eleven, but Lois was nowhere to be seen. Lee wondered where she slept, and why it wasn't at the Crystal Castle. She watched a man inside the store in a dirty flannel shirt and sweatpants buy diapers and a pack of cigarettes. Outside, he did a slow double take as he passed her, as though she were a ghost he couldn't be sure he had seen at all. For the past eight months she had imagined this moment of freedom in various incarnations—she'd be walking along the beach, through a park, along a downtown street, even on a silent and empty street such as this—but in none of them did she imagine she'd feel so alone. Lee thought of Edie. It was mid-August; she'd be saying her goodbyes and packing for college. Lee turned and headed back.

She was back inside and across the lobby when she heard the door open behind her. It was too dark to make out much more than the frame of a man, wearing a hat and a dark coat, silhouetted in the doorway. Lee ducked into the dark crevice behind the stairs just as he turned on a cell phone flashlight.

She saw a flash of gray stubble on the wattle of the man's neck as he passed and went up the stairs. He made it to the first landing, her floor, and headed up to the next. Upstairs. There was a knock, followed by a door opening and closing. Lee crept up after him. At the top landing was the door. Behind it she heard a woman's voice, not Ester's, and a man's reply but couldn't make out the words. Lee tested the knob. It was locked.

The next morning Lee awoke to the faint chords of Sly and the Family Stone's "Everyday People" coming from somewhere downstairs. She could hear voices and smell something cooking—pancakes, maybe, and bacon.

In the morning light she examined her room more clearly. The carpet was stained, and the windowsill was burned by all the cigarettes extinguished into it. Along the wall above the mattress someone had drawn a series of stylized mouse heads, seventeen in all—three neat rows of five, plus two. They were each identical, except for the eyes, which grew slightly bigger with each iteration.

"Sleep okay?"

Lee turned around to find Ester, backlit and haloed in dust motes, looking a little sleepy. She held a mug.

"Come on, we'll get you some breakfast, introduce you around."

Ester brought Lee down to the lobby, then through another door to a stairwell going down. She could increasingly hear the sounds of people talking over one another and of silverware clinking against plates. Ester and Lee came into a large basement space, where maybe two dozen kids Lee's age sat around a cluster of tables eating breakfast. One girl in a too-large Steelers jersey and no pants kept getting up and moving from one table to another, instigating something between the two groups, who were playfully trading insults back and forth. No one looked up when Lee entered the room, until Ester stuck two fingers in her mouth and whistled.

"Everybody," she called when the room grew quiet, and Lee suddenly felt all eyes on her. "This is Lee."

A chorus of voices sang out, "Hi, Lee!" Then they all turned back to what they'd been doing.

"And that's that," Ester said, taking two plates of food from a shirtless boy in an apron. She brought the plates to an empty table, and Lee sat across from her, pushing the scrambled eggs around her plate before taking a bite.

"So," Ester said, waiting for Lee to meet her eyes before continuing. "Tell me what you're good at."

"What I'm good at?"

"What you're good at. Everybody contributes, and so we try to start with what you're good at."

Lee thought about it. She did well enough at school but didn't excel in any one subject. She didn't cook. She wasn't especially strong, or fast, or artistic. She was a lousy typist. She could steal. And she could disappear. But these didn't seem like the kinds of skills you advertised.

"How are you with computers?"

Lee shrugged. She wasn't anything with computers. She began to feel useless.

"How about your personality skills?"

"What do you mean?"

"Never mind." Ester clicked her teeth. "Anything?"

Lee stuck a forkful of egg into her mouth so she wouldn't have to answer.

Ester seemed to sense Lee's shame, and her face softened. "Don't worry, there's room for you here. We just have to figure out what your role is. Everyone down here has a role; it's important. And no role is more than any other. That's also important. You understand what I'm saying?" She touched Lee's shoulder so tenderly it felt like a hug.

It was the kind of thing Steve would say, but coming from Ester, it was a warm blanket she wanted to wrap herself in. Lee looked away, afraid of her own emotions.

"God, you're pretty, though. And you don't even know it, do you?"

Ester was one of the most beautiful girls Lee had ever seen. She wondered what pretty looked like through those eyes.

"Here," Ester said. "Let me show you." She got up and pulled an old Polaroid camera from a shelf full of old books and came back. "Smile," she said, holding the camera up and clicking a photo before Lee could do more than gape.

She popped the photo out and waved it in the air until the image clarified. "Pretty as a picture," she said, showing Lee. "My grandmother used to say that. Pretty stupid, huh?" She dropped the photo into her bag. "You can do dishes for now. Everyone can do dishes." Ester gave Lee that smile that made Lee think everything was okay, then she got up. "Go see Doug when you're done." She nodded to the boy who had given her the plate. He was standing by an open trash can, scraping off a pan into it. "I'll come find you later."

Lee ate the rest of her breakfast by herself, watching as, one by one, the other kids finished their plates and stacked them in plastic bins before leaving. When she finished, she got up and went to see Doug about the dishes.

It took Lee nearly two hours to get through them all. Doug had pale eyes that never landed anywhere for long. He wore earbuds the whole time, taking one out only to answer her questions, and he left her to finish up before they were half through. But Lee liked being alone in the kitchen, and she liked the feeling of contributing something, even if it was only dishes. When they were all clean and stacked and put away and the floor was swept and the counters and tables were wiped down, she went back upstairs, looking for Ester in the rooms down the hall, then heading up to the second floor. Lee put her ear to the door. Just as she did, it opened and Lee nearly fell forward into a girl. She caught a glimpse of a nose ring and a pink lightning bolt tattooed across one shoulder and stammered something out about looking for Ester.

The girl shut the door in Lee's face without a word. Lee was still off balance but turning around when the door opened again and Ester was there. Lee caught a glimpse down the hallway behind her; it was just like the one on the floor below, except that these rooms all had doors. She could hear the low pulse of techno music throbbing out from somewhere. Ester squeezed into the stairwell, closing the door.

"What did I say about coming up here?" She wasn't smiling.

Lee cringed under the admonishment. She followed Ester downstairs. "I finished the dishes."

"Good." At the landing she turned to face Lee again. "And how was your breakfast?"

"It was good. Thank you," she said to the floor, ashamed she hadn't thanked her before.

"That's okay. But those breakfasts don't pay for themselves."

"Oh, I . . ." Lee could feel herself turning red as she dug into her pockets, knowing there was nothing to find there. What had she done? Ester's tone had changed completely.

"That's not what I mean. Remember what I said about contributing?"

Lee nodded.

"Ever spare-changed before?"

Lee heard the door open and close upstairs. She stepped aside as Doug shouldered past them, carrying a plastic tub full of dirty dishes back down. Ester didn't wait for Lee's answer.

"There's a right way and a wrong way to go about it," Ester said when they'd reached the first-floor landing. "But once you get it down, there's nothing to it."

Lee tried to imagine herself approaching strangers and asking for money. The thought of it made her a little ill. But the thought of disappointing Ester was worse. "Is there something else I could do?"

"Worried about cops?" Ester put an arm around her and squeezed. "Don't. Just keep your head down and you'll be all right. I get the feeling you're good at keeping your head down. And here—" Ester plucked a trucker cap from a passing kid, who kept on going without a beat; she plopped it down onto Lee's head. "Presto—incognito."

Lee pulled the hat down low, until it was nearly covering her eyes.

Ester winked at her. "You'll be just fine."

She introduced her to a girl named Kellygreen, who gave Lee a story, one she used herself all the time, she said—that she had left an abusive stepfather and all the shelters were closed for the night and she was trying to get enough together for a room—and told Lee a good corner to work where others would watch out for her. "Don't worry," she said when Lee seemed surprised at this. "We keep an eye on our own." Kellygreen had long strawberry-blond hair and waxy red cheeks and eyes that conveyed such trusting naiveté that Lee knew the girl had no trouble persuading strangers on the street to hand her money. Lee wasn't so optimistic about herself.

For an hour Lee paced her corner, an intersection crowded with tourists and students from nearby UPenn, and tried to work up the nerve to approach someone and tell her story. She tried to stay out of sight and measure potential donors simultaneously: this one looks too poor, this one has had a bad day and isn't feeling generous, this one seems like a creep, this one has the New Age stink of Steve all over him. The few who passed muster were long gone, down the block or into one of the restaurants or shops or cafés, by the time she had decided on them.

Kellygreen hadn't said anything about how Lee was supposed to break through the shame. By midday she was disgusted with herself. She imagined going to Ester empty-handed, and the shame of that was even worse. Lee thought about Lois, who just made up a cardboard sign and sat on a corner waiting for people to throw her a few scraps. Maybe she didn't take in much that way, but it seemed something Lee might at least be able to pull off. But then she might as well put up a sign for the cops to come harass her. Maybe she could steal something, but Ester was expecting cash.

"Excuse me."

Lee hadn't realized how deeply lost she was in her thoughts and was startled to see a man in front of her, middle-aged, in a tie and black cardigan, carrying a canvas satchel.

"You're looking a little misplaced. Can I help you out with any-thing?"

Maybe he was a professor at the university. Lee took comfort in his beard. "I'm just trying to figure out what to do," she said.

"Can I help?"

"Only if you can get me back to Cincinnati." The lie came so easily.

"Ohio?"

"Jack said we'd get work out here, he promised to take care of me. I'm so stupid. I'm sorry, sir, this isn't your problem, I'm just a little . . . I just need to figure out a way back home." It was as though someone else were speaking, another girl out on her own, looking to get home. She almost believed herself.

"I guess things didn't work out with your boyfriend."

Lee examined a squashed piece of gum on the ground. "No."

The man pulled out his wallet. For a moment she thought he was going to flash a badge, but then he took out sixty dollars, all that he had there. "I don't know if you're telling me the truth, and I guess I don't really care. I've got a daughter about your age, and I hope that if she ever did something as foolish as you, someone would do the same for her. Even if she wasn't telling the truth."

Lee didn't take the money until he placed it in her hand. She watched him thread through the crowd down the block until he turned the corner and disappeared.

Before Lee returned to the Crystal Castle, she bought a can of Coke with a twenty-dollar bill and asked for her change in ones and quarters. She would give this to Ester and call it a day's work. That way the sixty bucks could last her a few more days. Lee just hoped that eighteen dollars and change was enough. But when she gave it to Ester later that evening, Ester didn't even count it, just shoved it into her pocket and went off to see about something upstairs.

That night Lee showered in one of the bathrooms of the Crystal Castle, drying herself with a damp towel already hanging on the rack. Earlier, at dinner, a girl had spilled her spaghetti all over Lee's front. The girl had tried to play it off as an accident, but Lee knew it hadn't been. Lee looked at herself in a mirror and barely recognized the face staring back at her. Her hair was stringy and matted; her eyes were sunken and dark and somehow puffy, too. And she'd lost weight— she could see it in her jutting pelvic bones and in her sternum, which looked as white and brittle as a soup cracker. She got back into her dirty clothes stained with red sauce and fixed her hair as best she could. She took one final look at herself in that ridiculous purple T-shirt. TOUGHER THAN CANCER. Right.

That night, as she lay in bed trying to sleep, a young man passed by her room. He wore a funny little white suit, a white cap, and he carried a canvas bag slung over one shoulder. Lee didn't see his face beyond a flash of glasses. He knocked on the Station Master's door.

"You have it?" she heard the Station Master ask.

"It wasn't easy."

"The Priest?"

"I can handle the old man. He's trapped in a room, what's he going to do?"

"This will change everything. You understand—there's no going back."

"I know it."

"Give it to me," the Station Master said.

When the young man passed by her room again, he was no longer carrying the bag. Lee wished she had some business with the Station Master. He had told her to come to him anytime, that they were family. But what would she say?

It was late and Lee was finally falling asleep when she felt a presence in the doorway and jolted awake. She knew it was him. It was as though he had heard her thoughts. She could feel him enter her room and gave herself a moment before turning her head to him. He wore the same suit as the day before.

"I'm sorry to wake you; it's been a busy day. But I wanted to check in. Did you get enough to eat today?" He came into the room and sat beside her. He was holding a cup of tea.

"Yes," she said. "Thank you."

"But you ate alone, didn't you?"

It was true. After the girl had spattered Lee with spaghetti sauce, she'd spent dinner at a table by herself, pretending to read a book she'd found on the shelf. She couldn't figure out how to fit herself in with any of the other tables. It was just like high school, before Edie.

"Why not sit with the other kids? Nobody here bites."

"I was just reading," she said.

He handed her the tea, and she leaned back against the wall. The warm cup felt good in her hands.

"Nothing wrong with that. But the others are all curious about you. And you have a lot to offer."

Lee didn't know what she had to offer, but she liked the way he half smiled at her when she scrunched her face up.

"Will you do that for me?"

"What?"

"Make an effort."

"Okay." She didn't know what more to add. She could see him about to leave, and her head swam with something to say that might keep him a bit longer. "Can I ask you something?"

"Of course."

She liked that when he looked at her, he didn't look away. But she still couldn't think of a thing to say. "What's upstairs?" she blurted out.

"You tried to go up there this morning, didn't you?"

"I didn't mean to. I was just . . ."

"Do you understand desire, Lee?"

"What do you mean?"

"You are too young, I think, to understand yet the nature of desire. You know what it is to want, perhaps even to yearn, but true desire is something else entirely."

"I guess."

"You don't understand what I'm talking about, but you will. We are a community, we exist like an undercurrent beneath society. But to exist in concert with society, we need a currency that society values."

She could feel his eyes on her, and she kept hers on his shoes. She no longer knew what to do with her hands, so it felt good to hold the warm cup.

"You still don't understand, but you will. Society has cast you out. Determined that it has no use for you. How does that make you feel?"

Lee didn't think about it like that. It was her mother who had cast her out. Her mother and Steve who had no use for her. Society didn't even know she existed.

As if inside her mind again, the man said, "Even your family has rejected you. I am sorry to be so blunt. But I need you to know that you are not alone. Each of us here has felt rejected in some way—by family, by society, by our supposed community or friends. But now you are here, and you have found another place, another way. You have found another family."

She felt her emotions rising from somewhere in her chest like an undertow wanting to pull her down. Lee took the spoon from the cup and bit down on it, focusing on the hard bite of the metal. But she could feel herself losing the battle by degrees. The man took the spoon from her mouth and put it back in her cup, then took the cup from her hands. When he sat back down beside her and put his arm around her, Lee was sobbing. He said nothing, only held her as she pressed herself into his chest. He was so thin she could feel his rib-cage beneath his suit jacket, and his heart felt right there in her ear. It beat slowly, pumping a steady river of calm that slowed her sobs until they and his heartbeat were synched.

"The Crystal Castle is like a mansion with many rooms, but you have to earn the right to enter some of those rooms, and you earn that right through trust. When you've earned trust, you earn keys." He pulled a strand of her hair loose from behind her ear. "All in good time. Now, can I trust you not to go back up there until I tell you it's time?"

Lee nodded into his chest.

"I need to hear you say it."

"Yes," she said, sitting back up. "You can trust me."

"Good." He kissed her tenderly on the head. "I told you you'd fit right in." He got up. "We don't pull punches here. But you will see we take care of our own." He seemed about to leave, then paused, and Lee followed his gaze to the mattress. He bent down close, then pulled back the thin sheet. Beneath it was a large brown stain. "I'm sorry about that. It's improper. We'll get you another mattress. Until then . . ." He offered her his hand and helped her up, then tore the sheet off and flipped the mattress. He got down on his knees and carefully remade the bed for her, tucking the sheet tightly underneath. He went back to his room and returned with a square of tissue paper tied with string, which he laid on the end of the bed. "I heard about what happened in the eating commons earlier. I hope this helps."

When he left, Lee untied the package and opened it. She held up a folded dress. It was old-fashioned, a simple gray cotton drop-waist dress with white cloth-covered buttons running up the front, all the way up the neck. It felt ancient.

Lee put the dress down and lay back on the newly made bed, still feeling his lips against her head. She felt stupid and briefly dirty—the man was twice her age—but whatever she was feeling wasn't sexual;

it was something else. He saw her. When she was with him, she knew she was the only thing in his world at that moment, and she liked that. Lee shifted and faced the wall and tried to will herself to sleep. She rolled onto her stomach, then her back. Something was digging into her spine, a spring in the mattress. Lee shifted again but couldn't find a position around it. She got up and removed the sheet—even the stain was better than this thing in her back—when she noticed the rectangular outline beneath the mattress fabric. She felt around it, felt the spring of a spiral notebook, and pushed it along until she was able to squeeze it out through a tear in the side of the mattress.

The notebook was about the size of her hand, and when she opened it, a small card-stock club flier fell out onto the bed. Lee recognized the style; it was the same as the one given to her and Edie in the café. On this one was a mechanical insectlike figure below a cloud with three square cutouts in it. Within the cutouts was an announcement of an event put on by the Société Anonyme, along with a date some weeks past. At the bottom it read ADMIT ONE, with a Web address and a six-digit code. As with the other flier, there was no street address, but someone had scrawled one on the back.

The first half of the book was filled with sketches and cartoon figures. Some of the kids from her school, graffiti bombers, had kept books like this. The same mouse head as the ones from the wall kept popping up again and again, with more frequency as she turned the pages. Then, about halfway through, it became a diary. The entries were undated, but they were clearly demarcated by day—seventeen of them.

The girl—there was no name but Lee could tell that much—had started out much like her, homeless and drifting, before she'd been invited to a party at some place called the Silo. She'd met a boy at a prearranged spot, and he had taken her there with several others, to a place well outside the city. The girl had written down the name of the road in case she ever wanted to come back, but once there she'd met Ester, who'd brought her back to the Crystal Castle. The first entries brimmed with feverish excitement and spoke of all the new friends she was making—she was clearly more outgoing than Lee, and Lee hated to see that the girl had felt the same giddy anticipation at the visits from the Station Master. Except she called him Josef, and Lee felt an unexpected pang of envy that the girl had earned his name.

Lee tried to picture the girl, lying awake as she herself did, waiting for Ester or the Station Master to give her their attentions. She wondered what this girl's life had been before she was here. She'd run away from home, probably, with nowhere else to go. Had she been lonely before she came here? Where was she now?

About a week in, the entries became so scattered and self-referential they were hard to follow. She wrote of wanting to please Josef enough to earn his trust, of fearing something upstairs but wanting to see it so badly she dreamed about it at night. The last entry was a single line:

He came today. It's time. I close my eyes and see it.

The next day Lee went out again to ask strangers for money. She didn't want to return to the same corner, because she didn't want to see the professor again. Lee liked the idea of him imagining her on a bus back to Ohio. So she chose a spot near the steps of the Philadelphia Museum of Art, where tourists stood in line to take pictures mimicking the victory pose of a life-sized bronze of Rocky Balboa. The spot was full of competition, and Lee watched others—both older and younger than she—approach strangers and ask for handouts as easily as asking for the time. By midafternoon she gave up. She still had forty dollars, which she could stretch to two days' worth of supposed panhandling before she'd be forced to come up with something.

Lee wandered the streets downtown, winding a tortuous path back to the Crystal Castle. It was nearly five when she got there, late enough to call it a day. Lois was on her corner, wearing the orange smock from the JDC. "Spare some dough?" she said as Lee passed.

Lee stopped, waiting for Lois to look up, to see her, and finally to recognize her. "Where you get that dress?" Lois said, her eyes trained on Lee's legs.

Lee looked down at herself, running a hand down the starched cotton.

"They bring you upstairs yet?" Lois said.

Lee sat down beside her. Lois was as mean as spit, but Lee still wanted to help her. "Why don't you come in with me? It's a pretty good deal—place to sleep, shower, two meals a day . . ."

"So you doing Ester's job now?"

"What?"

"Recruiting?"

"No, I—"

"Forget it. I got no use for them. Anyway, you'll see upstairs soon enough."

"Why do you keep saying that?"

"He's watching us right now, you know," she said, not looking at the Station Master's window. "Probably."

Lee said nothing.

"He talk to you about trust yet?" Lois asked.

Lee didn't answer, but she knew her expression told Lois he had.

"Well, that sure was quick. Shouldn't be surprised, though, pretty girl like you."

"What are you talking about?"

"First he'll tell you you need to earn his trust. Then he'll tell you his name. Then he's gonna tell you it's time. Then you'll see what's upstairs. I never talked to anyone after they went upstairs. Never saw them again."

"I don't believe you."

"What's it matter to me you believe me?"

Lee got up. She knew Lois was only trying to scare her; she was just mean that way. Lee didn't care; for some reason she wanted to help her anyway. But she also knew you couldn't help someone who didn't want to be helped. "Okay," she said. "Suit yourself."

That night at dinner Lee made a point of sitting at a table with four other kids, one of them the girl who had spilled spaghetti on her. She was a black girl with tight bleached cornrows and sharp, pretty eyes. She pointed at Lee's chest with a fork and said, "How you like my dress?"

Lee looked down, embarrassed. She didn't know what to say.

"You know how long I been looking for that? You stole that from my room."

Another girl whispered something to the boy next to her and giggled.

The black girl stuck her fork into a piece of Lee's chicken and popped it into her mouth. "I want it back."

Lee looked down at the dress again, then around the room. It was just like what had gone down in the detention center with her shoes, but there was no Maria here to defend her. She stood, deflated. "Whatever. You want it? I'll go change and bring it back down."

"Uh-uh," the girl said. "Right here."

"Come on. I'm not even wearing a bra."

"Not my fault you're flatter than Nebraska."

Then the room went silent, as though a window had slammed shut, blocking all the noise out. Lee could feel the attention of the kids behind her shift, and she turned to see the Station Master, standing in line with a plate in his hands, waiting for food as the rest of them did. He was talking casually to a few kids in line, and Lee wished she could hear what he was saying. He noticed her and nodded. But then he turned back around, and she no longer had even that little piece of him.

He took his plate upstairs, and the room went back into motion as though the window had been opened again. The girl was staring hard at Lee, and Lee began to unbutton the dress, but the girl reached out and touched her arm.

"Hey, man, I'm just fucking with you," she said. "Of course that ain't my dress. And I like flat titties—my mom had nice big ones and you should see them now, like two socks holding grapefruits." She laughed.

"You're such a bitch, Ramona," said the boy.

By the end of the meal, Lee felt that they'd accepted her. Ester came down once and smiled at Lee sitting there at the table, and seeing that gap between her teeth made Lee feel good.

The Station Master came to her room again that night. He sat beside Lee on her bed and asked her how she was settling in. Lee felt an urge to answer in a way that pleased him, but she didn't know how. It was easier to know what to say to Ester, whose face couldn't help but display her emotions. This man was unreadable.

"I saw you sitting with the others today. See, nobody bites."

"Just making an effort."

He smiled. "Can I ask you something?" The man waited for her to meet his eyes before going on. "What did Lois say to you? Earlier today, on the corner?"

Lee knew she couldn't tell the man what Lois had said. "She's all alone. Why don't you take her in, too?"

"Lois is welcome to come in again any time she wants. She has an open invitation. She knows that."

"Again?"

"She was with us once, for a short time. But some kids are just . . . feral. They've been out on the streets too long, and they—they start to believe things, even to see things, that aren't there. They feel better out in the open. She's not in here with us, but we still look out for her. Once you're family, you're always family." He took Lee's hand and gently removed it from the lock of hair she'd been pulling, then took the hair and pulled it behind her ear. "Did she say something to you?"

The man leaned back and shifted behind Lee, taking Lee's hair, and began braiding it. Lee felt the skin of her neck prick with electricity.

She stared at the dark corner of the room. "Not really." He pushed her head around until he could meet her eyes, and Lee, without being able to stop herself, said, "Only that she had no use for you." Why had she said that? She hated herself.

The man went back to braiding Lee's hair into two ropes, which he wrapped around the top of her head, pinning them there. It was an act that might have been creepy from a different man, but from him it seemed mannered and old-fashioned. "Soon enough you won't be saying 'you,'" he said. "You'll be saying 'us.' But until then, I'd suggest staying clear of Lois. Like any feral animal, she's unpredictable, even dangerous. Do you understand?"

Lee knew he was wrong about this, but she nodded anyway.

He stood, took a long look at her. "When I first saw you, I thought it a coincidence."

"What coincidence?"

"But there is meaning, even destiny, in coincidence. Remember when we first met, I told you that you came here for a reason?"

"Yes."

"I'm quite sure you don't know what that reason is. Am I right?"

Lee said nothing.

"Well, I do know what that reason is. I don't think you're ready for it yet, but you will be. In time. Can you trust me until that time?"

Lee nodded.

"Thank you. Good night, Lee."

"Good night. Sir," she said.

"You should call me Josef."

When the Station Master was gone, Lee went down the hall to the bathroom. She buttoned the dress and stood back to inspect herself in the mirror. She didn't recognize the girl staring back at her. The chaotic tangle of her hair was made serene, even elegant. This girl was pretty and refined. Lee had felt a thrill run through her when he told her his name, as though he'd given her the key to a secret garden.

That night Lee dreamed that she was sharing her room with a girl, the same girl who had written the diary. Her hair was braided in the same fashion as Lee's, and she kept talking Josef this and Josef that. Lee felt herself grow annoyed when the girl put on Lee's new dress and kept flattening it down with her greasy fingers. Lee woke to footsteps down the hall, and the dream girl remained in the room with her, naked now, for several terrifying seconds before slowly disappearing into the air. Lee felt the dress on her and realized she'd fallen asleep in it.

Someone was knocking on the Station Master's door, lightly at first, then loudly. She heard the door open, heard the Station Master say, "What is it?" But after that only whispers. Lee pretended to be asleep as she watched the Station Master, looking pale and spindly in boxer shorts and a white undershirt, follow a boy down the hall.

Lee lay in the dark, letting the dream fade. She heard sounds upstairs, then raised voices that hushed quickly. The diary came back to her, and she pulled it out to read again: *He came today. It's time. I close my eyes and see it.* Upstairs. What had happened to her?

Lee stuffed the diary behind the radiator, then got out of bed. The hallway was empty. She stood against the Station Master's door and listened, then reached for the knob and turned, as slowly as if she were defusing a bomb. The door cracked open. She told herself to go back; she'd promised him he could trust her. But it was as though some machine had been set in motion and she was powerless to stop it. She edged into the room, closing the door behind her.

When she'd been here before, the Station Master had drawn all her attention; now that he was gone, the room carried a fuzzy residue of his presence. She could feel him, beneath the smell of old cigarettes and garlic, in everything he'd touched. The whole room seemed to hum with him. There was an old armoire in the corner beside the door, and a painting hanging above a dresser, a frenzied explosion of color and movement that made her a little dizzy to look at. Lee kept telling herself to leave, once even saying it out loud, but before she knew it, she had opened the armoire. Five suits hung inside. Each was dark, thick wool, old and slightly moth-eaten. Lee noticed an insignia on the sleeve of one of them, and she pulled it out. It was more of a uniform than a suit, even heavier than the others, a blue so dark it was nearly black, rumpled and ancient-looking. A matching cap, with the same insignia, rested on the shelf above. She thought of the uniform on the young man who'd paid the Station Master a visit that night. It was different but seemed of the same era. Lee let the suit swing back into the armoire.

The bicycle wheel sat there inert, its apparent purpose nothing more than casting shadows. Briefly she scanned the titles on his bookshelf, a lot of organic chemistry texts and books on art. A whole shelf was devoted to books about alchemy. On the desk was an old manual typewriter. Lee picked up a steel fountain pen and rolled it between her fingers, resisting the urge to pocket it—how delicious would that feel?—before setting it back down. She opened the desk drawer. His black ledger sat there, the one he'd been writing in when she first met him.

Its pages were filled with tiny, neat handwriting in black ink: dates going back nearly four years, followed by a series of numbers. Each number was followed by an "M" or "F," which was followed in turn by notes in shorthand or code. The last entry was from a few days before: #46, F. Beside it he had simply written a question mark and circled it.

Then Lee spotted something shining dully from beneath the bed. She crouched and pulled out an old metal lockbox. She placed it on the desk. Its lock was broken. Inside was a bound stack of Polaroids. When she twisted off the rubber band, the Polaroids popped out of her hand, spilling across the desk in a crowd of faces gazing placidly up at her. Teenagers, all of them, black kids and white kids and brown kids, hair short and long, braided and cornrowed and spiked, skin smooth and acned and freckled. An array of faces that could have come from the yearbook of her high school. On the back of each was a number.

Lee saw her own face among them; it was the photo Ester had taken in the cafeteria. On the back was written #46. And then she recognized another. As she held the photo up, Claire Faver's face stared back at her. Lee didn't know what to do with this information. She had been here a week—surely she would have seen Claire if she had been here, too. Then her eyes landed on another photo, framed and hanging above the desk. Lee put Claire's photo down and lifted the frame from the wall. Had it been here before? Lee couldn't remember, but surely she would have noticed it. The photograph looked a hundred years old, cracked at the edges and peeling. In it a young woman stood with her hands clasped in front of her, staring past the camera. Her dress was identical to Lee's, her hair pulled back in two braids tied above her head. More than that, she had the same nose as Lee, the same sleepy eyes. Lee looked more closely. It could have just been something on the photo, but the woman even had a dark mole above her lip, just like Lee's.

She was shaking now. The dress felt suddenly grotesque, and she wanted to rip the braids from her hair. How had she found herself here? Lee thought back to the man in the park who had told her to come to this place, find the Station Master. Had the Station Master been waiting for her all along? *First he'll tell you you need to earn his trust. Then he'll tell you his name. Then he's gonna tell you it's time. Then you'll see what's upstairs.* Her hands shaking too much to get the rubber band back around the photos, she dumped them back in the box and slid it under the bed where she'd found it. Lee was about to leave when she saw it hanging from a wood and metal coatrack on the wall: the satchel that the young man had brought the Station Master. She grabbed it. Footsteps were coming down the hall. There was no way she'd get back to her room without being seen.

She looked at the armoire—she could fit. Then she saw the fire escape outside the window. The window wouldn't open at first, and Lee almost smashed it before she saw the latch. It opened easily and she climbed out, shutting the window behind her.

The sidewalk was a long way down, too far to jump. Lee dropped the bag and pushed down on the ladder, but it wouldn't budge. He would be back in his room any second now. Lee wondered how much time it would take him to realize that someone had been there, and how much time from then to look out his window. Another ladder led up. Lee took it.

She climbed to the next floor, freezing when the landing groaned beneath her weight. Lee looked up, but the ladder stopped there. There was another window at this landing. Through it she could see a hallway lit only by the lights from the few open rooms; most of the others had their doors closed. At the far end was the door they kept locked. On the other side of that door was the main stairway, which led out to the street. If she could get there before the Station Master realized she'd been in his room, she might make it.

Lee lifted the window quietly and crept down the hallway. One of the doors ahead was open. She slowed as she got to it, angling her head around.

Inside the room a girl sat on a bed. She had ringlets of curly red hair and a face full of freckles, and she was dressed in a tight purple half top that pushed her breasts up and a tiny pleated purple skirt, with white stockings and matching purple pumps. She sat with her legs curled beneath her, staring straight at Lee, two big blue jellyfish eyes oscillating in her head. It was clear she both saw Lee and did not see her, that she was looking at Lee and through her at the same time. Her outfit, but more than that those huge nonseeing eyes, made her look like a cartoon. Lee felt herself go dizzy, trying to make sense of what she was seeing. She stood there, unable to move. Until the girl smiled at her, which was enough to break the spell.

Across the hall was another open door. In an identical room a boy, maybe fourteen and wearing nothing but a pair of tight blue underwear, swayed to music she couldn't hear. His big brown misshapen irises took in Lee as she passed him, but he said nothing. Lee had seen him before, and it took her a moment to place him: his was one of the faces in the Polaroids from the lockbox. His eyes had been normal in that photo. Lee took off running.

She was nearly to the door at the end when she was stopped in her tracks by three loud knocks. Lee froze. The same girl she'd seen manning the door before came out of her room. She kept her back to Lee as she opened the door. A man in a shiny suit came through but stopped when he saw Lee. He leered at her. "Who's that?"

The girl turned, and when she saw Lee, her face went stricken.

Lee made it back to the window in a half-dozen strides and exited so fast she nearly lost her footing and fell. She took the ladder down and looked up to see the girl staring down at her from the landing above. Then Lee felt another pair of eyes on her. She turned. The Station Master was on the other side of his window, facing her. He held in one hand the open ledger, his expression the bewildered look of a boy who'd just had his feelings hurt.

Lee looked down. She'd break her legs if she jumped; she had no doubt about that. She pushed on the ladder again, but it didn't budge. When she heard the window open behind her, Lee jumped on the ladder with all her weight and felt it give way beneath her. She held on and it took her to the ground, dumping her onto the sidewalk. Lee sprung up without checking to see if she'd been hurt. The bag was a few feet away; it must have tumbled down after her. She grabbed it and took off down the street.

FOUR

HER mom's old Geo Prizm was not in the driveway. Lee didn't recognize the newish green Prius that sat there instead, but the string of Tibetan prayer beads or whatever they were hanging from the rearview had the stench of Steve all over them. She went between her house and the neighbors' and around to the back.

With any luck her mother would be at work. Steve was always home, not having a job to speak of, but he was clueless, and if she was stealthy enough, she could be in and out without his noticing. Lee rolled an old wheelbarrow to the back of the house, upended it, and climbed on top. The window to her room opened easily.

For a moment she thought she'd come to the wrong house. It certainly wasn't her room anymore. All her stuff was gone, replaced by wicker tables holding orchids and scented candles. Where her bed had been, a pair of cushions sat facing a wooden cabinet, on top of which squatted a stone Buddha, sticks of incense embedded in a pool of sand between his legs. Where once was taped the picture of the female archaeologist, there now hung a bamboo scroll with lacquered Asian script and a woven mandala. Even the desk and chair where she used to do her homework were gone. The room smelled of burnt sage, and she stepped through quietly, trying not to gag, concentrating her anger to stay focused. It was as if they'd erased her.

She slid open the closet door. A neat stack of unopened boxes with Steve's company logo—a jolly laughing Buddha—plastered on each took up most of the space. But on the shelf above sat a row of old boxes. She pulled a few down. They were stuffed with her clothes. She grabbed a pair of jeans, a few shirts, a gray hoodie, underwear and socks, and her black Chuck Taylors. The guitar case was nowhere to be found. Lee began tearing the boxes apart, pulling them aside noisily, not caring if anyone heard. Then she saw it, leaning way in the back behind the tallest stack of Steve's boxes, almost covered by an unrolled sleeping bag. Lee exhaled. Maybe she'd take that bus to Ohio after all. She found herself thinking of Edie again, wondering where she'd gone to school, but pushed that thought from her head. She shoved the boxes aside and grabbed the handle of the case.

Lee could tell from the weight that it was empty. Her mother, who had once created an entire tinsel-strewn gala of old dolls and stuffed animals when no one showed up to Lee's sixth birthday party, had stolen her money, or had let Steve steal it, to buy a car and a bunch of plastic nonsense. She opened the case anyway. Everything she'd been saving for, her entire college tuition, gone. Her hope of a new start, gone. The only things left, in the corner of the case, were seventy cents and a little blue glass bottle, the tiny silver die still inside. Lee stuffed the clothes and the sleeping bag into the canvas satchel, pulled on her sneakers and hoodie, and shoved the bottle into her pocket.

Those fuckers. Lee didn't know why she'd expected her money to still be here. It wasn't theirs to take, and that had seemed enough. She wanted to scream, to smash everything in the room, to squat and piss on the stone Buddha. She grabbed the mandala and tried to tear the thing apart in her hands. It was the only silent act of destruction she could manage, but she couldn't even manage that—the mandala, which looked woven, was just a hard piece of colored plastic.

When she opened the door, Lee could see, down the hall, Steve's elbow scrunched into a leathery pouch against the kitchen table. As she made her way toward him, she heard the clank of a pan and smelled bacon cooking. Then her mother crossed into her sight line, and Lee froze. She asked herself what she hoped to accomplish by confronting them. Somehow her mom hadn't seen Lee, despite the fact that Lee was standing practically right in front of her, and when her mom turned away, Lee slipped into their bedroom.

Steve's wallet was lying on the nightstand, with two hundred and twenty-three dollars inside. Lee considered rummaging around to see if there was any more of her money stashed away but knew she shouldn't push her luck. Steve would call the cops on her without hesitation, and her mom would let him. One of his necklaces, a purple crystal with a leather cord tied around it, was hanging from the mirror. Steve called it his transcendental amulet, and he wore it when he was in special need of positive energies from the universe. Lee took it just to spite him.

A few bus rides and twenty minutes of walking later, Lee came across a fenced-off field of junk—engine blocks and rusting axles and radiators, old refrigerators and piles of scrap copper, spaced in neat rows like some sort of orchard of crushed metal. It was just as Maria, back at the JDC, had described it. SANTIAGO'S SALVAGE CITY was strung across the front gate in a sign made from twisted hunks of metal, broken lengths of pipe, and old golf clubs. Most of the lot was filled with the rusting heaps of cars. Some were stacked on top of each other, others so mangled Lee could smell the death on them. But one area was given over to cars that were more or less whole.

Lee slipped in behind a pickup full of scrap metal and ducked between a row of old appliances to where the intact cars sat. She chose an old van up on blocks because it had few windows. She was happy to find it carpeted inside. It must have been, back in its day, a real studmobile. Now it was a rotting hulk of metal that smelled of mold and stale beer and puke. But she had a change of clothes, a bit of money, and a place to sleep, at least for now. She thought about what she'd seen upstairs. Those kids. What had happened to them? And the Thrumm kids in Wonderland—hollowed out, adrift. They were the same. The diary girl. Had she become like them, too? Was that the fate Lee had just escaped herself? The thought of it made her sick with relief and rage.

The screech of crashing metal jolted Lee awake, and it took her several seconds to remember where she was. She crawled toward the front of the van and peeked out the driver's side window into the morning light. A few men were unloading junk onto a pile, and another was sorting through it. A flatbed truck was waiting to unload an old 1970s sedan with its entire rear end crumpled in.

For a moment she wondered if the past days had all been a dream. Then she saw the Station Agent's canvas satchel in the corner of the van. She crawled over and opened it. She tossed her clothes to the side. Beneath them was a small cardboard box. She took it out and placed it in her lap, then undid the flaps. Sitting on top of a nest of crumpled newspaper was a strange object: a ball of twine encased within two identical brass plates and held tight by four long screws. She picked it up. It looked very old. The top plate was about five inches square. Carefully painted in block letters, it read:

P.G.	.ECIDES	DÉBARRASSE.
LE.	D.SERT.	F.URNIS.ENT
AS	HOW.V.R	COR.ESPONDS

Lee turned it over in her hands. Along the bottom, in the same block letters, it said:

.IR.	.CAR.É	LONGSEA →
F.NE,	HEA.,	.O.SQUE →
TE.U	S.ARP	BAR AIN →

Something inside rattled when she turned it. Whatever she'd been expecting to find, this was a disappointment. Still, she hoped that it meant something to the Station Master and that part of him had died when he found it missing. She put it back in its box.

Lee hadn't eaten in nearly a day, and her throat was parched, but she huddled in the hot darkness of the van for several more hours, until she heard the sounds of men leaving and then the front gate shut. She waited a half hour more, biding the time by removing the cord from Steve's crystal and using it to fashion a necklace of her own around the little blue bottle. She turned her attention back to the twine-ball object for a while, trying to decipher the code. Lee had always liked puzzles; she and her father used to spend mornings and evenings working through a big book of brain teasers he had bought her for her seventh birthday. But after a while she grew impatient and tossed the object aside. When she was sure the yard was clear, she climbed from the van and out of the yard, slipping beneath a loose section of cyclone fencing near the back.

A mile down the road Lee found a gas station convenience store, where she bought a package of beef jerky, a bag of corn chips, a Coke, and a tin of sardines. As she chugged the Coke and the rush of sugar seemed to puff the blood back into her, her eyes landed on a bulletin board by the front door. A face stared back at her. It couldn't be, but it was. Lee wasn't used to seeing Edie in glasses, but in this photo she wore them, smiling, along with a tight red cardigan. Lee had stolen that sweater for her herself. Above the photo the word MISSING was prominent in big block letters, and below that EDIE OSWALD. Along the side were

Edie's statistics: her age, her height and weight, her hair and eye colors, her complexion. Lee tore the photo from the board and read the rest of it. Edie had last been seen the night of August 1, leaving her Belmont Village home. Nearly five weeks ago. The date triggered something, and Lee stared at it until it came back to her: August 1 was the date on the flier she'd found in the girl's diary. Was Edie in one of those rooms upstairs? Lee thought she might burn the Crystal Castle to the ground if she knew she could do it without any of those poor kids getting hurt.

That night in the van, every time she closed her eyes she'd see the face of the girl in the room upstairs. The eyes of that girl kept hovering there, just past her vision. Lee wondered what was going on behind those eyes. She thought of the men visiting upstairs. They didn't look like they were part of the Crystal Castle. They were clients. Lee remembered what the Station Master had said to her about the currency of desire. At the time it had sounded like something profound. Now it disgusted her. Whatever happened to those kids might have happened to Claire. And now maybe Edie. Lee wondered if Edie, too, had slept in one of those rooms at the Crystal Castle. If he'd told her his name, then invited her upstairs. It could have been Lee there, if she'd stayed any longer. It would be some other kid next.

Lee thought again about returning, slipping into the Station Master's room and stabbing him through his eye as he slept. She would never have the guts to do that. But she could do something. Lee found a phone booth a few blocks from the yard.

When the operator asked who she wanted to call, Lee didn't know. "The police?"

"Is this an emergency? If this is an emergency, you should dial 911."

"It's not an emergency."

"What district, please?"

"I don't know what district. Isn't there some kind of anonymous tip line or something?"

It sounded stupid when she said it, but it turned out there was exactly such a thing. The dispatcher Lee eventually got connected to sounded bored and unconvinced when Lee tried to explain to her what she'd seen. Even to Lee, the more she talked, the more fantastic it sounded. But the woman took down the intersection the building was on and promised that someone would check it out.

Lee hadn't been planning to go back—it was a stupid idea—but she just had to see with her own eyes who they escorted out of the building. If Edie was among the Thrumm kids, then at least Lee would have saved her from something. Maybe they could help her, bring her back to life. And to see the Station Master arrested and taken away in cuffs would be something. When she got there, the building was dark, lifeless-looking. She waited. About an hour later Lee saw a police cruiser silently round the corner and pull up in front of the building. She pulled herself into the shadows. The cruiser stopped in the middle of the street as a cop got out of the passenger seat, and one hand on his holster, the other holding a flashlight, he found the door of the Crystal Castle, opened it, and went in.

Lee waited, one minute, then two, wondering what to expect. Gunshots? A mass exodus? A rush of backup squad cars? But ten minutes later the cop emerged from the building, shut off his flashlight, and got into the car. The cruiser pulled away as silently as it had arrived.

Lee took her time getting to the door, skulking between parked cars, making sure to keep out of the sight line of the Station Master's window. The lobby of the Crystal Castle was pitch-black, but she could feel its emptiness as soon as she shut the door behind her. Lee felt her way to the stairwell and climbed up to the first floor. The only light was light from the streetlamps that washed in through the windows of the open rooms along the hall. Lee poked into each room that she passed. There were no mattresses, no clothes on the floor or posters on the walls, nothing to indicate that anyone had been here in years.

Lee didn't know what she'd expected to see in the Station Master's room, but the stark vacancy of it left her feeling disoriented.

Nothing remained of the man's presence—no bed, no armoire, no chess table, no desk or paintings or books or useless bicycle wheel— and she could feel nothing of him here anymore. Lee began to feel crazy. She was on her way out and was passing her room when she saw the series of cartoon mouse heads on the wall. She remembered the girl's diary.

She crossed into the room and felt around behind the radiator with her hand until her fingers brushed something hard. The diary was still there. She stuck it into her pocket.

When Lee emerged from the empty building, she looked for Lois. Maybe she had seen them leave. But there was no sign of her at all.

That night, slouching against the wall of the van and staring at the swaying shadows of the junkyard beyond the windshield, Lee felt as hollowed out as she had in solitary. When she pulled the diary out and opened it, the flier fell out onto her lap. Lee squinted at it in the moonlight. Its date was past, and there was no address, but there was that street name, which the girl had scrawled on the back. The Station Master might have pulled a disappearing act, but maybe he'd left a trail.

Outside the salvage yard looked extraterrestrial in the moonlight. The landscape felt lunar, emptier even than in the van. It began to rain, fat drops that beat against her neck and hands. Near the van was a heap of old bicycles, and Lee dug through them until she found one that was more or less intact. She pulled the bike under the fence and pedaled to the convenience store, where she had taken to buying most of her food.

She bought a bottle of Coke and a package of beef jerky. The clerk stared through her. She'd come in every day, sometimes twice a day for nearly two weeks now, and the same clerk just looked right through her every time. Before leaving, she went to a rack of Philadelphia road maps and pulled one out. She found the street on the back of the card, which looked like an access road off the highway, about six miles north of the city.

Lee pedaled through sheets of rain that soaked through her clothes before she'd gotten a mile. She rode along the side of the highway, cars honking as they sped past, until she found the overgrown dirt road. She would have missed it had she been driving by in a car. There was no sign, but it was the only access road she'd seen in miles, so she took her chances.

The road wound through a long, wooded area that brought back memories of her escape from the JDC. It opened up to a large dirt lot harboring twenty or so cars parked haphazardly around a tall concrete wall with barbed wire running along the top. A security camera was mounted on a pole high above the wall. It could have been a military complex, except for the undulant electronic beat that seemed to be emanating from the ground itself. The area was surrounded by pine woods, and there were no people, no other buildings, in sight.

As she approached a steel door built into the wall, a floodlight clicked on. Lee dropped her eyes. A voice behind a slot in the door asked for her invite. She kept her head down as she handed the card through a slot. The man ran a blacklight over it, and Lee saw the image of a bicycle wheel appear briefly on the flier. Then he turned it over.

"This invite's expired."

"I know," Lee said. "I missed it. I was just—"

"Sorry to hear that. Maybe you just weren't meant to come."

"I came all the way out here by bike. Isn't there some way—"

"Pull your hoodie down."

"What?"

"Let me see your face."

She didn't like the way he seemed to be leering at her. She pulled the hood off and stared into the slot.

The door opened with a loud, rusty creak. A fat guy with a bushy beard and glasses, spilling off an old metal stool and holding an open book in his lap, nodded his head at her, and she was in.

There was no building, no structure at all, on the other side of the wall. Just a large round concrete slab like a helipad, in the middle of which was an enormous inflatable . . .

Clown's head.

Its eyes had been modified with colored strobes, which flashed in time to music so loud it made the whole head tremble.

As she walked closer, Lee could see the purpose of the clown's head: it was covering a concrete-enclosed steel door, which opened onto a staircase. A light, chemical-smelling smoke wafted up from below. Lee looked back once more at the bouncer on his stool. What was she hoping to accomplish here? She had no plan going in, nothing to defend herself with, not even a story if anyone questioned her.

She held the red steel railing tightly. The music, a thumping, droning, ceaseless thing, only got louder the farther down she went, and the smoke thicker. By the time she got to the landing, it felt as if there was no more air, only smoke and the music, which throbbed in pulsing waves that beat against her body. There was another steel door at this landing, and the stairs continued down. Lee tried the door, but it was locked. She followed the music down.

Just as she reached the second landing, three kids stumbled out from a door to her left, laughing and shoving each other. The two boys had mustaches and wore old-fashioned suits. The girl wore a prairie dress with a doily collar. Her hair was short and slicked back beneath a wide-brimmed hat. She turned to smile at Lee as she passed.

The trio headed down a long hall toward the music and disappeared into the smoke. Everything down here was painted the same thick battleship gray. Exposed pipes and wires ran along the walls and ceiling, and the door they'd emerged from had a glass porthole. Like being in a submarine. Lee slipped past them into the room.

When the door shut behind her, the music became a ghost of what it was. She was in a large circular room with a concrete column rising from the center, from which a dozen standing racks came out like huge bicycle spokes. The racks were hung with old clothes.

"Find something dry to put on," a voice said.

Lee jumped. A man was sitting in a chair directly behind her, leaning back with his hands clasped around one knee. When he stood, she had to step back to look up at him. He wore an antiquated black suit, with a high-collared white shirt and a black tie. He had thick brown wavy hair brushed back from a high forehead.

The man touched her shoulder, guiding her down a rack of old clothes. Flapper dresses and ruched gowns, service uniforms and old suits, top hats and straw boaters and fedoras. Period costumes. Everything looked to be a hundred years old. Avoiding the man's eyes, she ran her hands along the costumes, briefly pulling out a beaded cabaret dress before putting it back.

"If I might," he said, and walked to the end of one row and took out a simple white wedding dress. Plain and straight, its only embellishment a curtain of beaded tassels at the hem.

"The Bride," he said. "No?"

Lee stood absolutely still. She looked down. She was still dripping from the rain, a small pool of water forming around her feet.

He ran a finger along the pale silk. "Here. Allow me."

He gently set the dress aside, then took hold of her soaked sweatshirt and lifted. He smelled of sandalwood. Edie'd had in her room a book of old black-and-white photos of actors and actresses from the golden age of Hollywood. Most of them looked unreal to her, flat and white as paper. But one of them, Rudolph Valentino, transcended every photograph he was in. He was luminous, otherworldly. This man's skin was as white as that.

He was part of this, Lee knew. She was so scared she couldn't do anything but follow the man's lead. She brought her arms up and let him strip the wet clothes off her body, first her sweatshirt, then her shirt. She pulled off her wet jeans herself. He turned her around and lowered the dress down onto her. When his skin touched her bare back, she felt a pulse of electricity. He zipped her up. The dress fit as if it had been sewn around her.

He turned her around to face him. He had narrow gray eyes. A thick lock of hair had fallen across his forehead. She felt he might lean in for a kiss. Lee didn't know what to do. Her instincts had shut down. She closed her eyes.

"It's perfect," he said. "And the party is full of bachelors."

When she opened her eyes, he was closing the door behind him. Lee stood there feeling stupid and small.

She poked through a pile of shoes on the floor before her disgust took over and she just pulled the soggy sneakers she'd come in with back on.

As she squished her way back down the tunnel, Lee passed a man costumed in what looked like an old policeman's uniform. He turned to watch her. The tunnel was corrugated steel, with a graffiti mural that ran the entire length. The music grew louder and denser as she approached a thick black curtain at the far end. When she pushed through, Lee found herself in a huge round space, like some sort of hangar, crowded with dancing bodies.

Up on a stage a DJ in an old European-looking uniform smoked a cigar and spun records. An antiquated projector splashed a black-and-white film onto the wall behind him, the images moving with the amphetamine speed of silent cinema: a pair of men gallivanting around a wheeled cannon; a bearded man in ballerina dress performing a grotesque pirouette; a pair of men playing chess on a rooftop. Seated in chairs on the stage, as though mirroring this part of the film, two men in tweed suits stared down at their own chess game, ignoring the throbbing chaos around them. They moved pieces quickly back and forth, but Lee couldn't help thinking it was all for show.

A girl in a black sequined dress flowed past her, and a boy wearing an old soldier's uniform twitched in place. Lee pressed herself against the wall, trying to make herself invisible. The music took residence in her with a kind of popping effervescence, so dense it hurt her teeth.

There was a hiss followed by a creaking noise so loud Lee thought a wall must have collapsed. People around her stopped dancing and looked up. Lee looked up, too, to see the concrete roof slowly split down the center as four enormous yellow hydraulic arms pushed the slabs until they were vertical. The room erupted with a cheer, and with the roof open Lee felt a cool wave wash over her and a sudden feeling of expansiveness. She looked up to the naked sky, the clouds gone, stars dotting the black canvas in a mist of light.

A girl with short blond lacquered hair was circulating the room, her beaded flapper dress winking as she threaded through the dancers. She carried in one hand an unlit cigarette in a long holder and in the other a tray of plastic water bottles. She was something to look at, oozing sex in that effortless way that Lee had always envied, and it caught Lee by surprise when the girl said something to her. Lee had to lean in to hear, close enough that she caught the smell of watermelon candy from the girl's neck.

"I said, welcome to Société Anonyme!" she shouted this time. "I'm Xenia. If you need anything, come find me!"

Lee felt some part of herself begin to unfurl toward the girl, the way she did when Edie had first approached her that day behind the gym, when Ester had outside the Crystal Castle. Like a dog rolling belly-up in hopes of a rub. She hated herself for it.

The girl placed the bottle of water in her hand. "You need to stay hydrated down here! Even with the roof up I've seen girls pass out when they didn't drink enough water. Don't make more work for me." She winked and went off the way she had come.

It was just like any other rave she'd been to—vintage suits and dresses and uniforms instead of phat pants and pony beads, and a repurposed missile silo in place of a warehouse or field, but in the end it was the same music and the same lost, unfettered kids. They were kids she could have gone to school with; she didn't recognize any of them personally, but they danced with the same hunger, looked inward with the same blank stares while wanting only to be seen. Edie was nowhere to be found, of course. She hadn't really expected her to be here, but a part of her had hoped. What had she expected to find? The Station Master? Ester? More Thrumm kids? At the Crystal Castle, the Thrumm kids were held upstairs; maybe they were being held somewhere out of sight here, as well.

Lee wove her way across the floor, navigating sweat-slick bodies and hands that darted about like pale hummingbirds. Looking without knowing what she was looking for. Nobody paid her any attention beyond a few stoned smiles that greeted her as they did everyone else. A boy danced around her, his feet sliding around beneath him like he was on ice.

Suddenly Lee felt herself being watched. She turned. The chess players were staring at her. It took her a double take to recognize the one on the right. He had shaved his beard down to the mustache, and the kindness was gone from his eyes, but it was him: the man who had given her sixty dollars for a bus ride back to Ohio. The professor. Their eyes met. He no longer saw in her his own teenage daughter. He didn't even have a teenage daughter.

A wave of sickness washed through her. She'd been playing a game with an opponent who was moves ahead of her. The tall man who'd given her the dress was watching her from across the room. She turned back to the DJ, recognizing him now, too—the homeless guy from the park, the one who'd told her to find the Station Master. Lee looked up through the open roof. The surface was there, three stories up, but there were no ladders, no way to get out but the way she'd come in.

The curtained doorway was across the dance floor. Lee made for it, slamming through the dancing kids. She was through the curtain and halfway down the tunnel when she stopped. The costumed policeman was sitting on the stairs at the end, smoking a cigarette and eyeing her curiously. Without hurry, he ashed his cigarette and stood. Lee felt her breaths turn to sharp pains in her chest, and she bent down, dizzy and collapsing inside, when she felt a hand on her shoulder. She wanted to scream, but she couldn't breathe. A voice said, "This way."

Lee couldn't see well enough to make out more than an old woman wearing a shawl wrapped around a head of gray hair. She wore a pair of black-framed glasses glinting green in the light. The woman hissed. "Come with me."

Lee looked back at the policeman. He was walking her way now.

The woman gripped her shoulder and pulled. Lee broke from her stupor and followed the woman back toward the doorway she'd just come through. But instead of going through the curtain, the woman turned quickly the other way, behind a different curtain. She shifted herself behind Lee and guided Lee's hand to a ladder welded into the wall.

Lee climbed. She could feel the woman behind her, her hands brushing against Lee's ankles. Step by step her breathing began to return to normal. Then her knuckles brushed a steel ceiling and Lee nearly hit her head. The woman grabbed hold of her. She was surprisingly strong. She reached around Lee and undid a latch. The woman pulled down. There was a click, followed by a tiny hydraulic gasp, then a sliver of light came through from above. Lee pushed and the cylindrical steel door popped open. She emerged behind the clown's head. Lee turned to help but the woman was already up, closing the door behind her. When she reached up and pulled the shawl off, her hair came with it. It was a wig.

The boy before her was short, shorter than Lee even, with a wide, squat face and wavy brown hair. Just a few years older than she.

When he reached out and grabbed her arm, Lee instinctively pulled back, losing her balance and nearly falling. She steadied herself and looked down. A good thirty feet below her the kids danced, oblivious to everything but the music. The chess players were gone, but the tall dark-suited man was staring up at her. Lee thought she saw him smile before she turned and headed quickly for the front gate. The boy followed. "Slow down," he said. "Take it easy." Lee slowed, but only because she thought the doorman might try to stop them. But he opened the door to let them through without even looking up from his book.

"Are you okay?"

"Who are you?" Lee said.

"Are you sure you're okay?"

"Why were you dressed that way?"

The boy raised an eyebrow at her, and Lee realized that of course she, too, was in costume. Everyone there was. "Can I give you a ride?" he asked.

She turned to see the boy holding open the passenger door of a boxy old black sedan. Her bike, she remembered now, was back by the entrance.

The black frames of the kid's glasses sat above a squashed-looking nose and seemed to hold his features in place, his flat, wide mouth and too-high forehead and his round, stubbly cheeks. Could he be one of them? Her gut told her otherwise, but her gut had been wrong before. She heard voices back by the front gate and the creak of the door opening. Lee got in the car.

She watched the boy as he drove. "Who are they?"

"What do you mean?"

"Those people. Who are they?"

"I don't know who you mean."

"You helped me escape. Why would you do that unless you know something about them?"

He looked at her, confused. "You were about to have a panic attack. My sister used to have them, so I know. You obviously needed air."

"So you weren't helping me escape."

"From what?"

"Those men. The Station Master."

"Which one was he?" When Lee didn't reply, the boy shrugged and turned to her. "Hey, you looked like you were having trouble breathing. I took you out the most direct route I know."

"You go to a lot of these?"

"Nah. A friend gave me the ticket. I was supposed to meet him there but he never showed. Who's the Station Master?"

Lee stared out the window. She didn't recognize anything about the neighborhood. "Where are we going?"

He smiled. "We are driving. Talking. I thought you might need to calm down. I can take you wherever. Or you want to come back to my place? I can introduce you to my crew."

He had the slightest hint of an accent, as well as a near formality that shadowed his diction. Like he wasn't born here but had lived here long enough to erase most of his past. Lee thought about her van in the salvage yard. The twitchy loneliness of it felt crushing.

"Fine," she said.

"Good," he said, pulling over to the curb. "Because we are here."

The boy's place was a four-story walk-up in Fishtown. He unlocked the door to an apartment, and Lee took a moment before she followed him in. "You want a beer?" he asked.

"Where are your housemates?"

The boy shrugged. "Out. Stay awhile. They will be back and you can meet them." He handed her a beer and flopped down on the couch. He took his phone from his pocket and tapped on its screen until a Sigur Rós album came on.

Lee stood awkwardly, thinking: this is a bad idea.

But several hours and three beers later, she was feeling relaxed. At some point the boy disappeared into his room and came out with a lit joint, which he extended to her. Lee hadn't smoked pot in over a year, and nothing good ever happened when she mixed it with alcohol. But she took a hit anyway, and then another before handing it back. The boy talked nonstop, a nervous, rolling chatter that Lee found herself coming in and out of. She'd tune in and he'd be telling her about the history behind some obscure European art movement, then she'd tune out and come back in a bit later to find him describing a childhood memory of fishing for eels using a horse's head. Soon she felt herself nodding, struggling to keep her eyes open.

· BOOK III ·

With Hidden Noise

FIVE

LEE awoke with her head buried in the cushion of a strange couch, someone's coat draped over her. Beneath it she still had on the vintage wedding dress.

The shades were drawn and the room was dark. She heard the flutter of fingers on a keyboard and turned to see someone at a laptop on the table behind her. The screen reflected two blue squares onto the lenses of a pair of glasses. It took a moment for the boy's face to unblur. "What time is it?" she asked.

"Almost five," he answered, without looking up. "P.M."

Lee rubbed sleep from her eyes. How was that possible? "How long have I been . . ." She trailed off, remembering now coming home with the boy, talking on the couch until she'd nodded off, and then half-waking at some point to meet a blurry cadre of housemates. There was a handsome shirtless guy in black leather pants and dark primped hair and mascara who'd introduced himself as Derrick before putting out his hand in an oddly formal gesture. And there was a couple, whose names she'd forgotten, an oxlike farm girl from upstate and her boyfriend, who resembled a high school shop teacher with his cropped hair, his Buddy Holly glasses and sweater vest.

"A long time. You must have been tired."

Lee blinked at him.

He got up and put out a hand. "I'm Tomi."

She shook it and let him pull her upright. "Where is that from?"

He smiled a little and went back to his keyboard. "From my mother, of course."

"No, the name. I mean, where did you . . ."

"I know what you mean. I am from the Czech Republic. Have you ever been?"

Lee felt stupid and hardly awake. She shook her head.

"It is beautiful. And some of it is ugly. But most of it is beautiful. My hometown is a fairy tale. Perhaps I will take you there sometime. It is where my mother waits, fat as a dumpling and missing me terribly." He smiled to himself, his glasses flashing dim blue against the screen.

She felt a twang of pain in her chest. "I'm Lee," she said dumbly.

He shut the laptop and his smile opened to her. "Can I take you somewhere, Lee? I would like to show you something."

By the time he pulled the car over beside a gray stone building blackened by years of soot and exhaust, it was nearing dusk. They were in an abandoned-looking industrial area by the river. Lee got out of the car after him and craned her neck up at the tumbledown three-story structure, surrounded by cyclone fencing and spotted with graffiti. It must have been grand once, with big granite columns flanking a huge steel door, the crumbling stone arch above it held up now by weathered four-by-fours.

"What do you think?" Tomi said.

It was just an old deserted building. There were hundreds like it all over Philly. She thought of the Crystal Castle, not nearly so grand but just as deserted in the end, and the thought of it spooked her.

"Come on," he said, holding open a section of broken fence.

Beyond the fence the ground was littered with trash—broken bottles and crushed fast-food containers and cans, a pile of old clothes.

"Hurry up. This is not the best neighborhood."

"It looks pretty sketchy in there, too."

"You won't regret it. But it is up to you." He didn't wait for her, climbing through the fence and, with two long strides, launching himself a few feet up a rusted gutter drain that ran up the side of the building. He shimmied up until he was near the top, then let go with one hand and grinned down at her before disappearing onto the roof.

Lee stood watching the top of the building, but he didn't show his face again. The street was quiet and deserted. Suddenly shadows all up and down the street seemed to be moving, disappearing when she'd look at them. Lee heard voices from down the block, then three dark forms took shape, loping toward her, their drunken laughter growing louder. She could either follow this boy she'd just met or take her chances out here. Lee looked once more up the street before climbing through the fence, then testing the pipe with her hand. When she pulled herself up, it was surprisingly easy, and before she knew it, Lee was standing on the roof. A black ventilation pipe turned in the wind. A series of broken skylights ran down the center. One of them was open. Lee stuck her head in.

The space below was obscured by the top of a large steel machine. Lee lowered herself onto it, catching her dress on a shard of glass. Silvery light filtered through the skylights, throwing a watery gleam over a huge room. The place had obviously been abandoned for decades. Most of it was brick and steel, great rusted turbines and valves that looked ancient, like something raised up from the bottom of the sea. Lee let her eyes adjust to the dim light, then climbed down a steel ladder to the floor.

Tomi was waiting for her at the bottom, but she ignored him. She ran a hand down the cracked gauges of one blocky machine the size of a refrigerator, feeling the old paint chip away beneath her fingers.

A set of gears as tall as she was leaned against one wall. The remains of an old water mill were collapsed at the bottom of a long concrete trench. The room was filled with old machinery like this, and Lee got close to each of them, fascinated by their decay. She didn't care that her dress was now smudged in rust and dirt, and torn beneath one arm. This was the most beautiful place she had ever seen.

"The Schuylkill Water Works. In its heyday this place pumped water for the entire city." He followed her as she walked through the space, gazing up at the huge rusting machines. "This turbine used to pump two million gallons a day. These generators created enough electricity to power half of Philadelphia. Of course, the city was smaller back then."

The turbine was a hulking steel tube with rivets wider than the span of her hand, and the generator consisted of four steel rings that dwarfed them both. He took her hand and she let him lead her through the debris and fallen angled pipes and up a steel staircase that seemed to be hanging together by bits of rust.

"Across here," he said, taking them down a narrow walkway.

She followed him through a door and into a long room with brick walls and raw wood floor planks, empty except for several brutish metal tables with benches standing end to end. She could see only by what faint light came through the soot-covered windows.

"Wait here," he told her.

He disappeared into the darkness at the other end of the room. She could hear him feeling about, rustling and clanking something together. Then a low, subterranean hum filled the room, and something at the other end began to faintly glow. It was as though some sort of moss, covering the tables at this end of the room, had been stimulated into bioluminescence. As she edged closer, she made out hints of waving tendrils, vibrating like a field of white grass on a breezy day.

He bent down to insert a plug in an orange extension cord that ran out one of the windows, and the wall beside her began to glow with the same pale light. A long, narrow canvas spanned nearly the entire wall, a tableau painted in earthy, mulchy colors, the paint peeling and bubbling on the canvas. The skin of something dark and oily dredged up from a bog. Glued to the surface of this skin were archipelagoes of amoebic islands—each one a clear lacquer base with a field of white vibrating tendrils embedded within.

"You made this?" she said.

"You are the first to see it."

Standing next to it gave her goose bumps. "You haven't shown it to anyone else?"

"A man I respect very much once said that 'the great artist of tomorrow will go underground.'" His accent was slight, just a softening of the consonants and an elongation of the "s" sounds, but it gave everything he said an air of earnest delight.

Lee thought about being underground. Disappearing. Something about the idea appealed to her. She'd ghosted through her entire life unnoticed and had hated it, wanting only to be seen. But now she wondered whether that wasn't her natural state, something to be embraced.

Tomi reached down and unplugged the work, and the room went dim again. Lee could just make out the boggy shapes he'd painted on the canvas. "The same man said that when a million people look at a painting, they change it. Just by looking. I guess I just want to keep my work as it is. It's perfect, no?"

"It is."

"Do you know what aura is?" he asked.

Steve used to talk about auras all the time. Auras and chakras and dharmas and tantras. One morning while they waited for her mother to finish making breakfast, he squinted at her, then leaned across the table and told her quietly that her aura was as gray as old fish, almost as if there were nothing there.

"You know how when you are in a museum, standing in front of a Picasso, it feels different than when you see it in a book?" he said. "This comes from being in the presence of the original. That's aura."

"I wouldn't know," she said.

"You've never seen a real Picasso? Seriously?"

He waited for her to respond, but she gave him nothing. She had known kids like this in school, wearing their arcane knowledge like a collection of medals. She wasn't going to let him make her feel stupid.

But he was smiling, a little sheepishly, more embarrassed by sharing his passions than she was by not sharing them. And suddenly she liked him. He wasn't wearing any medals after all, and he wasn't judging her for not getting what he was talking about.

"Can I show you what I mean?" he said.

Lee had been inside the Philadelphia Museum of Art before, but only as a child with her father, and the vast, high-ceilinged entryway, with its stone columns and statue of Diana, brought back the feel of his body next to hers. Tomi had lent Lee a gray hoodie, which she wore over the dress. When he paid for the two tickets, bouncing back and forth off the balls of his feet as he pressed himself up against the desk, the cashier informed them that the museum would be closing in thirty minutes.

"We won't be long," he told the man and grabbed Lee's hand.

She followed Tomi up the stairs and through several galleries until they stood before a portrait of a woman seated by a vase of flowers. She wore a long leopard-fur coat, and her features were Asian and her hands were large and misshapen, the fingers flabby noodles across her thigh. Everything about the painting was flat, and the colors were out of a child's paint box.

"Matisse," he said, watching her take it in.

"All right," he said finally. "You're not feeling it. I get it."

He took her to another painting, a boat sailing beneath a bridge, and to another, a long-necked woman with sleepy eyes, and to an Impressionist field in the rain. They stood in front of several sculptures. He didn't say much, allowing her the space to experience whatever it was she was supposed to be experiencing. And it was sweet. But she wasn't going to pretend to feel something she didn't.

A bell went off, and a man's voice came over the PA to inform them the museum was closing in fifteen minutes. As the guards began herding the people out of the room, Lee started to follow the crowd, but Tomi took her arm and led her the opposite way, skirting behind a sculpture to avoid a guard, and then into a room where they were alone. There was a door at the far end. Tomi led her to it and then took a key from his pocket.

"What are you doing?" she asked.

He unlocked the door and led her into a dark room. A single red light from some sort of meter gave off enough light for her to see that they were in a utility closet. They huddled there for over an hour, surrounded by the fumes of cleaning agents. She tried to ask him questions—Where had he gotten the key? What were they doing? How long were they going to wait there?—but he brought a finger up to shush her each time. Lee began to wonder why she had let him bring her in here in the first place, and why she had stayed. It was too late now. Now she was forced to trust him.

She was stiff and cramping when Tomi finally stood, listened at the door, then opened it and ushered her out. After hours, the museum was lit only by low-wattage bulbs set near the floors, giving the place a monasterial solemnity. How had she gotten herself here? Had the thrill of it simply turned off something in her brain?

"There are two guards on this floor," he whispered to her. "We have to time it right, but we can stay between them."

They passed through an exhibition of Japanese prints, another that was all tapestries, and several rooms of an exhibition called "Investigating the Insignificant," a curation of works whose value seemed to be based on the amount of time they took to complete. There was a life-sized model of a 1961 Lincoln Continental Limousine made entirely of toothpicks (3,762 hours, according to the wall text); a huge fish tank containing exactly 821,309 grains of black sand (a number corresponding to one estimate of the deaths in the Armenian genocide) and a single grain of white sand (significance unexplained), all counted and added to the tank grain by grain by the artist (4,699 hours); and a 3:1 scale portrait of Pauly Shore constructed completely from coat hangers (1,775 hours). Lee tried to imagine spending that much of her life dedicated to something so inconsequential. Then she thought of what she *had* spent time on in her life, and what it had amounted to.

After a few rooms Tomi started in on a steady, whispered patter about the art surrounding them. He talked her through the evolution of the movements whose representatives they passed, from Impressionism to Art Nouveau, Fauvism to Futurism, Expressionism to Cubism to Dada and Surrealism, Abstract Expressionism to Pop Art to Photorealism. Lee found herself unable to concentrate, afraid that someone would hear him, despite the fact that he was whispering so close she could feel his breath in her ear. She got distracted by a photograph so big it took up nearly the entire wall, and stopped to gaze up at it. It was just an old red barn, falling to pieces in the middle of an overgrown field, but Lee couldn't help but be drawn to it. Wherever it was, she wanted to be there, feeling the speckled sunlight on her shoulders. Tomi grabbed her arm and pulled her away. "That's just a photograph," he said. "By definition, it has no original and so can have no aura. Come on."

She didn't care about aura, but she followed him anyway. "Paintings have aura, because they are one of a kind," he went on. "To go and see a painting is a kind of pilgrimage, a ritual."

He stopped her in front of another painting. It was one they'd stood in front of before, when the museum was open. The rainy field. "You feel it now?"

It was a dark Impressionist landscape painted in thrusting vertical lines. If it was supposed to look different to her now, it didn't.

"I know you do. You're not as cold as you pretend. Walter Benjamin would say this painting has aura because it's an original, not a reproduction. Painted over a century ago with Van Gogh's own hand. But I think aura is more than that. I think that aura exists somewhere in the space between this painting and us." He waved at the air in front of the painting, as though wafting smoke away. "Aura is not in the thing but in the relationship between the viewer and the thing. Think about it: when we were here before, standing with a dozen other people crowded around, how different the experience was."

"It's different because if we get caught here now we're going to jail," she said. The thrill of trespassing had faded, and in its place came not fear but anger. That he was risking everything without even asking. For what?

"No," he insisted. "It's not about that. Risk has nothing to do with it."

"But I'm not feeling anything. What is it? A child's view of a field. I don't care that it's a Van Gogh."

Tomi was grinning. "I know you feel it."

He was still holding her hand, and she pulled it away, annoyed. He had tricked her into this, and now she had no choice but to go along. Lee hadn't told Tomi this, but today was her birthday. She was eighteen now. What would she have been doing tonight if none of this had ever happened? She'd be somewhere else, for one thing. At college, with Edie. Edie would have done something special. In the end, Edie cared only about herself, but when you were part of her world, you felt singular, chosen. Lee had felt that way in the presence of the Station Master, too, and the thought of that made her sick. Was she that easily manipulated? Is that what this boy was doing now? Lee didn't think so; Tomi was trying too hard to impress her. With Edie and the Station Master, it was always Lee trying to impress them. Eighteen, though. Edie would have thrown a hell of a party. Then Lee had the sudden realization: if they got caught, she wasn't going back to the JDC. She'd be headed to an adult prison this time.

"Let's go," she said.

"But we just got started."

"Please." She turned and looked at him with pleading eyes. "Please just take me out of here."

He must have seen something in her face, because his tone changed. "It's okay. I've done this before. Stick with me, you will be okay. I promise. Okay? Come on," he told her. "I just want to show you one last thing."

She didn't move.

"One of the guards is behind us," he said. "If we stay too long, he'll catch us. I know the route, and I know the timing. But if we stay here or go off course, it fucks up all of it."

She let him lead her into a new room and then into another room and another beyond that. Lee was staring up at a spiky, medieval-looking thing hanging from the ceiling when she nearly walked into a towering double-glass panel mounted in the room's center. She stopped and gazed up at it.

The sculpture came up vertically from the floor, at least ten feet, framed in steel and bisected horizontally at the center. A lattice of cracks in the glass webbed down from the top right corner to the bottom left of the upper plane, then from there to the lower right of the bottom plane. Between the glass panes were a coterie of sepia forms that seemed engaged in a kind of mechanical ballet. A circle of abstract figures, like alien chess pieces, took up the bottom left corner of the work.

She didn't remember ever seeing the work before, though there was something familiar about it. Lee couldn't figure it out. The whole thing left her feeling strangely agitated, and she wondered for a moment if that was its aura.

"Marcel Duchamp's *The Bride Stripped Bare by Her Bachelors, Even*. Probably his greatest work. But not the one I wanted to show you."

As she kept gazing up at it, she felt him take her hand, and she turned away to follow him to a dark alcove just a few feet away. At the far side of the alcove was an ancient-looking wood-slatted door recessed into a brick threshold.

"Go up. Press yourself against it," he told her.

"The door?"

"Go on."

She walked up to it and pressed herself against the door as he said but felt nothing. She tried to turn around, but his hand was on the small of her back, keeping her there. She felt a brief panic, the man behind the Dumpster coming back. But Tomi's touch lightened.

"Stay there. Now close your eyes."

"Why?"

"Trust me."

Lee didn't know that she did, but she closed her eyes anyway, feeling the cool grain of the wood against her cheek, the iron bar that ran through the door's center pressing into her belly. Somewhere she could hear the footsteps of one of the guards. Lee held her breath.

When she felt Tomi's hands move to the back of her head, a tingling ran through her. He maneuvered her head down, then a little to the left, and held it there. "Now open them," he said.

She heard the guard's footsteps recede into the next room and exhaled. When Lee opened her eyes, she saw the strangest thing. Her eye was pressed against a hole in the door. And through that hole was another room.

Inside this room, lying supine on a dense thicket of dried brush, was a woman, naked, her legs open, skin as white as plaster. The angle of the peephole didn't let Lee see the woman's head, only a few wisps of blond hair wrapping down around her shoulder. Lee would have thought her a corpse left in a field if not for the antique lamp she held aloft in her left hand. Beyond her was a vista that seemed ethereal in its artificiality: a pale blue sky spongy with clouds, a range of trees in reds, oranges, and greens, and a glittering waterfall. Except for the fact that the woman was completely nude, the landscape reminded Lee, in its pure shimmering plasticity, of a beer advertisement hanging from the wall of a dive bar.

"It's called *Étant donnés*."

Lee jumped. She'd somehow forgotten that Tomi was there.

"Duchamp's final work. He worked on it in secret for the last twenty years of his life. The most influential artist of the twentieth century, and everyone thought he'd retired to play chess."

"What's it supposed to be?"

Tomi shrugged. "Duchamp thought that the viewer completed a work of art. That something sparks between the viewer and the work, giving it its meaning. So whatever it is for you is what it is. In your universe. In my universe it might be something different. So in a sense we're looking at two different works right now. As far as what *he* meant it to be, Duchamp was never very forthcoming about his intent."

Lee was still tingling. "It looks like a crime scene."

Tomi leaned in and pressed his eye to the hole. "My universe is more romantic than that. In my universe she is the same figure from his work in the other room. *The Bride Stripped Bare*. Only in that work she is a seductress. Here she is sleeping off a good roll in the hay. Everything Duchamp ever did is a continuation of previous work. And everything he ever did is erotic."

It sounded like nonsense, but she couldn't help but feel the sex of the thing, like a warm glow pushing through the cracks of the door and suffusing the room. The old wedding dress was clinging to her, and she realized she was sweating. She'd never felt aroused by an artwork before, but it was happening now. She tried to shut it down. "So he was just a pornographer?"

"Well . . ."

Suddenly she wanted Tomi's mouth against hers. She didn't know why, but she was trembling.

Tomi pulled away from the hole to eye her with suspicion. Before he could speak, she pushed him up against the door and kissed him.

He pulled back. "Wait. There's something I want to tell you. I brought you here for a reason."

Lee bit him on the lip. She couldn't have him talking right now. Pushing him up against the door, with her other hand she got his pants down.

As they fucked against the old wooden door, she felt a splinter go into her back, but the pain of it was subsumed in the moment. There was nothing else. The guards, the paintings and sculptures, the adrenaline of the trespass, the *aura,* whatever the hell that was— all of it was subsumed. She'd never disappeared so completely.

Afterward, as they lay on the stiff-carpeted floor of the alcove, Tomi nuzzled into her neck, but she pulled away. The moment was gone. Her torn dress was bunched up around her ankles. She got to her feet and pulled it up, then looked around for her other shoe. It was lying against the far wall.

"Lee—"

"If you say another word about aura—"

"I was just going to say that that was fun but we better get the fuck out of here. I did not plan on this. We have been here too long. I've lost track of where the guards are." Tomi dressed quickly and stopped by the doorway. "I will go ahead to scout."

His sudden pragmatism caught her off guard, and she felt inexplicably hurt. She pulled her shoe on.

As Lee left the alcove for the next room, she passed a rectangular white pedestal with a clear Lucite box on top. It was empty, except for a sheet of paper taped to the top. On the paper was a photograph of a familiar object and a note stating that it had been stolen on August 20 and offering a reward for information leading to its return. She grew a little dizzy as she tried to make sense of what she was looking at: it was the thing she'd taken from the Station Master's room, the ball of twine sandwiched between two metal plates. The thing she now had in the van.

Tomi poked his head back into the room and gestured to her. She felt numb, confused by the coincidence of it all, but she followed him through the halls. He seemed to know exactly where to go, when to stop and hide to avoid the guards. When they got to a door, he stopped her. "The alarm will go off as soon as we open it. But we don't have a choice. Just follow me, okay?" He pushed on the door without waiting for her response.

They ran like hell.

It was one in the morning when Tomi dropped her off at a corner that was near the salvage yard. He'd asked when he would see her again, but Lee just smiled as she shut the door. "I know where you live," she told him. "I'll drop by." She had no intention of seeing him again and felt a sense of relief as she watched his car slowly drive away. Lee went straight to the van, grabbed the Station Master's bag, then headed through Fishtown to the river. At the river she sat on a rock and watched lights flicker off the water. What did it mean to stumble upon a wanted sign for the very stolen art piece that she now had in her possession? Was the universe just trying to fuck with her? The universe, she thought, could fuck itself.

Lee took the object out of the bag. Turning it over and over, she liked the feel of it in her hand, the sharp edges against her skin, the obvious age of it. Maybe this was aura. Because the object itself was nothing more than a whimsical curio she might have picked up from a table and held with only momentary intrigue. And she'd had little interest in it before. But now this thing contained a kind of energy that seemed to vibrate in her hands.

Why had she taken it in the first place? It didn't matter now; she didn't want the thing. This wasn't a sweater from a department store; it could be worth millions, for all she knew. It would mean serious prison time if she was caught with it. Adult prison, she reminded herself. She'd just chuck the thing into the river. Lee weighed it in her hand and swung her arm back. The water looked cold and depthless.

Her arm slumped down by her side. She couldn't do it. The thing, whatever it was, had sat in a museum. Who was she to destroy it?

She dug around in a trash can until she found two bags, one

paper and one plastic. She sealed the object in the plastic one, then wrapped that in the paper one. She went back to the rocks along the river until she found a crevice big enough to stuff it into.

It was a long walk back to the salvage yard. By the time she got there, the yard was just opening up, and she wanted only to crawl inside the shitty old van and sleep. But when she got into the yard, she found that the van was gone. Lee looked around, as though it had only been misplaced; but then she saw it, compacted into a cuboid of steel and crushed plastic the size of two mattresses. All her belongings in the world—her sleeping bag, her clothes—compacted inside it.

SIX

DERRICK didn't look surprised to see her at their door, but he didn't look happy, either. He didn't look much of anything, not even awake, as he stepped aside for her to come in. Then he slouched back off to bed without a word, leaving her alone in the living room. She heard his door shut and then lock. Lee sat on the sofa, thinking about the destroyed van with all her stuff, about the stolen museum piece, and about the fact that she was about to put herself at the mercy of a guy she hardly knew.

A clock above the TV read just half past seven, and it was another hour before the girl housemate shuffled past to make herself coffee. She smiled blearily at Lee and disappeared into the kitchen. Fifteen minutes later she appeared with a mug for herself and one for Lee.

"I'm Allison," she said.

"We met last night."

"Oh, yeah. Sorry. I'm barely awake. What's your name again?"

"Lee."

"That doesn't sound right. Are you sure?"

"Pretty sure."

Allison shrugged, took a sip, and grimaced. "Jesus, I make terrible coffee. Can you make good coffee?"

"I don't drink much coffee," Lee said. "So I guess I don't know the difference. It tastes fine to me."

Allison smiled. "I like you. Will? My boyfriend? He wouldn't drink this. He'd pour it out and then spend half an hour hand grinding the beans, boiling water to a precise temperature, blooming the grounds, pouring a bit at a time with that precious little swirling motion . . . I swear I'm usually asleep by the time he's finished. I mean, I get it, he wants to be a chef, and that's his thing, but sometimes I just want to have a fucking sandwich, you know?"

Lee was trying to follow, with mixed results, but it didn't seem to matter. Allison just seemed to like to talk.

"Is that vintage?" Allison asked.

Lee looked down at the wedding dress, now soiled and torn. She wanted to cover it up.

"You're rocking it," Allison said. "I couldn't get away with that, but I get what you're doing. It's, like, Riot Grrrl redux. So how do you know Tomi?"

"We just kind of met."

"You guys just friends? Because Tomi doesn't bring a lot of ladies home."

"Just friends."

"Well, don't hurt him, is all I'll say. Or I'll have to murder you."

Lee was deciding how to respond when she saw Allison looking over her shoulder.

"Speak of the devil," Allison said. "You could have at least given her a blanket."

Lee turned to see Tomi, his confused expression turning to delight. "When did you get here?"

"I'm sorry," she said. "I . . ."

"Is everything all right? You need a place to stay or something?"

Lee was glad she didn't have to ask. She didn't even have to respond. She watched Tomi look at Allison, and Allison's shrug seemed to settle it.

"As long as you need, honey," she said. "And if you ever need anyone to talk to, I'm a freaking vault."

"Is there more?" Tomi asked, nodding at Allison's coffee. He went into the kitchen without waiting for an answer.

"Tomi is the only one who can stomach my coffee," she said. "But he's Czech. He makes it worse than I do."

Lee stayed on the couch again that night, beneath a blanket that Allison gave her that smelled of old milk. Over the next several days she tried to keep herself inconspicuous within the small apartment. She read novels she found around the house and watched cooking shows with Will on TV. She learned that Will and Allison had a silent channel of communication running between them, that they seemed to read each other's minds in a way that was spooky. Lee hated the idea of someone else inside her mind, but their closeness tugged at her. Allison liked her, Lee could tell, but she also had a jealous streak. Lee learned to avoid getting too close to Will and not to borrow his clothes, which fit her better, and to accept Allison's instead, which left Lee in overlarge gingham prairie dresses and lumpy sweaters. Lee stuck with Tomi's thick gray hoodie, and after a while it was understood to be hers.

She found herself spending most of her time with Tomi, too. He liked having her around as he worked at his laptop, pressing his face to the screen and typing clumsily while he'd spin stories to her of his childhood in a small southern Bohemian town, of his sister's Doolittle-like rapport with animals, or of his crazy uncle Sasha, who seemed always at the end of these stories to be covered in shit. And sometimes after his work she'd meet him down at the Water Works and hang out in his studio while he'd work on his paintings.

They all had occupations that brought them in and out of the apartment at various times—Tomi had a day job at a data recovery firm,

Allison was studying architecture at Philadelphia University, Will worked in the kitchen of a Whole Foods, and Derrick was supposedly a barista, though he spent much of his time in his room with his door closed—and Lee found herself alone in the apartment for long stretches. She liked to clean the place when they were out; it made her feel like she was contributing.

Dinners were communal, and Will, the aspiring chef, cooked most of them. Lee couldn't cook a thing, but she liked to help him prep and happily washed the dishes afterward. When she asked Allison if she could borrow a shirt, Allison told her she didn't have to ask, to just go help herself, which made Lee unexpectedly happy. By the end of the week everyone but Derrick seemed to have warmed to her.

As the days went on Lee began to feel that she was becoming less a boarder and more a part of the family. Will revealed that he was saving to go to a culinary academy and that his five-year plan was to open a restaurant that Allison would design. Tomi wanted to save money and someday return to his hometown, where living was cheap and he could afford to paint full time. Tomi kept weird hours. She'd wake up from her spot on the couch and find him slipping out or coming back in at all times of the night. She always pretended to be asleep. One day she asked him where he went at night.

"You want to come with me sometime?"

"You haven't told me what you do."

"We'll see," he said. "Maybe one of these nights I will take you." He left it at that.

Even Derrick could be charming when he wanted to be, especially when he was talking about his own dreams: he wanted to start his own data security business and make a lot of money. When she asked him what he would do with a lot of money, he told her he would take care of his autistic younger brother, whom his parents had stuck in a group home. Lee thought she might cry, until he started laughing at her gullibility.

Lee couldn't figure Derrick out at all. Most days he treated her like a stray cat who'd wandered into the apartment, but every now and then, when the others were gone, he'd open up and actually be a human being. One night he came home late from a party and Lee was still up, reading one of Tomi's science fiction novels on the couch.

He was dressed in a thin but expensive-looking leather jacket with a white V-neck beneath and wore thick eye shadow and dark lipstick that had smudged across his face. His freshly dyed hair was blue-black and messy. He took two beers from the fridge and offered her one without her asking. She didn't want a beer, but he had never offered her anything before, so she took it.

He slumped down in a chair and pulled it up close to the couch, putting his feet up on it and arranging himself into a position that seemed at once studied and louche.

"Good party?" she asked.

Derrick leaned his head back and talked to the ceiling. "The DJ was spinning all retro jungle bullshit, but the teenyboppers like it." He looked at Lee and smiled. "No offense."

"None taken."

"You go to school in the city?" he asked, looking away now, as though it was a casual question and not the interrogation it felt like. He had been trying clumsily to siphon information about her past from her since she'd arrived.

Lee thought carefully about how to answer. "I was home-schooled," she said.

"Your parents some kind of religious nuts?"

"Something like that, yeah."

"Well, you didn't miss much. I hated high school."

"How come?"

Derrick smirked wistfully. "Nobody can take a joke. I got expelled my senior year and never looked back."

"For what?"

"For hacking into the school's network and changing all the links to live webcam porn. They could never prove it was me, but they found a way to expel me anyway. Best thing that ever could have happened to me. I used it as a calling card to join a hacker crew after that. That's how I met Tomi."

"He was part of that crew?"

"No, he was a lone operator. But we both happened to be hacking into the same system at the same time. It's like if you were spelunking some network of hidden caves way out in the middle of Buttfuck, Nowhere, and just happened to run into some dude. You bond."

"So you took to each other right away, huh?"

"We hated each other at first. Each of us tried to sabotage the other at every turn. But it was just good-natured rivalry. So we decided to meet IRL and teamed up. We started our own crew not too long after. We figured out we both love the same things about hacking—the social engineering, the personal risk, the codes of ethics. And the cryptography. That's where Tomi and I really found our common ground."

Derrick stared at her, in a way that began to feel uncomfortable. She thought about the object she had found and the code on it.

"But then he got into that goofy urbex shit, and the hacking world pretty much passed him by. That world moves fast. He's pretty much nothing but a script kiddie these days." Derrick looked down at his beer and puckered his lips. "Anyway," he said, finishing it, "you want to come to bed with me?" He asked it as if he were asking if she wanted to share a smoke.

"That's okay," Lee said, amused but trying not to let the smile go to her face. "I think I'll go to sleep."

"Suit yourself." Derrick left his bottle on the table and disappeared down the hall. She could hear the clicking lock of his door.

Lee went back to the novel. It was a book about a man who was hired to investigate another man, unaware that the man he was investigating was himself. Only the man being investigated knew that the man doing the investigation was himself. Lee was on the last chapter when a large card slipped out from behind the back cover. At first she thought it was a postcard, until she picked it up. It was a Société Anonyme invite. Just like the one that the man had given to her and Edie at the café, over a year ago.

She confronted Tomi the next day, removing the card from the book and dropping it onto his laptop keyboard as he sat hunched into the screen. Tomi stopped typing, picked up the card, and squinted at it. If he was taken off guard, he didn't look it.

"What's this?" he said.

"You told me you'd never been to one of these things before you met me."

He turned the card over, then handed it back to her. "I hadn't."

"This is your book, right? I took it from your bookshelf."

"I was telling the truth. But I don't see why it matters. What would the difference be?"

"The difference would be . . ." Lee realized she couldn't tell him why it made a difference without telling him about the Crystal Castle and the Station Master. Or her missing friend Edie. Or Claire. The Thrumm kids. Her escape from Juvie. And she wasn't ready to do that. Not until she knew she could trust him. "The difference would be that you lied to me. Why?"

"I told you a friend gave me the ticket."

"So?"

"So that friend was Derrick. He borrowed that book a while back. He must have left it in there. You want me to ask him about it?"

"Forget it," Lee said, feeling foolish. "I'm going out for a walk."

It was midafternoon, and Lee kept her hoodie up. As she walked she began to think about Derrick in ways that she hadn't bothered to before. Derrick always locked his door, both when he was in the room and when he'd leave, and she wondered what kind of person did that. He was hiding something, but was he part of all this? She wondered if there was a way to get into his room.

When Lee returned, the house was empty. She was tired from a night of no sleep, but when she tried to take a nap, it wouldn't come. She couldn't get the idea out of her head that this wasn't just a coincidence. That Derrick was in with the S.A. in some way, or at the very least knew more than he was letting on.

She called out a few times to make sure the house was empty, and knocked on all the doors. She knocked on Derrick's the loudest. When Lee was a young girl, her father kept an old locked chest in the back of the closet. She used to obsess over what could be in it, until one day when she was home alone she figured out how to pick the lock with a paper clip. There wasn't much in the chest, just a lot of photographs and some things that seemed to be from a past life, and she was disappointed when this mystery was solved, but she liked that she had been able to figure out how to get past the lock, and every now and then she'd pick it again just for fun.

The deadbolt on Derrick's door was not some old chest lock, and it was not going to give way to a few jiggles from a paper clip, no matter how much Lee tried. She tried a nail file and a hair clip, too, but soon realized that, despite her previous success, she knew nothing about locks. The door remained closed.

For a good while none of them asked her outright about where she came from, about her past or her family. They were obviously curious, but she was cagey enough that they must have decided collectively to leave it alone. But when Allison offered to help Lee with the dishes one night, Lee knew something was up—Allison never offered help with the dishes. And Allison didn't waste any time. "You know we have no problem with your staying here. You stay as long as you need to. But we're all wondering, you know . . ."

"Yeah?" Lee made a big show of scraping off a bit of pasta barnacled to a plate.

"What's your story?"

She scrubbed harder at the now-invisible spot of food. "My story is I ran away from home a few months ago."

Allison nodded, as if this was the answer she was expecting. "How old are you?"

"Eighteen, now. But I was seventeen when I left home, and not finished with high school. I'm an adult now, free to do what I want, so it's not like you're harboring a real runaway or anything. I just can't go home."

Allison had stopped even the pretense of washing dishes and now leaned against the refrigerator, looking not at Lee but at Lee's reflection in the window over the sink. "Where were you staying before this?"

Lee knew she couldn't tell Allison about any of it, but Edie once told her that to get away with a lie, you mix it with truth. "I was sleeping in an abandoned van. In a junkyard."

"Seriously?"

Lee smiled. "Here is better."

"Yeah, I mean, of course . . . can I ask you, what . . . I mean, why . . ."

"Why I left home?"

"Yeah."

"You won't tell anyone?"

"Steel vault, remember?"

Lee just said, "My mom's boyfriend," and Allison let her leave it at that.

That night Lee felt a hand on her shoulder, shaking her awake. She rolled over to see Tomi squatting down, his face right up in hers. "What's going on?" she said.

"Get dressed."

"Now? What time is it?"

"A little after two."

Lee sat up and reached for her jeans. "Where are we going?"

He just handed her a dark hoodie and shouldered a backpack. "You said you wanted to come with me sometime. Now's the time."

She hadn't said anything of the sort, but she pulled on the hoodie and followed him out the door.

They rode bicycles through the city, Lee just trying to keep up, all her tiredness gone, invigorated by the cool wind. Tomi stopped suddenly, veering his bike onto the sidewalk and dropping it behind a hedge. The street was well lit, and an enormous stone wall, maybe thirty feet high, ran the entire block, paralleled by the hedge, which spanned its length. Lee followed.

Tomi walked along the inside of the hedge, his eyes to the ground, until he stopped, bent down, and took a short metal tool from his pack. He squatted, and Lee watched him use the tool to unscrew a bolt in a grate at his feet. He inserted his fingers in the grate and lifted.

A concrete tube with a rebar ladder went straight down into darkness. Tomi pulled a headlamp from his back and strapped it on, then handed one to her. He went down first. Lee put on her head-lamp and followed. About twenty feet down the ladder deposited her onto the floor of a square concrete tunnel.

A ways down they found another rebar ladder and climbed up, emerging onto a patchy yard. It was hard to tell in the moonlight, but the wall seemed to contain within it nearly an entire city block. Across the yard she could barely make out the top of a smokestack, and be-low it a long, low building. "Wait here," he said. "I'm going to go take a leak."

She watched him walk off to the wall. Why did guys always need something to pee against? Lee turned back to the structure, curious what it was, and headed toward it. The building was old, made of the same stone as the walls, and there was an enormous, gaping doorway at its center. The doors were wide open. Before she knew it, Lee was walking down a long hall. When it got too dark to see, she turned on her headlamp again. Along both sides were cells, with wood-slatted doors set into tracks. The place had to be an old prison. Lee shined her light into one of the cells, then walked in. The walls were peeling gray plaster, and a rusted iron bed frame sat in one corner. It smelled damp and old, and she imagined what these walls had absorbed over so many years: the fear and anger and loneliness of decades of prisoners. Lee could hear Tomi calling to her in the distance and turned toward his voice, but then she tripped over something and was hurled headfirst into a wall. Her headlamp saved her forehead, but the lens cracked, sending her into total darkness.

Lee felt a moment of weightlessness, the ground gone beneath her feet. She reminded herself to breathe, then felt around until she could make out the door to the cell. Back in the hallway, she could still hear Tomi's voice, but it was growing more distant. Which way had she come from? She could no longer remember. She tried to follow the direction of the voice, but it was hard to tell where it was coming from.

As she inched her way down the hallway, fear began to take hold. She should have hit the doorway by now. She couldn't see any light or hear anything but her own breathing. Her breaths grew shallower until they stopped bringing air in at all. She put out her hand to find the wall, but there was no wall. She stumbled, hands out, but there was nothing in front of her and she fell, skidding to the ground and feeling the cool flash of a scraped knee. Her palms burned. She got onto her hands and knees and crawled, ignoring the pain, needing the ground, the only solid thing to cling to. Then something sharp bit into her knee and she collapsed there on the concrete floor.

She could wait here until morning, lying on her side and holding herself. Or she could get it the fuck together. Lee got up onto her feet. She thought back to the time she was four and her father was looking after her while her mother was working a graveyard shift. Late at night he had woken her to go to the store with him, and he had left her in the car, telling her, "Be right back." She had waited there for what felt like an hour but could have been minutes, slouched low in her seat and watching rats move in and out of the park that bordered the parking lot, before she let herself out of the car. Lee went into the convenience store, but her father wasn't there. When she came out, she followed sounds from the park, then stood in the middle of the grass watching her father hugging another man against a tree. Both men had their backs to her, and Lee could hear her father whispering something into the man's ear. When she got back to the car, she found that she had locked herself out of it. As she walked back home she remembered wishing he had shared secrets with her, too. It was an unfamiliar route, and yet she had hummed a made-up song and found her way back without thinking about it. When she let herself in, her father was home waiting for her. He was wild-eyed, pacing, and he had hugged her so tightly she thought he would squeeze the air out of her as he promised never to leave her alone again.

As she remembered again the sensation of walking home by herself that night, she slowly became aware of something happening. Her surroundings, even in the dark, were becoming clear. She was not in a hallway but in a room. The room was circular. She could not see this, but nevertheless she knew it to be true. Lee took a step, then three, then turned. There was a wall in front of her, maybe four feet away. She could sense it. She took two steps, put her hand out, and felt it. Lee backed away and turned. She walked forward again. She could feel a hallway to her left. She kept walking. Another hallway. Lee made a circuit of the room, and by the end she could see it in her head: a circular room with a series of hallways leading into it, like spokes into a wheel hub. She circled the room again and counted. Nine of them. Incredibly, she knew which of them was the hallway she had come through, and she also knew in which direction the grate was and even in which direction the apartment was.

Lee spun herself around in circles for thirty seconds, then stopped. She was a little dizzy, but she still knew the direction of the hall she'd come through and the direction of the grate. She knew that the room was empty except for something solid about six feet to her left. She walked in that direction and felt around. Her hands touched something made of wood and glass, a display case of some kind.

Lee started walking. She picked a direction and went down one of the other hallways, slowly at first, afraid of bumping into something, then picking up speed, faster and faster until she was running full tilt through the dark. A blob of light took shape at the end, and she ran toward it. When she emerged back out into the yard, she was laughing. She looked down at herself. Her jeans were torn and her knee was scraped raw, bleeding into her shoes. She saw then that something had caught against the bottom of her sneakers and torn the canvas nearly straight through. She pulled off her shoes and tossed them one at a time across the yard. Standing there in the dark space, barefoot in the grass, Lee was happier than she could remember ever being.

She found Tomi ten minutes later, by his flashlight. He was so angry with her he said nothing the whole way back, but Lee didn't care. She had discovered another world.

Over the next few days, Lee wanted to ask Tomi everything about this hobby of his. She'd heard about people who explored abandoned places, but nothing about it had appealed to her in the abstract. Now she wanted to do another one, as soon as possible. Lee couldn't explain the feeling of freedom and power she'd had, knowing her way in the dark, but she knew she wanted to experience it again. She was on her way out of the apartment, intending to surprise Tomi with a sandwich at his studio, hoping to convince him to take her again, when she heard voices in the stairwell below. Lee backed away and listened.

"She said she didn't have anywhere else to go. What was I supposed to do, just turn her away?" She heard Tomi say.

"So what, she's homeless? Do you even know how old she is?"

"Are you asking did I card her, Derrick?"

"She could be fourteen for all we know. You know what that would make you?"

Lee bristled at the implication of what Tomi might have told them.

"She's eighteen," Allison said. "She told me."

"What else would she say? I'd be willing to bet she hasn't even seen sixteen yet. Just find out who her parents are and call them to come pick her up," Derrick said.

"We don't know anything about where she came from," Allison said. "Maybe she was abused or something. You just want to send her back?"

"Not our problem," said Derrick. "Look, she's a nice kid. But we're not running a shelter, and we don't know anything about her. We could get into trouble just for having her here."

"I told her she could stay here," said Tomi. "She's my responsibility."

"For a few days. It's been weeks now. Are you going to start paying her rent, too? Paying for the food she eats?"

"I don't mind sharing my food." This was Will. "It's mostly stuff from Whole Foods they're gonna throw out anyway."

"Fine," said Derrick. "I don't care about the money, either. I just don't want to go to jail for harboring some teen runaway. I'm getting too old for this shit."

"You're twenty-seven, Derrick."

"Exactly."

"I told you she's my responsibility," Tomi said. "I'll take care of her."

Lee went back in to the apartment before she could be found out. She was quiet all that night, the conversation burning a hole in her stomach. She felt shitty enough about not contributing any money. She did what she could around the house, but it didn't seem enough. That night, when they were all asleep, she put her shoes on and took them off twice, always on the verge of just slipping away. But Tomi was right: she didn't have any place else to go.

A few days later she was coming home from the supermarket when Derrick came up behind her, taking a shopping bag and opening the door. "Let me get one of those for you," he said.

She thanked him and followed him up the stairs, but then he stopped, so suddenly she walked into him. Lee tried to move past, but he blocked the way.

"How long you planning on staying with us?" he said. "By the way."

Lee tried again to get past, but he blocked her again. "I don't know."

"Because everyone here pays rent, utilities, groceries. You're in a hard place and I understand. I'm not a bad guy, you know. You need a place to crash until you get your shit sorted out, I get it. But sooner or later everyone has to pay their own way."

"I know, Derrick. And thank you. Really and truly. And that's exactly what I'm doing, trying to sort my shit out so that I can pay my own way."

"So you're looking for work?"

Lee was not looking for work, she couldn't, but she also couldn't tell him that. "Yes."

"Where?"

"Where?"

"What kind of work? Maybe I can help."

"I don't know," she said. "Anything."

"You ever do any acting?"

"What do you mean?"

"Movie acting."

"What? No. Why?"

"Or more like webcam acting. Anything like that?"

It took Lee a moment to understand. She could tell he was enjoying this.

He leaned against the wall and ran a hand through his hair. "You're eighteen, right? I know some guys. I could hook you up."

Lee heard the door open and close upstairs, then the sound of footsteps. Derrick turned as Tomi rounded the staircase. "I was just looking for you," he said to Lee. "I'm going to my studio. You want to come?"

Lee turned to Derrick. "Bring this one up for me, too?" She handed the other bag to him without waiting for a reply, then followed Tomi down the stairs.

Tomi called the excursions creeps, and over the next two weeks Lee went on eight more with him. They visited a derelict hospital, an abandoned aquarium on an island, the rooftop of a half-constructed high-rise, an old theater in ruins, a crumbling hotel, two factories, and a network of tunnels beneath a rail yard that seemed like a vast catacomb of industrial corpses. Like any explorers, they sought out places unsullied by the footprints of previous urban explorers. Posting the first photos of a site on an urbex forum was like planting a flag. Others could explore it now, but they would always be following in another crew's footsteps.

He called his crew the Philadelphia Urbex Society, and when she asked who else was in it, he said, "Just you. Assuming you'd like to join."

"Really?"

"It's a very exclusive crew."

"So before I came in, you were a society of one?"

Tomi smiled. "No one else has made the cut."

Urban exploration altered the way Lee saw the world. The corner of Oxford and Broad was no longer an office high-rise under construction, a movie theater, a subway station, and a department store. Now when she passed by she saw a ladder of scaffolding leading to rooftop access, open windows like invitations, and minimally secured underground access tunnels.

Lee loved the feeling of being lost in an empty building, the nebulous, directionless sensation of passing through an unknown space with no idea what might be ahead. The funny thing was that her internal compass always knew where she was and where the exits were. She'd challenge herself by going as deep into a building as she could, sometimes turning her flashlight off for minutes on end or closing her eyes and spinning in circles. But she always found her way in the end.

One night she and Tomi were exploring a crumbling high school, empty since the mid-'80s. As Lee ran her flashlight over old lockers and along the heaps of trash and sludge at the bottom of the drained swimming pool, she found herself by the pool bleachers, remembering that last moment with Edie before the cops came to take her away. It seemed so long ago. What a child she was then.

Tomi had gone on ahead, and she caught up and followed him down a stairwell. At the bottom they emerged into an enormous basement warehouse, shining their lights over a block of old textbooks as massive as a Greyhound bus. Decomposed to near disintegration, the stacked volumes looked fungal, like something growing in a forest. She wandered the damp room on a floor of books as soft as moss, the smell—earthy and thick with mold—making her lightheaded. It was fantastical down here, like an enormous underground cave.

Lee lay on her back in the middle of the room, her flashlight pointing up, losing herself in the dark expanse of the peeling ceiling. Down here the JDC was a distant memory, her mother was a character in a book she'd read a long time ago, and the Crystal Castle was a dream, the Station Master a phantom within it.

Tomi sank into a spongy pile of books that collapsed around him like a beanbag and lay back next to her. They listened to the faint ticking of the decomposition around them. She loved how alone she could be here. It was different being alone in the real world; there she just felt missed, invisible. But here, in the underground darkness, she felt whole. She didn't mind that Tomi was here, too, because he saw her. It was as though he made it real just by witnessing it. Lee picked up an old geometry textbook, so soggy it came apart in her hand.

"It's like a necropolis of the written word down here," he said finally.

It wasn't anything like that here. And he'd ruined her moment by saying it. He must not see her after all, she thought. "You've been waiting this whole time to say that, haven't you? Why does everything need a headline?" Lee felt bad the moment the words left her mouth. She didn't know why she sometimes felt the urge to be mean to Tomi. He made it no secret that he had feelings for her, that he wanted more from her; maybe it was his nakedness that drove her to swipe at him as she did. He was never hiding anything of himself, which made Lee uncomfortable.

She thought she'd hurt his feelings, but after a pause Tomi laughed and told her what a bitch she was, and she figured they were okay. "What's Derrick's story?" she asked.

"Why? You like him?" Tomi looked resigned to the idea, as if he had come to the conclusion some time ago.

Lee wanted to laugh. "What are you talking about?"

"You told me you thought he was handsome."

"He's also a fucking creep. Did I not tell you that, too?"

"So you're not into him?"

Lee found Tomi's palpable relief kind of sweet. He'd never brought up their tryst in the museum and hadn't made a move, though she'd expected him to and half dreaded it, hating the idea of hurting him. She braced herself for a move now, but Tomi just got up and walked toward the stairs. Even in the darkness she could tell he was smiling.

As they walked back to the apartment that night, Tomi told her about his crazy Czech family, his three childhood cats—Bolo, Tomo, and Gogo—and the reasons why, if he could pick any year in history to travel back in time to, it would be 1917. He rarely pried into her life, and she liked it that way, but tonight he ventured a few questions about her past and Lee was forced to choose her words carefully, offering details that she didn't think could ever be used to pin her down. She could sense the rawness of his nerves around her, and she liked watching him weigh her answers, as though there were something in them to weigh.

Some nights they'd go out and eat sandwiches by the pier or picnic in a half-constructed office building, in the middle of an emptied public pool, in a derelict bank's vault. Once they snuck into a Cineplex to view a late-night showing from the rafters up behind the screen, legs dangling and staring down at the film in mirror image. Tomi opened his backpack to show it stuffed with popcorn, then reached in and pulled out a flask of whiskey buried inside. As they passed the flask, Lee watched his face, his skin pale silver under the reflected light of the projector, and felt a tenderness for him she hadn't known was there.

Most of all she liked coming to his studio at the Water Works, liked to watch him work as he moved back and forth along the length of the canvas, which he'd tack down on the floor across the entire room. He didn't talk when he painted, but he would when he took breaks. He asked her opinions on things. He asked her if she'd felt anything like aura when they'd creeped the museum that night, and seemed delighted when she told him she thought she'd felt something standing in front of the big glass sculpture by Duchamp.

"What happened that night? After the museum. When you showed up at the apartment the next morning." When she didn't answer he said, "Allison told me you were living in a van in a junkyard."

Some vault. But Lee didn't blame Allison. "I was. After you dropped me off, I came back to find it flat as a pancake." She tried to laugh, but he just looked at her sadly.

"All your stuff, too?"

Lee brought her hands together in a crushing motion.

"What was in there?"

Lee thought about her clothes, her sleeping bag, the girl's diary. "Everything I owned." She shrugged. "Not much."

Tomi held that sad look on his face and returned to his work.

She liked that Tomi saw her, and yet he seemed always to know when she needed to be alone, too. She liked especially when he'd turn off the lights and plug in one of his paintings. She'd hear a hum, then the little vibrating tendrils would come to life. In the dark the white fields glowed radium green and seemed to free-float in the air like small, trembling clouds.

At first she thought it was a random, possibly accidental, blip of a highlighter pen: someone had highlighted the word hello halfway through the book she was reading. The book was a bloated paperback historical novel that Allison had plucked from her bookshelf for Lee to keep herself occupied with, and Lee was burning through it. A half-dozen pages past the highlighted greeting was another word, lee, highlighted in that sickly neon yellow, extracted from the word "bleep." Lee flipped forward, finding what highlighted a few pages in, do on the page after that. The word you was highlighted a few pages later, followed by see on the same page. She flipped forward until the word through jumped out at her, followed by your a few pages after. Lee couldn't find another highlighted word until nearly the end of the book, when she landed on the word windows. A bit down the page was a highlighted question mark. Then there were no more highlighted words.

Lee shut the book and sat there, listening to the hum of the silent apartment. It was three in the morning and everyone was asleep. "Hello Lee what do you see through your windows?" Was this Tomi's doing? It seemed the kind of coy, oblique game he might play. But what did it mean? It could have been someone else. Allison could be playful like that. Derrick had been agitating to kick her out since the beginning; maybe this was just him trying to fuck with her head. She had been out earlier that day, without the book. It could have been any of them. Lee scanned the living room, landing on the windows. She got off the couch, dragging the blanket with her, and pulled up the shade.

All she saw was her own face staring back at her in reflection. It took her a moment to realize that she was seeing, beyond that, her face again. Lee turned off the light. A picture was taped to the glass from the outside: a rectangle made of photographs of men—black-and-white and from another time, all of them in old-fashioned suits and ties and overcoats, all of them with their eyes closed—surrounding a single Polaroid photo: the same one Ester had taken of Lee in the cafeteria of the Crystal Castle. Someone had cut out her eyes, replacing them with big, sightless engorged eyes that sucked all sentience from her face. Lee tried to open the window, but it was painted shut. They were four floors up.

· BOOK IV ·

Nude Descending a Staircase

SEVEN

THIRTY-SIX days. A long time to have something growing inside you. How could she have gone so long without knowing? But she had known. Isn't that why she stole the pregnancy test in the first place? She stared down at the white stick now, wondering how big the thing was and how it would feel to kill it. She wondered too what it would feel like to let it keep growing, taking up space inside her. She couldn't help but imagine it as one of the creatures in the diorama in front of her, some Cambrian thing from the bottom of the sea crawling around in her belly, tickling her insides with its antennae, clawing to get out.

Lee had cried when she first saw the little pink plus sign begin to appear on the stick; she had nearly stopped breathing. She had wanted to smash everything around her. Then her sobs stopped, as suddenly as they'd started, and she told herself that this, like everything else, could be taken care of.

Lee forgot about all of it, if only briefly, when she plucked the little scroll of paper from the diorama and unrolled it to discover the photo of her twin from a hundred years ago. Lee had gotten only a glimpse of it in the Station Master's room and had mostly written off the resemblance as her adrenaline playing tricks on her. But she had taken it in for nearly an hour now, and the resemblance was undeniable.

"A.T. Juli 1911." It wasn't much to go on. But the note below the cryptogram was clear enough: "Return what you have taken."

If she'd had the object on her, she would return it; she'd give anything for all of it to just go away. Lee wondered if they could be here now, watching her. She turned quickly, shining her flashlight across the room, the beam glancing off empty tanks, old exhibition signage, defunct fossil displays. She flicked the light off and listened. No sound; nothing at all. She was alone, she knew it. Still, the place was no longer hers.

As Lee motored the little boat back to shore, she thought about what to do. The apartment was no longer safe. She'd left it two nights before, stuffing a few things in a bag and slipping out as soon as she'd found the photo taped to the window. The abandoned aquarium was the most isolated place she knew. Earlier that day she'd gone back to shore for food, using what little money she had. She'd lifted the pregnancy test on a whim, just to ease her mind—missing her period had to have been a side effect of the stress of the past month—stuffing the empty box behind a milk carton and slipping the stick into her waistband. That must have been when whoever it was had come to the aquarium and left the scroll for her to find. Whoever it was had known she liked to sit and stare at the diorama. Which meant that he or she had been watching her. Tomi had been the one who showed her the place. Who else would know that she would come here? Lee began to consider the very real possibility that Tomi was behind it. He had been at the Silo party, after all, just happening to be there to whisk her away. Had her rescue all been engineered? But why? If that was the case, then he'd had her right there—why let her escape, only to come after her again?

If Tomi was with the Station Master, then they had been toying with her from the beginning. Lee began to run through it all in her head, from the Silo party to his studio to the night in the museum—because of which she was now carrying Tomi's baby, which made her feel sick—to all their explorations together. But why choose now to start taunting her with notes? Tomi was her friend, had been her lover, too, if just for a night. He had feelings for her, she knew that, or thought she did. Had he fooled her about that, too? Lee watched the oily black water ripple by and thought about what it would feel like to sink into it and simply disappear.

The boat hit the shore without her even realizing it was there, nearly knocking her into the water. She'd missed the dock completely. She killed the motor and doubled back to it, then tied the boat up but just sat there for a long time. She'd known Tomi for only a little over a month, and yet she'd felt like she'd known him her whole life. What do you do when the one true thing in your life turns out to be a lie?

It was late at night but warm for early October, warm enough to be wearing only what she'd left the house with: a gauzy tank top of Allison's and a thin, zippered hoodie and jeans from Tomi. Lee walked. It suddenly seemed as though everyone was watching her, casting backward glances or peering at her past their cell phones. She kept on in a directionless, circuitous nonroute, which took her past shipyards and collapsing warehouses, residential neighborhoods lined with yellowing duplexes, a cyclone-fenced car dealership whose artful owner had piled tires in towering columns like great black obelisks. Lee kept walking. She stood in the middle of an empty parking lot carpeted in shards of broken auto glass glinting cruelly up at the streetlamps. Everywhere the streets were nearly empty, and Lee felt swallowed by that emptiness. She now had no apartment, no friends, no money, and any site she had visited with Tomi she had to consider unsafe.

As the sun was just beginning to pinken the water of the Delaware River, Lee found herself in a neighborhood of columned manors and expensive German sedans. A dented Toyota crawled the street; a man inside flipped newspapers out the window at the manicured lawns and stone walkways. He flicked a lit cigarette onto the road, and Lee picked it up and inhaled from it, stopping in the middle of the street to watch a couple scrambling to head out for a vacation, she guessed—the husband loading the back of an Audi station wagon, his wife dragging their luggage out the front door of a large white house. Lee watched as the woman bent and checked inside one of the bags; she seemed to take inventory, marking in her head the things they had and the things they might need. The man was already in the front seat, watching this all through his rearview with glowering impatience. Then Lee felt eyes on her, and she met the gaze of a teenage girl, younger than Lee but not by much, staring at her from the backseat. The girl had sleepy eyes that seemed held open by the tight bun of her brown hair, and Lee saw in them a mix of curiosity and envy.

And then the woman was in the passenger seat. The man had started the car and was pulling away even before the woman had buckled herself in. That was when Lee noticed that the mother had forgotten to close their front door—it stood half-open, and Lee could see into a dim foyer, a burgundy runner leading up to a set of stairs. She was about to yell something to them when she looked up to see the car breaking to a stop just inches from her knee. The father honked his horn and yelled at her to get out of the damn street. She stepped aside and met the girl's eyes one more time.

Behind the drawn shades the house was dark and blanketed in silence. Lee pulled off her shoes and stood looking past the dining room into the kitchen, then up the stairs to a darkened landing. She went up and entered the first room she found, the master bedroom, where she opened drawers at random and ran her hands through the woman's clothing, her camisoles and yoga pants, bras and underwear and silk scarves. She flipped open a box on the dresser and pushed her fingers through a loose array of jewelry that felt like a pile of pebbles and sea glass. In the closet she found a short mink coat, which she turned inside out before putting on, sinking into the feel of soft fur against her arms and neck.

She peed in their toilet, then ran a bath, stepping downstairs into the kitchen as it filled. From the refrigerator she took a package of sliced ham, which she ate by rolling the slices and dipping them into a jar of mayonnaise. She followed this with four hard-boiled eggs from a Tupperware container, dipping them, too, in the mayonnaise, then licking her fingers clean and wiping them on her jeans. The bath was nearly overflowing when she got back upstairs. She turned off the faucets and waited for the excess water to drain before undressing and stepping in. The tub was large, and she submerged herself completely in the hot water, staying under until she was forced up, gasping. How could that thing inside of her breathe? She came up to hear the sound of the downstairs door slam shut.

Lee's breath caught in her throat. She cupped a hand to her mouth to stifle her coughs. She crept from the tub, picking her jeans up from the toilet seat and pulling them on over wet legs. There was only one window in the bathroom, too small to be of any use. Lee's shirt had dropped to the floor and was a wet rag, but she put this on, too, before creeping into the bedroom. She heard a woman's voice mutter, "Shit shit shit," followed by a series of beeps. Lee thought of her sneakers, sitting at the bottom of the stairs, of the mess she had left in the kitchen. It would be only a matter of seconds before whoever was downstairs realized that someone was in the house. Lee crept across the carpet to the large bedroom window and peered out. Downstairs in the driveway, the family's station wagon was idling, its passenger door open.

Lee popped her head into the hallway. There were two doors across the hall, but she'd have to pass the stairway to get to them, exposing herself to the downstairs. She had no choice. Placing her foot on the runner, Lee froze when she heard a creak. Carefully she brought the other foot around, then angled her head for a view downstairs, just in time to see the door close. She heard the car door slam shut outside, followed by the squeal of tires. Lee waited, completely still, for another minute. She was alone again. To the right of the door, beside a keypad, a red light was blinking.

She figured she could stay here as long as the family was on vacation, but she was trapped inside. Once she left, she'd trigger the alarm and there'd be no coming back. Lee stripped her jeans back off, threw her shirt on the banister, and sunk back into the tub.

She called them the Orbisons, after the Roy Orbison CD that had been left in the stereo, and they had enough food in their house to last Lee for several weeks—canned fruit and tuna, SlimFast diet shakes, frozen hash browns and meat patties. They'd cleared out most of the perishables, which led Lee to believe they'd be away for a week at least. She found a laptop in the girl's room, brought it downstairs, and powered it up. Lee didn't know why she hadn't bothered trying to investigate any of it before; maybe she had hoped it all would just go away. But the search proved fruitless in any case. Googling "Crystal Castle" pulled up a Canadian electronic music duo, a 1980s arcade game, and an Australian New Age tourist destination that smelled of Steve, but nothing that seemed relevant. "Société Anonyme" came up as a generic French term for an anonymous company, the name of an Italian clothing store, and, significantly, the name of a small art collective formed in 1920 by Marcel Duchamp. He, like the Station Master, seemed to be following her everywhere she went. Lee typed "Marcel Duchamp" into the browser.

Henri-Robert-Marcel Duchamp was born on July 28, 1887, in the tiny French village of Blainville-Crevon, to a notary father and a mother he once described as "placid and indifferent," a stance that the Web page said Duchamp would take on as a kind of guiding principle throughout his own life. Lee brought up an image. He was handsome, even as an old man, with a face as serene as a summer lake. As she scrolled through more images of Duchamp both young and old, she found herself captivated by his nose, whose straight bridge ran down from the protrusion of his brows before curving delicately in at the tip. It seemed to take on a different cast depending on the tilt of his head. He had intelligent eyes and a thin, facetious mouth, which never smiled directly but in every picture contained an almost imperceptible curve of mirth. He wore his thick brown hair brushed back from a high, square forehead. He often smoked a pipe. In many of the photos he was playing chess.

Then Lee saw a picture of the bicycle wheel mounted on a stool. She felt the presence of the Station Master in the room with her. She closed the laptop and went upstairs. It took her a long time to get to sleep.

She spent her first two near-sleepless nights in the Orbisons' palatial bed, but after that she gravitated to the daughter's room, which had only a double mattress but which Lee found suited her better. It had walls plastered in magazine photos of old actresses like Audrey Hepburn and Grace Kelly. Band posters and fashion spreads.

The floor was strewn with paperback YA novels and schoolbooks, binders full of notes and dreamy, elaborate doodles. The girl's name, Lee gleaned from one of those binders, was Annie. Over the next week—as Lee nested further into that room, wearing Annie's clothes, dancing on the unmade bed to the music on Annie's iPod—she allowed herself to forget about the person or persons stalking her, about the thing growing inside her, and imagined that she and Annie were friends. In the photos on her computer, Annie had shoulder-length brown hair, usually swept back in a headband; she had quiet brown eyes and light rosy makeup, and she dressed the way the rest of her friends dressed, in plaid skirts and pastel blouses and ballet flats, plastic rings and friendship bracelets. At first Lee scorned her for her sameness, her lack of imagination or originality—Annie was the girl who'd sneered at Lee behind her back, then hit her up after school to lift a sweater for her from Macy's; the girl who'd ask her to score her a bag of Molly for a party she was throwing, then not invite her. But as Lee dug further into Annie's diaries, her e-mails and iPhoto albums, and her Facebook and Instagram pages, she saw a side of the girl that she kept hidden, and Lee yearned to protect her, to save her somehow from the pain Lee could see in her eyes. Annie was sixteen, a junior at a private high school, and secretly in love with her best friend, Oona, a preppy blonde with an equestrian's demeanor. In every photo Oona seemed to treat those around her with a kind of benevolent mastery. Lee found herself hating Oona, the entitlement she wielded like a riding crop, the way she corralled her friends and set them against one another, and then Lee was thinking about Edie and felt a surge of guilt. For a long time after seeing the MISSING flier, Lee had lain awake at night wondering what had happened to her. But she hadn't thought of Edie in a while.

As Lee tunneled deeper into Annie's longing, she lost track of the days. She ate when she was hungry, slept when she could no longer keep awake. Keeping the shades drawn bled day into night into day, and so she was caught completely off guard when, descending the front stairs naked and dripping after a bath, she first heard a sharp click, then watched the front door open.

Lee froze midstep, hand grasping the banister, water dripping from her hair in slow motion, two drops, then three. When Mrs. Orbison came in and immediately turned her back to punch in the alarm code, Lee took the moment to spin and launch herself back up the stairs. She crept into Annie's room and took quick stock of her situation. Lee had known when the Orbisons were returning home— she'd found it marked on a kitchen calendar. She'd been planning for this moment, she knew her escape route, but she had planned on getting out a day before. She was going to clean the place, take her trash with her, erase all traces of herself. But now clothes were strewn about the house; her shoes were downstairs, where she'd left them that first day. A week's worth of dirty dishes; books and magazines and CDs scattered all over the living room. She couldn't believe it had been ten days.

Lee was standing in Annie's closet pulling on one of her shirts when the door opened. Annie stood there in the flesh, hand frozen on the doorknob, gaping at the half-naked girl in her room. Both of them remained perfectly still, as though to move would set some terrible machine into motion. It was strange seeing Annie in person, the girl standing in front of her set up against the girl Lee had grown to know through her words and her photos, her taste in music and the jagged, angry slant of her handwriting. As Lee reached down slowly for a pair of Annie's jeans a look passed across Annie's face and Lee knew Annie recognized her, from when they'd locked eyes in the street. Lee tried to hold that moment of recognition between them.

Annie nodded almost imperceptibly and backed out the door. Lee knew she didn't have long. Her only hope was that Annie could stall her parents long enough for Lee to . . . to what? She grabbed a tote bag, stuffed in a few random items—a T-shirt, socks, underwear—before grabbing a pair of Annie's sneakers and opening the window. She climbed out and onto the roof of the carport, then reached in and grabbed the bag, just in time to see Annie at the door, pointing at Lee, her father beside her, white-knuckling a baseball bat.

You little bitch, Lee thought, dropping down onto the grass of the lawn and walking quickly away.

EIGHT

THE Royal Greene Hotel stood a stone's throw from an abandoned theater in North Philly that she had once creeped with Tomi. At the time she'd paid little attention to the empty shell of a hotel, its east wall scorched from a fire that had destroyed the adjacent building. Some of the plywood used to board up the windows was singed as well, which meant that the fire had come after the hotel had been condemned. It might have been the result of some junkie's cooking mishap, but now the building was so damaged even the junkies avoided it.

The building had no running water, no electricity. The third-floor room she slept in smelled of human waste. The first thing she'd seen when she came in was a black velvet painting of a nude woman that some dude had clearly shot his load across. Lee took it and hung it above the bed, in the middle of which was a cigarette burn bigger than her fist. A small thicket of used syringes sat rusting up the bottom of the bathtub. But the room provided easy egress out the only window, and Lee set up an alarm system using rat traps she'd found stored in a utility closet. She mined the floor with them around the front door and up the stairs. She'd gagged when she first came into the hotel, but she settled in anyway, and a week later she noticed the smell only when she'd return after having been out.

Worse than the smells were the night sounds, the exchanges of prostitutes and dealers on the street below, the quiet wailing of a man who seemed to circle the block constantly in conversation with himself about something he'd lost. She stayed awake most nights with this sound track in her head, sure that as soon as she fell asleep these people would make their way into her room. But the silence of the day was worse, the light from the window casting the room's history in stark relief—the stains and smears across the mattress and walls, the pile of empty Sterno cans, the garbage, the ring of feces left behind from the bucket she had moved to another room at the end of the hall.

Still, she didn't want to leave the room. She peed in the toilets of other rooms and ventured outside just once a day to use the gas station restroom at the end of the block, to shit and wash and fill a plastic bottle with water. She'd try to scrounge or steal some food, then return to the hotel and not go out again until her bowels or pangs of hunger forced her to. When she went out, every person she saw seemed like one of them, every homeless kid an agent of the Station Master.

As it had in the van, or in solitary, the loneliness was what got to her most. Alone in the hotel was not the same as being alone on a creep. Here she was besieged by unwanted thoughts. She thought about her mother more than she wanted to. About all the little betrayals she'd endured, especially since Steve had moved in. But she thought about before that, too, when Lee and her mother were close, and that was just as bad. She thought about the time she was seven and her mother, called in from work, defended her against the school principal and her second-grade teacher, who had accused her (accurately but without proof) of stealing Howard, the class guinea pig. Lee had watched two boys torturing the poor creature earlier in the week and had assembled a plan to liberate him. She snuck him out of the class during recess and set him free in the park beside the school. When she returned to check on him the following day, she found him a few feet from where she had left him, his body stiff and cold. But her mother had been a different person then, before Lee's father had left them.

It was Lee's seventh night in the hotel when she heard the clack of a sprung trap downstairs, then another. She had been half-asleep, but the sound shot her into a panicked terror so immediate and primal she was out the door with a length of broken pipe in her hand before she even realized it. At the bottom of the stairs: Tomi, howling and slapping at his legs, a cacophony of rat traps popping up around him like grasshoppers disturbed in a field. He offered up an embarrassed smile, relief flooding his face.

Lee tightened her grip on the pipe, waiting for him to get close enough to crack him in the skull. "How did you find me?"

Tomi lifted a wrapped deli sandwich from a grocery bag. "Aren't you going to invite me up?"

"You just disappeared," he said. "Not even a note. I won't say it didn't hurt."

Lee sat with her back against the wall, the pipe beside her on the floor. In the end she simply couldn't bring herself to do it. After everything, she still missed him. And if she listened to her gut, she trusted him, mostly, and knew he'd never do anything to hurt her. If he knew more than he was letting on, she would get it out of him. "I got *your* note," she said.

Tomi was perched awkwardly on the edge of the mattress, as though trying to touch as little of it with his person as possible. He stopped chewing and looked up. "What note?"

"Why pretend?"

He looked genuinely confused. "I've been really worried about you, Lee. We all were. Why did you just take off like that?"

"I needed time to think."

"You have been gone two weeks. What have you been thinking about?"

Because Lee didn't want to get into the kinds of things she'd been thinking about, she told him about her time at the Orbisons.

"So you broke into someone's house, and lived there? And that was better than living with me?"

"I enjoyed every minute of it."

"Do you enjoy living here, too?"

Lee looked carefully at his face, wondering if he really knew as little as he seemed to. She pulled her bag close and rifled through it until she found the photo of the woman. She tossed it to him. "Who is she?"

Tomi squinted at the woman's face. "She looks just like you. Is she a relative?"

"You've never seen her before?"

Tomi turned the photo over to the cryptogram on the back, and his face changed, but just for a moment. "Where did you get this?"

"I got it exactly where you left it for me."

As he met her eyes, he shook his head; he really didn't know, she could tell.

"What about that photo of me, with the eyes, surrounded by men—'What do you see through your windows?'"

He handed the photo back. "I swear to you, I have no idea what you're talking about."

Lee scrutinized his face. "Tell me what you were doing at the Silo that night."

"Implying what?"

"I'm just trying to figure out why you're always just a couple of degrees away from all of this shit that keeps happening to me."

Tomi looked as though he was about to say something, but then he stopped himself. "Look, I get that you don't trust me. But I can help you. You can't keep staying here."

"Why not?"

"Jesus, Lee, don't be an asshole. Look at this place. Look at yourself. You look like a little broken bird in here."

Lee felt her anger flare. "Don't ever call me that."

Tomi deflated. "Okay. But I can't go home knowing you're sleeping here."

Lee looked around her home of the past week. She was getting used to it, and that scared her a little. "I'm not coming back to the apartment with you."

"I get that. But maybe I can help you go underground. Not like this. For real."

"Underground." The word sounded like an actual place when he said it, but she knew there was no *underground*. There was only wherever she happened to be, when she happened to be there. "How?"

"Leave that to me."

"I want to know what's going on. Who these people are that are following me. And what they want from me."

"Maybe I can help with that, too. I will try if you tell me more. But we need to get you out of here first. Please."

"For real, Tomi, how did you find me?"

Tomi laughed. "Pure chance. I saw you come out of an Aldi yesterday."

"And you followed me back here? Why didn't you say something then?"

"Obviously you did not want to be found. I'm sorry, but I couldn't give you the chance to just vanish again. Now I get it. But I can help you disappear."

She could see gears moving in Tomi's head. "How?"

The next day Tomi returned with a twenty-some-page sheaf of paper. Lee squinted at it in what light came in through the boarded window. Just a long list of names, addresses, and dates.

"Okay," Tomi said. "You said you were squatting the home of some family on vacation."

"Yeah."

"Well, it occurred to me that there must be hundreds of people like that leaving their homes vacant every week."

"It was just dumb luck I found one of them."

"Okay. But what if . . . " he said, reclining back on the room's mattress with a self-satisfaction that Lee couldn't help but find a little irritating, "you were able to know when they were going out of town?"

"I wouldn't lie on that," she said. "I wouldn't get near that thing."

"The mattress?"

"God knows the junkie juice it's soaked up over the years."

"Where do you sleep?"

Lee gestured toward a rolled-up foam mat she'd found in one of the rooms. "Right behind you, that big stain on the wall?" She waited for him to crane his head. "I think that's where someone shot himself."

Tomi got up and moved to the floor. He nodded at the paper in her hand. "Take a look at that list."

"What are these?" she said.

"My work, it gives me certain accesses." Tomi day-jobbed as a data recovery technician, spending his work hours digitally spelunking into damaged hard drives, salvaging what could be salvaged. "One of our clients is a travel agency. Not many people use them anymore, but folks with money still want someone else to do their shit for them. So this agency brought in its server a few months back. The thing was totally fried. Someone spilled coffee onto it, and the dummies never had a backup."

"So?"

"So I was able to restore eighty-three percent of it."

"So?"

"So we keep backups of all the data we restore. I went through it last night and hey! Logins and passwords there for the taking. So I took a peek at their current database of airline and hotel bookings. I set parameters to grab trips one week or longer, with two or more travelers from the same address. That way it's pretty much all vacations, no business trips leaving the wife and kids behind. Shall we go house hunting?"

The first home on the list was a two-story brick colonial in the southwest suburbs, pushed far back along a grass walkway, and they circled back around to check it out. "Keep your eyes open," he told her, and jogged up to the front door and peeked in through the mail slot.

"No good," he said when he got back.

"How could you tell?"

"Mail is stacked up on a table, nothing on the floor. It means someone's been coming in to check on the place."

"You've thought this through, haven't you?"

Tomi blushed a little as he checked his list for another residence. He took her hand and started walking. "Come on, we're a couple on a stroll."

The next house was a stone and wood two-story Tudor with a peaked roof, and Tomi let go of her hand and picked up a rubber ball that had rolled to the edge of the driveway. He bounced it a few times, took a few steps, then kicked it into the yard.

Lee watched as he ran to get it, taking his time about it, checking through the mail slot, then going around the side to stare up at the windows.

When he got back, he told her, "I think this is the place."

They went around the side of the house to the back. Tomi showed her the cracks in the magnetic tape around the windows, which told him the alarm system was likely old and defunct. He pulled a thin strip of steel from his bag and used it to get under the window pane and jimmy the latch, which fell open easily.

"How do you know this stuff?" Lee asked.

Tomi shrugged. "The Internet."

Lee felt her heart race, not unlike the rush she used to get shoplifting. She climbed in feetfirst and dropped to the floor.

In the gunmetal light they moved past a furnace and water heater. Stacked all around was the detritus of someone else's life: rusty bicycles and boxes stuffed with camping gear and old clothes, gardening equipment and tools and a stack of board games in torn cardboard boxes, an orange kayak hung from the rafters. Lee followed Tomi across the basement to another set of stairs. At the top was a door that Tomi jimmied open with a crowbar.

The owners had been good enough to leave a few lights on, and Lee left Tomi to investigate upstairs. The rooms were spare and decorated in cool grays. Each was a showroom, nothing out of place. In a tidy little office she picked up a metal comb from a shelf and ran her fingers along its teeth. She went into the bedroom and lay down, trying to get a feel for the place, but there was nothing. Even in the hotel she'd felt the presence of people who'd been there before her. The people who lived here were blanks. It made Lee feel very alone. When she returned to the living room, Tomi was on the couch, eating peanut butter from a jar and reading a magazine.

"So what do you think of your new digs?" he said. "Okay for a week?"

She took the peanut butter from him and ate it from the knife. "I guess so."

He pulled the list from his back pocket, smoothing it over the coffee table next to the map. "There's enough food in the kitchen to last you that at least. There's no pet bowl, no house plants, which means no one'll be coming by to feed or water anything. I went through the list, and check this out: Mr. and Mrs. Lunske—that's these good folks—they get back next Friday. But if you leave on Thursday, you can stay at the Gilberts', here"—he pointed to a dot on the map—"or here, at the Talbots'."

Lee stared at the map, tried to imagine the houses of these people, but all she could think about was the mutilated eyes of her own photo staring back at her. "You said you'd help me find out what's going on. Why these people are harassing me."

Tomi folded the map. His eyes went to her face. "Okay," he said. "But you have to tell me everything first. Start from the beginning."

Lee hesitated.

"I can't help you if you don't."

She had confided so little to anyone about what had happened to her since the JDC it felt strange talking about it now, like she was repeating someone else's story. But she stumbled through it, starting with her high school arrest, then gaining momentum as she described the JDC and her escape, the man in the park, finally taking Tomi to the Crystal Castle. She told him about Ester, the Station Master, and how he'd talked to her. She told him about sneaking into the Station Master's room. When she told Tomi about what she'd seen upstairs, she felt the familiar sickness and rage run through her.

"What did you find in his room?"

"There was an old ledger. Numbered subjects—I think he was recording the kids there. I was one of them."

"What else?"

"That photo. The woman I showed you. I first saw it there before I found it left for me at the aquarium. Who is she?"

"I can try to research her. Anything else?"

Lee hesitated, then plunged forward. "I took something. Someone delivered something to him that night. It was a work by Duchamp."

"Why did you take it?"

"I was holding the bag, but I didn't know what was in it. When I heard him coming back, I panicked. Later, I saw it had been stolen from the museum . . . what kind of coincidence is that?"

It sounded more and more fantastic the further she went. If Tomi was skeptical, he didn't show it. "Where is it now?" he asked.

Lee shook her head. "I can just return it. Maybe they'll leave me alone if I do."

Tomi frowned. "Maybe."

"But I want to know who they are," she said.

They went upstairs to the office, and she sat beside him as he powered up the computer. When he got a private browser window up, he said, "Where should we start?"

"I want to know about the Société Anonyme. The Station Master's connected to them somehow. But I already tried that. The only mention is of some old artists' salon founded by Duchamp in 1920. They disbanded ages ago."

"Well, maybe they've re-banded," he said.

"And now they throw raves and push drugs?"

Tomi shrugged.

"You think Derrick's involved? He had at least two of those invites, for two different parties. The one he gave you and the one he left in your book."

Tomi shook his head. "Derrick's a scenester. Whatever the cool thing to do is, he wants to be there. But he's not a joiner. He hooks up with girls where he can, but mostly he just sticks to himself."

Tomi scrolled down the search pages, one after another, coming up blank.

"I told you," she said.

Tomi pulled a keychain out of his pocket. The ring was attached to a blue rabbit's foot, which he pulled off to reveal a USB stick. He inserted it into the computer's port, opened a folder, and then clicked on an icon. A different browser opened. He laid into the keyboard with a burst of typing.

"What are you doing?" she said.

"Have you heard of the Darknet?"

"Is that one of those underground Internet sites where you can buy drugs and hire hit men?"

Tomi laughed. "You can also order stolen organs. But that's just a small part of it."

"So are we going to order a kidney or have someone knocked off?"

Tomi smiled. "Neither. Most of that is scammers, anyway. How do you think Derrick makes his money? How do you think he affords all that gear—that SLR camera, that watch? As a barista?"

Lee thought about his webcam offer in the stairwell. "Derrick traffics in human organs?"

"He'll pose as a doctor in the Ukraine, or Mumbai, tell his customer he has access to kidneys and livers, lungs, even hearts. Or he'll be an ex-marine mercenary willing to kill anyone for a fee. He gets husbands and wives paying to get rid of their spouses. Then he just takes their money and disappears."

"How does he get away with that?"

"Anonymity, and knowing how to navigate. The Darknet isn't a site; it's more like an area. And it's part of an even larger area called the Deep Web, which is like a hidden Internet. The Deep Web runs beneath the public Internet, but you have to know how to access it. It's huge, maybe five thousand times as big as the World Wide Web. Most of it is just forgotten information stored on servers in governments and institutions around the world. But within the Deep Web are areas like the Darknet, which is both hidden and anonymous. And embedded within the Darknet are different sites and groups and organizations. It's like a termite hill. We're going to a site called the Subnet right now. A lot of the urbex crews communicate via the Subnet. Aside from housing the main urbex forum, the Subnet serves as a kind of trading outfit. It's how we trade maps and locations, post photos without being found out. When I need something, I contact this guy in the Subnet and he finds someone who has it. We agree on a fair trade, and the Subnet gets a broker's fee. Everybody's happy."

To reach the Subnet, Tomi told her, he had to log in through a special browser that was cloaked to hide his identity and keyed in to access Darknet sites. Once in, he clicked on an icon of a door, which sent an electronic knock to the Subnet site.

A window opened on the desktop. Below it was a little avatar of a flying turtle monster that Lee remembered watching on TV as a kid, and the name H3rm3s beneath that.

"Is that you?" Lee asked. "Hermes?"

"Messenger of the gods. Protector of thieves, travelers, and border crossings. Guide to the underworld, bitches."

Below Tomi's avatar, another avatar came up, a hostile-looking troll holding a key, the name Papoola beneath it.

"Papoola's a gatekeeper," Tomi explained. "Everyone who logs on to the Subnet needs to provide a visual to the gatekeeper first. It's more secure than a password."

Tomi typed: subnet access, which was followed by an immediate response:

[Papoola]: Ready for vid-ver.

Tomi adjusted himself within the monitor's webcam. No image of the person on the other end came up, but a voice, modulated to eliminate all hints of gender, said, "Hello, Hermes. How can I help you today?"

"Just research," Tomi said.

"You realize your account is currently two months in arrears."

"You know I'm good for it."

"And who is that behind you?"

Tomi grinned. "A new friend."

Lee stepped back into the shadows and lowered her head.

"Why is she hiding?"

"She's shy."

Tomi turned the desk lamp on her, and suddenly there was no place for Lee to disappear. She didn't like being looked at when she couldn't tell who was looking.

"I want to authorize her full access on my account," Tomi said.

"You are vouching for her?"

"Of course."

"Very well. Sit in front of the webcam, please. Pretend I'm taking a passport photo."

Tomi stood so that Lee could sit down. Lee thought about Ester taking her photo in the cafeteria. "That's okay," she said.

Tomi looked at her, confused. "What's okay?"

"I don't want my picture taken right now."

Tomi spoke to the computer: "Could you give us a second?" He turned off its microphone.

"Listen, I've already vouched for you. I let you see me access the Subnet. You can't just walk away now."

"Why not?"

Tomi was silent, as though considering how to put it. "You know how, in a movie, if drug dealers want to test whether someone is a cop, they make them try some drugs first? It's like an insurance policy."

"But I'm not a drug dealer. Or a cop."

"But you understand what I am saying. If you say no now, it looks bad. For both of us."

Everything in her gut was telling her not to do this. But if she was going to trust Tomi as far as she already had, she had to trust him with this, too. When she sat, the face she saw in the monitor stared back at her, eyes dark and tired but cheeks flushed. She heard a click, and her image froze for a moment.

"You are now L2 authorized," the voice said. "You will give her an orientation, Hermes?"

"Of course," Tomi said.

"And assume responsibility for her presence on the Subnet?"

Tomi looked at Lee. "I will," he said. Lee felt as though they were getting married.

"If she wants unsponsored access, she will have to set up an account of her own, which will require a monthly bitcoin deposit. Is there anything else?"

"Nope."

"Proceed," the voice said, and the troll avatar disappeared.

Tomi brought up a browser window. It looked exactly like a Google home page, except for a tiny "s" attached to the bottom of the first "G" in Google. He typed in "Société Anonyme," and suddenly the screen was full of hits that hadn't been on the normal browser. "You see—the Subnet's even got its own subWikipedia."

The subWiki page included a mention of the original Société Anonyme, but most of it was dedicated to the regenerated S.A. According to the site, the group was begun in 2001 by a man referred to only as the Priest.

"I heard the Station Master use that name," Lee said. "When he was talking to the man who delivered the Duchamp piece."

"What did he say exactly?"

"Something about the Priest being an old man."

"Anything else?"

"How the Priest was trapped in a room somewhere? And how what the guy was delivering would change everything. I don't know, it's hard to remember." She sat back on the bed. "But now that I look back on it, it sounded like there was a split within them. I think they were working against each other. Maybe we can use that?"

Tomi considered this. "Maybe, but we'll need more than that." He looked like he was considering something.

"What is it?" she said.

"Do you remember *The Bride Stripped Bare,* the Duchamp work from the museum, the tall glass panel?"

"Yeah."

"Near the bottom of the work is a circle of nine figures. Duchamp called them the Bachelors. They were all typical male roles of the early twentieth century. There's the Delivery Boy, the Gendarme, the Cavalry Soldier, the Policeman, the Undertaker, the Busboy, the Flunky, and get this: the Station Master and the Priest."

"Does everything lead back to Duchamp?"

"From what I can tell, he is like a patron saint to them."

She thought about the men in old uniforms she'd seen at the Silo. "So maybe there are nine of them in the S.A. That's something." Lee's eyes were tired. She sat on the sofa, behind him. "What else?"

Tomi turned back to the screen, paraphrasing for her. "The Société Anonyme started out throwing salons and exhibitions around modernist avant-garde art. They dressed in early-twentieth-century clothes and reenacted exhibitions and performances of the time. Like a performance of a Duchamp musical composition with notes chosen by chance. Or a production of Alfred Jarry's play *Ubu Roi*. They reenacted Dada sound poems from the Cabaret Voltaire in Zurich; they did a Futurist symphony using industrial machines as instruments."

Tomi clicked to bring up a page full of blurry pics of fliers from these events and others. Lee's thoughts were still on men in old uniforms. The Station Master, she'd seen a uniform in his armoire. The man who brought him the Duchamp work, he had on a funny-looking old uniform as well. Maybe he was the Delivery Boy? The tall man in the antiquated dark wool suit—which one was he? She remembered a policeman, and a few men in old military uniforms. Lee had had an uncle on her mother's side, and every June he and his friends used to dress in period clothing and reenact the assassination of Archduke Ferdinand. Her uncle and the other men (they were all men) in his little club had all been earnest and harmless. But the S.A. was something else. She thought about those kids upstairs.

Tomi was scrolling through pages, looking for anything that might be relevant. He stopped on something.

She got up to read over his shoulder: "'Members of the Société Anonyme are rumored to include scientists and engineers, but they are also said to be involved in more esoteric areas, such as consciousness exploration, metaphysics, alchemy, and technological singularity.'"

"They have their fingers in a lot of pies," Tomi said.

"What's technological singularity?"

"It's the idea that one day artificial intelligence will make a super-leap forward and will become of such a higher order it will make us look like insects in comparison."

"Are they just a bunch of cranks? There's got to be something here. Who is the Priest?"

Tomi shook his head.

"When they took me in at the Crystal Castle, the Station Master treated me . . . I don't know, as if he knew me somehow. Like he'd been waiting for me. And that man in the Silo, the way he acted, too. Like he'd been expecting me."

"You must mean something to them."

"It's got something to do with that woman," she said. "They think we're connected."

"These people are not . . . they don't seem to look at the world like the rest of us."

"So what am I supposed to do?"

"Don't do anything. Just lie low. Let me ask around, see what I can find out. The Subnet has long arms. Maybe there's someone who can help." Tomi got up and put his jacket on.

"Where are you going?"

"Home. I've got to go to work tomorrow morning, and it will be better for me to leave now, while it's dark."

She was so grateful to have him back, more than she'd realized, and the need for him to stay the night came unexpectedly.

He saw her face and added, "I'll be back tomorrow night."

She nearly told him then of the thing growing inside her, the thing that might have his eyes or his squat nose, the cleft in his chin. But she didn't know if she'd be telling him because he had a right to know or because she knew it would make him stay. So she said nothing.

He wrote his number on a slip of paper. "I know you don't have a cell, and you can't use the landline here to call anyone, so this is just for an emergency. If you need to call me, find a pay phone."

Tomi left the way they had come in, and Lee cracked the curtain to watch him disappear down the street. When she could no longer see him, she stood in the middle of her new home and listened to the clicking of the empty house.

Lee couldn't sleep that night, and so she stayed up watching TV, flipping channels until she began to feel the loneliness gnaw at her insides. She browsed the single bookshelf, but the Lunskes weren't much in the way of casual readers. Most of it was devoted to law texts. There was a lone book on chemistry, and she remembered the bookshelf in the Station Master's room. All those books on chemistry, but also a whole shelf devoted to alchemy. She went back online.

Alchemy, according to the Internet, was a kind of proto-chemistry, going back to before the twelfth century. It was, so far as Lee could interpret, a garbled mess of religion, magic, and coded mystical jargon. Its aim seemed to be either to turn base metals into gold or to achieve a means toward immortality. Alchemists saw the universe as made up of opposing forces and elements, and alchemy was an art that focused on the marriage of these paired opposites. The key to all of it was something called the philosopher's stone. Nobody knew exactly what it was, but it was the thing they were all after. It just seemed like magic tricks to her. Were the S.A. nothing more than a bunch of cheap magicians?

Lee opened a new private browser and typed in "Marcel Duchamp alchemy." There were people who found encoded alchemical symbolisms in his work, especially *The Bride Stripped Bare*. But Lee was only able to locate one quote on the subject from Duchamp himself: "If I have ever practiced alchemy, it was in the only way it can be done now, that is to say, without knowing it."

Lee sank back in the chair. None of this was telling her anything. She closed her eyes, but sleep wouldn't come. She wished Tomi hadn't gone. She wished she'd been able to ask him to stay. Lee did the math in her head and then typed "fetus 7 weeks" into the search engine. She deleted it, shut the laptop, then opened it and typed it again. She hit return. A click on "images" brought up a page of pink tadpoles. Lee opened one, fitting it to the screen. It had a big, misshapen head with dark eyes and tiny flippers. About half an inch, according to the Web site. She lifted her shirt and looked down at her belly. The thing was in there, floating in its little sac. Lee went to the living room and found the liquor cabinet. She opened a bottle of gin, tipped it back and chugged for a good three seconds. Then she went into the bathroom to throw up.

In the morning she made herself eggs and toast. Everything in the house seemed harsher in the daylight, and she walked through it picking up random things—a blue glass vase, a faux deco lighter, a tiny copper lamp—and trying to get a sense of the place. At the Orbisons, everything in the house felt like something they had all touched; the whole house was infused with the presence of the family. Walking through the Lunskes' was like walking through a furniture showroom.

That afternoon someone let himself into the house, waking her into a state of animal panic. Lee hid in an upstairs closet, praying the person wouldn't come up to find the tangle of unmade bedding and the dirty dishes she'd left on the nightstand. Eventually, after rattling around downstairs for what seemed like forever, the person left.

Lee gathered her things, made sure she had left no traces behind, and went out the way she and Tomi had come in. She had no money, but she had Tomi's list.

The next house was a yellow, aluminum-sided single-family home behind a picket fence. Lee let herself in through a second-floor window. No alarm went off, but Lee was sitting at the kitchen counter, eating a package of deli meat from the fridge, when the family's teenage son came home. He walked right past the kitchen and into the living room, where he turned on the TV and began calling friends to set up a party while his parents were out of town. Lee slipped out the kitchen door and through the yard of the house behind. It was dark out. She walked quickly, zigzagging streets until she hit a main boulevard and found a gas station restroom. She splashed water over her face until her shakes subsided. Lee dried herself off on her sweatshirt, went into one of the stalls, and sat on the toilet seat.

"Are you all right?" The voice outside of the stall sounded hesitant, as though the woman had been debating with herself whether to get involved.

Lee hadn't realized she'd been crying, little hiccups that must have sounded like someone choking. She could see the woman's shoes, brown leather pumps, and white stockings. She imagined a woman her mother's age, in a scarf and cardigan. If she opened the door and the woman saw her, the woman might take pity, invite her to stay at her home for the night, or even a few. Lee would eat French toast in the woman's kitchen and answer her questions politely, lying to her with carefully chosen words.

But when Lee opened the door the woman was already gone.

Outside Lee stood at a pay phone, holding the receiver but unable to dial Tomi's number. He would be sick with worry—for that alone she owed him a phone call. And she missed him already, missed his stories, missed their late-night creeps and their long walks home, missed wanting him to stop talking. But the encounter with the woman in the restroom had made her feel so needy and weak she disgusted herself. She remembered her rising panic when Tomi had told her he was leaving, and her visceral desire for him to stay. She refused to need anyone like that.

The next house proved to be a winner. She spent three days there skimming novels whose titles all seemed to reference someone's daughter, and eating steadily through the contents of the refrigerator. Every day it became easier to be alone, and every day the prospect of calling Tomi seemed more remote. He would be better off without her, in the end, and she stood a better chance of disappearing on her own. She knew how to be invisible, it was in her blood. But she couldn't be invisible with someone else. On the fourth day, she went out again and scouted her next residence, came back and erased every trace of her presence. She left that night, dropping a bag of her trash into a neighbor's bin.

By her third residence, Lee had worked out a system of rules. One: leave as small a footprint as possible. This meant cleaning up after herself constantly, washing and drying her dishes and putting them away as soon as she'd finished. It meant making the bed every morning and doing a run-through every night. Two: draw the shades and leave the place in darkness. Usually the homeowners would leave on a light or two anyway, which gave enough illumination for her to get by. Sometimes she allowed herself a dim reading lamp in a back room if the shades could be drawn tightly enough. Three: always have an escape route mapped out, with her things in a bag and ready to go. And four (the hardest): never take anything from the homes that she didn't bring in.

She was beginning to feel nauseated, close to vomiting, several times a day, and sometimes she'd sit with her cheek against the cool porcelain of the toilet and wait for it to come, but nothing ever came up. Once she came close to finding a clinic and getting it over with, but then she imagined herself walking in and the questions they would ask. She had no money, and even if they gave her the procedure for free, she had no ID and no way to prove she was over eighteen. She knew how young she looked. She would have to figure out a way, at some point, but she still had time.

NINE

LEE perpetrated her first burglary on a November night around 1 a.m. She had intended to squat the house, a columned colonial mansion that was tonier than her prior residences. After drifting from room to room to let the feel of the place sink in, Lee had settled down in the kitchen with a bowl of cereal when she saw the note for the cleaning woman on the counter. It didn't say when she was expected, but Lee knew she couldn't stay.

The list was shrinking fast. It would take her through another month, if she was lucky. Lee began to think about what she would do when it ran dry. Philadelphia was no longer safe. There were too many people looking for her.

There were cities she'd always wanted to see: New York, Miami, New Orleans, Chicago, Los Angeles, San Francisco, Seattle. If she could scrape together enough for bus fare, she could have her pick. Lee imagined herself stepping off a bus in New York, saw the crowds rushing around her as she stood under the fluorescent lamps of a downtown Greyhound station. But then what? She'd still need money for food, an apartment, at least until she could get some kind of job. She saw herself behind the counter of a bookstore or washing dishes at a restaurant.

Maybe there was something valuable in the house. If she wasn't staying here, then her no-stealing rule didn't apply, did it?

She returned to the bedroom where she remembered seeing a black lacquer box on the dresser. The box was filled with necklaces and earrings and rings, and she picked through it for anything that looked valuable, careful not to take too many pieces. The longer it took these people to realize they'd been robbed, the better. Lee left with a gold bracelet, a set of earrings inlaid with large blue stones, a ring, and an old brooch, because she liked the image carved into the ivory inlay—the profile of a young woman.

After settling in at another home from the list, she went out the next night and found a house whose lights were on at three in the morning. No one left their lights on that late unless they were awake or away. Lee peered through the windows until she was certain no one was home, then broke in through the garage. Two nights later she broke into a third house. Each time she went straight for the jewelry, taking only a few pieces—the ones that looked the most valuable.

That night she lay all the jewelry out on the bed of the home she was squatting and held each one, gauging its weight. There was good money here—there had to be—but only if she could find someone to buy them. Lee had never had a fence in high school, when her fingers had been the stickiest. She'd never needed one, always selling her stolen goods directly. But now she thought of Maria from the JDC. She was a thief, like Lee, but unlike Lee, Maria took no pleasure in stealing; she did it because she had younger siblings to help support but couldn't hold a job for more than a few weeks. And because her uncle Vasco, who ran a pawnshop, knew what to do with stolen property. Lee wondered how Maria was doing inside. She wished she could visit her, even write her a letter, let her know that she wasn't forgotten. And thank her for her connections. But Maria knew she wasn't forgotten; she was always getting visits from family and friends, including, on at least one occasion, her uncle.

Lee took a bus out to Fairhill. It was a neighborhood of Mexican bakeries and tire stores and shops that seemed to cater exclusively to proms and quinceañeras, and Lee asked store to store for nearly an hour before someone finally directed her to an old converted garage in the middle of an alley.

The man at the counter looked to be anywhere from forty to sixty, either old or young for his age. Beneath his thin, pressed white shirt, she could see a ropy torso patchworked in faded tattoos. He was rubbing carefully at a pocket watch with a clean white rag and didn't look up when she came in. His shop was not a shop at all, just a counter behind which leaned shelves made from unfinished boards stacked on old TVs and holding a slew of things Lee could never imagine anyone buying: old tape decks and clock radios, a scorched hot plate and a torn beach umbrella and a black-bottomed stockpot filled with old kitchenware. Boxes of laundry detergent, diapers, instant coffee, Similac. A stack of school notebooks and a few boxes of pens.

"Are you Mr. Velasquez?" she asked.

He didn't look up when he spoke. *"¿Estas muy lejos de tu hogar, verdad?"*

"I'm sorry," she said, taking an uncomfortable moment to register this other language. "I don't speak Spanish."

"¿Tu crees que este barrio invita gringas perdidas?"

Hoping gold might be a common language, she came to the counter, upended her bag, and spilled the small pile of jewelry—three bracelets, six rings, three pairs of earrings, three necklaces, and a brooch—onto the space in front of him. The man put down the watch and looked at the jewelry. He spat out something else in Spanish and picked up the entire pile in one fist. Then he pulled her bag across the counter and dumped it all back in. The man nodded at the door, picked up his watch, and returned to polishing it.

"I'm sorry, I just thought . . ." Lee turned to leave, feeling stupid. "Never mind."

"You thought what?"

She turned back. "You speak English?"

"I've lived here over forty years. Of course I speak English. Now what are you doing here?"

Lee looked the man in the eyes. "I'm a friend of Maria's."

"You know how many Marias I know?"

"Your niece. We met in the detention center."

He took a moment to regard her. "Tell me about my niece."

"She's got long black hair and a tattoo of a boy's name on her wrist. One of her front teeth is chipped in half," Lee added.

"Anyone can describe a photograph."

"She was kind to me. When I first got there, I didn't know anyone. All the girls ignored me. One girl stole my shoes. Maria gave me a pair of her own."

The man nodded. "That could be. What else?"

Lee hesitated. She really didn't know Maria well at all. "And she helped me get out," she blurted. Which wasn't true, but she could see in the man's face that she had unlocked a door.

"You are the escaped girl? Maria told me about you." He put one hand out, gesturing to the bag. When she handed it to him, he dumped it back on the counter, spreading it out in front of him with two fingers. "Where did you get this?"

Lee shrugged. "My mother."

The man stopped what he was doing. "If we are to have a relationship, you are going to have to learn not to bullshit me. It is clear that this is not all the jewelry of one woman. I see three, maybe four women here. Now, where did you get these?"

"I stole them."

"Good." He pulled out piece after piece, throwing each aside with an epithet in Spanish: *"Basura. Bisturia. Barato. Barato. Barato."* He looked at her. "Now, why did you take these?"

"Because I need money," she said, meeting his gaze.

"No. Why *these* pieces? Why did these look good to you?" When Lee didn't answer, he continued: "Because they are shiny, they gleam like money. You have the eye of a small child. This," he said, picking up the brooch, the intricate silver oval with the sad woman's profile, "is the only thing of any value here." He handed it to her. "See how dull it is, how tarnished with age? This has history, probably someone's heirloom. You have stolen a part of their history. You are okay with that?"

Lee thought about it. "I can't really return it now, can I?"

"If you were back there right now, in this woman's bedroom, knowing what you know now: that this is something that might be the only thing she owns that holds the memory of a loved one. Would you still take it?"

Lee thought about this too, about how honestly to answer. "Yes," she said.

"Good."

Before she left, he gave her sixty dollars for the brooch and told her to dump the rest in a storm drain.

Lee came back two days later with a Ziploc bag full of jewelry she'd lifted from three more homes. She'd sifted carefully through the boxes to find the oldest and most tarnished pieces. To prove that she was not saddled with sentimentality, she took an old lighter as well, a brass World War II–era Zippo with a heart etched into the side and PFC JOHNNY CAPP: BORN TO BREAK above it. Mr. Velasquez examined the lighter cursorily before pocketing it, but he barely looked at the other pieces. Instead he wiped off his hands and grabbed keys from a hook on the wall. "Come," he said, without waiting for her to follow. Whatever test it was, she hadn't passed, and something in her gut fisted up at the thought of her failure.

Mr. Velasquez was already halfway down the alley by the time she stepped outside. He rounded the corner and she ran to catch up. When she got to the street, she found him holding open the passenger door of a white-paneled van with OROZCO BROS. PLUMBING stenciled on the side.

The interior was worn but neat; the seats were torn in several places but had been resewn. She moved a clipboard filled with estimate sheets and sat down. As he started the car, the radio came on to a classic rock station, and Mr. Velasquez was silent as he drove, a half-hour trip that took them onto a freeway and then up into the southern suburbs. Quiet tree-lined blocks of large single-family homes, all of them two or three stories, made from brick or stone, with lots of yard between them.

Mr. Velasquez pulled over, turned down the radio, then reached across her lap and opened the door. She sat there, growing increasingly uncomfortable as he put on a pair of glasses, took a yellowing paperback from his glove compartment, and began to read. When she didn't move, he looked up and nodded at the door. Lee considered trying to wait him out, but something about the way he peered at her over his glasses let her know she would lose. She climbed out and shut the door. Inside the van, Mr. Velasquez put the book down and pulled away. She watched him disappear, blue smoke trailing the van out the exhaust pipe.

Lee stood there for a while, waiting for him to return. He was testing her, or messing with her, but he would come back. He could have driven her anywhere in the city, and yet he drove her here, to this upper-class suburb of old trees and lawns littered with kids' toys and SUVs in the driveways. Did he think she was some suburban rich kid? Was it a message for her to just go home?

She returned to his shop early the next afternoon, and if he was surprised to see her, he gave no sign, looking up only briefly, then returning to run numbers from a ledger through a bulky adding machine. Lee pushed up against the counter across from him and read from a torn piece of paper she pulled from her pocket:

"Five-four-five Sherwood Street. Two, um, stories, no alarm, second-floor . . . second-floor *window* in back, open a crick? A crack. Rain gutter looks climbable. Seven-six-four Sherwood. One story, storm cellar unlocked. Newish BMW in driveway. Fifteen-eighty-two Drexel. Drexer? Drexel. Three stories. Looks well locked, but garage window may be . . . be something, I can't tell."

She went on like this for six more houses, as Mr. Velasquez added numbers. He pushed a tally button, and the machine spit out a final inch of tape. Mr. Velasquez put out his hand. She gave him the paper.

"This is English?" he said, squinting down at it.

"I wrote it so no one can read it," she said. "In case I got questioned."

Mr. Velasquez nodded curtly, but Lee thought she caught a smile.

He drove to each of the addresses on her sheet, pointing out which houses she had chosen well and which not. This one has a dog, he pointed out. This one is silent-alarmed. This one hires regular landscaping service. These people look retired, and retired people are always home. This one has potential. When he was finished, only two of the nine houses from her list had passed muster. He drove her around for two more hours, and he showed her which neighborhoods held promise and which did not. The neighborhood should be well off but not obscenely wealthy: too much wealth meant state-of-the-art alarm systems or hired security. He taught her to look for neighborhood watch signs and well-maintained houses and lawns and to avoid these places. In neighborhoods with a lot of older residents, neighbors were always home, snooping out their windows.

Lee learned to spot homes with dogs by chew toys or water dishes on the porch or scratches on the doors. Mr. Velasquez told her that alarmed homes made good targets, because alarms meant something valuable to be protected. You just had to know how to bypass them. He taught her how to case neighborhoods on foot, rubber-banding menus to doorknobs and peering through windows, or walking around with a clipboard door-to-door, claiming to be selling magazine subscriptions.

The following week he taught her to pick locks, starting her on a clunky steel padlock, then moving on to a series of deadbolts he'd screwed into a two-by-four. His hands were small and fine, and the picks seemed extensions of his fingers. He made it look as easy as combing his hair. Lee thought briefly of her father, who had taught her a bit of the guitar, even cutting down one of his picks to fit her child hands. She would sit on his lap and he'd finger the chords to "Three Little Birds" or "Sweet Caroline" while she strummed. Mr. Velasquez, fixing or polishing something at the counter, would make her stand for hours as she worked her way up the progressively difficult totem until her fingers began to cramp and bleed. It took her sixteen hours over four days to finally defeat the most complicated lock, a bump-resistant double-cylinder deadbolt, and when she did and showed him, she couldn't remember ever having felt so proud. But he just nodded and made her do it again. And again. Until she could move up the line and open them all within six minutes. When she did, he gave her without ceremony a small leather pouch containing a series of steel lockpicks, some nearly as fine as wires. The pouch was well worn, the leather supple and cracked. He said nothing about it, but Lee imagined it was the set that he himself had once used. That night she slept clutching it in her hand.

Lee dreamed of a salamander in her belly. In her dream it turned and flopped inside her and she knew that it was hungry, but she walked the aisles of an abandoned supermarket, the shelves empty but for the husks of dead bugs. She woke with a nosebleed.

Mr. Velasquez taught her how to bypass alarms by using second-floor ingresses, how to identify alarm systems by their manufacturer, and how to disable these alarms using wiring diagrams. He had a big rubber-banded folder bursting with the diagrams, and when he spread them out across his counter, she sat cross-legged beside them and in-haled the oil in his hair as he showed her how to read them. He taught her how to block the modern wireless alarms with a simple cell phone jammer. He taught her how to fool motion detectors with a square of white wood. He taught her to answer a phone if it rang while she was inside a residence, because it might be the security company saying that a silent alarm had been triggered. He taught her to stall them by telling them she was a houseguest and looking for the password the owners had given her; this would buy her time to disappear before they alerted the police. If it wasn't the security company, she should just tell them wrong number and hang up.

Lee had been at it for over two weeks now. Some nights she'd go out on her own and slip into empty homes and come away with her pockets stuffed with jewelry. She'd take it back and lay it out and try to guess what had value and what didn't. But Mr. Velasquez refused to even look at any of it. Without his help none of it was worth any-thing anyway, and she wasn't going anywhere.

He taught her to look for access through second-story windows, or through the garage, which allowed more cover than the front of the house. He taught her to break windows by duct-taping them first to muffle the sound, and he taught her that one sharp noise rarely aroused any lasting suspicion, whereas multiple noises always did. He taught her to be in and out of a place in no more than twelve minutes, to always have an exit strategy in place, and to avoid rooms without window egress when possible. He taught her to go through a house in this order: master bedroom (dresser drawers, bedside table, mattress, and bathroom medicine cabinet), then the kitchen, then the living room if there was time. He told her to never take anything bigger than a fist—"in your case, two fists," he said, with a rare smile—unless it was a gun or drugs. Guns and drugs were the easiest things to sell. Otherwise, he told her, stick to jewelry and cash. He taught her never to steal cell phones or laptops, because you might as well be carrying a tracking device. He taught her which prescription drugs to look for in the medicine cabinets. He taught her to skip the kids' rooms. Nobody ever hid anything of value in a kid's room.

Mr. Velasquez gave her a small magnet and taught her that precious metals had no magnetism. He taught her about the different precious-metal stamps and what they meant, and the kind of patina to look for in gold versus silver, and that platinum had none. He taught her how to spot a fake diamond using a glass of water and a flashlight, and that if one piece of jewelry was fake, then the rest likely were, too. He taught her about dummy jewelry boxes, and that a house with nice things will have the real stuff hidden somewhere; you just had to know where to look. He taught her how to search a kitchen: for a plastic bag at the bottom of a flour bin, for a can of tomatoes that had been opened from the bottom, for foil-wrapped packages in the back of the freezer. For secret doors built into the bulkheads of cabinets. He taught her how to feel for hard lumps in the cushions of sofas, to shake paintings and listen for something hidden inside the frames.

He taught her to open a simple safe using a small amplifier and a pair of earbuds. Lee practiced at her squatted homes, using the amp on a series of combination locks. One home she squatted, the home of a married couple, had a small safe hidden in a compartment in the closet, and she spent hours on it, finally getting it open to reveal a digital camera, on which Lee found photos and videos of a series of different young women, all wearing the same blond wig and pale blue fairy outfit, which was also in the safe. It made her think of the kids upstairs at the Crystal Castle. Lee couldn't help herself, and broke her cardinal rule of leaving no trace behind. Before heading out, she took the camera and the outfit and laid them on the couple's bed.

Over the following two weeks Lee blossomed under Mr. Velasquez's mentorship. He was a man of very few words and even fewer facial expressions, but she was always watching him for signs of approval. His children were the only ones who ever got a true smile out of him. Lee would watch the twin boys harass their dad, grabbing hold of either leg and making him walk them around his shop, or the daughter show off her grades from school, and he always put down what he was doing to indulge them. Lee wished she had the power to make him smile like that. Once she began to tell Mr. Velasquez how she lived, squatting from one empty home to the next, but he stopped her. He didn't want to know. It was as though he knew she was only confiding in him as a way to get closer, and the implied rebuke stabbed her a little.

One day as she was sweeping the space, she asked if she could ask him a question. He didn't say no, so she went on. "Why are you doing this?"

"Doing what?"

"Helping me. Teaching me."

"You are a friend of Maria's, are you not?"

"Sure. But we weren't even that close."

"I know this. She protected you because she was paid to do so. You, on the other hand, you sacrificed yourself for her, for what? For—"

"Paid? Who paid her to protect me?"

"I thought you knew. Someone wanted you kept safe. I assumed someone close to you."

Lee shook her head, too stunned to speak. The information numbed her. Could it have been her mother? Lee knew it wasn't. Or had Edie actually gotten her father to help after all? Lee's heart fluttered a moment, but she knew that wasn't the truth, either. It had to have been the Société Anonyme. Even in the detention center they had been watching her. It also meant they had been trying, at least back then, to protect her. Why?

"When I was a younger man, I was aimless," he told her. "A kid hustling drugs like the rest. I had no skills, no ambition, no future. But a man, a man I had actually tried to rip off, he took me in, taught me things. The things I am now teaching you. He had no reason to trust me, but he saw something in me. And he is the reason I am the man I am today. You understand?"

"I guess."

"I have no one else to pass this on to. Maria is incarcerated, and besides, she is too . . ."

"Hotheaded?"

"Yes. You know, if you had not taken the fall for her, they would have sent her to the block for violent offenders. It would have changed her forever. You saved her from that."

"What about your own children?"

"My daughter, my sons . . . I don't mean to offend, but I have other wishes for them. Other things to give them. You understand?"

Lee felt herself grow warm and embarrassed with the pleasure of his trust. She took the broom from where it leaned against the wall and began to sweep what had already been swept.

One day Mr. Velasquez put a box of jewelry in front of her and brought out a stopwatch. Without a word he started the clock. Lee knew what he expected. She began sifting through the box, feeling the weight of each piece, examining maker marks, testing strings of pearls against her teeth. When she had set aside five pieces and closed the box, he stopped the clock, picked up one of the pieces, and put it back in the box. But she got her nod, and she carried it around with her the rest of the day.

There were down times. She'd spend hours in his shop, sweeping up or running chores or errands around the neighborhood. The neighbors all came to know her, the corner boys and the grocers, and they called her *Ladroncita* when she passed by or came into a shop on an errand. Mr. Velasquez laughed at the name when she asked him what it meant, but he never translated it for her. When there was nothing to do, he let her hang out in the storeroom, a place even his children were not allowed. It was just down the alley, through a steel door that took three keys to open. The room had a narrow hallway lined with shelves holding boxes of jewelry, cameras, iPhones, old coins. In a box of gold jewelry she saw a necklace that she recognized as one she'd stolen herself. Everything was neatly arranged and cata-logued. The far end of the room opened up to accommodate a table with four chairs, a small refrigerator, and a sofa. There was a blocky old television on a crate in the corner, but it didn't turn on. A TV mounted on the wall, a new flat-screen hooked up to cable, turned on fine.

Often one of his children or sometimes his wife would come in with food, usually a plate of tortillas and meat and beans, that he would share with her. Mr. Velasquez's wife was a stout woman with bright, intense eyes under heavy mascara. She had nearly as many tat-toos as her husband, and Lee could tell she had seen things that had hardened her, but still there was warmth in her eyes. She never paid Lee any mind, except to bring a second plate when Lee was there.

Often she and Mr. Velasquez would eat in silence, but sometimes he would talk, and when he did, he would tell her about his dreams, not for himself but for his children. Every dollar he could spare he put away for them so that they could go to a college or trade school and make something of their lives. Lee once started to tell him about her own college aspirations, but he had to take a phone call and she never brought up the topic again. His daughter was nine and wanted to be a veterinarian, and his twin boys, only four, were already reading. Sometimes the boys would sit together in her lap and Lee would help them get through a book, each one vying for her attention. Other times they would bring in a book in Spanish and teach her the simple words, laughing at her pronunciation. Lee liked listening to Mr. Vel-asquez's dreams for his children, and she liked that she could be the beneficiary of the teachings he would never bestow upon them.

Lee bounced from residence to residence. Still keeping to Tomi's list, she ventured out of the suburbs and learned how to access apartment buildings in the city, posing as a bike messenger to get into the build-ing, then picking the lock of the apartment door. She spent her time indoors, watching TV and reading books but also online. She didn't have access to the Subnet browser that Tomi kept on his USB drive, so her information was limited, but there was plenty to learn about Duchamp. As for what he might mean for the S.A., Lee could find nothing of any help. Nor could she find anything about the woman in the photo.

Outside in the world she imagined signs of the Société Anonyme everywhere: a man in an old-fashioned suit reading on the bus, a vintage doctor's satchel at his feet; a group of panhandling kids, one of them watching her intently, then breaking away and seeming to follow her as she passed; even an old cracked urinal sitting on the curb in front of a ramshackle bar seemed like some sort of sign left for her. One night downtown a group of people emerged from a hotel, all wearing animal costumes—coyotes and pumas and raccoons. One of them, a fat brown squirrel, ran up to her and hugged her tightly, clicking playfully behind his mask. Lee looked into its big cartoon eyes and vomited on the sidewalk.

Lee tried to ignore the baby metastasizing in her belly, but it reminded her of its presence every time she felt so stomach-sick she'd have to hang over the toilet, metallic-tasting saliva strands dripping from her mouth. Her breasts were bigger now, too, stretching at her bra in a way that made it hard to breathe sometimes.

One evening as she was straightening up Mr. Velasquez's shop before leaving for the day, he came in and looked at her funny. "You all right?"

Lee followed his eyes to her stomach, which she was holding with one hand. It was something she'd been doing lately, unconsciously putting a hand beneath the slight swell of her belly, and she took it away and smiled at him weakly. "Something I ate," she said.

He seemed to regard her for a moment. "Tomorrow," he said, "when you come back, bring in what you have."

Lee took a moment to decide if he was saying what she thought he was saying.

"I know you have been going out on your own. Show me what you have taken. I will tell you what you have."

The next day she brought in her backpack, which had the weight of a bowling ball and which she carried by hugging it to her chest. She dropped it onto the counter with a dull thud. Mr. Velasquez opened it and dumped the contents in front of them, a great pile of gold chains and rings and watches, necklaces, earrings, prescription drug bottles, and a few loose stones. He picked through it quickly, his fingers pecking in and out of the pile like two chickens over a bag of seeds, until there were two heaps, one much smaller than the other. It only took Lee a moment to know which was which, but she took comfort knowing that most of the things in the larger, worthless pile came from the early days of his tutelage.

He dumped this pile back into her bag and told her to dispose of it. The rest he went back over more carefully, examining each piece and then punching a number into his old adding machine. When he'd gotten through all of it, he hit Return on his machine, peered at a number on the tape, then reached into a drawer and counted out some money for her onto the counter. Six hundred and eighty dollars. Lee felt the same giddy rush of pleasure she'd felt when Edie had invited her over to her house the first time. She took eighty and gave Mr. Velasquez the rest back. "Will you hold onto it for me?" she asked.

He only shrugged and placed the money in an old envelope, which he put back in the drawer.

Again Lee began to imagine the things she would do once she'd made enough to leave. She no longer saw herself settling in one place. She wanted to see the coast of Northern California, where she'd once seen a photo of a forest of redwoods that ran right down to the ocean. She'd go camping in Yellowstone, visit the Carlsbad Caverns, see Hollywood, the Golden Gate Bridge. She could travel to Mexico, South America. Even Asia or Africa. But she'd start with Europe. Tomi always told her that Český Krumlov, his hometown, was the most beautiful city in the world and that to wander its streets at night was to walk through a fairy tale. She felt a pang of sadness when she thought of this place. She missed Tomi so much. She wondered what he felt when he thought about her. Was he worried? He had every right to be. Angry? He had a right to be that, too. While she had no right to feel anything but guilt and loss.

As more days passed, the Crystal Castle began to seem like more and more of a dream. She stopped seeing signs of their presence everywhere she went. Once she saw a man on a vintage bicycle ride past and Lee felt herself freeze up inside, all that fear rushing back, but he never spared Lee a glance.

It was past 4 a.m. when Lee climbed through a rear second-floor window of her current residence, the apartment of Wally Flemish, insurance executive, his wife, Joy, and their two young children. She could tell immediately upon stepping inside that something was wrong. She waited in the room, completely still. When she could be sure of the silence, she crept down the hall, checking room by room. Everything seemed in place. Then she saw a light on downstairs. She was certain she hadn't left any lights on.

Lee went straight for the closet, where, while excavating the life of the Flemishes, she'd found a nickel-plated revolver with a black rubber grip. Sometimes she'd take it out and hold it in her hand, marveling at the feel of it. She'd never felt anything so perfectly weighted in her life, so exquisitely molded to the hand. The gun was in a box pushed to the back of the top shelf of the closet, and Lee had to pull a chair up to reach it. It was loaded.

The gun felt clumsy, now that she might have to use it. Still, it seemed simple enough—just point the thing and pull the trigger. She headed back into the hallway and took the stairs quietly, avoiding where she knew the creaks to be. The light was coming from the living room.

When she poked her head around the wall, the gun at her side, she nearly pulled the trigger in her surprise. No one was in the room. But someone had leaned the lamp from the end table onto its side, sending a spotlight along the floor. In the center of that spotlight something had been laid out on the carpet. She got closer. Lee couldn't decipher what it was meant to be, only its simple, implicit threat: we found you.

· BOOK V ·

The Juggler of Gravity

TEN

TOMI'S new place was tiny, a studio in Fishtown with an actual Murphy bed and a kitchen consisting of a little gas stove and a little fridge and a little counter and a little sink by the window. A lot had happened in the five weeks since she'd last seen him. Allison had gone home to take care of her mother, who had cancer, and Will had gone with her. And then Tomi had had a falling-out with Derrick.

When she'd called from a pay phone in the middle of the night, he'd been silent for a while. "I'm so mad at you" was the first thing he'd said. Tomi then told her that he'd let himself into the Lunskes' home while they were in their living room, watching TV. They'd just stared at him in mute horror as he backed away. "I didn't know what happened to you. I thought you'd been arrested. I tried other houses on the list, but I couldn't find you. You just disappeared."

Lee hadn't considered what might happen when he came back to the Lunskes'. "I'm sorry," she said. She hadn't wanted to call at all. She felt horrible bringing him back into this. But they seemed to find her wherever she went, and Tomi was the only one who knew enough to help her.

When he first saw her at the door, he hugged her so hard she couldn't breathe. She thought he might cry, and then for a moment she thought she might, too. All she knew was that she felt safe now, with him. Tomi's relief at having her back was all around her. It felt like sitting in a warm tide pool. She told him nothing of Mr. Velasquez, only that she'd been hopping from residence to residence, until she realized they'd found her again. "I left right away," she said. "I didn't have anyone else to call."

"Did you leave anything behind, anything they could trace back to you?" he asked.

Lee was on his sofa, pulling bits of stuffing from the cushion and rolling them between her fingers. She had a little pile of balls by her feet. It helped her keep her hand from her belly. "I didn't leave anything behind." She got up to pace the small room. He owned more books than he had room for, and they were piled everywhere.

"Did you take anything?"

"Just this."

"Jesus, put that back. Is that thing loaded?"

"Of course it's loaded." Lee tossed the gun onto Tomi's couch.

She opened his fridge and helped herself to a carton of milk. It felt good to be back with him again. She dropped back to the couch and drank thirstily.

"Three pieces of string on the floor?" he said. "That's it? How do you know it's from them?"

"Because I recognized it." Lee opened his laptop and did an image search. She brought up a page and turned the laptop around. The image showed three vertical strings on a blue backdrop, roughly parallel, each in its own white frame.

"I know that work," he said. "That's Duchamp's *Three Standard Stoppages.*"

"What's it supposed to be?"

"Duchamp dropped three meter-long pieces of string from the same height onto a canvas, then glued them down. He used these to create a new length of measurement based on chance."

"But what's the message? *Their* message."

Tomi shook his head.

"The object that I took from the Station Master had a ball of string in it," she said.

"That's true."

"Do you think that's significant?"

"I think everything is significant to these people."

"I'll just give it to them. I should have done it a long time ago. Do you think that will end this?"

Tomi looked up from the computer. "You still have it?"

"No." Lee finished the milk. "I mean I have it, it's safe, but—"

"Where is it?"

She put the carton to her mouth again, realized it was empty, and threw the carton aside. "Maybe it's time for me to go get it."

Lee returned to the riverfront to retrieve the thing herself. She half expected the object to be gone, or waterlogged, but after searching for less than five minutes, she found it, right where she'd left it, dry and intact.

It was the middle of the night, and Lee hadn't slept going on twenty-six hours now. As she sat on the near-empty train back to Fishtown, alternately nodding and starting awake to the car's gentle rocking, she half watched a young man sitting across from her. He stared down the whole time, looking forlorn. Lee tried to imagine the boy's sadness—a breakup maybe, an unrequited love—wishing that these were the kinds of problems she had. Then the boy looked up and met her eyes, and she found herself staring into two floating blue jellies.

Lee was so exhausted by the time she got back to Tomi's that all she wanted was sleep, but Tomi was fired up. "Did you get it?"

She pulled the old object from her bag. "Why is this thing so important to them? I guess it must be worth a lot of money."

He reached for it, but she held on to it, feeling the sharp corners against her fingertips. "Not compared to some of the other things they could have stolen," he said. "That museum is full of Picassos, Van Goghs, Gauguins, you name it. There are little Chinese jade dragons in there that would buy you a house in the suburbs. Comparatively, the Duchamp piece is peanuts."

"So it must be something else. What do you know about it?"

"It's one of his readymades," Tomi said. "Basically the idea was that anything could be a work of art if an artist named it as such. In the early twentieth century, art was still all about beauty, and the tastemakers were the ones who decided what was beautiful. Duchamp called it retinal art, art that was only meant to be taken in with the eye, and he despised it. Readymades were a big fuck-you to the arbiters of taste at the time. This isn't a pure readymade, like the urinal or the bottle rack; it's what he called an assisted readymade. Which just means he had a hand in making it."

She set the object down on the desk, and it just sat there on its four brass legs, an old ball of twine sandwiched between two metal plates. How could this thing be anything more than a curiosity? "Tell me what's special about this. I mean now, not a hundred years ago."

"Duchamp wasn't all that well recognized in his time. It wasn't until near the end of his life that people saw him as a visionary."

"You're still not telling me anything. Why do these people want it?"

"How would I know?"

"You seem to know a lot of stuff."

He looked up at her. "You still think I'm involved with them?"

"You just happen to know a lot about the man the people after me seem to consider some kind of—what did you call him?—*patron saint*?"

Tomi bristled. "I don't just happen to know anything. Duchamp was the most important and influential artist of the twentieth century. I'm an artist, too, and like any artist I work in his shadow." He seemed to consider something. "Shadows. These people keep to the shadows, but not any shadow—Duchamp's shadow. They don't want to be seen. They're so deep underground there's not even a mention of them on the Internet. Why?"

"You told me something a while back," she said, "about the artist of the future living underground. Was it Duchamp who said that?"

"It was."

"Don't you see?" she said. "That's what these people think they are. Artists of the future. Working underground in Duchamp's name. Only they've twisted everything he stood for into something else. But I think the real question is, they have a component that's above-ground, the Silo parties—why?"

He considered this. "They must need to be seen for some reason."

"And why? Why do we need to be seen?"

Tomi shook his head. "An audience? Recognition?"

"Maybe," she said. "But what about advertising?"

"What do you mean?"

"Maybe they need to bring people in."

"Why?"

Lee thought about what Lois had said about recruiting. "I don't know." She turned her attention back to the thing on the desk. "So what's this thing called?"

"*With Hidden Noise*. Duchamp made it in 1916. Everything had a double meaning for him." Tomi picked the piece up. "Before he screwed it all together, he gave it to a friend, with instructions to deposit something inside the ball of twine."

"When I held it, something rattled inside!" Lee took it from him and shook it next to her ear. She felt like she did when cracking a safe and hearing a tumbler click. "What's in it?"

"Nobody knows. The friend never said, and Duchamp claims not to have known." Tomi took it back and shook it as well. "Maybe it's Schrödinger's cat."

"What?"

"Nothing, just . . . for all we know it could be another of Duchamp's jokes. Everything Duchamp did was both serious and one big gag at the expense of anyone who took him too seriously. Whatever it is, the S.A. thinks it's important."

"Why don't we open it and find out?"

Tomi looked pained.

"Aren't you curious?"

"Of course I'm curious. But we would be destroying it." He stared at her. "I couldn't live with myself. Could you?"

Lee put it back on the desk. "I just want to know why these people are following me. I want it all to go away."

"You can't destroy it. Duchamp might be the most influential artist since da Vinci. It's one of a kind. It would be like you somehow destroyed a color. Orange. No one will ever see the color orange again, because you destroyed it. Gone forever. You want that on your head?"

"I don't care. I'll just give them the damn thing and maybe they'll leave me alone."

Tomi picked it up. Holding it seemed to transport him, and he very gently placed it back. "It doesn't belong to them. How about we put it back?"

"What? Just waltz into the museum and put it back where it was stolen from?"

"Why not? I'll take care of it."

"No," Lee said. "It's my responsibility. I'll do it."

Tomi sighed. "Fine. Get some sleep; we'll return it tonight," he said. "Together."

"How?"

"Leave that to me."

When Lee woke, Tomi was at his computer, the object on the table in front of him, a bunch of notes strewn around it. Lee peered over his shoulder.

P.G.	. ECIDES	DÉBARRASSE.
LE.	D . SERT.	F . URNIS . ENT
AS	HOW . V . R	COR.ESPONDS
.IR.	.CAR .É	LONGSEA →
F.NE,	HEA.,	. O . SQUE →
TE.U	S.ARP	BAR AIN →

He'd been trying to decipher Duchamp's cryptogram, with letters filled in, attempts at sentences, others crossed out.

She went to the fridge but it was as empty as before. "Did you find anything?"

"No. I suppose I'm just amusing myself with it. Some of it is in English; some of it is in French. Do you speak French?"

"I took a little in high school. Not enough."

"It doesn't matter. Plenty of others smarter than me have had a go at it. There's a professor in California who wrote a 350,000-word treatise on it. He considers the work a kind of sculptural cosmogram."

"A what?"

"A cosmogram. A representation of the origins and the fate of the universe."

Lee picked the object up, turned it over in her hands. Once again its meaning remained mute to her.

"It's just the theory of some academic," he said. "But many cosmograms feature a circle and a square, just as this does."

Lee looked at the mess of papers on the table. "That seems a stretch."

"Okay, but look at this . . ." Tomi typed something into his browser and brought up an image of a flat grid. "This is a two-dimensional representation of space. Basically how we envisioned space until Einstein came along. An endless plane. But what happens if we add a bit of matter, say a massive star, into the mix? Before Einstein, we would have said nothing happened. But Einstein's theory of general relativity tells us that the gravity generated by the mass of the star causes the space around it to warp. Like placing a bowling ball in the middle of a big rubber membrane. It distorts the very fabric of space surrounding it." Tomi picked up the object again. "Now look closely at this thing. The two metal plates—you see?"

Lee looked. The four screws holding the metal plates against the ball of twine pulled the corners in, if only slightly. "The plates are curved," she said.

"Because they represent space. The ball of twine is a star or a planet or something. Some massive gravitational object."

"And what about the noise? When you shake it."

Tomi stared at it blankly. "Maybe something to do with time? In Einstein's conception, space and time are interwoven. Space-time. So really, it's not only space that's warped by the mass of an object; it's time as well. Duchamp once said that art is a path toward regions not ruled by space and time. But you want to know the weirdest thing about all this?"

"What?"

"Einstein first presented his theory of general relativity on November 25, 1915. Duchamp's *With Hidden Noise* was made a few months later, in April of 1916. But I found Duchamp's notes on the piece, dated September 1915—almost three months before Einstein let his theory into the wild."

They slalomed their bicycles through empty, wet city streets. Lee liked to feel the damp night air against her face. As she rode past, she could see two men through the windows of a bar stacking chairs. It was nearly 3 a.m. by the time they reached the museum grounds, and they kept to the shadows as they timed the patrolling security cruiser. After the cruiser passed a third time, they jogged to the rear of the building. When they reached four metal grates in the ground that ran along the wall of the museum, Tomi slowed and Lee crouched down with him.

Tomi pulled a folded sheet of paper and a small tool from his backpack. "I got this blueprint from the Subnet. It won't help us get through the drainage tunnels, but once we find our way into the museum subbasement, we're golden."

He inserted the tool around the bolt and turned it easily. Lee helped him lift the grate. They stood looking down a large rectangular shaft. Lee descended first and Tomi followed, pulling the grate back behind him.

Not far down they hit a horizontal tunnel so narrow they had to wriggle along using their elbows and hips. Pushing through a thin slew of muddy water, Lee kept the flashlight in her mouth and had to stop every few feet to clear cobwebs from their path. It was slow going, and Lee was covered in a layer of mud and dust that she felt in the folds of her skin, in her pores, and in her lungs by the time the pipe opened up into a small concrete room. She had to do some maneuvering to turn around and drop to the floor with a splash.

The drainage tunnel they'd come through was about eight feet above them now, dripping a steady stream of dark, viscous water, several inches of which they were standing in.

Tomi shined his light over her. "You look like a muskrat."

"And you look like a big Bohemian turd," she said. It felt good to be creeping with Tomi again, the world right once again. But creeps were all about discovery, they had no goal beyond that, and Lee had to remind herself that they had an actual mission tonight.

Behind him was a rebar ladder leading up. They'd both been on enough creeps to know that this was what they were looking for: an access into the building proper, built so that city workers could have a way into a building's gas, water, and sewage systems. At the top was a rectangular iron cover heavy enough that it took both of them to push it up. Lee pulled herself up into an enormous room.

Tomi came up beside her, shining his light along with hers over the vast space. "Talk about your motherfucking aura," he said.

An enormous marble statue loomed over them, a nude man

straining against some unseen force. Milk-blue in the beam of the flashlights, he stood on a wooden pallet a few inches off the ground on a forklift. Other statues lined the space behind him: centuries-old stone deities, black granite Egyptian kings' heads, a squat Indian Buddha. Some were covered in heavy canvas cloths.

A shelving unit on a scaffold held dozens of busts in stone and plaster and bronze, each with a number hanging from its neck. Across the room were rows of steel floor-to-ceiling shelves, set into a track. Paintings were stacked five or six deep and three levels high on each unit. She grabbed hold of a hand crank and parted two of the shelves enough to walk between them, flanked by works that had been painted a hundred years ago, two hundred, five hundred.

She pulled out a long map drawer, revealing dozens of small stone figurines nestled in tissue paper and laid out like eggs. Tomi unfolded the blueprint and spread it out on top. He pulled a tiny compass from his pocket, checked it, and shined his light up at the ceiling. His beam landed on the slats of a ventilation cover. "There," he said.

They wheeled a ladder over, and Lee climbed up to get to work on the screws. When the cover came off, she shined her light inside. "The entry's pretty tight, but it opens up inside."

They'd gone ten feet when the vent spit them out above another room. Lee grabbed hold of an exposed pipe that ran along the ceiling, shimmied until she was over a table, and dropped. Tomi was right behind. They were in a large, square room with a single door at one end. She shined her light over walls painted in layers of thick green paint that dripped in hardened pools around a concrete floor covered in a patchwork of Oriental rugs, frayed, full of holes, piled three high in places. Lee walked slowly across the room, feeling the rugs sink beneath her, deep and boggy in spots. "What is this place?"

She turned to a bookshelf. They were all science titles, books that looked to be anywhere from a hundred years old to recent. Titles on physics, chemistry, quantum mechanics. Neural mapping. They didn't look like layman's books at all. Lee pulled one down at random. *Helium Cryogenics.* She opened it, flipping through pages of equations as meaningful as crop circles.

"Maybe it's just some kind of library for the museum," Tomi said.

Lee moved to a bank of laboratory equipment, shining her light over glass jars and beakers and flasks of different colored liquids. She picked up a large glass ampoule milky with age, and shined her light into it. Inside was nothing but air. A few bulky and complicated-looking machines connected to an old computer stood idle in the corner. Behind it a huge chunk was gouged from the wall, and the paint around it was charred, as though there had been an explosion at one time. "I don't think so," she said.

Tomi pulled out the blueprint and shined his light over it. "This place isn't even on here. It's some sort of hidden room. But we should be right below where we need to be."

Something flashed in the corner of Lee's vision, and she found herself staring up at a large glass panel framed in steel and bisected at the middle. Etched into the glass were forms that cast oblong shadows across the wall. The whole panel had been hung on a hinge so that it could be swung back and forth.

"I recognize this. I saw it upstairs, in the Duchamp room."

"It's *The Bride Stripped Bare*," he said. "It must be a replica."

"It has the same cracks. I thought the cracks happened by accident—why reproduce them?"

"I don't know. But to Duchamp, chance was integral to the work. Cultivated chance. Domesticated chance, he called it. When *The Bride Stripped Bare* shattered in transit back from its first exhibition, Duchamp spent a year piecing it back together, shard by shard, gluing each piece back in place, like a jigsaw puzzle. When he was done, he declared it finally finished. The cracks became part of the work."

"Something's different about this one."

Tomi looked up at it, turning it back and forth on its hinge. "Could be."

Lee took a photo, the flash illuminating the room in stark relief.

As Tomi returned a book to the shelf and began sorting through a pile of detritus on the table, Lee looked over a second bookshelf. *Five Treatises of the Philosophers Stone. Athanasius Kircher's Mundus Subterraneus. The Hermetic Arcanum. Corpus Hermeticum.* She'd seen some of these titles before, in the Station Master's room. "This place is connected," she said. The room seemed suddenly very small.

Tomi was sifting through papers on the desk. "Connected to what?"

Books on alchemy and cryogenics. "Cryogenics—that's freezing people, right?"

"The theory goes that the body can be revived sometime in the future. When we have cures for things we don't have now."

"Is anyone doing that?"

"I don't know," he said. "I think it's mostly hypothetical."

She thought about what she'd read about alchemy. "A way of becoming immortal?"

Tomi didn't answer. He was flipping through a sheaf of papers. His face looked stricken.

"What is it?"

"Nothing," he said, replacing the papers on the desk.

She stood beside him. "What?"

"Don't freak out," he said.

There were six or seven stapled pages. On the first was a photograph of her, caught midstep emerging from a subway entrance. She had longer hair than now, a surprised expression on her face. Lee turned to the next page, a printout containing her name, her date and place of birth, her mother's address, her high school. Her phone number. Her father's address was there, an apartment in Albuquerque, New Mexico—*she* didn't even know where her father lived. Her height, eye and hair colors. The next page was her arrest record, followed by a copy of her arrest warrant, issued by the State of Pennsylvania, a week after her escape. Her file from the JDC, stating that she was considered "psychologically unstable and potentially dangerous." And then, on the final page, another photo, black-and-white: Lee, in the old wedding dress, looking off past some hidden camera. The pages had several staples, as though they'd been added to, and date stamps along the bottom. Lee turned back to the first page. It was dated September 3, over a year ago. Before the Crystal Castle. Before the JDC. Her birthday. The day that big, childlike man with the antique camera had accosted her in the street.

She felt a wave of anger and humiliation run through her. "Who are these people," she said blankly. Her eyes fell on the door across the room, and she went to it. Tomi reached for her, but she shook him off. "How are they down here, beneath the museum?" Lee remembered what the man had said to the Station Master when he'd delivered the object to him: that the Priest was just an old man, *trapped in a room*. Was it here? She tried the knob. It turned. She pushed the door open and shined her light down a long hallway with a door halfway down and another at the far end.

Tomi grabbed her arm. "I don't feel good about this. Let's just leave the thing here and go back out the way we came."

Lee ignored him. Halfway down the hall was an old wood-slatted double door, surrounded by a brick threshold. Exactly like the one upstairs, the one that housed Duchamp's last work. And like the one upstairs it had two small holes at eye level. Lee pressed her eye to one, her flashlight into the other.

She got only a glimpse inside before she heard voices at the far end of the hall, behind another door. In that brief flash she saw something she didn't know how to describe. A large metal contraption, enshrouded in shadow, seemed to be hovering in midair. She clicked off her flashlight. Tomi was hissing at her to come back.

As the door at the end of the hall opened and a large dark figure stepped out, Lee managed to just make it back into the room and shut the door. Whatever had gripped her to confront these people was gone now. Voices came from the hall, growing louder.

"Look." Tomi pointed.

A ladder she hadn't noticed before. Built into the wall and leading to a small square door near the ceiling. She was up it quickly,
unlatching the door and crawling through. She turned to help Tomi
up. They shut the door just as the light in the room below came on.

They were in a tiny room, a dim, flickering artificial glow emanating from the old gas lamp, held aloft in the hand of a nude female
mannequin, casting a bluish luminescence over the waterfall behind
her, the crinkled tinsel and the bushy pastel trees of the backdrop.

"Holy shit," Tomi whispered. "This is *Étant donnés*. We're inside it."

She could hear below the low voices of two men. Lee couldn't
make out words, but she knew it wouldn't be long before they were
found. There wasn't room enough to stand, and she had to stoop as
she picked gingerly around the body of the mannequin, which, Lee
could see now, had no face, no head at all, only a wig of coarse blond
hair wrapped around the empty space where her face should be.
Blocking the wood double doors was a brick wall with a hole in the
middle, too small to crawl through. But when Lee grabbed hold of it,
she found that it swung outward. The door itself was more difficult,
but Tomi ran his hands around it until he found a hidden catch. The
doors swung open.

She was about to step out when Tomi grabbed her shoulder.
"The guards could be anywhere. We're going to have to just make a
run for it. I'll go ahead and make sure it's clear. Remember what we
came for: just take the thing out and leave it in the room somewhere."

Tomi pushed the doors outward. He crept into the room and
then into the next, leaving her behind. Lee approached the empty
Lucite box on the pedestal. She took *With Hidden Noise* from her
bag. The thing inside rattled. They were here, beneath the museum,
and they'd been after her before she'd even been in possession of the
thing. She thought back to the uniformed man in the café, how he'd
told her she looked like someone and then given her and Edie tickets
to the Silo party. It had gone back that far at least. Giving the thing

back wasn't going to end anything. They wanted her for something else. She remembered standing in the old wedding dress as the tall man looked her over. There must have been a camera somewhere. Peering into every secret corner of her life. Fuck them, she thought, stuffing the object back in her bag. I'm not giving them shit.

ELEVEN

EVERY book was on the floor, spines bent, bindings torn out. Shelves were upended. The little refrigerator was on its side, some fluid pooling out from its cracked door. The dresser drawers were all overturned, clothes strewn everywhere, the bed and sofa gutted, tufts of stuffing littering the small room. Tomi picked up an old glass-fronted box from the counter. It was smashed and its contents—a nest of tiny mechanical circus figures—were strewn across the floor.

Tomi tried to collect the little figures and bend them back into shape. "My sister made this for me." Then he dropped it all back onto the counter with a crash. "Fuck it."

They picked through the carnage in silence for a while, until Lee gave up and sat on what was left of his couch. "I'm sorry, Tomi. This is all my fault."

Tomi tried to smile as he shook his head, but Lee could see the heartbreak in it. "Well, you returned the thing. Maybe now they'll leave us alone."

Lee looked down at the floor.

"You left it there, right?"

Lee shook her head.

Tomi let the books he was holding drop. "Isn't that the whole reason we went down there?"

She got up and looked out the window, onto the street below. One of them was probably down there now, staring up at her from the shadows somewhere. "Why do they know so much about me? Why do they know where I was born?"

Tomi picked a book up from the puddle and wiped it against his jeans. "I don't know." He propped the fridge back up. "Are you sure that gun is loaded?"

Lee took it from her bag, popped open the cylinder, and showed him.

"You know how to use it?"

"No." She picked his laptop up from the floor and placed it carefully on the desk. "They didn't take your laptop."

"It's not what they were after." Tomi knelt under his desk and untangled a little bronze statuette from a rat king of loose cables. "Goddammit," he said.

"We have to go," Lee said, wanting to cry at what she'd brought down on them but holding it together. "They might be watching us." He stopped, as though considering this for the first time, and dropped the statuette to the floor.

The house was one of the last on Lee's list. Its residents, George and Patricia Caldwell, a childless couple in their midfifties, judging by the photographs along the stairs, were booked for a solid three weeks at a resort along the Mayan Riviera. They decorated their home like a beachfront time-share, full of macramé-framed photos of marinas and seaside villas, goofy little figurines made from seashells, nautical ephemera all over the place, and a glass coffee table over a beach tableau of sand and shells.

The Caldwells must have left in a hurry, because the fridge was full of milk and cheese and yogurt and berries, eggs and tortillas and bacon. Tomi called in to work and rasped into the phone that he'd come down with the flu and would be out for a few days at least.

"Why couldn't you just leave it there, like we talked about?" It was the first time she'd seen him look angry with her. They were sitting at the kitchen table, eating leftover chicken from the fridge. "It could have ended this."

She put the chicken down, her appetite gone. "Did you see that photo of me? Do you know when that was taken? Over a year ago. These people have been following me for over a year, and it has nothing to do with the Duchamp thing, whatever it is."

"Maybe not, but they want it back," he said. "Let's just give it to them and maybe their incentive goes away. We'll go somewhere they can't find us."

"And where is that?"

"Let me think about it. I'll come up with something."

They took separate rooms. That night as Lee tried to sleep, she kept seeing the girl upstairs at the Crystal Castle, staring at her. Lee knew that there was nothing behind those eyes but blissed-out emptiness, but she couldn't help seeing something else. *Don't leave me,* they kept pleading.

Lee couldn't sleep without seeing the girl, so she paced silently through the dark house. Finally she opened the back door and cut between the houses to the street, where she walked beneath a clear night sky filled with stars. How had she become so trapped? She kept walking.

The next morning Lee came downstairs to find Tomi in an apron, wielding a spatula over the stove. There were two plates, two mugs, two place settings laid out.

"I saw you go out last night," he said. "I won't ask where."

"Good."

He pushed a mound of scrambled eggs onto each plate. "I didn't know if you were coming back."

"What made you think I was?"

"Nothing but hope," he said. "There is a saying where I'm from: Hope is fuel for life; despair only gums up the engine."

She scanned his face, trying to tell if he was putting her on.

"It sounds much better in Czech."

"Say it."

"In Czech?"

"Yes."

He looked into her eyes long enough to make her feel uncomfortable. *"Celý můj život moje srdce toužilo po něčem, co jsem nedokázal pojmenovat. Teď to má jméno, a to jméno jsi ty. Slibuji, že Ti budu vždy nablizku."*

Lee sat, taking a fork and staring down at the eggs. "You're right, it's very pretty."

"Told you."

Tomi took to the life quickly; he seemed to be enjoying going underground with her. They were trapped inside, but it never felt that way. He took it upon himself to entertain them, and it wasn't long before he had them both putting on clothes ransacked from the closets, Tomi in Mr. Caldwell's golf pants, his short-sleeved polyester shirts, his double-breasted naval jacket and sometimes his suits, sleeves and cuffs rolled up. Patricia Caldwell was big as well, and Lee found herself engulfed in her flower-print evening dresses, her flowing pantsuits. Tomi would make up occasions of various degrees of formality—birthday parties and pool parties and cocktail parties and dinners—for the Caldwells to attend, and he and Lee would dress for that occasion and mimic the Caldwells in their natural habitat, Tomi getting fuzzy on ill-measured concoctions from the liquor cabinet, Lee pretending to.

Lee liked it most when she would wake and come downstairs to find that Tomi had made a breakfast of coffee and eggs and defrosted bagels and he'd let her sit and eat in silence, lost not so much in thought but in a feeling that this moment might somehow be sustainable.

But silence with Tomi was rare. He liked to talk about their future, the places they would travel to, the places they would live when the curtain went down on all of this. Sometimes they lived on the coast of Ireland, in a cottage on a cliff; sometimes they managed a little music store together in Oslo; sometimes they ran a tourist shop out of some beach village in Thailand. More than once they lived in a little farmhouse by a lake in the Czech Republic. Lee avoided playing along; his fantasies were so naked they embarrassed her. Still, the idea that they might carve out some sort of life worth living gave her something close to hope. But then Lee thought about the thing growing inside her, about how much it would need, and about how impossible it made the future, any future, even one fashioned on wishes and twine.

When she was alone, she'd sit in the den at the Caldwells' ancient computer and pore over everything she could find online on Duchamp, trying to find something, anything, she could use. There must be some way to get to them, but Lee had no idea what she was looking for. She'd put the old photo of the woman up next to the screen and look for women connected to Duchamp, or Google "Duchamp A.T." and sift through images until her eyes hurt.

Tomi kept at it, too, focusing on Duchamp's works and on the notes to his works, which Tomi found archived online. "I'm not sure," he told her one night, "but I may have found something." He had that excited look he'd get when he was about to show her something. "I think we've been looking at the wrong work. It's not *With Hidden Noise* we should be focusing on at all."

Lee pushed a chair up next to his and stared at the now-familiar image he had up on the screen, the vertical steel frame bisected horizontally across the center, the webs of shattered glass over sepia forms.

"*The Bride Stripped Bare by Her Bachelors, Even*, aka *The Large Glass*. Duchamp conceived it in 1913, began constructing it in 1915, and more or less completed it in 1923. But he never finished it as planned. He says he simply grew bored, but I think there's more to it than that. If there is anything we know about the man, it's to never take anything he says at face value."

"Did you find something new?"

"I've read Duchamp's notes on the work. They are typically inscrutable, but they helped me figure something out."

"Tell me."

"Okay. The entire work is a system. A machine. Caught in a moment in time near the end of its run. Duchamp called it a 'delay in glass.' We're supposed to imagine all its elements moving."

Lee looked closer at it, tried to envision the whole thing in motion, but it just existed there on the screen, inert. "I don't see it."

"That's okay, just follow along for now. The upper half is the Bride's domain." Tomi pointed to a figure hovering in the top left of the frame. She looked like some sort of mechanical insect. "The Bride is a motor; she runs on what Duchamp called love gasoline. It is the blood of her desire, and it powers the whole machine."

"The man at the Silo, when he had me put on that old wedding dress. He called me 'Bride.'"

"I told you, these people see connections everywhere."

"The woman in the photo—she's the connection. But I can't find out anything about her. She looks so much like me I thought at first it was Photoshopped, but it's not."

"Just think of how many people have been born throughout all of history. We must all have doppelgängers, if you go back far enough. We just rarely get the opportunity to see them."

Lee supposed that must be true. "So you're saying it could just be a coincidence."

"Yes. What else?"

She remembered something that the Station Master had said to her, about there being meaning, even destiny in coincidence. For them, there were no coincidences. Everything had meaning. It seemed dangerous to her in a way she couldn't put her finger on.

Her eyes went to the top of the glass, where a cloudlike formation with three square cutouts drifted out from the Bride's head. She recognized it from one of the S.A. fliers. "What's that?"

"That's the Bride's Cinematic Blossoming. Essentially, it is her libido. Imagine erotic images projected in the three empty squares."

"Like what, porn?"

Tomi laughed. "Sure."

"Okay, so the Bride is floating there, lost in her sexy thoughts. Then what?"

"Her pornographic fantasies are projected onto these three screens for the benefit of the Bachelors. The whole region down here," he said, touching the bottom half of the work, "this is their domain." Tomi pointed to a ring of forms at the bottom left of the frame. "These are the nine Bachelors. The Delivery Boy, the Gendarme, the Cavalry Soldier, the Policeman, the Undertaker, the Busboy, the Flunky, the Station Master, and the Priest. They exist purely to follow the Bride and live only in hopes of seeing her undressed. They are her servants."

Lee wondered which one was the tall man. She refocused on the whole work, squeezing her eyes shut, then opening them, trying to see the thing as something recognizable. It was all so abstract. "It doesn't look like anything to me."

"That's because the world of *The Bride Stripped Bare* is all invisible forces in flux. The top half represents the forces of Desire. The bottom half is the physics of Chance and Fate. And remember, the whole thing is a machine in constant motion. We are seeing it in a single frozen moment."

Lee thought about what she'd read on alchemy. That it saw the universe as made up of opposing forces. The marriage of opposites. The Bride and the Bachelors. Above and below. Lee looked at the work closely again, trying to see in it whatever it was those men saw. Then it occurred to her: "Maybe it's some kind of map."

Tomi perked up. He seemed to see it, too. Then his face scrunched up in confusion. "Er . . . how do you mean?"

"Everything you're telling me is an abstraction," she said. "But these men must be looking for something concrete. Is there some way that this could be pointing the way to whatever that is? Or maybe it's not a map itself, but . . . It's all glass, right? Maybe you put a map behind it and it shows the location of a hidden treasure or something."

"I like the way you're thinking; it seems like the kind of trick Duchamp might play."

Lee stared at each element, trying to piece them together, but the work wasn't giving her anything more. "Okay, take me through the rest of it."

"Okay. So while the Bachelors are getting all aroused, the Bride starts stripping."

"Getting undressed?"

"A striptease, yes. Which gets them all riled up to consummate with her. Something they'll never do, because she's just a tease, and she knows the power she wields."

"So basically she strips down and gives each of these guys a look at her beaver, knowing full well none of them are getting any. It all sounds very erotic." Lee recalled herself standing naked in front of the tall man. She remembered what he'd told her after he'd put her in that dress: *the party is full of bachelors.* There had been a camera in that room. Lee thought of the men she'd seen at that party, how they had all been staring at her. She felt a wave of disgust.

"The Bride simply wants to be seen. She saturates the Bachelors with her pheromones, and they get all hopped up on desire."

Lee wanted to be seen, but not like that. She focused away from the image, and onto a point on the wall just above the screen. Lee reimagined the work onto this blank space, and tried to see it in motion again. This time the Bride began to move, slowly at first, as a piston rocking awake, then faster, spewing a rain of love gasoline down on the Bachelors, who began to lurch and spin below her like a ramshackle carousel.

"The Bachelors respond by emitting an illuminating gas, which flows through these tubes, where it becomes a fluid. Meanwhile, all this stuff down here"—Tomi pointed to a corral of rickety-looking contraptions—"represents the forces of Chance and Fate, and they operate the Scissors, up here, which snips the emerging fluid into distinct spurts, and each spurt travels upward, through the Eyewitnesses, here"—Tomi indicated a series of rings—"past the threshold and into the Bride's domain. Their aim is for the windows of the Bride's Cinematic Blossoming, because if they can hit one, they can consummate their desires. But they always miss and end up spattered into the ether."

"The money shot," said Lee.

"And so it goes, repeated again and again."

"I guess I can see it now," Lee said, and she thought she could.

"So this is where it gets interesting. When we were in that room beneath the museum, remember the reproduction you found? You said you thought there was something different about it."

"I remember."

Tomi popped his zip drive in the Caldwells' computer and brought an image up on the screen. "Here's the photo you took. Notice anything?"

It took her only a moment to see: the reproduction contained several new forms not in the original. On the bottom right of the Bachelors' domain, below the Eyewitnesses, was a long, winding spiral thing; and above the Eyewitnesses was something that looked like it could have been a diagram from geometry class. Just above that, in the Bride's domain, was a mechanical-looking figure standing on four spindly legs that sent a spiraled appendage up toward the Bride.

"The story is that Duchamp got bored with it and left it 'definitively unfinished.' He even claimed to have abandoned art for good after that. We know now that isn't true: he was working on *Étant donnés* for over twenty years, in secret. But what if in fact Duchamp didn't stop work on *The Large Glass* because he grew bored but, instead, purposefully left out some key elements?"

"You're saying this was how he saw the final work."

"Exactly. This thing here"—he pointed to the geometry problem—"Duchamp called the Boxing Match, and it functions as a kind of electrical coil. Without it the machine can't even start. And this"—pointing to the spindly-legged figure—"Duchamp called the Juggler of Gravity. His job is to catch and deflect the spurts of the Bachelors."

"So the reproduction beneath the museum shows how the whole system, when complete, was supposed to look." Lee got up and paced the room. When she closed her eyes, she could see it, the whole system in motion all around her. "You said that without the Boxing Match, the machine can't even start . . . "

"That's what I understand from his notes. Like I said, they were pretty—"

"I was wrong. *The Bride Stripped Bare* isn't a map. It's a blueprint."

"What do you mean?"

But Lee could see that Tomi was getting it. "He left out the Boxing Match, and the Juggler and the rest," she said, "because without them the system can't work. It's as though I gave you the schematics of a car but left out the ignition coil. You could build the car, but it wouldn't run. It would just sit there. But why leave these elements out of the final piece? After working on it for so long—it seems like he was almost there."

"I don't know. But it's all starting to make sense." Tomi got up and began to pace the room, the way he did when he was either agitated or excited. "Remember how I said that *With Hidden Noise* might have been a cosmogram that predicted Einstein's general theory of relativity? There have been dozens of attempts to decipher *The Large Glass*. Most interpret it as a theater of frustrated desire. But Duchamp was more scientist than humanist." He put one hand to his head, as if he couldn't believe what he was thinking.

"What? What is it?"

"The Juggler of Gravity. Of course. It makes so much sense now."

"What? What are you talking about?"

Tomi stopped pacing. He removed his glasses and faced her. Lee had to suppress an unbidden urge kiss him. Where had that come from?

"Gravity. General relativity is all about gravity."

"And?"

"What if this work contained within it the answer to something world-changing, something not even discovered to this day?"

"Like what?"

"Have you ever heard of the unified field theory?"

Lee shook her head.

"There's a contradiction in physics that no one has yet been able to solve. Einstein's theory of general relativity precisely explains the workings of the large-scale universe—from solar systems to planetary bodies to objects as small as a grain of sand. And quantum theory explains with equal precision the workings of the subatomic universe—photons and neutrons and quarks and all the rest. The problem is that these two theories are incompatible. They can't be reconciled. What works to explain the macro-universe goes contrary to what works to explain the subatomic universe, and vice versa. Both can't be correct, and yet somehow both are." He paused, waiting for her excitement to catch up to his. "For both to be valid, there must be a theory that ties them together. A unified field theory. It's only hypothetical, but it's the Holy Grail of physics. There are those who say that solving it would be akin to reading the mind of God."

He had put a blanket over her. The computer was shut down, and all his notes were stacked neatly beside it. She must have fallen asleep while he'd stayed up working. She looked through the notes briefly, though it didn't appear that he'd made much more progress. He'd written "BLUEPRINT??" on the page and then an arrow to a circled "UFT."

Lee went into the bathroom and stood naked in front of the full-length mirror. She would be about twelve weeks now. She wasn't showing, not as she thought she'd be. She remembered stories of girls who'd carried their babies to term without anyone knowing they were pregnant. Still, she felt bloated and heavy, as if someone had pumped her full of water, and her breasts were full and sore.

She could smell food cooking as she came downstairs, but the kitchen door was locked. She knocked.

"Go away!" Tomi shouted.

Lee pressed her eye to the keyhole but couldn't see much. "What are you doing in there?"

"Alchemy!"

She could have picked the lock, but she decided to let Tomi do his thing and went back upstairs. A bit later he brought up a breakfast of coffee and toast but then returned to the kitchen.

Lee spent her time upstairs poking through the Caldwells' bedroom, rifling through drawers and closets, opening boxes and searching for secret hideaways, but the Caldwells were dull folk whose bookshelves were full of Christian cowboy romance novels and a series of *Left Behind* books as long as her arm. The closest she could find to interesting was their wedding album. A big black book with old color photos behind plastic showed Mr. and Mrs. Caldwell when they were young, in a series of shots that were all staged but that struck Lee as so sweet and earnest it made her a little sad.

Later that afternoon, after she'd abandoned the Caldwells' album for a bloated novel that promised to "uncover the erotic secrets of ancient Rome," Tomi called up to her, "Come on down!"

The smell of food filled the house, reminding her how hungry she was. At the bottom of the stairs Tomi stood waiting, wearing a suit of Mr. Caldwell's, pale blue with a little plastic flower stuck into the wide lapel. He untied a white apron from around his waist and hung it on a chair. Behind him, the dining room table was under a white tablecloth, and on top of that was a wilted brown turkey on a platter, the skin puckered and burnt. He'd fashioned little frills from two of Mr. Caldwell's tiny novelty golf club cozies to put over the legs and surrounded the bird with roast carrots, apples, celery, and onions. There was a squat cylinder of cranberry sauce still holding the mold of the can and a bowl of stuffing made from chunks of sliced white bread. He'd put out glasses and a bottle of wine.

"Happy Thanksgiving!" he said, arms spread wide.

Lee felt more shame than delight. It was a gesture that she never in a million years would have thought of. She stared down at herself:

dirty socks, the same threadbare jeans she always wore, one of Mr. Caldwell's oversized white shirts. "Let me go change," she said.

He pulled her chair out. "Don't be ridiculous. You look beautiful."

As quickly as it came, the guilt vanished. Tomi didn't expect any big gestures from her. He was just happy when she accepted his own.

She waited as he carved out a few jagged, meaty chunks for her plate and cut off a jiggling tower of cranberry sauce. She waited as he served himself and poured them both wine, and she held her glass up across the table as he leaned in and clinked it. "To domesticated chance," he said.

She took a small sip and put the glass back, then turned to the food.

Lee found herself less and less in need of alone time. She came to enjoy listening to his fantasies of another life for them somewhere. One night she asked him to come sleep with her, and he moved from the guest room and into her bed. She still wasn't ready to have sex with him again, not with his child growing inside her, but she liked falling asleep with his arms around her, the feverish warmth of his body, his erection pushing against her rear, and sometimes she would take his hand and put it on her belly, always on the verge of telling him.

But she couldn't. Since the night in the museum he had clung to a promise of a future for them, but Lee couldn't shake the threads that seemed to tie him to these people—his knowledge of Duchamp, his being at the Silo the night she'd been lured there, the fact that the S.A. kept finding them—and every time she thought about it she felt like she was drowning.

Ultimately, though, all these threads were coincidental. Deep down she trusted him. And being with Tomi was easy. But she couldn't let go of the fact those people knew everything about her. For a long time, long before she'd even arrived at the Crystal Castle, they'd been studying her like a mouse in a maze. How had she ended up at the Silo that night? More to the point, how had Tomi? Then she recalled who he said had given him the ticket.

TWELVE

HE answered the door wearing only a pair of tight black underwear. He ran a hand through his hair and looked sleepily at Lee's chest. "If you came to pick up your shit, I threw it all out. And if you came to return any of mine," he said, shutting the door on her shoulder, "keep it."

Lee pushed past him into the apartment. "Is anyone else here?"

"What the fuck. It's"—looking at the clock—"three fifteen in the morning. Last time you did this you stayed a month. You can stay the night if you sleep with me; otherwise get lost." He went into the kitchen and came back with a beer, slumping to the couch and picking up a magazine, pretending to ignore her. Finally he looked up. "You still here?"

She took a chair and sat across from him. Derrick was a bully, but like all bullies he was also a coward, and Lee knew that the best approach didn't involve a lot of finesse. She took the old S.A. flier from her pocket, unfolded it, and dropped it on his lap. Derrick barely glanced at it.

"Where did you get this?" she said.

He looked up from his magazine long enough to give her a dead stare. "From you. You just dropped it on my lap."

"Where did you get it, Derrick?"

"Fuck you. You think you can just come into my home and make demands? Accuse me of . . ." He picked up the flier, looked at it as though he'd never seen it before. "I don't even know what you're accusing me of."

"You gave it to Tomi, invited him to that party. All I want to know is who was behind it. Where'd you get it? Who's the Société Anonyme?"

"Bunch of French faggots? I don't know. I don't know what you're talking about."

Lee calmly took the gun from her bag. She held it at Derrick's chest, or his stomach. Her hand was shaking so much she couldn't tell where she was aiming. She started feeling nausea in waves and couldn't tell if this was morning sickness or the feeling of pointing a loaded gun at someone and not knowing if you will fire it.

Derrick just started laughing. Great coughing laughs that might or might not have been forced, it didn't matter; it angered Lee so much she nearly shot him. Except that her finger wasn't even on the trigger.

"You're gonna shoot me?" Derrick said. He kept laughing. "You're not gonna shoot me. But I admire your ladyballs. That's so gangster of you. Just point that thing somewhere else; it might go off."

Lee let the gun drop to her side. Derrick finished his beer. He looked like he was enjoying this. He held the bottle out. "Get me another, will you?"

"I won't shoot you, you're right. But I have some folders I copied from your hard drive. A cache of photographs, a few videos, a ton of e-mails, and some very revealing search histories that I may very well let loose into the wild."

"Bullshit. My door is always locked."

Lee casually walked to his bedroom door, took her kit from her pocket, and picked the two locks in less than thirty seconds. She opened the door. She had never actually peeked inside before. Derrick's room was so neat and ordinary it could have been part of a showroom display. The bed was made, his desk was clean, and all his clothes hung tidily in his closet, organized by color. The walls were covered in posters and fliers. Lee returned to the chair.

Derrick's eyes got narrow and mean. He stood and towered over her. "You little bitch." But Lee could tell that his resolve was gone.

"Why not just answer the question?" she said.

"Drop it. The less you know the better, believe me." He collapsed back on the couch. "Look, some girl just hired me to hand those things out to the kids. She called it a recruitment drive."

"What girl?"

He seemed shriveled now, his skinny pale body in his little black underwear, and Lee felt a sudden disgust rising up. "What's her name?" she said.

Derrick mumbled something but wouldn't meet her eyes.

"What?"

"I don't know. Tall. Long blond hair. Lotta eye makeup."

Ester's gap-toothed smile came into Lee's head, and she felt her world spinning away from her. "Were you at the Crystal Castle?"

For the first time Derrick looked genuinely rattled. "I don't know what you're talking about."

"You know what goes on there?"

He picked up the bottle and began tearing away at the label. "It's just rumors."

"They're not rumors. I've seen it. And I'll bet you have, too. Big eyes like fucking blow-up dolls? About as conscious? Maybe you've even made use of a few yourself?" Lee watched Derrick tense up, followed his eyes to the gun, which she hadn't realized was pointed at his chest again. "What happened to them?"

Derrick shook his head.

Lee pulled a seat up close. "A few clicks and the contents of that folder are uploaded onto 4chan. Do I have to remind you what's on there?"

Derrick looked like he was in genuine pain. "I'm not telling you anything that anyone in the scene hasn't already heard."

"Tell me."

"It's just *rumors*. I don't even believe half of it myself."

"What's the connection with the Société Anonyme?"

"Don't be stupid. It's all Société Anonyme. The Crystal Castle is just an arm of it."

"How deep are you in with them?" she said.

"I'm not anybody," he said. "I recruit for their parties sometimes. It gets me in, gets me free drugs and stuff."

"Don't lie to me, Derrick. You're closer to them than that. You know more than some outsider would."

"It's like any corporation. There's a hierarchy. I'm not just starting out in the mailroom, but I'm not on the board, either."

"So what are you? Middle management?" She almost felt sorry for him. "Tell me. Everything you know."

"The S.A. are drug manufacturers."

"What kind of drugs?"

"It started out with club drugs: crystal meth, Ecstasy, GBH, LSD. Kids could buy them at the Silo and party all night. They even had a room for them to sleep it off. But then . . ."

He told her that about two years ago the Société Anonyme had a steady manufacturing operation going and had been trying to synthesize DMT when something went wrong. "A few molecules got rearranged," and they ended up with a new drug, a synthetic psychotropic that made LSD or mescaline or anything else on the market look like strong coffee. Named Thrumm because of the humming subterranean vibration the user felt at the drug's onset, it was a body-centric catalyzing agent that made one feel as though all the world was vibration and all vibration was from a single source. Any division between body and mind became erased, and those who ingested the drug reported hours-long states of pure, humming energy.

But one of the early batches went bad. There were reports of kids found drifting through the city, their eyes engorged and jellied, their wills eviscerated. They were placid and docile, wandering, aimless, and helpless to survive on their own. They floated through the streets with their huge, unblinking eyes and near-constant smiles, giggling as though at some private joke. They strayed into restaurants and shops, annoying customers, but were otherwise harmless. Because they were open to suggestion and willingly followed simple commands, these kids became quick prey for local pimps, who herded them around like cattle and advertised them as living fuck dolls who were game for anything.

The S.A. isolated the two strains of the drug—one of which a user would come down from, while the other would leave a jelly-eyed zombie in its wake. And so the Crystal Castle was born. Pretty young runaways were recruited into the fold and given the latter version of the drug. The girls were dressed in tiny skirts and baby-doll shirts, the boys in skinny jeans and buckled jackets; with their oversized eyes and dreamy otherness they were like living anime.

When Derrick was finished, Lee stayed silent for a while. She'd dropped the gun in her lap. "What do you know about a man called the Priest?"

"The Priest started the S.A. He was running it all until there was some sort of schism."

"When?"

"About three months ago."

Right around the time she went to the Silo. "Why? What happened?"

"I don't know exactly. Something between him and the Undertaker. I don't think the Priest was down with what he and the Station Master were doing to those kids. Everyone involved was forced to take sides."

"The Undertaker—he's the tall one in the black suit? What's his role?"

"He runs the whole show at the Silo. And he's not someone you want to fuck with. I told you, leave this alone. Just leave it be."

"What else?"

"That's all, I swear."

Lee got up to leave, and Derrick blocked her at the door. She raised the gun, and he put his hands up and backed away. "Give me the disk."

"What?"

"I told you what you wanted to know. The stuff from my hard drive, you must have it on a disk. Give it to me."

Lee laughed. "There's no disk."

"Bullshit."

"Derrick, like you said, there was never a moment your door wasn't locked. You've got secrets in there. I never went into your room, but chances were good—"

Derrick looked pissed. "What if I'd called your bluff?"

She smiled. "Then I guess I'd just have had to shoot you."

When Lee came out of the building, Tomi was leaning against a lamppost, waiting for her. She ignored him, too angry to speak, unlocking her bicycle and pedaling off without looking back. She could feel him, following just behind. "Lee, hold up," he said. "At least slow down."

As she pedaled, she went through everything that had happened since she'd left the detention center, trying to piece it together. How did they keep finding her? She'd been sloppy somewhere, though she couldn't figure out where.

Lee was dizzy with fatigue by the time they got back to the Caldwells', and she tore off her sweatshirt, ran to the bathroom, and vomited. Tomi came in and touched her back, but she shrugged him off.

"You went to see Derrick. Why?"

She washed her mouth out at the sink and turned on him. "You do not follow me."

"Lee, I was—"

"*They* are following me. *You* can't. My life is my own. I can take care of myself."

Tomi put up his hands in surrender. "Okay. Okay." With a towel he tried to wipe her mouth off, but she took it from him and did it herself.

She walked past him into the bedroom, then sat on the bed with her hands around her face.

"But why did you need to see Derrick?"

"He's involved with them. He told me things. Just as I suspected, there was a split within the group. Just a few months ago. If that's true, it means one hand doesn't know what the other is doing. But they both want *With Hidden Noise*. That's how we get to them. We figure out a way to play them off against each other. Get them to destroy themselves from the inside."

"Why? Lee, let's just leave. There's no reason to stick around anymore. We could make a life together."

"You don't know what happens to those kids. You haven't seen it."

Tomi approached again, and this time she let him put his hand on her back.

"If you did, you'd understand. You wouldn't be able to just walk away, either." Lee paused, suddenly suspicious. "Tomi, you need to tell me now. Is there anything you're not telling me?"

"You still think I'm part of this, don't you?"

"I don't know. Not all of it, maybe, but—"

"I don't know what to tell you so that you'll trust me. But if I was with them, what would we even be doing here? Wouldn't I just hand you over? I'm sorry I followed you. I just want to make sure you're okay. I lost you before; I don't want to lose you again."

She took his hand and led him to the bedroom. She fell onto the bed with her clothes on and fell asleep with his arms around her, his hand wiping a pasty strand of hair from her face.

When Lee woke up, it was barely light out. Tomi was at the computer, his face washed in the glow of his laptop. His hand hovered above the trackpad as though afraid to touch it.

"What is it?" she said.

When he didn't answer, she looked over his shoulder. He'd gotten an e-mail:

From: rroseselavy1887@gmail.com.

Subject: why not sneeze?

"What is it?"

"It's from them."

"How do you know?"

"Rrose Sélavy was Duchamp's alter ego. It has to be from them."

"Are you going to open it?"

She had to grab Tomi's arm to break him out of his trance. He clicked open the e-mail.

There was no text, only an attachment.

"Open it."

Tomi logged off from the Subnet and turned the wireless off on the laptop. He ran a program. "It seems clean."

"Open it."

Still Tomi hesitated, so Lee pushed his hand away and clicked on the attachment.

A single photo opened up. Lee doubled over beside the desk, her breath coming in quick, shallow bursts, no air reaching her lungs.

In the photo Derrick was in the bathtub, fully clothed, a large chunk of his head taken away above the right eye, blood and brains spattered on the tile behind him.

Tomi bent down to help her to the bed. "Breathe into this," he told her, fishing a plastic bag from the wastebasket and putting it to her face.

She crumpled it in her hands, unable to take her eyes from the photo.

"It's a fake," Tomi said. "Derrick's just trying to get back at us."

Lee wiped her mouth and leaned in closer.

"Look at that." Tomi pointed at the picture. "All that blood, like from a zombie movie. It's so bogus."

Then she saw it in Derrick's hand, dangling between two fingers like a cigarette, the little white plastic pregnancy test.

"What is it?" Tomi asked.

"I have to go back."

"What?"

"Just . . . I have to go back."

"What is that?" Tomi began to zoom in on the object, and Lee swiped his hand away and closed the screen.

"Never mind what it is. If the cops find it, they will trace it to me."

In the garage they found two nearly new bicycles that looked as though they hadn't been ridden in many years. Tomi agreed to stand sentry outside the apartment while Lee went in and did what she had to do. It was clearly a setup, but what choice did she have? Tomi was right, Derrick's death was probably a fake. But their end goal was clear. If they wanted to set up an exchange—*With Hidden Noise* for the pregnancy stick—she'd do it. The door was unlocked. When she entered, the first thing she noticed was how quiet it was. She'd never felt such silence in this apartment; it felt quieter than any abandoned building she'd ever been in.

On her way to the bathroom she saw something that she'd never seen before. Derrick's door was open, just a crack. She stood next to it, listening, then whispered: *"Derrick."* There was no response, and she pushed the door open.

She looked more closely this time at the posters and fliers and programs plastered all over the walls. All of them were Société Anonyme. It was the room of a dizzy teenager in love with a band. She left the room and headed for the bathroom.

The photo had done very little to prepare her for the reality of Derrick's body slumped in the tub, the line of blood and brains streaked from his head up the tiles behind him. His eyes were still open, but they were no longer eyes anymore; they were sightless, occluded with a graying film. Lee pulled the shower curtain shut, then desperately wiped at it and everything else she'd touched with the sleeve of her sweatshirt, fumbling so much she nearly brought the curtain down. She had held a gun to his face a few hours ago, and Lee remembered what it had felt like to want to pull the trigger. Her stomach cramped painfully. She may as well have pulled the trigger—Derrick was now dead because of her.

Lee held her breath and opened the curtain again. The little plastic stick was still in his hand. She covered her mouth and tried not to vomit again. The last thing she needed was to leave more of her DNA behind.

She had two fingers on it and was easing it from his hand when she heard someone come in behind her. Lee collapsed forward, nearly falling onto Derrick's body. A hand grabbed and steadied her. She heard Tomi's voice: "Lee . . ."

Lee thrust the stick into her pocket and pushed past him. She took the stairs three at a time, feeling pressed in, sick at herself for what she'd just done—Derrick was a scumbag, but he didn't deserve this. She wished she were in the bowels of some dark, forgotten building. She wanted to be alone.

When she burst out onto the sidewalk, the bright afternoon light wilted her. Tomi was right behind. "Lee—wait."

She slowed despite herself, waiting without turning. He came up beside her.

"*They* did that to him," she said.

"I know."

She was feeling lightheaded again. Derrick was really dead. She didn't know how she was supposed to feel about this, except in her body, which seemed to be trying to shut down. She had to keep herself from simply flopping to the sidewalk. "Jesus, I think I need to throw up."

"Come on, let's walk it off."

"Walk it off? Did you see him?"

Tomi looked at the ground.

"We never liked each other, but I never . . . He was your friend."

"Come on, we have to go. They might still be around." They began walking. Lee kept her hoodie up and her head down. Tomi kept looking behind them.

Derrick was dead and she was alive. Was that fair? He'd been involved, apparently, but he wasn't at the center of it, as she was. Just collateral damage. Lee wondered if they'd killed him just to send her a message. She couldn't understand how things had gotten to this point. "How did they even get him in the shower?" she said. "Do you think he knew what was going to happen? Did you see him? His eyes . . ."

"I saw him."

"It's my fault."

"No."

"Who, then?"

"Derrick was involved with those people," Tomi said. "Obviously he knew what they're capable of."

"I didn't know they were capable of *this*."

"Why would they have killed him?" Tomi said.

"To get us back out in the open." She stopped and looked up and down the street for someone watching them. Only a couple pushing a stroller, and farther down, a man walking his dog. "They must have lost track of us, but now they've found us again." Lee waited until the couple were out of earshot. "How much money do you have?"

"On me?"

"Not on you. In the world. I can get six hundred dollars."

"What for?"

"Let's get out of here. Out of this city."

"And go where?"

"Anywhere. Anywhere."

"Okay. Yes. Finally."

"Really?"

"Yeah. Really."

"Tonight?"

"Sure. Tonight."

"We'll go to the Greyhound station."

"Lee."

"We'll pick a bus at random."

"Lee. I saw you take that thing from Derrick's hand. What was it?"

"Nothing."

"That was a pregnancy test."

Lee looked away.

Tomi's confusion was naked on his face. "Is it his?"

She pulled her hoodie back up and quickened her pace back to their bicycles. When he grabbed and spun her around, he froze and stepped back, and Lee could only imagine how she must have looked to him.

"How far along are you?" Tomi looked stricken, but she could see him trying to suck it up. "I don't care if it *is* his. We'll do whatever you want. I'm still with you."

Eyes on the ground, she thrust her hands into her pockets. "Twelve and a half weeks."

Lee waited for him to do the math and watched this new information take root in him. "Is it mine? It's mine, isn't it?"

She turned away and unlocked the bikes. Lee began pedaling, in any direction, she didn't care. He was right behind her, shouting in her ear: "We'll raise her in the country, teach her to hunt and to farm! I'll teach her to hack before she can talk. Why am I thinking it's gonna be a girl? It doesn't matter, we'll have two, she can have a little brother to take care of. What do you think about New Hampshire? I've always had good feelings about New Hampshire—"

Lee stopped so suddenly Tomi was a quarter block away before he was able to adjust and turn around. He wheeled up to her. "They'll get as big and strong as grizzly bears!"

"I'm not going to keep it."

Tomi let go of his bike. He stumbled to the curb and collapsed. The bike lay there in the middle of the street, one wheel spinning. A car honked. Lee rolled hers to the sidewalk. "Come on," she said. "We have to go. They could be following us right now."

"I don't care."

Lee sat down next to him. "This is exactly why I didn't want to tell you."

"You want to kill her?"

"I didn't say that."

"You just did."

"I don't know."

"But you might. You might kill her."

"Yes."

"Can I feel her?"

"What?"

"Before you decide. Can I just feel her?"

Lee unzipped her sweatshirt, then lifted her shirt and leaned back. She stared up at the sky. Tomi's hand on her belly was cool; it felt good. "I can't do this," she said, pulling her shirt down and yanking his hand away.

"What?"

"You don't get to be part of this." Lee ran to her bike and pedaled off, not looking back until she was sure he wasn't behind her.

When they arrived back at the Caldwells', Tomi began packing immediately. Both of them knew they could no longer stay there. Lee had only her small bag, already packed and ready to go. "What now?" Tomi said.

Lee realized how deep over their heads they were. Saving Thrumm kids, past or future, was a fantasy. "Name six cities," she said. "Anywhere. Some place where nobody knows you."

"San Francisco. Portland. Detroit. New Orleans." He stopped. "Are we really doing this?"

"Chicago," she added, writing them down and numbering each. "Albuquerque." Lee almost scratched the last one out—after all, they knew her father lived there—but then she didn't. If fate meant for her to go there . . . She pulled the little blue bottle from around her neck and shook it, staring at the die inside. She looked at it, then the paper. They were going to Detroit.

"Okay, then," he said. "Good urbex community there. So we go to the Greyhound station?"

Lee opened Tomi's laptop and looked up the bus schedule to Detroit. She looked at the clock. "There's a bus leaving in an hour, but we'll never make it. There's another tomorrow at noon, though. We can make that."

They left together but split up, with an agreement to meet in two hours at a café downtown. Tomi wanted to come with her, but Lee knew that if she was being followed, she'd have an easier time losing them if she was alone. The whole way she made sure no bikes were following, and she cut through several parks and even a restaurant to lose any cars that might be on her.

Mr. Velasquez didn't seem surprised to find Lee at his door, though she could never glean much from his expression. She thought she could see a small, dark face peering at her from behind the curtain of his kitchen window. He didn't invite her in but headed to his shop without a word. It was cold, but she was drenched in sweat and panting, the ride having taken everything out of her. She must have looked pathetic, but he said nothing about it.

He didn't ask where she'd been, though she'd stopped coming to see him some weeks ago. When they got into his shop, he closed the door and faced her.

"I need my money," she told him.

"You are in trouble?"

"It's nothing."

He stared at her a long time before reaching behind the counter and taking out the envelope stuffed with cash. He handed it to her, and she stuffed it in her bag.

"There's something else," she said. She took the object, wrapped in an old dishrag, from her bag. "I need you to hold something for me."

"And what is that?"

Lee unwrapped it on his counter, and he just stood regarding it, as though not wanting to touch it. In the dim light of the garage, it looked even older than it was, like something unearthed from the bottom of a tomb.

"Just until I figure something out."

"It looks like the kind of thing my cousin Marco makes from trash on the street. And he's not all there in the head." Mr. Velasquez wrapped it back up carefully. "I suppose it must be worth something?"

"I guess it is," Lee said, heading out to the alley.

"Wait," he said.

Lee turned to see him holding something out to her. She took it.

It was the lighter she had stolen when she had first come under his tutelage. He had cleaned it up, and it shined coolly in her hand. He'd had it engraved on one side, LADRONCITA in elaborate gothic script, and below that, FROM VV in small block letters. Lee flicked it open and sparked it lit. The small orange flame warmed her hand, and the smell of flint and lighter fluid made her a little dizzy.

THIRTEEN

THE signage of the Heart O' Philly Hotel had a red neon heart in place of the "O." Tomi insisted on their best room, and the clerk seemed amused at this, obligingly charging him another twenty bucks. Lee guessed that all the rooms were exactly the same, but she didn't say anything. Since they'd left the café, Tomi had been aggressively protective, shielding her from cars a half block away, carrying both their bags in one hand as he wrapped his other arm around her.

Lee liked this side of him; it was assertive but sweet. When the clerk asked them if they wanted a single king-sized bed or two doubles, Tomi looked at her, then at the clerk. "One bed," he said. She took the keys from the man and headed off, leaving Tomi to take care of the rest. She didn't feel especially safe in a hotel, had argued they'd be better off sleeping in an abandoned building, but Tomi had insisted.

The room was small and clean enough, with a big bed and a TV. Lee pulled the shades, stripped off her clothes, and stepped into the shower. She stayed there a long time, sloughing the horror of Derrick's bathroom from her skin in a pool that swirled around her feet and into the drain. The image of his body kept flashing in her head, and she had to look directly at the light to make it go away. Lee emerged feeling somewhat human again.

Tomi was sitting cross-legged on the bed, his laptop open. On a sheet of paper was a drawing of a chessboard, just a few pieces remaining on it.

"What are you doing?"

He didn't look up. "Playing around with an idea you gave me. I found this in the room beneath the museum, in that stack of papers. It's a copy of an announcement Duchamp did for an art exhibition in 1943. He attached a chess endgame problem to it. It's done on translucent card stock, with the announcement on the front and the problem on the back."

Tomi held it up for her to see, but Lee didn't play chess, so the pieces on the board meant little to her. Below the board was written "White to Play and Win."

"You're trying to solve it now?" she said. "I thought we were leaving all this behind."

"I can't help it. And I'm not trying to solve it, exactly. Many chess players have tried their hand at it. Grand masters, even. One person designed a computer program to attempt to solve it. The consensus is that it is a problem with no solution."

"So what are you doing?"

Tomi turned the paper over and showed her a sketch of a little cupid, upside down and seemingly plummeting, pulling back on his bow mid-fall. "It's meant to be held to the light." He demonstrated, holding it up against the lamp, and now she saw the cupid transposed over the board. "You can see that he's pointing his arrow right at this pawn."

"So is that where the solution is? With that pawn?"

"Others have thought as much, though there's nothing in that pawn that wins the game. But I thought of something else."

"What?"

Tomi let the paper fall back to the bed. "Duchamp's entire lifetime of work is a lattice of connections. Each of his works refers back to prior works, embedding them and referencing them again and again."

"And there's a reference in here somewhere?"

"Maybe. Something you said about *The Large Glass* got me thinking. What if this weren't a chess problem at all. What if it was more like . . . a map."

"Or that you held it over a map," she said, getting it, "and it pointed to something. But what are we supposed to hold it over?"

Tomi shook his head. "I wish I knew."

Lee lay back on the bed, the towel wrapped around her. "It doesn't matter," she said. "This time tomorrow we'll be on a bus to Detroit with all this behind us." Lee turned on the TV to avoid thinking about the girl upstairs.

She didn't know how long she'd been asleep when she heard Tomi click the door shut behind him. He took a carton of chow mein and a liter of Coke from a bag and left them on the desk, then disappeared into the bathroom. Lee heard the shower go on. She didn't wait to dive into the bag, swigging from the bottle, then holding chopsticks in a closed fist and shoveling hot noodles into her mouth.

By the time he came out of the shower, she was nearly asleep again. He climbed into the bed with her, still wet. Lee had never really been attracted to Tomi. She had liked being with him, even needed him. But he was hairy in all the wrong places, and almost as short as she was; his eyes were dewy and nervous, and his nose looked like it belonged on another face. She had felt drawn to him the first night of the museum but never since. Lee could feel Tomi's breaths on the back of her neck, and she turned to face him. With his glasses off and in the gauzy light of the room, he actually looked handsome. His eyes, unmagnified, were intelligent and kind, and his mouth turned down willfully, as though suppressing a smile. Without the glasses, his nose looked right. Tomi had lost some weight over the last month, and Lee could see it in his cheekbones and cleft chin. More than anything she could see in his eyes how much he loved her. His breaths were falling on her mouth now, and she pulled him close and kissed him.

It was different from the night in the museum. This time was slow, fumbling and tender. Lee wasn't sure if she loved him, but for the first time she thought that maybe she could. When they were finished, he sat up in the bed and ate chow mein from the carton and told her a story from his childhood he'd never told her before, one he said he'd never told anyone. He said he used to read books in the library while his friends played soccer in the streets. Not because he was a particularly studious kid but because he had a crush on the librarian. She was tall and blond and unsmiling, and she looked exactly like Nico from the Velvet Underground. She was also at least a dozen years older than him. He would sit at a table near the circulation desk reading books on art history, not because of his own interest but because he had gleaned that it was hers. But somewhere over the course of a year, his interest turned from her to what was in the books, and that was how he had decided he wanted to become an artist. He was telling Lee about moving to America at thirteen, about getting a paper route to pay for art supplies, when the open laptop awoke. He went to shut it down when he looked at the screen and stopped.

"It's an e-mail," he said. "From them."

"Open it," she said.

Tomi shut the laptop. "No. We stick to our plan. No matter what."

Lee grabbed the laptop from him. The e-mail came from the same address as the last one, the subject: LHOOQ. Lee opened it.

There was no message, just another attachment. When she clicked it, the video started immediately: Lee in Derrick's bathroom, his body slumped in the tub.

Lee watched herself stoop over, gingerly pluck the little white stick from his hands. She watched Tomi come in behind her, and she watched herself shove the stick into her pocket and flee the room. The video was no more than ten seconds long, but it looped on an endless repeat, over and over.

Lee was feeling dizzy when another e-mail came in. Tomi opened it this time. There was a single line of text: Enough games. Where is it?

Tomi seemed frozen. Lee moved in and typed: fuck you.

Almost immediately, another e-mail came back: Let us meet and be done with it. Otherwise the video gets sent to the police.

She typed: where and when?

The old aquarium. Two hours.

It was a little after midnight as she cycled through the streets, slaloming between shadow and pools of yellow streetlight. She would retrieve the stupid object and arrange to give it back to whoever the fuck wanted it so bad, and that would be that. She would find a future with Tomi, somewhere in one of his impossible fantasies. Maybe there was something to build there; maybe the strength of his belief was enough to carry them both. Maybe at some point she would stop seeing the girl upstairs whenever she'd close her eyes.

Lee knew something was wrong from a block away, the red and blue lights of a parked cop car illuminating Mr. Velasquez's three children, the little girl staring into nothing, the two boys with their heads buried into either leg of their mother, her face shiny with tears, talking to a police officer.

Lee ducked her head and pushed her bike slowly up the alley, past the crowd surrounding the yellow crime scene tape. Someone muttered something in Spanish. She got a glimpse beneath a man's tattooed arm. The body was covered under the tarp, but Lee could see Mr. Velasquez's shoes sticking out from underneath.

She stood there for much too long, unable to move. Derrick had been involved with them somehow, but Mr. Velasquez had nothing to do with any of this. He simply had something they wanted. And he must have refused to give it up. The phrase "I'm so sorry" came to her lips and wouldn't leave; she just kept mouthing it again and again. A man beside her gave her a quick glance before returning his attention to the scene inside the police tape. Lee couldn't stop repeating the phrase. She pushed her bike to the other end of the alley. Everything, her entire world, was unreal. Not a dream, just unreal. Like none of this could be happening. He was just lying there, in front of his own shop. He had been good to her. For no reason, he had been good to her, and this is what he she had given him in return. She realized she was still repeating the same phrase aloud, and she made herself stop, telling herself to breathe, making that the phrase instead, until she was sobbing so uncontrollably she lost sense of everything around her. It seemed to have no bottom.

She came to lying on a swath of broken auto glass, her cheek pressed into it so tightly she could feel shards sticking to her skin as she sat up. The crime tape was still up, though the alley was empty. She could see the back of a police car at the corner. They had taken his body. She got to her feet and held herself steady against the wall. The door to Mr. Velasquez's storeroom was a few feet away. It was open. Lee edged in and shut it behind her, waiting in the dark and listening before turning on the light.

Someone had laid waste to the room. All along the floor lay upturned bins, their contents strewn across the floor. Appliances were smashed, and even the walls had been torn open. The steel safe, which stood beside the little refrigerator, had been cracked, and its door hung open. So maybe they had found it. But that wasn't his style; Mr. Velasquez would never put anything truly valuable in a safe. And if they had found it, then why would they send the e-mail? They must have sent the video after they'd torn the place apart. So they must not have found what they were looking for.

Lee kicked through the piles of broken junk on the floor, looking for someplace they might have missed. She began going through the bins herself, knowing it could be anywhere, knowing that Mr. Velasquez hadn't necessarily even hid the thing in here, when something occurred to her: when she had spent some of her off time in this room, she'd tried to turn on the old TV, but it hadn't worked at all. Mr. Velasquez was fastidious. It wasn't like him to leave something lying broken in his own shop. She rifled around in the debris until she found a screwdriver, then undid the eight screws in back of the TV. The back slid off to reveal a hollowed-out space behind the tube. There was the fist-sized object, still wrapped in its dirty rag.

She raced through the streets, ignoring traffic lights, skirting delivery trucks, and nearly running into a group of guys coming out of a bar who called her a dyke faggot and insisted a real man would fuck her straight. She pedaled faster. Tomi was waiting, just where she'd told him to meet her. When she saw him, she hugged him so tightly his back cracked.

The little motorboat was there, as it always was, tied to the dock. Lee held it while Tomi wobbled his way to the center, then half fell down onto the seat. He grabbed the sides and held on. Lee untied the boat at the dock, then jumped in and took hold of the oars. She pushed them off and rowed. She was exhausted, but running the motor this late would risk too much attention. There were no lights on the western side of Petty Island, and so she had to keep herself straight using the silhouette of the pier building backlit by the faint light of the city.

"Keep a lookout behind me for other boats," she told him. "They still run shipping freighters down this route, and they won't see us."

"I'm pretending we're on the lake by our house, the one out in the country. It's just you and me and our daughter, and we're taking her out on a picnic to a little island in the middle of a lake. There's an apple grove on the island, and a spring." His voice sounded hollow, like he was somewhere else.

Lee wanted to tell him to stop, but she knew it was just his way of coping. She scanned the still, oil-dark water behind them as Tomi talked, watching the tiny wakes expand outward into darkness. There was no house out in the country with a farm and a lake and picnics on an island, but maybe they could still find a way together.

"We're here." Lee turned the boat around and found a spot along the concrete wall where she could tie it to one of the rebar ladders running down the side. She cast her flashlight down both walls, but there were no other boats. They might be here already, which would be good. But whoever they were meeting could also have taken another route. Lee steadied the boat while Tomi climbed from it to the ladder.

At the top of the concrete pier, they could see the lights of the refineries on the north end of the island. To the east, where they were headed, was mostly darkness, beyond which a few lights shone from the shores of New Jersey across the reach. They picked their way through dry marsh, then a copse of woods. Soon the silhouette of the Blizzard came into view, the old roller coaster looking like the skeletal remains of a mountain.

She led them around the area where CITGO employees must have been illegally disposing of the old industrial-sized tires for years, to the front of the aquarium and down the ramp to the rear. They crawled beneath the opening in the loading dock door, Lee taking the lead through the rear offices, up the employees' hallway, and through the door into the aquarium itself.

Lee turned off her light, Tomi did the same, and they stood listening. She could usually tell when someone else was in an empty space with her. She sensed nothing now. She turned her flashlight back on and led them past the empty alligator pit, the cashier's desk, the rows of empty tanks and dioramas.

Tomi stood in the Paleolithic Room, silently regarding a 1960s imagining of early humans in a Stone Age dwelling. There were no figures—someone must have taken the mannequins long ago. There was only a crude structure and beneath it a bed with blankets made from animal hide, a fire pit, and a few primitive cutting tools.

Lee put a hand on his shoulder and flicked off her flashlight as they sat on the bed. They remained as still as possible in the darkness while Lee listened. When she smelled sandalwood, she knew they weren't alone. A match hissed from somewhere across the room, and its flame touched the wick of an old gas lantern. A figure stood holding it. "Shall we get on with it?" the man said.

The lamp washed an orange glow across the pale face, his dark eyes and thick, brushed-back hair. He wore the same black suit he'd worn in the Silo, when he'd given her the white dress. The man approached with slow, deliberate steps, then stopped. "It's nice to see you again, little Bride."

Before Lee could stop him, Tomi stood in front of her and pulled something from his jacket. She thought it was his flashlight until she saw the dark outline in his hand. This was not what they had planned—they would hand the object over and be done with it. She hadn't even realized he'd taken the gun from her bag. Tomi wrapped his arm back around her and held her behind him.

"We only want the Duchamp piece," the man said. "Afterward we never need to cross paths again."

"How do I know you won't give that video to the police?" she asked him.

"You have my word."

"What am I supposed to do with that?"

"We don't deal with the police. I'm sure you can imagine that giving them that video would make for needless complications. It is only a last resort. We only want the Duchamp piece now. We no longer even care about you. Obviously, you are not who we thought you were. Now, do you have it?"

The man hadn't seen the gun yet. Tomi was holding it down behind his leg. "We have it," Tomi said.

"May I see it?"

Lee reached into her bag and took out the object. The thing inside rattled as she held it out in front of her. With her other hand she held on to Tomi's arm, the one with the gun. She tried to project her thoughts into his: *Let him take it. Don't be stupid.*

When the glow from the lantern found the object, the muscles in the man's face relaxed and he let out the lightest of sighs. Lee saw him close his eyes. Tomi's gun hand came up, and Lee knew then that he would shoot the man. She heard a pop behind a flash of yellow. Lee felt the weight of Tomi's body shift. His breaths stuttered out in three lumpy coughs.

Lee had a hard time arranging the pieces of what she was seeing. The gun she was looking at was not Tomi's but an antique-looking thing, dull and gray. The man's mouth twitched into an almost embarrassed smile. She felt Tomi slump downward, and then the gun he was holding was in her hand. She fumbled it, aiming it at the man, but before she could fire he squeezed the trigger of his pistol again. She heard only a click. Tomi dropped to the floor. Still holding the lantern, the man tried awkwardly to unjam his pistol, but Lee raised her gun first and fired.

The lantern dropped and went out. She heard him swear, and then she heard him stumbling backward before he disappeared completely in the darkness. Lee fired more shots in his direction until the gun only clicked. She dropped to the floor and grabbed Tomi's face, trying to see his eyes. Her hand passed along his chest and came back bloody. She felt a horrible compression inside her, her whole body contracting into a state of absolute helplessness. Lee shook him, pushed her hands into his chest like she'd seen done on TV, planted her mouth on his and puffed air in, but even then she knew he was dead.

Lee sat in the dark, listening, her hand gripping the gun. After a time she turned the flashlight on and set it standing on the floor. She couldn't take Tomi with her, couldn't tell anyone about him. But it didn't feel right, leaving him here in the middle of the floor. Lee took his hands and dragged his body across the dirt floor, into the shelter of the Paleolithic Man display, and onto the age-worn bed of animal hide. Then she pulled the blanket on top of him and covered him. Above him on the ersatz cave wall was someone's rendition of an early cave painting: a drawing of a bison besieged by arrows.

Lee grabbed her bag and Tomi's, too. The smashed lantern lay on the ground. Near it a trail of blood led out of the room. Lee followed it. She would find him, wounded and dying somewhere in the woods, and she would finish this. But by the time she made it to the docks on the south side of the island, Lee knew he was gone.

When she made it back to the boat, it was nearly daybreak, the sky bleeding from black to gray and purpling along the horizon. She climbed onto the boat and rowed. When she reached the dock, Lee eased the boat in and tied it off. She stood on the concrete pier, not knowing what to do. She had nowhere to go. Nothing to her name. Tomi had been holding all their money. Lee dropped the bags to the pier, squatted, and opened them. She took out the flashlights and then the gun and threw them into the water. Tomi's laptop went in after them. Then she took out *With Hidden Noise*. She held it one last time before setting it gently on the pier.

Lee walked away, toward the broken slabs of the shore. She found an old length of rusted pipe and returned with it. Lee stood looking down on this thing that had brought with it nothing but misery. She hated herself for ever taking it. She raised the pipe over her head and came down with it again and again as the thing bent and crumpled and then the ball of twine burst open and Lee flopped down onto the concrete, out of breath. She picked up what was left of the thing. She could still hear it rattle. She jammed a finger into the hole of the twine and dug around until she could feel a small round object, then pulled it out and held it up to the dawn light.

· BOOK VI ·

The Bride Stripped Bare

FOURTEEN

WHEN the Daywater Medical Center closed its doors for the final time in August of 2002, creditors had stripped it of everything they could put a price tag on: medical and office equipment, from desks to cabinets to CT scanners and dialysis machines and ultrasound bays, wheelchairs and gurneys and beds, sold in lots to hospitals, nursing homes, and clinics. An agent from Ghana bought a $220,000 lot to crate up and ship back to Accra. What the creditors couldn't sell, they left behind, and for several weeks the building fell prey to looters, who harvested everything from sundry medical supplies to the copper wiring on the first two floors, and to junkies, who squatted the break rooms and nodded through the halls in jaggy stupors. Neighbors threatened the bank owners with lawsuits, so a crew was hired to seal the building up tight, chaining the doors and boarding up the windows on all four floors. Which gave the once dully modern hospital the look of something out of a postapocalyptic film set.

But Lee rarely saw the building from that angle, as access in and out was now limited to a single underground tunnel, through a drain cover behind a Dunkin' Donuts parking lot a block away. The tunnel led to the hospital's subbasement, a room of peeling concrete walls and rusted pipes and wires hanging like fat black vines from the ceiling. From there a set of stairs led up into a mechanical room, cluttered with boxy vent housings and plump white ducts and a bank of circuit breakers, beyond which was a second stairway into the hospital lobby. Inside the hospital, the first and second floors had been stripped clean of everything not bolted down, the walls gouged in trenches from the wiring being stripped out. Junkies had left their detritus in small piles around the waiting rooms and emergency room bays, and Lee could tell where they had gone through ferocious ransacking episodes, tearing open locked cabinets and smashing in janitorial closets in hopes of unearthing some undiscovered cache of prescription drugs. Somehow the third and fourth floors had for the most part escaped destruction, and so these were the floors that Lee called home. Up there were rooms full of Reagan-era medical apparatus too outdated to be sold: beige plastic operating lamps, a cracked CT scanner, an antiquated iron lung sitting like an abandoned escape pod in an otherwise empty room. She slept in an office on the fourth floor, a modest room whose desk and chairs had been sold, but it still had carpeting and a coffee-stained couch and even a shelf of medical books left behind in the aftermath of the hospital's sudden implosion.

Because all the building's windows were boarded up, very little daylight leaked through, giving every passing day the gray hue of a fog-enshrouded morning. For the first few nights Lee stalked the halls in this underwater twilight, exploring rooms without seeing, with none of the fascination or abandon that used to typify her creeps with Tomi. And it was during this time that Tomi began talking to her. Only simple sentences, asking about her and how she was, but always coming around to the baby: *You didn't get rid of her, did you? Can you feel her yet? I'm thinking about names.* She ignored him at first, and when he didn't go away, she tried pounding her fists against her head, then running as fast as she could from one end of the main hallway and back until her lungs gave out and she'd collapse from exhaustion. When he came back again, she trashed a doctor's office, upending and throwing about the room anything not bolted to the walls. None of which did anything to drive Tomi's voice from her head.

Lee soon discovered, though, that when Tomi's voice did go away, she yearned for it to return. It no longer mattered that hearing it meant she was crazy—she would take that, if only she could have him with her. She found herself walking the halls, looking for his voice to come back, sometimes talking to him, too. Lee had never known what it was to miss someone so totally, to feel as though they had been wrenched away so violently they left nothing but a gaping wound behind. Her father had left a hole behind, but Lee had been a little girl then, and that loss was a different thing, deeper but dulled. There was nothing dulled about the loss of Tomi. It was a sorrow so intense it felt as though something was stabbing her in the heart again and again.

The electricity had been shut off years ago, and so at night the hospital took on a blackness so total that it threatened to consume Lee entirely. She had trouble sleeping in such absolute darkness, and being awake in it was worse, so sometimes she would exit the hospital through the tunnel and wander the night-lit streets. Even those few hours a day when she did find sleep, part of her was always half-awake, hoping for Tomi to appear. The lack of sleep began to take its toll. She walked the halls and the streets feeling wobbly and disoriented, and she began to see movements from the corners of her eyes. The Crystal Castle, the Société Anonyme, the cops—she didn't care about any of them anymore. If they wanted to find her, they could have her. Even the Thrumm kids no longer mattered to her. When she closed her eyes, the girl upstairs was no longer there with her, only blackness.

She scrounged scraps of food in Dumpsters behind supermarkets and restaurants. There was no running water; she did her business in buckets and washed once or twice using a hose in the basement of the adjacent building, where she also filled containers with drinking water. Once she caught sight of her reflection in the glass pane of a conference room. Her face looked like someone had hollowed it out with an ice cream scoop. Her hair was tangled and mangy. Only her belly, which sloped out from her body like a gentle white hill, did not look cadaverous. She took in the image for a long time, wondering who was staring back at her, before digging up a pair of surgical scissors in one of the upstairs cabinets and cutting away at her hair until it was nothing but patchy lumps on her head.

Lee was aware of the baby inside her as she'd never been before. Its tendrils had grown deep, wrapping around her insides and clinging there like kelp to a rock. It lived with her in her rare dreams, which were always underwater, the little flippered thing swimming with her in brackish prehistoric pools.

She began to spend most of her nights walking the streets. No one ever bothered her. Lee knew it was because she was a ghost.

The red and green lights began to come out that week, just a few at first, decorating front doors and hedges, spreading a soft wash of color over her as she'd walk through a neighborhood at night. Soon elaborate tableaus were sprouting up, big plastic Santas skidding sleighs across rooftops, overworked elves jigging across lawns, quiet little nativity scenes awash in the surrounding light show.

The nights of long walks in the freezing cold had taken their toll. She was sleeping more during the day, but when she was awake, small black spots hovered in the periphery of her vision, making the world dance with tiny dark sprites. Her tongue felt swollen in her mouth, and she was hot and feverish all the time. She was having a hard time even standing, and it took more and more each night for her to go out.

Lee knew she was spiraling into a place she was never going to return from. She'd just fade away quietly in a forgotten room of a forgotten hospital. She couldn't bring herself to care, until she thought about Tomi. He never visited her anymore, but she knew what it would do to him to see her this way. She thought of how protective he'd become after he found out about the baby. She should have listened to him. If she'd returned the thing when she was supposed to, he would probably be alive. Lee thought about everything she'd never told him. How much she liked having him there with her. How much she needed him. She knew now she'd loved him, and she'd never told him that, either. Even if she couldn't save him, Lee wished she could have been strong enough just to utter the words. Would it have meant anything if those were the last words he'd heard?

There was nowhere for her to go, but the hospital was nowhere to stay. Lee struggled down the three flights of stairs into the hospital maintenance room and its subbasement, and up through the access tube a block away. She knew she wasn't coming back. The black spots in her eyes had gotten larger, and by now her vision was like a dark, cloudy tunnel, with just a small iris of light at the end. Lee began walking, without a destination, until she heard a bus wheeze to a stop beside her and she got on, knowing she was invisible, knowing no one would stop her. She sat in the back and quickly fell asleep. She hadn't planned to come out to this part of the city, but when she awoke, something about the neighborhood seemed familiar. She couldn't place it, but she recognized the trees and some of the houses. Had they stayed here? Maybe Tomi would visit her here. Maybe she could tell him then what she had never been able to tell him before. She got off the bus.

It was snowing, and in this neighborhood the holiday spirit was out in force: giant inflatable Santas and plastic reindeer trains colliding into roofs, great grapelike clusters of blinking lights. Through the front windows she could see Christmas trees drooping with tinsel and hunkering above stacks of wrapped gifts. A man with a snow shovel scooped out a path to his house. Lee limped past it all without seeing, her tunnel vision deepening, unable to distinguish between the fat gray snowflakes and the spots swarming her vision. It was snowing, but she was burning up. She stumbled, righted herself on a hydrant, and kept going, moving on instinct more than memory. Nothing looked familiar to her. And then something did. When she saw the front door, it came flooding back, the bubbly rush of fear and exhilaration she'd felt when she'd acted on a whim and slipped inside. The cool silence of the house as she'd moved from room to room, the whole place still and perfect like some life-sized diorama for a museum of the future: Early 21st Century Suburban Home.

Lee came to half buried in snow on the sidewalk. She pulled herself to her feet and stumbled across the street and into the Orbisons' yard. Lights were on downstairs, and their car was in the driveway. She went along the side of the house and to the back, where she used her remaining strength to climb onto a garbage can, up to the garage roof, and to the girl's window. Lee grasped the bottom of the window, sucked in her breath, and heaved up. It wouldn't budge. She looked inside, at the latch. It wasn't locked. She closed her eyes, breathed in, and heaved up with all the strength she had left. The window opened. Lee climbed into the room. Then she fell onto the girl's unmade bed and passed out while remembering the girl's name.

When she awoke, Annie was standing over her, looking down at Lee with an expression that was more curiosity and annoyance than anything resembling fear. Lee tried to say *Please*. Nothing came out. She felt her lip crack, tasted her own blood.

"You want some water?" Annie said.

Lee nodded.

Annie picked up an open Coke and handed it to Lee. It slipped out of her hands. Annie ignored the spilled Coke on her comforter and handed the can to her again. Lee managed to get it to her mouth and spill a few drops past her lips.

Annie sat down on her desk chair and leaned forward. "I recognize you from before. Who are you, and why are you in my room? Again."

Lee took another sip. The moisture and the sugar allowed her to speak. "I came here to die," she said.

Annie leaned back, unimpressed. "Here? This is like the last place I'd want to die. When I die, I want to be as far away from here as possible."

"Please . . ."

"Please what? Here," she said, pushing Lee upright and into the corner, where she could stay up. She handed the Coke back. *"Please . . ."*

"Please don't tell your parents."

"It so happens I'm not speaking to my parents right now. So you're in luck."

"I'm sorry. I just wanted to be in your room again."

"Before you die? I was about to go downstairs and eat. Are you hungry? My mom's a douche, but she's all the time in the kitchen, and there's usually something around."

Lee shook her head.

"You should eat something anyway. You look like a concentration camp."

As soon as Annie left the room, Lee passed out again, but she awoke to the smell of grease and meat. She opened her eyes to a plate sitting beside her, on which was a slice of pizza, a chicken leg, and a lumpy beige mess sitting in a pool of warm oil.

"Don't worry, that's not dog food like it looks. It's tuna casserole, I think. I forget."

Annie left her alone again, and Lee felt the room swim around her. She could feel what little strength she had hemorrhaging out of her in dark waves.

Then Annie slapped her. Not hard, just a light flick to each cheek. "Uh-uh. You don't get to do that again. I want to know who you are and why you're back in my room. Here." She lifted the pizza up to Lee's mouth and stuck the tip between her lips until Lee bit down and began chewing. Then Annie held up a Coke, newly opened, with a straw this time. Lee sucked hard on it, then winced and coughed.

"Please, just . . ." Lee coughed again, felt something come up into her mouth, phlegm or blood or a piece of lung maybe, she wasn't sure. She swallowed it back down.

"Please what? I'm trying to do some good here, but you won't tell me why you're here. I can tell my dad you're here. He'll recognize you, too. And he'll press charges, he's that much of a little bitch."

Lee could only shake her head.

"Then tell me."

Annie waited for her to speak, but Lee had nothing to give. She felt herself fading away again until Annie stuck another bit of food into her mouth. Chewing came easier this time.

"Fine," said Annie. "Eat first, talk later."

Lee passed out again after finishing half the plate. Annie let her sleep.

When she awoke, daylight was fingering in through the blinds. She was still in Annie's bed, alone in the room. None of it had been a dream. On the floor beside her was a tray with a bowl of cereal, soggy in milk, a can of Coke, three pieces of cold toast, and a mug of creamed coffee with so much sugar in it Lee thought at first it might be cocoa. A sheet of paper was folded in three beneath the cereal. The note was in the jagged scrawl that Lee knew well from Annie's diary.

> Dear Strange Girl in My Room,
>
> Good morning. I'm sorry for being such a cunt last night, but you surprised me at a bad time. My life at school is shitty as hell right now, and my parents are dicks of the highest order. But it looks like things aren't going so well for you, either. I have to go to my shitty school and spend a shitty day there, but my shitty parents will be at work and I'll get home before them and we can figure out what to do with you. Just don't kill yourself—as you can see by my room, I'm not good at cleaning up messes.

She signed off the note with a smiley face with x-ed out eyes and the letter A.

Lee found that she was able to eat most of what was on the tray and that when she was done, some of her strength had come back. Her vision was still spotted with small black blobs, and her equilibrium was off when she attempted to stand, but her mouth was less swollen and the pounding in her head had subsided to a quiet thump. She coughed up something thick and phlegmy into the coffee cup.

Lee slid to the side of the bed and put her feet on the floor. Annie had taken her shoes off. Gingerly, grabbing the chair for support, Lee stood. She felt wobbly, something rattling inside her skull. She collapsed, not even making it to the bed. She remained on the floor, in and out of consciousness, until she heard the door click shut downstairs and the beeping of alarm buttons. Then Annie was squatting above her, the back of her hand on Lee's forehead.

"You're burning. You want me to get you a doctor?"

Lee shook her head.

"Suit yourself. I had an idea while I was at school. Think you can walk?"

Lee didn't know if she could walk; she was so awash in fatigue that even lifting her head took effort. But she pushed herself up into a sitting position, and Annie helped her to stand. With Annie holding her around the waist, she managed to stagger out into the hallway.

"You're heavier than I expected," Annie said. "Considering. And we got a lot of stairs in front of us—can you manage?"

They made it down the stairs into the foyer, one slow step at a time. It seemed to Lee to take forever, and she felt herself nearly buckle with each step, but Annie was surprisingly patient, urging her on with little sounds of encouragement. They went through the kitchen and to the door that Lee knew led to the basement. Still holding her around the waist, Annie opened the door and flicked the light on. The stairs were harder here, with no carpeting and deeper steps, but in the same way they made the first flight they made this one.

The basement was a clutter of old boxes and forgotten things: a wooden crib on three legs, a buckling wall shelf full of old paint cans and solvents and oil containers, a roll of old carpeting leaning against a bundle of skis. Annie ran her fingers across the wood wall along the stairs until she found an edge to grasp. She pulled and a door hinged open.

Inside was a small space beneath the stairs. It had been carpeted floor to ceiling in the same carpeting rolled up just outside, with a small mattress, a beanbag, and a child-sized chest of drawers taking up the entire floor. A sleeping bag was bunched up against the wall, and on the table was an old boom box with a pair of headphones attached. The carpeted walls were tacked with posters: Blink 182 and Eminem and Insane Clown Posse. Annie helped Lee into the room and eased her down onto the beanbag. She closed the door, flicked the switch of a lamp, and flopped down onto the bed.

"My brother put this together when he was my age. He'd come down here every day after school before our parents got home and work on it. While he was supposed to be watching me. My parents never found out about it. But I did, of course. I got curious and snooped around, and I could see the light through the cracks in the door one day. He fixed it after that—you can hardly see the door if you don't know it's there. After that he let me come down some days and hang with him if he didn't have a friend or a girl over."

Next to the beanbag was an abalone shell used as an ashtray, and a foot-high purple plastic bong beside it. Annie reached into one of the drawers and pulled out a small baggie. She took a bud out and packed it into the bong. "Henry's dead. He got killed two years ago in Afghanistan. So now the room is mine."

Annie took a long gurgling hit and exhaled, dense smoke filling the small space immediately. She offered the bong to Lee, but Lee shook her head.

"Well, it's here if you want it. I hope you don't mind if I come down and smoke out sometimes. There are some CDs in the drawer, but it's mostly shitty bro rock. He was a good guy, but he had terrible taste in music. I left his posters up in his memory. I'll make you a mix of good stuff if I remember. Could you stand something to eat?"

Lee could feel a buzzy little contact high coming on, and her whole body seemed to settle a little. For the first time in weeks she was actually hungry.

Lee didn't know how long she had been out, or whether it was day or night, but when she awoke, there was a tin of sardines with a chunk of baguette and a Coke on a plate beside her. The smell of oil and fish was nauseating, and she felt encoffined in the tiny space—helpless, delirious, wishing for the endless open maze of her hospital. Mostly she missed Tomi, his voice beside her as she'd wander the city. She took a long swig of the Coke, wanting water instead, then another, finishing the can.

The black spots were still tunneling her vision, but less so now; they were less dense, and she could see through them in parts. Lee found the light switch, plunged herself into darkness, and passed back out. She woke and passed out again and again over any number of hours or days or weeks or months or years, Lee had no idea. Sometimes she was so hot she sweated through her clothes and tore them off; other times, so cold she curled herself into her sleeping bag and chattered herself to sleep. Lee had hazy visions of Annie coming in and out, her voice filling the space, though Lee could recognize no words. She had a vague sense of plates of food coming in and out at various times, and sometimes of eating something and sometimes not, but being thirsty, always thirsty. Sometimes instead of Coke Annie brought large plastic jugs of water, which Lee consumed quickly.

With Annie's help Lee would make it to a toilet in a room off the basement, and once Annie stripped the room of her sleeping bag and Lee of her clothes, Lee thought maybe because she had relieved herself there in the room but she wasn't sure. All time, all movement, all moments waking and dreaming had swirled and condensed into a single amorphous event that she felt at once inside and outside of.

Then one afternoon she woke up and she wasn't sweating, and her body wasn't wracked with chills. She didn't know how she knew it was the afternoon, but her internal clock had started moving again, and she felt, for the first time in memory, somewhat lucid. There was a plate beside her, containing a tuna sandwich, a bag of chips, and a half jar of applesauce. She ate all of it, tasting food for the first time in a very long while, licking her fingers clean when she was finished, wanting more. An empty paint can sat at the foot of her bed, half filled with urine, and she noticed the smell of the room for the first time, how rank it was. Filled with her sickness. Lee pushed open the door and breathed in, relishing the bloodrush to her head. It felt good. She looked down at her belly for the first time in she didn't know how long, running her fingers along its easy slope. She thought of Tomi, and the pain of his absence came back, as though it had never gone away. She put herself into one of his fantasies, the two of them raising a daughter on a farm by a lake. For a moment she smiled at the image, until Tomi disappeared from it and she was left there, alone and filled with a dull emptiness. Suddenly the space was too small. She crawled out. Light bled in through the high basement windows.

Lee stood still and listened. No one upstairs. It was afternoon light, which meant the Orbisons would be at work, Annie at school. Something smelled terrible. She scanned the basement, seeing it clearly for the first time. A lot of stuff that must have been Annie's brother's was piled up down here. Not much that looked like Annie's, except for an old dollhouse listing in one dark corner. Lee crouched to peek inside, but the windows of its pale blue French doors had been glued shut and the glass painted black. Only now, her nose close to her crotch, did Lee realize that the awful smell was coming from her. Lee found an old hose coiled by the washing machine and attached it to a faucet on a big metal basin. She stripped her clothes and stepped into the paint-spattered basin and ran the cold water over her body. Her skin was tender all over and the water stung, but still it felt good. She found a dirty bar of soap and cleaned every inch of herself, then used it to wash what matted tufts of hair she had on her head.

When she was finished, she stood, wet and shivering, unwilling to put her filthy clothes back on her skin. She stuffed them into the washer, along with the sleeping bag, and while her clothes washed, she drained the urine from the can, cleaned and straightened the tiny room, and sat naked on the beanbag hugging her legs until the washing machine buzzed and she could transfer her clothes to the dryer.

She was pulling on her dry clothes, relishing the clean warmth against her skin, when she heard Annie come home upstairs. There followed some clanking around in the kitchen, Annie humming a song Lee vaguely recognized. Lee found herself eager to see Annie without a fog of delirium between them. And feeling weirdly shy. She got her hoodie up just as Annie opened the door.

When Annie saw Lee sitting up and not curled up in a feverish ball, she froze, just stared at her slack-jawed. They stayed with their eyes locked for what seemed like forever, as though each were weighing the other's intentions. Then Annie broke into a smile and nearly dropped the plate in her excitement. "You're back!" she cried, loud enough to hurt Lee's ears. "And you cleaned up. The place doesn't smell like a bus station toilet." Annie climbed in and shut the door behind her. She handed the plate to Lee, and Lee took it, eating before she even knew what was on it.

Annie watched silently as Lee forked in mouthful after mouthful of cold chicken and potatoes and vegetables. She was ravenous, feeling as though she hadn't eaten in days. A fist of food caught in her throat, and she tried to wash it down with a swig of Coke, but it stuck there and she nearly choked before it finally went down.

"Careful, there. How ironic would it be for you to choke to death after I brought you back from the dead. You did look dead, you know." She took Lee's finished plate and set it beside her. "Like a corpse. But look at you now. You've actually got color in your face."

Lee flinched back a bit as Annie reached over and pulled down the hood. "Oh, my God. You're so pretty. I wish I could get away with cutting my hair like that."

Lee tried to smile but wasn't sure how it came out.

"Can you talk? I don't think I've heard you say more than 'Please' since you got here. I've been dying to hear you say something. Go on, say something."

Lee knew she could talk. But right now she couldn't get a word out. Nothing seemed appropriate. "Thank you," she said finally.

Annie came down much more often over the next several days. She'd stay with Lee as Lee ate, and they'd talk about Annie's miserable school life and her miserable parents, which Annie hated in equal measure. Lee wanted to ask specific questions about Annie's school troubles, and especially about Oona, though she wasn't supposed to know about any of it and wasn't about to let the girl know she had spent her previous time here reading Annie's diaries and going through the photos on her computer. It didn't take Annie long to get into it, though, to fill in backstory that Lee already knew and to add details that Lee didn't. She was as open with Lee as she was in her diary. Lee didn't open up in turn, and evaded most of Annie's questions with vague nonanswers. All she would say was that she had no home and hadn't in some time. Annie seemed intrigued with the idea of homelessness—it had a romantic allure to her—and she peppered Lee with questions about how she'd survived. Lee was more forthcoming about this. She told Annie about her weeks squatting homes of people on vacation.

"Why'd you come back?" Annie asked. "Here, I mean. Why my house?"

Lee didn't know how to explain, even to herself. "I thought I was dying. It seemed as good a place as any to do it."

Annie nodded thoughtfully, as though this seemed reasonable. "I guess I foiled your plans, huh?"

Lee smiled, realizing that her lips hadn't cracked when she did. "I guess you did."

The room no longer seemed a coffin to her; now it was more a ship's quarters, and she imagined a vast, flat ocean outside the door instead of the dim, cluttered garage that greeted her every time she went to the bathroom. Sometimes she read the books Annie would bring down; sometimes she listened to a mix CD Annie had made for her, which she'd titled "ADHDmix" in her jaggy scrawl, a mishmash of techno tracks that all sounded the same to Lee. Sometimes she could hear Mrs. Orbison come down to do laundry, and Lee would tighten herself into a ball and make as little noise as possible. She could hear the three of them in the mornings, during their breakfasts just above, and at night over dinners. More often than not, they were fighting, Annie's indignant trill rising over her parents' voices, usually presaging the screech of a chair and the stomping of feet. Lee liked these times most of all; she would turn off the music or put down her book or stop whatever else she was doing to lie back and listen and imagine herself as part of the family upstairs. In Lee's home they had never fought, but that was because they rarely spoke. Steve thought there was too much chatter in the world, and he designated "hush zones" most mornings and mealtimes. Lee was not allowed her headphones, or to eat alone, and during these times Steve would smile at her or her mother in a quiet, approving way that always made Lee want to stick her fork deep into his mouth and twist. The voices upstairs, arguing or not, made Lee think of her month living in the apartment with Will and Allison and Derrick and Tomi, how they had been the closest thing she had to family.

Lee found her hands unconsciously circling the round swell of her belly again, and more and more the fact of the baby began to return. She still was barely showing, though when Annie came down, Lee made sure to keep her midriff covered. How far along was she? She counted the weeks in her head since the night Tomi had taken her to the museum. Something like fifteen. She wondered if she had damaged it as much as she had herself over the past weeks. The thought of it made her sick.

As her strength returned, she became more and more antsy to clear out but also afraid knowing that once she did there'd be no coming back. One morning she woke up to the sound of choir music upstairs and knew that it was Christmas. She imagined Annie taking presents from beneath the tree and ripping them open with childlike pleasure, a rare moment of family between her and her parents.

Steve always said Christmas was a corporate brainchild and refused to acknowledge it in any way. Before Steve, when it was just her and her mother, Lee remembered picking out a small tree every year from a lot up the street and rolling it back in her Radio Flyer wagon. She remembered decorating it with her mom's jewelry. On Christmas morning she would give her mother a drawing and her mother would give her a single gift, a doll or a book or a sweater. When she was twelve, a month before her mom met Steve and the last year they celebrated Christmas, her mother gave her a pair of gold earrings and pierced Lee's ears herself, using a cork and a needle. They went to a movie that day, and Lee remembered fiddling with the hoops in her lobes the whole time, and how sweet that pain had been.

Annie came down later, a plate of leftover turkey and stuffing and gravy and cranberries in one hand, a little wrapped box in the other. And under her arm was a laptop. She handed this to Lee first. "My parents gave me a new MacBook for Christmas, so I thought you could have my old one," she said. "But that's not the real present. Here." She handed Lee the box. "Open it."

Lee took the box, feeling a rush of shame for taking so much from this girl and giving nothing back. It was just like with Tomi— Lee had no idea what Annie got back from all the care she had lavished on her.

"Go on, open it. If there's one thing you should know about me, it's that I hate waiting."

Lee unwrapped the box carefully, feeling herself reddening under the girl's gaze. Under the wrapping was an old cardboard box. Lee opened it.

"He doesn't look like much, but he was my friend all through my childhood. You can see Tedward's been through a lot."

Lee pulled out an old teddy bear, as flat as a deflated balloon, with one eye missing and a hole at the pad of his foot.

"He helped me through a lot of lonely times," Annie said. "I thought he could do the same for you, down here, when I'm not here to keep you company."

"I feel bad," Lee said. "I don't have anything for you."

Annie looked stricken. "What? Give him back. Go on. I give something to you, you give something to me. That's the deal."

Lee thought for a moment, then removed the leather cord from around her neck. She handed Annie the little blue glass bottle.

Annie sat frozen, refusing to take it. "I was only kidding. I can't take that. It looks . . ."

"Worthless?"

"It looks like it means something."

Lee leaned forward and put it over Annie's head.

Annie looked down at it, took it in one hand, and shook it lightly next to one ear. She peered closely at it. "What's inside?"

Lee shrugged. "Domesticated chance."

"What?"

"Nothing. Just a die."

FIFTEEN

BEFORE Annie left Lee to go to church with her parents, she pulled the little bottle out from under her shirt and made Lee hold it in her hand and swear on it not to go anywhere. "Now that you're good enough to get around, I don't want you running away again."

Lee didn't point out that the last time she'd run off was because Annie had brought her bat-wielding father in tow. She had no thought of leaving, though. The hospital no longer felt like a place to go. It had no resources, no Internet, no food. It was nice having Annie around, and the fact that Annie now wore the little blue bottle around her neck made her feel good.

Lee opened the laptop and bounced around online for a while, scrolling through news of a world gone by, events and people she didn't recognize. How quickly the world changed when you looked away. She searched back through the *Philadelphia Inquirer* until she found articles about Derrick's murder. The first was brief, with scant details, and didn't name him, only said that he had "suffered a gunshot wound to his head," his body was discovered by a neighbor, and he was pronounced dead at the scene. A later article named him—Derrick James, a "27-year-old barista and aspiring DJ." Something about the murder—the gruesomeness of the crime scene, or the fact that he was a young white male with a shadowy life online—gave the story legs, and Lee clicked around the brief media flurry that had quickly devolved into speculation about drug running and occult circles. No mention of his old housemates. Lee wondered when Tomi's body would be discovered and what would happen then.

She logged in to an urbex site that Tomi had introduced her to, just to escape the rabbit hole of these thoughts. These were people she had never met in person, with online names like JinxMagnet and Volume-Control. She didn't even know what they looked like, but she knew their personalities, or at least the online versions of their personalities. She just lurked, not wanting to engage with anyone, in particular wanting to avoid the question of Tomi, whose disappearance from the boards other members were chatting about. She closed the browser.

Her eyes were tired, but she opened a new browser window anyway and, before she could think better of it, typed "Tomas Cernak" into the search window. Only a few links came up. She lingered on one photo for a long time, Tomi posing in front of one of his paintings at some local gallery show. She felt the tears well and tried to knuckle them back into her eyes. Whatever she had hoped to gain from this, it was only making her feel worse.

She took out his key ring, which she'd found in her bag and was the only thing of his she owned, and helplessly rubbed the attached rabbit's foot between her fingers. It came apart in her hand, and she remembered what was inside. When she inserted the USB stick into the laptop, a folder appeared on the desktop, labeled simply +/−. Inside were more folders. She opened the one labeled Subnet, clicked on the icon, and typed his password.

The Gatekeeper's troll avatar came up, and Lee typed subnet access, just as she'd seen Tomi do so many times. The box replied back:

Ready for vid-ver.

Lee hesitated, then clicked on the laptop's webcam.

"Hermes! I guess you—" The voice stopped. "I remember you," the voice called Papoola said finally.

Lee felt naked. She resisted the urge to pull her hoodie up.

"Is Hermes with you? Nobody's seen or heard from him in a while."

"Tom—Hermes is not here."

"So he's not with you?"

"No."

"He's authorized you to use his account, so I'll give you access. But he hasn't logged on in some time, and there is a lot of speculation as to his whereabouts. Can you tell me where he is?"

"He's fine."

"Okay. Well, the forums haven't been the same without him, and we'd all like him back. Will you pass that on to him?"

"Okay."

"Are you all right?"

Lee wiped her face with her sleeve. "I'm fine."

"Are you sure?"

Lee stared straight at the webcam. "May I please have access?"

"Of course."

There was no discernible sound, but Lee could tell she was alone again. She brought up the Subnet Google and typed "Tomas Cernak" into the browser window. It didn't bring up much more than the regular Internet search had. She was about to shut it down but then typed in "H3rm3s." She didn't know what she had expected, but it wasn't this: hundreds upon hundreds of hits, Tomi's screen name the subject of discussions, the generator of discussions, and often the last word. She went through the threads one after another, finding his voice again, no longer in her head but archived in these pages, and it was a different voice than the one she'd known. It was confident, knowledgeable without being showy, with none of the anxious insistence that characterized so much of the Tomi she knew. Lee spent nearly three hours burrowing down into the hive of these threads, linking to other threads, circling back. She found a thread in which he mentioned the penitentiary creep and was reading it when a small chat window opened. Below it was a name she recognized from the forums, alongside an avatar of a fractal. Then someone on the other side of the Subnet messaged her.

[Teutonik23]: Hello!

Lee stared at the screen for a long time, unsure what to do.

[Teutonik23]: Are you there?

She typed: Yes?

[Teutonik23]: We heard that H3rm3s's girlfriend was on the Subnet. We wanted to meet her.

Then another user popped on.

[DreamClown]: Will you settle a bet for us?

Lee typed: Who are you?

[Teutonik23]: The bet is about H3rm3s. He is legendary for being ungirlfriendable. So some of us think that your existence is a ruse.

Lee felt her face flush.

Fuck off.

[DreamClown]: You see? I told you. H3rm3s wouldn't know what to do with a girl if she sat naked on his lap.

You knew him? she typed, then changed "knew" to "know" before hitting Return.

[Teutonik23]: Of course we know him. He has not mentioned me?

No.

[Teutonik23]: I'm hurt. He has mentioned you. You are all he talks about anymore. He's pined for you for so long he has become boring.

[DreamClown]: Boringboringboring.

What did he tell you about me?

[Teutonik23]: He told us you have eyes like Anna Karina. The philistine beside me here will have to Google that.

[DreamClown]: He told us he had sex with you. My German friend here will have to Google *that*.

[Teutonik23]: What he did not tell us was your name.

[DreamClown]: If we knew your name, we could tell you where you were born, what your favorite food is, and what the doctor found from your last pap smear. We could tell you the porn your father surfs while you and your mother are sleeping.

[Teutonik23]: He told us you were a stray cat. He wants to rescue you.

Lee bristled at that.

I'm not giving you my name.

[DreamClown]: Can we get back to the wager? There's bitcoin on the line. Just tell us if he really landed you.

Lee didn't answer.

[Teutonik23]: He was famously a virgin before you, you know.

[DreamClown]: I think that he still is.

You are really betting on this?

Lee felt her anger rise.

[Teutonik23]: Do not take it personally. For what it is worth, I believe him.

I don't care what either of you believes.

[DreamClown]: I told you he was making her up.

I'm right here. I'm typing this to you.

[DreamClown]: Then prove it to us.

How?

[DreamClown]: Turn on your webcam. Show us your face.

What will that prove?

[DreamClown]: Show us your face and tell us that you are H3rm3s's girlfriend and we will believe him and I will apologize to him on my knees.

Lee didn't see why she had to prove a thing to these idiots. But something about their thinking that Tomi was incapable of having a girlfriend irked her.

Show me yours first.

[DreamClown]: Show me yours and I'll show you mine?

There was a watery bloop, and the chat boxes turned to video screens. In one was a man, in his forties maybe, balding on top but with long blond dreadlocks. She counted four cats in the room, one of which was attached to his lap like a furry gray fungus. Behind his wire-rimmed glasses were the eyes of someone who had taken a good deal of psychedelic drugs in his lifetime. DreamClown, in the other box, couldn't have been more than sixteen, with black, heavy-framed glasses. A Deadmau5 poster with glowing green eyes loomed behind him, and above that was a Toronto Maple Leafs banner. He sucked from a Big Gulp.

"Hello," said Teutonik23. His thick German accent was unmodulated.

"Now you," DreamClown said.

Lee sucked in her breath, clicked on the webcam icon, and stared directly into the lens. Her own image came up in a box on the screen.

It had been a while since she'd looked in a mirror. All her baby fat was gone, and her cheeks were sunken. Her whole face, as pale as bone, had taken on a sculpted gauntness, all but her mouth, which seemed fuller with so much of the flesh around it taken away. Her eyes looked caved in and dark around the edges, though she had no makeup on, and her hair, grown out but patchy in spots, was so black against the white of her face that it looked dyed.

Lee heard DreamClown clear his throat. "Okay, so you're real. But no way you're Hermes's girlfriend."

"What were you expecting?" Lee said.

"Something more . . ." Teutonik23 pushed his face toward the monitor and squinted. He shook his head and gave up.

"Poodle-haired? Meaty? Like a booth worker at a Ren Faire?" DreamClown chimed in. In his striped T-shirt and with his mossy red hair, he looked like any anonymous boy from the back of her high school cafeteria. He would have sat there every day with a few friends, and maybe he would have shyly approached her one day to ask her to steal him a necklace he could give to another girl.

"So what now?" Lee said.

"Now?" Teutonik23 adjusted something on his screen, and Lee caught a brief glimpse of a terrarium in the background.

Lee heard a door shut, then the sound of Annie's footsteps coming down the stairs.

"Now you show us your tits," said DreamClown.

Lee brought both hands up to the camera and gave each guy a middle finger. She closed the laptop just as Annie opened the door and popped her head in.

"Hey," she said, a little out of breath. "Who were you talking to?"

Lee stared at a point past Annie's head. "Who would I be talking to?" she snapped. Then, "I'm sorry. Sometimes I talk to myself."

"I guess you must be getting pretty stir-crazy in here, huh?"

"I've hardly left this room in weeks. I feel like I'm made of wood."

Annie smiled, but there was pity in it, and Lee turned away.

"I need to sleep," Lee said.

"But that's all you do," Annie said.

All this talk about Tomi had left Lee agitated. The frustration of weeks being cooped up inside a box came flooding through her. "It's all I *can* do. You're just mad because your little playdoll has a mind of its own and doesn't want to amuse you right now."

Lee could see how hurt Annie was, but then Annie's eyes narrowed. "I fucking saved you. Without me you'd be dead. Literally dead. You wouldn't have even gotten Christmas," she added, ridiculously. "If it was me, I'd be fucking grateful."

She was right, and Lee felt terrible, but no words came. Lee turned away, then heard the door click. Annie was gone. She went to sleep holding Annie's bear, wishing she had found the right words.

But when Annie returned the next day after school, she was excited, all the unpleasantness of the day before erased by whatever it was she had buzzing around in her head. She scooted into the little room and shut the door. "I got you, ladyfriend."

"You got me?"

"I'm taking you out."

"Where?"

"Dancing."

When Annie pulled and unfolded the thick card stock from her back pocket, Lee felt a swell of nausea wash through her.

Annie scrunched her face up. "Are you all right?"

The text on the flier read "L.CUN.E FUTUR." above a turn-of-the-century-looking lithograph of a suited man in a bowler hat holding on to a rope dangling from a streamlined silver Zeppelin. The Zeppelin had a dozen old-fashioned phonograph horns erupting from its tail, and a group of dandyish revelers in the gondola were looking down and laughing at the man with the rope. A little "S.A." was imprinted on the bottom corner. "Where did you get this?"

"I was at the Java Hut with Oona. This weird dude gave them to us. It's a New Year's rave. It's like the universe is telling us to go out and have a good time."

"You can't go to that."

"What do you mean? I'm taking you. *We're* going to it. And Oona will be there—you'll get to meet each other."

"No."

"Seriously, don't worry. I've got it all planned out. I'm going to tell my parents—"

"Listen to me. You can't—"

Annie snatched the flier back. "So you're my mom all of a sudden? I thought we could have some fun. You said yourself you're going crazy in here."

"We'll go someplace else. I'll take you on a creep. There's an abandoned foundry on the south side that used to make ship's propellers."

"I don't want to go to any of your nasty old factories or hospitals or sewage plants or whatever. I don't want to do any of that homeless shit. I want to go someplace where there are people our age. People like us, not like the stuck-up kids from my school. You owe me *something,* Lee. This, at least. The only way I could get Oona to agree to go was if she could meet you. I can't go alone."

"You told her about me? Who else have you told about me?"

"What does it matter?"

Lee didn't like that at all, but knew she'd better drop it. "Well, I won't go, and if you won't go alone, then I guess it's settled."

"Fine," she said. But it wasn't settled at all, Lee could tell.

"Annie, you have to trust me on this." Lee saw she was squeezing Annie's shoulders and released her grip. She closed her eyes and took several deep breaths. "Just don't go to that thing," she said.

"Then tell me why not."

Lee debated whether to tell her anything, but how could she and not tell her everything? And that just wasn't possible. "I've been to it," she said finally. "All I can say is, it's not what it seems."

"What is it?"

Lee had no idea how to explain it or even where to begin. "It's like . . . a cult thing or something. Gross old men hitting on young kids."

"Eew, really?"

"Really. You have to tell Oona, too."

"Okay. Fine."

"Look me in the eyes and promise me."

Annie leaned forward and narrowed her eyes. "I promise, whatever. It sounds really gross."

"We'll do something else. I promise."

"I know. And Lee?"

"Yeah."

"I'm sorry about what I said about your homeless shit."

Lee just laughed. The girl had no idea.

SIXTEEN

LEE recounted the events of Tomi's death along a tortuous path full of gaps she had to double back on to fill in. Trying to explain the S.A. and who they were made it all sound so fucking crazy, but she told it anyway. It took her a long time to get to the moment of his death, though that feeling of Tomi's weight changing in her arms kept rising up inside her. No matter how many routes she used to get there, the story would end the same way. Lee knew she shouldn't be telling a couple of strangers on the Internet; she didn't know if she could trust them. But they had proven they were friends of Tomi's, and she wanted them to know.

When she was finished, neither Teutonik nor DreamClown said anything for a while. Neither of them would even look at her.

"We will have a memorial," Teutonik said finally. "Over the Subnet. I'll take care of it."

Lee thought of Tomi's body, abandoned in an empty aquarium. "Does anyone know anything about his family?" she asked. Tomi had told her a million and one stories about his family, but as Lee tried to bring up the details, the only thing she could bring back was the image of him as a teenager in a library, one eye on a book, the other on a blond, statuesque librarian. "I think they are in the Czech Republic."

Teutonik was still staring at his keyboard. "None of us talk about our families much. It is the nature of online anonymity. Hermes used to talk about you, but that was an anomaly."

"Why were they after you?" asked DreamClown.

"They wanted something I had. We were trying to give it back. And then that man shot him." She thought about what it would feel like to plunge a knife into the Undertaker. To watch the light go out of his eyes. She wanted to burn the S.A. and everything they'd worked for to the ground.

"What were they after?" said DreamClown.

"An artwork." She hadn't meant to bring it up, but there was no way of explaining Tomi's death without it. She'd destroyed it, but still it wouldn't go away.

"Like a painting?"

"Not a painting. A thing. An object."

"What did they want with it? Was it worth a lot of money?"

"It was a hundred years old. Maybe it was worth money," Lee said. "But it didn't look like anything." It felt like something, though. Lee remembered when she first picked it up, how she thought maybe she understood aura for the first time. "I just wanted it gone. The thing was cursed. It's fucked my life since the moment I took it."

"So they have it now?" DreamClown asked.

"No. I smashed it to pieces." Something bit into her hand, and Lee looked down to see she was crushing a Coke can, hard enough to break the skin.

"That's too bad."

"Why? What do you care?"

"You said you want to get back at them," DreamClown said. "It'll be easier if you still have something they want."

"Most of it is at the bottom of the Delaware," she said. "But there was a piece inside."

Lee rifled around the bottom of the bag until she found it: a little brown ball not more than an inch across, made from some hardened resinlike material. She laid it in the palm of her hand and held it up in front of the monitor.

"It looks like a turd," said DreamClown. "Are you sure it's not a petrified dog turd? Put some light on it."

Lee angled the light onto it and watched Teutonik lean forward into his monitor, his eyes growing big on the screen. "Could you hold it closer, between your fingers?"

Lee did as she was told, waiting for the webcam to focus, then rolling it a bit between her thumb and forefinger.

"Do you know what that looks like?" Teutonik said, leaning back in his chair again.

"I still think it's a dog turd," DreamClown said.

"It looks almost like a Calabi-Yau space."

Lee held the thing up to the light, examined it again with this new name attached. She'd never looked at it very closely before. It wasn't a perfect sphere; it was lumpier than that, with a ridged surface full of pockets and folds. It was as though a flat ribbon had been folded again and again until it was a ball of planes and ridges with small cavities running through. She rolled it in her palm. "Is that something?"

"Oh, yes."

DreamClown sucked on his Big Gulp, unimpressed. "Enlighten us."

"A Calabi-Yau space is a physical representation of multidimensionality."

"Fuck you." DreamClown opened his drink and tipped back an ice cube, which he crunched as he talked. "English, you ancient German bastard."

"If you want to represent a single dimension, you do so with a single dot on a piece of paper. Two dimensions can be represented by the piece of paper itself, pretending for a moment that the paper is of infinite thinness. Three dimensions might be represented by folding the paper into an origami cube. The fourth dimension is time, and so four dimensions might be represented by throwing the cube through the air to show the passing of time. But what if you want to represent more than four dimensions?"

"I didn't know there *were* more than four," Lee said.

"String theory proposes that the universe exists in eleven."

"I don't even know how to process that," Lee said.

"Exactly. Which is where a Calabi-Yau space comes in."

Typing, DreamClown giggled to himself. "So this one goes to eleven?"

"Spare us your vacuous pop-cultural references, you homunculus. You do not see many three-dimensional representations of a Calabi-Yau space as small as this one. The task must have been painstaking. Carving out all those folded dimensions by hand, I can't imagine. Usually they are larger, or two-dimensional renderings of a computer program." Teutonik typed something into his keyboard and another window popped up on Lee's screen, showing an image of something that looked a lot like the little object she held in her hand.

"When did you say this piece was made?" Teutonik said.

"Nineteen sixteen," Lee said. "Duchamp supposedly never knew what was inside it. He had a friend put something in it and seal it up."

"Well, it can't be a Calabi-Yau, then. The Calabi-Yau space was not even conceived of until many decades later." Teutonik picked the cat up off his lap and set it on the floor. "It is interesting, though, that this little object was wrapped in a ball of string . . ."

"Why?"

"Well, string theory would be the obvious reference. Have you heard of the unified field theory?"

Lee remembered what Tomi had told her. "The attempt to solve the contradiction between the laws of the macro-universe and the laws of the subatomic universe."

Teutonik looked impressed and Lee tried not to let her pride show.

"String theory is the closest we've come to solving it. But string theory wasn't even conceived of for decades after this work of Duchamp's."

Lee thought of *Three Standard Stoppages,* its three parallel strings. Was it all coincidence? Her heart quickened. She was close to figuring something out, she knew it. She wished Tomi was here.

DreamClown still seemed unimpressed. "For old conspiracy-theorist farts like you, the world is nothing but dots waiting to be connected."

"So what does it do?" Lee said.

"What do?" Teutonik said. "A Calabi-Yau space doesn't *do* anything. It *represents*."

"Then why do these people want this thing so badly?" Lee said.

"That would be the question. But if this were in some way related to string theory, it could be huge."

"Huge how?" she asked.

"Nobody knows, not really. String theory posits that all matter, at the most fundamental subatomic level, is made up of strings. These strings are smaller than the smallest known particles, and they all vibrate at different, specific frequencies. The frequency of their vibration determines the behavior of the particles that form mass. So in a sense, these frequencies determine the nature of reality itself. If one were able to prove the fundamental principles behind string theory, then that means one could conceivably manipulate those principles. To play those strings, as it were. It could usher in a new era of scientific breakthrough. Quantum computing, leaps in artificial intelligence that would be positively hyperevolutionary."

"Technological singularity," she said.

"Yes! Exactly."

"To what end?"

Teutonik frowned. "It's all hypothetical. The possibilities are not only endless but beyond our current comprehension. But whoever discovered it would certainly stand to gain billions."

Lee remembered the bookshelf in the room beneath the museum. The books on neural mapping. "With that kind of computing power, could a person map a human brain?"

"Hypothetically, yes. You could copy it as you would information on a computer hard drive."

Gold and immortality, she thought. Modern alchemy. Is that what all this was about—piles of money and an eternal life in which to play with it?

"Some say that solving it could allow us to alter space-time itself."

"Don't listen to Teutonik," said DreamClown. "Too much LSD has expanded his poor brain past the point of usefulness. We need to remember what we are doing here. You want to get back at these people or what?"

"Why don't *you* do something useful, homunculus?"

DreamClown stopped typing and looked at the monitor. "While you've been connecting imaginary dots and lecturing us on abstractions, I *have* been doing something useful. You know what I just acquired?" He put a diagram up on the screen that looked like something out of a science fiction film. "These are the blueprints of the Atlas missile silo purchased in 2004. You want to get back at these people? Here's your way in."

Teutonik removed his glasses and wiped the lenses with his shirt. Without the glasses he had the small moist eyes of a forest animal. "I've done some research of my own."

"Do tell," DreamClown said.

"Something was discovered beneath the Philadelphia Museum of Art. In a secret room. Some say in the 1980s, some say the '90s, some say much earlier."

Lee thought back to the machine she'd glimpsed through the peepholes of that door. "What was it?"

Teutonik was staring at another screen. He shook his head. "Nobody seems to know. But the Société Anonyme appears to have been founded on that discovery."

Lee tried to remember what she'd seen in that room. A large metal thing glinting from the shadows. It had seemed to be floating in the air.

"Take this all with salt," Teutonik said. "The Darknet is an ocean of information, but it is populated by ships of conspiracy theorists and hoaxsters and archipelagoes of rumor and misinformation. Many of us want nothing more than to be the originators of modern mythologies, and thus many of us value the beautiful myth over the mundane truth. Sometimes it can be difficult to tell the island from the sea."

"Oceans and islands. Teutonik could list for you all the drugs he's ingested over the years, but it would take the rest of the day."

"I've seen it," Lee blurted.

"What?"

She told them about the room.

"What was in there?" asked DreamClown.

Lee shook her head. "I don't know. It was dark. I only saw it for a second."

"Close your eyes," Teutonik said. "Try to remember details."

She tried again. This time a long, spindly figure came into focus, armored in dark metal, and above it a hovering cumulous form. Beyond that it was all shadows and her fear of being discovered. "I just didn't get a good look."

It was dark when she awoke, not remembering having fallen asleep. Her head was marshy with sleep, and for a moment she wondered where she was. Then she saw Annie's bear, facedown on the floor. She picked it up and held it as she opened the computer. The Subnet browser was still up, as were the video screens, empty now. Artifacts left behind from a conversation that seemed like a dream. She looked at the time: 10:41 p.m. Had she really slept that long? Annie hadn't come down to bring her dinner, something she always did after her parents had turned in, which they usually did by ten. She'd bring down leftovers and Lee would eat and they would talk and sometimes Annie would fall asleep against her. She had never missed a night.

Lee crept out from her space and stood up, looking up the basement stairs. She hadn't been up in the main house since she first returned to the Orbisons' home . . . how long ago was it? Lee placed a foot on the bottom step, then another, testing each for creaks. She took her time, clumsily at first, making more noise than she should, but before long found herself at the top of the stairs. She opened the door into the kitchen. Yellow light from across the street cast over the white linoleum table. Lee took a chicken leg from the fridge, eating as she moved into the foyer. She paused again at the bottom of the stairs, listening for any signs of waking life. Just the silent buzz of a house asleep.

Moving up the stairs, then down the hall, Lee was surprised at how naturally her stealth came back to her. Now she wasn't making a sound. She stood at the Orbisons' door, looking in on the two inert mounds on the bed. She moved down the hall.

Annie's bed was empty. Lee closed the door and turned on the light. She opened Annie's laptop and looked at the date: December 31, New Year's Eve. Lee searched around for the flier, knowing she wouldn't find it. She walked across the hall to the bathroom and looked out the window into the driveway. The car was gone.

They were both there the minute she logged back on. "She's gone," Lee said, pushing down the panic. "I think she went to the Silo."

"Who?" DreamClown said.

"If they so much as touch her . . ."

"Who went there?"

"Annie. My friend. She had a ticket. I told her not to go, but she went. I have to go get her."

Teutonik frowned. "I don't think that is a good idea. They are dangerous people. We aren't ready yet."

"I know how fucking dangerous they are. Are you going to help me or not?"

Teutonik and DreamClown looked at each other through their monitors.

"You promised you would."

"We did more research," Teutonik said finally. "They are very shadowy. Everything we have is only rumor."

"Tell me."

"They are . . . behavioral scientists," DreamClown said.

"That is a generous term," Teutonik said. "They run experiments on humans."

Lee thought about Annie, and her panic began pushing itself back up. "What kind of experiments?"

"Exploring the limits of human consciousness," said DreamClown.

Teutonik scoffed. "Behavioral control is more accurate."

"I'm not defending them. I'm just going by what we were able to dig up."

Teutonik pulled on his beard. "You are too young, but my country has a history of such experiments. Your country too—the CIA in the 1960s. The subject pools are the same throughout: throwaways and prisoners and castoffs, people who won't be missed."

"Who are they?" Lee asked. "They must have names."

"Just pseudonyms," DreamClown said.

"I know all this already," Lee said. "Anything on a man called the Undertaker? Or the Priest?"

Teutonik looked to his notes and shook his head.

"Can you help me at all? Give me something I can use?"

"You're intent on going to get your friend?" DreamClown said.

Lee felt something bristle inside. "Yes."

"We can get you things."

"You're in Philly?"

"Of course not. But the Subnet has members everywhere. People who can be relied on to deliver things. Can you get to the Central Library?"

"Sure. But it's closed, isn't it?"

DreamClown just smirked.

"We don't know your name," Teutonik said.

"I'm not giving you that."

"What do we call you, then?"

She thought for a moment. "Bride," she said.

Lee pulled out a bicycle from the basement that looked like it hadn't been used in years, checked the tires, and eased it up the stairs to the kitchen. She pulled on a pair of Annie's gloves, zipped up her hoodie, and stuffed her right pant leg into her sock. The cold air outside bit at her cheeks and fingertips, and Lee rode as fast as she could, her blood warming quickly. But in just a few minutes she felt herself getting winded. After four weeks of sickness and several more weeks recovering in a room the size of a shipping crate, she had very little in her. She knew how to get to the Silo, and she knew how far it was, and she also knew there was simply no way. Lee turned around.

The lights were off when she pulled up, panting and exhausted after just fifteen minutes pedaling through the slushy Philadelphia streets. She walked the bike back behind the house and leaned it against the wall, then crept up to the back door and listened. She heard only the faint click of a furnace igniting. Lee climbed in the same way she had a few months back, through Steve's meditation room, the lingering smell of incense making her gag a little. She sat on a pillow to catch her breath and settle herself for what she had to do next. But the room made her anxious and angry, and she got up quickly and paced before going to the door.

A swath of light washed in through the kitchen window at the end of the hall, and Lee could see her mother and Steve's closed bedroom door. She edged her toe onto the hardwood, listening for a crack. She didn't have a lot of time, and so she moved forward faster than she would have liked, each creak of the floorboards sounding like cymbals in a marching band. By the time she'd edged as far as the bedroom, she was sweating. Steve was a reptile who hated the cold, and so he kept the heat to a precise eighty-one, day and night. The house was a fucking terrarium.

Steve was a man of habit and ritual—he took a shit at seven every morning, a bath at six every evening, and a cup of herbal tea at eleven every night—and Lee tried to remember where he put his keys when he came home. She closed her eyes and envisioned him opening the front door, stepping into the house, and putting his jacket in the closet. But that part of her life seemed distant and foggy now, and she could see little past his hanging his coat. In the living room she checked the table by the door, the bowl on the coffee table, Steve's jacket in the closet. No keys, but she did find his wallet there and took the fifty-six dollars he had and then his credit cards because why not? She hoped she wouldn't have to go into the bedroom.

She found the keys on a wall hook in the kitchen. Lee paused by two pictures magnetted to the fridge—one of her as a child, tiny as a foal and swallowed up in a too-big sweater, standing in a playground and staring, unsmiling, at the camera as kids ran amok behind her. The other was a picture Steve had taken at her mother's behest, Lee (at thirteen) and her mother standing on a bridge near Niagara Falls. It was a weekend trip not long after her mother had begun dating Steve, and Lee could see the hostility toward Steve already in her own eyes. She reached up to pull the photos off—she didn't like the thought of any part of herself, even a picture, being in this house. But her mother had put them up since Lee had left. Lee's hand fell back to her side. She couldn't bring herself to take them down.

The kitchen door was dead-bolted. Lee was flipping through the keys, trying to find the one for the door, when she felt the presence of someone behind her.

"Lee? Is that really you? What are you doing?"

Steve's voice was still sloughing off the sleep, and Lee thought if she could just get the key in before he realized what was happening, she might be okay. She fumbled the ring in her hands and put the wrong key to the lock. She was trying a second key when she felt the pressure of his hand on her shoulder.

"Relax," he said. "It's okay. Come into the living room. I'll wake your mom. We've been worried sick."

Lee felt herself shrink under his touch, all her will draining. He stood there in his tight red underwear, the only other thing touching his skin the bead necklace he claimed was given to him personally by the Dalai Lama. He seemed to have aged in the past months; his eyes were creased and tired. He had grown his hair out, as though to compensate. She let him lead her to the living room. He sat her down on the couch, then plopped down beside her, leaving no room between them.

"The police were here. After your escape. They put your mom through no end of hell."

Lee stared at a brown stain on the carpet, trying to remember if it had been there before.

"Guess it was pretty bad in there. For you to have to leave like that. You want to talk about it?"

Lee thought about the JDC, how far away it seemed now. She couldn't stand Steve's eyes on her own, and she shifted her gaze to a huge new flat-screen TV mounted on the wall above the fireplace. Wires beneath ran to some sort of video game console. Her college tuition.

"You don't have to go back. We'll fight it. We just want you home." He put a hand on her knee and turned her chin to face him. "You understand?"

Lee nodded. She hated how frozen she felt, how helpless to do or even say anything.

Steve squeezed her knee and got up. "I'm going to wake your mom. We'll all stay up and work this out. Okay?"

Lee nodded.

"You want some coffee? It's going to be a long night."

Lee shook her head.

"Okay, then."

He left the room and Lee sat in the dark, still living room, unable to move. She stared at all the things she'd left behind—the chair she liked to sit and read in by the fireplace, the little jade elephant on the mantel she used to rub between her thumb and forefinger, her mom's collection of antique perfume bottles in the case by the window. They were as cheesy as hell, but at least Lee had something to give her mom every year for her birthday. She picked up an atomizer and put it to her nose, but there was nothing left to smell.

When she looked up, her mom was standing in the doorway of the bedroom, clutching her nightgown around her waist, her eyes dark and tired, holding a sorrow Lee had never seen before. Her mom shut the door behind her, then came into the living room and sat on the couch. She waited until Lee sat down across from her before speaking.

"Where have you been staying?" she asked. Lee had a hard time meeting her eyes. "You think it was easy for me to let you go to that place. But it wasn't. You were out of control, Lee. We found drugs in your room. All that money . . ."

"That was my money. I was going to pay for college with that money. You had no right."

"We had every right. If the police had found it, or the rest of the drugs, you know we could have lost the house? What were you thinking, Lee?"

Lee felt something sharp bite into her palm. She looked down to see her hand squeezing the atomizer.

"We visited you. Do you know how much it hurt when you refused to even see me? Did you get my letters?"

Lee put the little bottle on the coffee table and stood. "I've got to go. It's good to see you, Mom. It really is."

Her mom got up, too. "Where will you go?"

"I'll be fine. Are you going to tell the police I was here?"

Her mom came around to be beside her. Lee could tell she wanted to hug her. "Of course not. What about those people?"

Lee stiffened. "What people?"

"A young woman contacted us after your escape. She told us they'd taken you in. She wanted me to know you were safe, or that you had been safe, living with them, but that something had happened and that you'd been separated from them. They were looking for you."

"What did you tell them?"

"What could I tell her? I thought maybe Edie would know."

Lee thought about that MISSING sign. "You told them about Edie?"

"Steve did. He talked to them more than I did. Who are they? They said they were a home for youth who had lost their way. It sounded so much better than the detention center."

"What's Steve doing now?"

"He went back to bed."

This didn't seem right. Steve never took himself out of the picture like that. Lee went to the door but stopped short of opening it. Steve was whispering, she couldn't make out his words.

She walked into the kitchen and picked up the phone. Steve's voice: ". . . said I would, didn't I? You told me she'll be safe, I just want to make sure."

"I assure you," a man's voice said. "We want what's best for her, too. Prison is not that. She needs family, and since you and your wife are, unfortunately, not an option . . ."

Lee hung up. As she made her way across the living room, she could feel her mother reaching for her but shrugged her off as she opened the front door and then slammed it behind her. The newish Prius sat in the driveway covered in a dusting of snow. Lee pushed the button on the key, and the car beeped and winked its lights at her. She got in and moved the seat up. It had been a while since she'd driven a car; in fact, she'd taken driver's ed but never the driving test itself, so she had no license. She stuck the keys in the ignition and twisted, feeling the car hum to life. Something beeped and a light shone on the dash. Lee tried to remember what to do next. It was too dark to see, and in trying to turn on the headlights, she ran the wipers instead, which cleared the snow from the windshield and revealed Steve, stomping out in his underwear, barefoot, his eyes lit with panic. Lee could see her mother silhouetted in the doorway behind him.

Lee grabbed for the shifter, but Steve was already at her door, pulling it open and reaching in. Lee pulled against him, but he was too strong. He had a hand on her arm and was yanking her from the car when Lee reached out with her other hand, for anything, found an ice scraper, and shoved it as hard as she could at his face. It only glanced his cheek, but hard enough to cut, which shocked him into letting go. He dropped to his ass on the cold concrete. Lee slammed the door shut. Steve was on his feet again, shambling toward the car, when Lee punched the gas. The car squealed in place until she remembered to put it in drive; the car lurched forward, smashing Steve onto the hood, his pale skin squashed against the windshield. As he flipped around and scratched at the glass for some sort of purchase, Lee found reverse and slammed out of the driveway, throwing Steve to the pavement.

Lee screeched out of there, feeling the sweet rush of adrenaline turn her panic into a wave she could ride. She watched in the rearview as her mother ran from the house and stooped over Steve's pale form. He was sitting up, holding his elbow and grimacing as he watched her go.

· BOOK VII ·

The Bachelor Machine

SEVENTEEN

THE library had been closed for hours, but picking the lock of the back entrance proved little problem. Inside it was silent and dark. Lee found a spot at one of the computers out of view from the windows, turned it on, and logged in to her Gmail account. There was one e-mail, sent a half hour before, by DreamClown. It contained only a single Dewey Decimal number. When she went to the stacks and got close to the number, her eyes running down the line of artists' monographs—Dalí to Degas to Delacroix—it became quickly obvious that someone was having his fun. There among the volumes on Duchamp, about three shelves of them, Lee found the number she was looking for. She looked both ways down the empty aisle, and pulled the book out. Behind it, wrapped in brown paper, was a package the size of a shoebox. It was heavier than she had expected.

Beneath the wrapping was an old child's lunch box, the Super Friends fighting crime across each side. Lee sat back against the bookshelf and held the box in her lap. Someone had put a sticker with the Subnet logo on it. Inside the lunch box was a small black revolver, five twenty-dollar bills, a Maglite, and a cell phone.

She popped the cylinder, pulled one bullet out, and rolled it between her fingers. She fumbled it back in, then stuffed the gun into her bag. She turned on the cell phone. It was brand-new, with a single contact added: DC. The number had a 416 area code. She checked the time: 1:39 a.m., January 1.

There were more cars parked around the site than the last time she was here. A few kids clustered around an old pickup, drinking and shifting to a low heavy bass from the truck's speakers. Lee pulled Steve's car in behind a beat-up minivan. She saw the Orbisons' Audi right away; it stood out from the old beaters that populated most of the lot.

Lee hunched between the cars, avoiding the kids as well as the closed front gate. She cut into the pine woods and circled around to the back, trying to skirt the sight lines of the cameras along the wall's perimeter. At the rear corner a tree had blown down onto the wall, providing a ladder right up and over. Every now and then you get a lucky break, she thought. Sometimes you even get a streak of them. Lee jumped up and shimmied to the top of the wall easily, then dropped down.

The area in the back had been neglected. Dried brambles grabbed at her hoodie and crunched underfoot. The only spaces clear of weeds or debris were two large concrete slabs set flush with the ground, a tight steel-lipped seam running down the center. The roof was closed tonight, but she could still feel the beat of techno music throbbing up from below. Passing a rotting utility shed, she nearly tripped over an open air vent. The vent had no grate, and had she fallen in, she could only imagine how far she might have dropped.

Using the monstrous clown's head for cover against the gate guard, Lee made her way around to a place she could watch him from. He sat slumped on his stool, reading a book. Lee waited, completely still, squatting in the shadows.

A few minutes later the motion lights outside the gate popped on. The doorman inspected some tickets, then opened the gate. The teenagers from around the pickup came flopping in, one of them offering the doorman a beer, which he slid into his jacket pocket. Lee walked quickly toward the door and attached herself to the group just as they went into the stairwell. As she descended, the smoke got denser and the music louder. She came to the green-lit tunnel at the bottom in time to see the kids disappear into the costume room. Lee stepped aside to let a newly costumed couple jostle past on their way out. Their clothes were shiny and metallic, the guy in bulbous Moon Boots and a kind of neoprene leisure suit, the girl in a pearly hoop skirt and a top composed of kelplike strands of silver tinsel.

Then a man wearing an old policeman's uniform came out of the room. Lee ducked her head. He was the one who'd been heading for her when Tomi had first found her. Thinking of Tomi, knowing he would not be here to save her this time, made her splinter a little inside. She waited in the shadows for the man to pass, then slipped into the costume room. The four kids she had followed in were laughing to themselves as they rifled through a pile of clothes on the floor.

Lee had to act quickly. She shuffled through the racks, searching for something bulky enough to hide her bag. She was halfway into a World War I Russian soldier's uniform when she saw what the others were wearing: tight-fitting rubber exoskeletons and loops of opalesque plastic, crinkly silver Mylar bodices and hazmat-sized coveralls. Lee remembered the flier Annie had shown her, with its nod to the future. The section beside her was all clothes made from plastics and acetates, stiff-ribbed corsets and Mylar dresses and tops with architectural lines or exaggeratedly rounded forms. She held up a dress made entirely of little iridescent bubbles, replaced it, and picked up a suit constructed from a weave of black rubber. Lee kept combing through the racks until she found a hooded-cowl thing made from a series of concentric circles of thick gray wool. It was heavy and scratchy, but when she pulled it on over her clothes, it cocooned her.

She caught a glimpse of herself in a mirror; what stared back was a monk from a science fiction film. But when she pushed the cowl up, her face disappeared into shadow, and that was enough.

Inside, the big room was much as it had been before—a mass of dancing kids compressed into too small a space—except that they were all dressed as denizens of some future Lee hoped she would never have to live in. The dumb, throbbing techno was the same. She wended her way past kids decked out in latex minis and wrapped in surgical garb, wearing tubular halters made from rings of sausagelike balloons, looking for Annie. Lee kept her head down as much as she could while still scanning the faces of the kids on the dance floor, catching only glimpses between each flickering strobe. The last time she was here, she had come in search of Edie and failed. She wouldn't fail again.

Lee kept her eyes out for men in vintage suits and uniforms but saw none this time. There was no chess table on the DJ platform, and the DJ was a girl with bright red dreadlocks in a dress made from glow sticks. The air was humid with the heat and sweat of the crowd. She suddenly felt the weight of her costume, the thick wool itchy against her skin. A smiling alien boy in a silver net shirt and Mylar lederhosen handed her a bottle of water, and she drank half of it in a gulp.

She needed a better vantage. The DJ platform was on the far side, and Lee edged her way toward it, pushing through a copse of dancing kids. Though she was hidden in her wool cocoon, the costume still seemed to mark her. Most of the kids were half-naked, some covered by nothing more than strips of silver tape they had wrapped around their bodies.

Lee kept scanning the room for Annie, panic beginning to claw at her chest. A slide show was being projected onto the wall behind the DJ, and Lee paid no attention to it until the corner of her eye caught something that made her turn. Blown up to life size, it left no doubt, if there ever had been any. It wasn't the cheekbones, or the nose, or the downward turn of the mouth. It wasn't even the mole.

It was the eyes. The woman in the photo had the same eyes as Lee, the same intensity and distance in her stare.

When Lee spotted Annie, it was clear why she'd missed her: Annie had shaved her head, and her scalp was slick with sweat and sparkling with bits of silver glitter. She was lost in herself on the dance floor, her eyes closed. She wore a little plastic dress made up of alternating bands of opaque blue and milky translucence. Lee hopped down from the platform, nearly tripping in her hurry to reach the girl. When Lee grabbed her shoulder, Annie opened her eyes, and her awareness seemed to rise slowly up to the surface and buoy there.

Then she pushed her face into Lee's cowl, squealing with de-lighted recognition. "Oh! Lee! You're here!"

"What did you do?"

"What do you think? You see—I look like you now!" Before Lee could react, Annie pulled Lee's cowl down, exposing her to the room. "We're practically twins!"

Lee saw the Policeman who'd passed her in the corridor. He was walking straight for her, and Lee started to measure out routes of escape through the crowd. But the man's gaze passed right through her, and Lee pulled her cowl back up. "We have to get out of here. Come on." Lee grabbed Annie by the arm, but the girl just slipped through, her skin slick with sweat.

"Dance with me! This place, it's nothing but music! This music, it's the closest I've come to being on drugs. Is this what being on drugs is like?"

"What did you take?"

"What?"

"You're on something. What did you take?"

"I'm so confused and so happy right now."

Lee felt the music popping beneath her skin in little carbonated bursts. She grabbed Annie by both arms. "We have to go. Now. Will you follow me?"

"I'll follow you anywhere, Lee! You know that. Just one more song! Oh, I love this song—dance with me!" Annie was spinning again, and Lee could only watch her, frozen between trying to rip Annie free of her spell and following her. Just for one song.

An oozing plasma was moving through Lee in the form of the music, a percolating beat with a high female voice layered and transposed until it was no longer music and words, only vibration. All of it, everything, was only vibration.

Something was happening inside her, some alien, noncorporeal entity taking over her body from within. She thought of the baby lurking there, its tendrils fanning out through her veins, inhabiting her completely. Then she shook the image away. It wasn't the baby; the baby was just floating there, a tiny cosmonaut in her womb. This was something else, something laying siege to the cells in her body, invading her consciousness. She tasted the salt of her own perspiration running into her mouth, and swigged the rest of the water. And as the last swallow went past her lips, she understood. The water. It was in the water.

An orchestra was waking from somewhere inside her, tuning its strings and preparing to launch the first notes of a full-blown symphony. She was losing control. She couldn't afford to lose control. Fighting against it only made her start to shake uncontrollably. She felt as though her flesh was folding in on itself over and over, forming . . . Lee needed to see her eyes. It felt as though they were being inflated inside her head. A boy in reflective sunglasses was dancing by himself, and she grabbed the glasses from his head and used them to see her reflection. Were her irises bigger? She thought of the Thrumm kids she'd seen, tried to compare theirs to hers. She couldn't tell; everything was throbbing, changing colors, losing shape.

Lee closed her eyes and tried to shut it all out, but when she did, she saw the baby floating amniotically inside her. Its eyes were two big blue jellyfish. She mouthed *I'm sorry* over and over and felt herself falling, into the same pit she'd fallen into when she was looking down on Mr. Velasquez's body, realizing that it was all her fault. She was supposed to be protecting the baby inside her—what had she done? Lee pushed through the pulsing bodies, looking for anything that resembled a bathroom. She grabbed Annie to pull her along, but when she looked back, she was holding the hand of another kid, a boy with a nose ring and his hair shaved into leopard's spots. Lee let go and stumbled back through the bodies, looking for Annie, wondering if she had ever been here at all.

A young girl with one arm wrapped in thick glow bands, her hair a glossy white eel-slick helmet, took Lee under the arm and led her through the dance floor toward a thick black curtain at the other end. She had a long, exotic face, with a pointy beaklike nose and big black avian eyes; the girl radiated serenity and for a moment the ropes of sickness were loosened. The crowd parted for them as the girl led Lee toward the curtain, which she eased aside, then into a bathroom. A series of toilet stalls lined one end, and there was a bank of steel sinks as well, but the girl led Lee toward a kind of metal trough, lined with a series of spigots. The metal's patina was diaphanous, swirling.

With one cool hand on the back of her neck the girl helped Lee kneel. Her touch was calming and Lee relaxed into it, until the sickness pulled her back and she grabbed hold of the side of the trough. The girl stooped beside her, drew Lee's cowl back, and whispered into her ear. Lee vomited thick black strands that came alive in the bottom of the trough, curling and writhing like ropy flukes, the sight of which brought up more, and then more, until she was so empty it hurt. The girl stayed by her side the whole time, whispering at her to let it out, all the toxicity of her life; that she could make a clean start after this, and then everything would be okay. The girl helped her up and led Lee to one of the sinks. Lee stared at herself in the mirror. Her eyes looked normal, her pupils dilated as hell but normal. The girl turned on the water and gently pushed Lee's head toward it. She splashed it over Lee's face. It felt good, and Lee stuck her entire head under, softening under the cool water, feeling somewhat normal again. She came up and looked the girl in the eyes for the first time.

The girl's irises were almost nonexistent, two pale blue halos circling the darkest pupils Lee had ever seen. Lee thought she could see herself twinned in them, and as she leaned closer to see, the girl smiled. "How do you feel?" she asked.

Lee felt as if her flesh were liquid, but she could express nothing more than a soft moan.

"It will come and go. You just have to learn to ride it. Like breaking a horse—she will buck you at first, but once you break her, she's yours. It's a journey. Not an easy one, but one that you will see will be worth it in the end. Trust me."

Two strains of Thrumm, one of which left a field of half-sentient vegetables in its wake. Which one was working its way through her? She felt like she might throw up again, but there was nothing left inside her.

"What's your name?" the girl asked.

"Lee," she managed before she could stop herself.

The girl's stare lasted seconds, then minutes, then an eternity as Lee felt herself swimming in those dark pools. "God, you're pretty, though. And you don't even know it, do you?"

Lee looked down self-consciously.

"My name is Xenia."

Xenia. Where had she heard that name before? There was something else Lee had forgotten. But whatever it was was gone now. She had a hard time placing where she was. The smell of the room, like sweat and vomit masked by a chemical strawberry perfume, began to seep in, and she started to feel sick again. Xenia helped Lee up; she hadn't even realized she'd been on the floor. "Come on," Xenia said. "Let's get you to a good place."

She led Lee out of the bathroom and back through the curtain to the dance floor, and as the music pulsed back through her and the mass of dancers came into focus, Lee suddenly remembered: Annie. She turned, trying to figure out where she had left her. Xenia was pulling her along, and Lee tugged against her, but Xenia was surprisingly strong, and Lee felt all resistance drained from her and could only follow. But she was looking for someone. Who again?

The crowd parted for them as Xenia led Lee toward the exit. Once they passed the curtain and the volume of the music dropped, the green-lit haze of the corridor became something she could hold onto. Xenia pulled her down the corridor as the green smoke pulsed and throbbed around them.

"I can always tell someone's first time. It can be a little scary. We'll get you settled down in a quiet place, and it will become beautiful. You'll see. You'll see things you never thought were possible."

As they passed the tunnel mural, Lee came away with fractured snapshots of hands and legs, arms and feet, and the face of an old woman, eyes heavenward.

"They used to launch ICBMs from here. Or were prepared to, I guess. It's built to withstand a nuclear blast. Now the place is the center of some positivity, at least."

She took Lee up a flight of stairs and stopped at the first landing, propping her against the wall with her shoulder as she fumbled with a key attached to one of her bracelets. As she opened the door, Lee stumbled backward and nearly fell back down the metal staircase into darkness, but Xenia caught her. "Hold on," she said. "We don't want you to hurt yourself." She flicked on a light and helped Lee into the room. She shut the door behind them. The music was gone now, just a memory in her skin.

Lee found herself standing on a dull green carpet in a large round room, with beanbags peppered about like enormous red mushrooms. A makeshift industrial kitchen took up one wall, with a long wooden dining table and chairs on the opposite end. Two dirty white couches faced each other, and behind them sat a cold war–era bank of controls, all dials and knobs and big square buttons and colored lights, and above it a bank of twelve blank monitors. As in the costume room, a large round concrete column rose up from the center of the floor to the ceiling.

"Sit down," Xenia said. "I'll get you some water. You need to stay hydrated down here!"

Lee flopped down onto a beanbag and took the bottle but didn't drink until Xenia drank from it first and handed it back. Lee heard the music again, pumping in from the dance floor somewhere far away, so low she could hear it only on a subterranean level. Perhaps it wasn't there at all, it was all just inside her now. Lee swigged from the bottle until she was coughing.

"Easy, now. No need to drown yourself. How are you feeling? Can you talk?"

Lee tried. "Am I saying something?"

Xenia smiled. "I can see you trying. Which is good. The sensation will come and go, so if you start feeling it come on again, it's okay. I'll guide you through. Do you trust me?"

Lee didn't know, but nodding seemed the easiest thing to do, and so she did.

"Good." She sat in a bag beside Lee. "Because here you have to let go. Of everything you've been holding on to. I can tell you've been through some rough times. Am I right?"

Lee had no words.

"You don't have to say anything, I can tell. How are you feeling now?"

Her mouth tasted tingly, metallic. Her body was fighting waves of nausea. She wanted to throw up again, but she nodded anyway.

"Good. Settle into it and don't fight it or it will drown you. Let it take you by the hand."

She *was* drowning. The more Lee thrashed against it, the deeper she sank. She closed her eyes and felt an unraveling inside her guts, candy-colored tentacles unfurling like kelp. The music, even so far away, was moving inside her. A cumulus of images swirling inside her head: Paleozoic underwater arthropods; a fetal, floating cosmonaut; the white, spread legs of a nude woman lying supine in a thicket of dried brush. She opened her eyes to the eyes of the girl, Xenia, and the images vanished.

"Now. Is there anything you want to clear away?"

Lee shook her head, then nodded, then shook it again. She didn't know what to do with her head.

"Anything weighing you down. When we carry negative psychic energies around with us, these energies keep us tethered to our fears and our anxieties. You clear these energies, and you release yourself from your fears. Is there something you would like to let go of?" Lee began to tremble, and Xenia steadied her with a hand. "It's okay. I'm here to guide you. Will you do something for me?"

Lee nodded.

"Close your eyes."

"No." The word felt phlegmy, like something she needed to eject from her body.

"You have to trust me, Lee. Do you trust me?"

Yes, Lee thought, *yes.* Her gut was speaking to her, and so Lee closed her eyes and plunged into the darkness of the empty aquarium. Tomi was there. She couldn't see him, but she could feel his presence.

The girl was there, too. Lee heard her voice: "Where are we?"

Lee spoke without words, her thoughts traveling the darkness. She knew Xenia could hear her. *In the aquarium. We have to go. It isn't safe.*

"What are you afraid of here?"

The Undertaker.

"What does he want?"

The hidden noise.

"Where is it?"

Lee wanted to tell the girl, but she didn't want to bring her any danger.

"Lee. Where is the hidden noise?"

He'll kill us for it.

"Unburden yourself. This is part of the clearing. Tell me where it is."

Lee felt naked. Sick in her body, the thing inside—the baby? Oh God, is that the baby?—slithering around, flapping in her guts. It was moving through her, contracting her organs, its long tendrils fibrillating beneath her skin.

"Go ahead. It's okay. Clear yourself and it will all go away."

Lee began to see that the space of the aquarium was not completely dark. She could make out the outlines of glass tanks, and figures from old displays, everything invested with a pale silvery hue. She still couldn't see Tomi, but she knew he was there with her. She heard his voice in her head. Competing with the voice of the girl. It was far away, a pale echo of a voice, tugging at her. She tried to follow it, but Xenia's voice, stronger and more urgent, kept her rooted in place.

"Let go of it, Lee. Let me carry it. See it in your mind. Describe it."

The light source, wherever it was, was expanding and the outlines around her were beginning to take shape. She smelled something familiar, milky and sweet. Sandalwood. Then she saw a human form begin to take shape with the rest of it. He was only a dark shape surrounded by a silvery aura, but she knew him. She opened her eyes.

He was standing behind the girl. He wore the same suit as before. Lee felt the black tendrils unfurling again.

He said, "Do you know the expression 'A single spark can start a prairie fire'? The world is an arid field, Bride, and you hold the match."

Lee felt bile rising again, and Xenia, as though reading her mind, brought her a steel bucket, which she held for her as Lee emptied the remainder of her stomach into it. Xenia handed Lee the water bottle, drinking from it first again without prodding. Lee drank in great, gulping swallows until she nearly felt sick again.

The Undertaker held one hand out to her. His other arm hung slack at his side, as though wires inside had been snipped. "I want to show you something."

He took her hand. Xenia helped her to stand, and Lee stumbled after him across the room. His hand was moist, like something attached to a rock at low tide. She felt a hatred rising, but it had nowhere to go, and so it churned inside, some restless, raging animal. She pulled back, but her hand stayed within his.

The animal inside her clawed to get out, tear his eyes from their sockets. He just smiled down on her. "It's too late for that," he said, as though reading her thoughts. "Your moment of retribution has passed."

He took one hand and raised his other arm, then let it flop back down to his side, as though to show her a fault in its constitution. No more useful than the arm of a marionette. "Your bullet shattered the humerus, snapped the biceps tendon, and destroyed the median nerve. When it broke apart, it left shards all up and down through the tissue. Little bits of lead are still finding their way up. Every now and then one comes, pushing through my skin like a tiny metal worm. The nerves are gone, too. I can't feel a thing." He put his good hand on her head. "If you feel the need to taste the bitter wine of retribution, have a look at my arm."

Lee spat. "I'll have more than your arm."

He just laughed. "But look at you. You're trembling, little girl. Believe me, there is an easier way."

Lee was doing all she could to suppress the rage telling her to claw the man's face away. The drug was gone, as suddenly as it had come; she could no longer feel it working through her. She maintained her thousand-yard stare.

The man nodded to Xenia, who left the room. He turned to the control panel and flicked a switch. The twelve monitors buzzed to life, little portals into places throughout the complex: two outside views, the dance floor, the costume room, and other spaces Lee hadn't seen before. He scanned them one at a time, looking for something. "She's here somewhere," he said.

With the man's back to her, Lee strained to maneuver her arm back into her costume, trying to reach her bag.

"I just wanted to show her to you," he said, his eyes still on the monitors. "Your friend. To show you she's all right."

Lee saw her, dancing, now with a boy. The man did, too. He zoomed the camera in on Annie's eyes. "A little dilated, to be sure, but she'll be fine." He turned. If he was surprised to see the gun in her hand, it didn't show.

Lee thought she had gotten used to the feel of a gun, but now it was unwieldy again, her fingers like balloons. He was maybe six feet away, one hand out in some sort of gesture of absolution, the other, attached to the shattered arm, slack beside his body. He made no move toward her. She could finish this now.

"Well?" he said. "What are you waiting for?"

The gun felt too heavy in her hand. She could barely keep it up. "You deserve it."

"Perhaps. In your system of justice and karma, I suppose I do. So why hesitate? Do you relish the moment so much?"

Then Lee saw something that made her stomach sink. One of the monitors was rotating through a series of nearly identical rooms, and Lee recognized in one of them a poster she had seen before: a black Deadmau5 head with glowing eyes. And, just before the monitor switched to a new room, a trash can beneath the desk overflowing with Big Gulp cups.

"He's with you?" she said.

"Who?"

"DreamClown."

"DreamClown." He said the name as though it amused him. "Our Busboy. Yes."

Lee thought back to the first time she'd spoken to Teutonik and DreamClown, in Annie's basement. How could she have been so stupid? She had let them lead her here. She had played right into their hands. Mourning Tomi had made her sloppy.

"You are feeling betrayed right now. By someone you trusted."

"You don't know anything about betrayal."

He moved toward her but stopped when Lee raised the gun to his head. "What would you say if I told you that your boyfriend, To-mas Černák, that he, too, had betrayed you."

Lee adjusted her aim toward the third button of his jacket and squeezed the trigger.

She saw him smile before she heard the crack from the gun, so loud in the little room. She stared, not comprehending. How could she have missed? The man stood not five feet from her, and yet she had missed the big black square of his chest. She brought the gun up by an inch and fired again. The man looked at her with pity. Lee aimed for his head this time and fired three shots in quick succession. He flinched, closing his eyes against the flash, but still he stood there.

Lee pulled the trigger again, which only clicked now, but she kept pulling it. Her ears rang. The room smelled of cordite. The Undertaker walked toward her until he was standing over her. "All done?"

Lee slumped to the floor. She was so fucking stupid. Of course they were not real bullets. The man wrapped his hand around the gun, removed it from hers, and put it in his pocket. He laid his good hand on her head, almost affectionately. All the fight suddenly drained out of her, and Lee felt her face go hot with shame and helplessness.

"Don't be hard on yourself," he said. "This world is so much bigger than any of us." He was stroking her hair. She could feel his breath on her neck.

Lee thought about the cell phone that DreamClown had left for her. They must have been tracking her the whole way, known exactly where she was all this time.

"It's just the two of us," he said. "I thought we could talk, just you and me, wash away some of the nastiness between us. I think we understand each other better than you know."

He helped her up and guided her to the couch.

"Let me help you out of this ridiculous thing," he said, pulling the costume up over her head and laying it on the couch. "The bridal dress suited you so much better." He took an old slide projector out of a cabinet and set it up on the end table by the couch, facing the big white wall by the door. "I'm sorry about Tomas. His death is not something I wanted on my hands. I hope you understand it was self-defense." He popped the carousel in and plugged in the machine. It awoke with a dull hum. "And understand, I was defending not only myself but nearly a hundred years of work and planning. We have within our grasp the solution to the only problem that matters, and he was willing to throw that away. For what? For love?" He turned off the room lights, and there was only a swirling wash of dust motes in the light of the projector and an empty white rectangle on the wall.

He picked up the remote, and a slide came on with a click. The work was so familiar by now, the tall steel frame bisected horizontally along the center, the web of shattered glass, the menagerie of mechanical forms.

"I think you're familiar with Duchamp's *Large Glass,* are you not?"

The Undertaker clicked the projector to bring up another slide. It was *The Large Glass* again but with the missing elements, the Boxing Match, the Spiral, and the Juggler of Gravity, intact. He used the shadow of his finger to point them out. "We know that Duchamp left out certain key components from the final work. Components that his notes make clear he had planned to include. So we come to the question: why? Was it simply that he abandoned the work as unfinished? Out of boredom? I cannot believe this. Duchamp was a man who was never bored a moment of his life. Everything he did had a purpose. So why? As he conceived it, *The Large Glass* is what he called a 'delay in glass,' a static image of a dynamic system. What might this system look like if realized in its true form and put into motion in the world? What might it reveal? My belief is that he knew we weren't ready for this knowledge, and so he was forced to leave certain key components out of the blueprint to keep us from realizing his vision until we were ready."

"The Boxing Match. He left out the ignition coil."

The Undertaker looked surprised but pleased to hear her speak, and Lee hated that she hadn't stopped herself. "Indeed," he said. "But the Boxing Match isn't an ignition coil. Nothing so prosaic. The Boxing

Match is a device to collapse space. This is how it moves the Bachelors' spurts across the horizon to the Bride. By collapsing space-time itself."

Lee felt the drug coming back on, the couch made of soft moss molding itself around her. She shook it away and the man's voice came back.

"In 1912, as Duchamp was conceiving the work, the idea of a space-time continuum was just percolating to public consciousness. Duchamp himself was playing around with ideas of collapsed multi-dimensions. In the same way that objects held up against a light project a shadow in two dimensions"—he held his hand up against the light to demonstrate—"Duchamp believed that the everyday three-dimensional objects around us are but the shadows of a fourth dimension. That our entire universe is but a pale shadow of a deeper order. But what is the nature of that order? What lies beyond?"

The Undertaker seemed mesmerized as he spoke, and Lee felt the madness in him like a third presence in the room. "Why are you telling me this?" she said.

"It's essential that you understand the importance of our work. Because like it or not, you are part of it. Why do you think it is you've been allowed to live as long as you have, while others have died? Did you ever ask yourself that?"

She still felt muzzy with the drug, and her head swum whenever she moved it. She could no longer define where she ended and the couch began.

"It's more than just *With Hidden Noise* and the fact that you happened to have it. In fact, we hardly think it a coincidence that you came into possession of the thing in the first place. Can I explain to you what I mean?"

He took her silence as leave to continue. "Allow me to backtrack a little: Heisenberg suggested that at a quantum level, particles exist only when they are colliding with other particles. Think about that: matter exists only in those nanomoments when it is paired with other matter. Otherwise, it's simply not there. The world does not consist of objects.

The world consists of the relationships between them. Even Einstein could not initially get his head around this. It is two things coming together that create not only meaning in the world but existence."

Lee had been alone her entire life. Invisible. It wasn't until Tomi came into her life that she'd felt seen for the first time. It was as if she suddenly existed, in a way she never had before. After he was gone, she'd nearly disappeared again. Was this what life was? Long periods of invisibility followed by short bursts of existence?

"Einstein's theories of relativity, quantum mechanics, string theory—Duchamp referenced all of it before the world's scientists had even fully conceived of such things. You can see it hinted in his work, going all the way back to 1913. But Duchamp was not simply a soothsayer, any more than was Einstein or Heisenberg. Duchamp was an engineer. An engineer not of the mechanical but of the unseen forces that exist all around us. The id, the ego, the anima, fate and chance, the unconscious, the collective unconscious, time itself. Just as there are forces that govern the physical structures of the universe, from planetary systems down to quantum particles, there are forces at work that govern human consciousness."

Lee couldn't stop thinking about Tomi, about the possibility that he really had been with them. It didn't seem possible. She *knew* him. He had loved her, she was sure of that. "You're a liar," she told him.

The man turned to her, looking confused. "Just listen, try to see, then you will understand. For nearly a century people have been too close-minded to grasp the truth behind Duchamp's greatest work. Allow me to put it this way: When Einstein conceived that space and time were all part of a single space-time continuum, it astounded the world. When the physicist David Bohm put forward the idea that human consciousness and the matter that makes up the universe are similarly of a single continuum, it caused barely a ripple. Was this because the idea was not as profound? On the contrary, the idea is so profound that no one is willing to even entertain it. Just think about it: all separation—between you and this wall, between you and me, between your consciousness and mine—is an illusion, a product of perception and the mutual unspoken agreement that things must have boundaries, they must remain separate."

Lee shifted, trying to separate herself from the couch, but it moved with her. She felt the man inside of her, too, and tried to push him out, but his voice anchored him there.

"Remember that the observer effect tells us that the observer affects the thing observed. Bohm suggested that the observer *is* the observed. That on a quantum level there is no difference. He used a holographic model to illustrate this. In a hologram, each part contains within it the whole. In a holographic universe, every part of it, no matter how small, contains within it the entire universe. If we had the know-how, we could access a moon of Jupiter through the leaf of a tree. All time as well. We could see thousands of years into the past, simply by knowing how to look at a drop of water."

Lee remembered what Tomi had said about the unified field theory, that solving it would be like reading the mind of God. Is that what had driven these men to kill three people, to empty out all those kids and traffic them as living sex dolls? "You pretend to want to see the mind of God," she said. "But what do you think God sees in you?"

The man stayed seated, focused on the image on the wall, but something in his posture changed, and she thought maybe she'd rattled him. "Let me answer it this way," he said. "Duchamp saw not only that all matter and consciousness is part of the same continuum but that we are governed by certain laws—absurd laws, in his view—that make for the deterministic dance we all participate in. But what if we found a way to break these laws? To bypass them or manipulate them? The work in front of you is nothing less than a blueprint for a machine that, when set into motion, will do just that. A machine to transform human consciousness as we know it. So you see, I don't want to see the mind of God. I want to change it."

"But you have the machine," she said. "That's what I saw beneath the museum, isn't it? Why not just set it into motion? What the fuck do you need me for?"

The Undertaker put the remote down and looked at her curiously. "Why, I thought it was obvious. Because you have the key."

The key? Of course that's what it was.

"Who knew we had been sitting on it for so many years? When Duchamp asked Walter Arensberg to put something into the center of a ball of string and seal it between two steel plates, he told the world that he had no idea what that object was. But if there's one thing to know about Duchamp, it is that everything he says must be taken with some salt. He was a man who embraced contradictions. He was dedicated to chance, and yet he never did anything without maintaining control. There is no way he would have let anyone, even someone as close as Arensberg, determine such a vital part of a work. Of course he knew what the object was. The whole thing was pure obfuscation, all done so that no one would figure out that inside was a key. A key to a work, a device, that he wouldn't build for decades. It became so clear when you stole it. A coincidence? Hardly. For Duchamp, there was no coincidence, only chance.

"And now here you are. Here both of us are. I was hoping that I might convince you of the importance of this project. That we could wash all the past misery behind us. I really am sorry about Tomas. All I can say is that he was armed as well. He drew first. And so it was a good old-fashioned duel. He died in as good a way as a man can. He died looking into the eyes of the one he loved."

All she could think about was how thirsty she was. She watched the dust motes swirl in the light of the projector. When he leaned in and put his hand on her belly, she flinched but she didn't move. "Come," he said. "Tell me where it is. Let's unlock the universe together."

Lee tried to gauge the angle of his body in relation to hers. With her eyes she followed the projector cord to the wall. It was the only source of light in the room. She calculated the distance between her and the door and kept an image of the route in her head. Then she launched herself forward and dropped to the ground, feeling his hand swipe the air above her head. Had she any hair, he might have grabbed her by it. As she rolled away from him, she took hold of the cord. She yanked, expecting the room to go dark, but the gray light from the monitors still glowed. Lee was on her back on the floor and the Undertaker was standing now, looking down on her curiously. Lee managed to get to her knees by the time he'd reached her, that blank, curious expression never leaving his face.

Lee swung the cord with all the strength she had, and it whipped through the air, the heavy three-pronged plug slashing his face. He winced and put his hand to his nose. His expression changed, all the placid curiosity erased in an instant. He reached into his suit pocket and came out with a flat silver wand, which opened to a straight razor, the steel glinting dully.

Lee launched away from him, across the room. She reached the door, grabbed the handle, and yanked it open just as she felt the man grab her by her hood and yank her back and up. As if she were a puppet made of straw. With one hand he held her off the ground, then slammed her against the wall. Instinctively, she turned so that her shoulder took the impact and not her belly. Lee felt the wind nearly leave her. He let her crumple to the floor.

The man picked the razor up and held it against her cheek, then slid it down in a slow caress. She felt the blood flow down her neck before she felt the cut itself. Lee reached into her pocket and brought the little object up between them. "This is what you want?"

His mouth went a little slack, and he became completely still, as though afraid moving might destroy it. He pocketed the razor and reached out a trembling hand. "May I?"

"You want it?" She spat in his face, a warm mix of blood and saliva, then threw the thing as hard as she could across the room. The man got a panicked look on his face as the thing hit the monitor bank. It bounced off, and for a moment Lee hoped she'd broken it, but then she saw it roll, intact, across the room. She took that moment to launch herself at the door again. But he grabbed her and smashed her head against the wall. This time everything went black.

EIGHTEEN

SHE didn't know how long she'd been down—the combination of the drugs and the head blow made time untrustworthy—but when she opened her eyes, she was alone. The room was silent. Even the music, faint before, was now gone.

Lee got to her feet using the wall for balance. Her costume lay draped across the sofa like a molted skin. The little Calabi-Yau space, whatever it was, was gone. The monitors were black. Lee went to the controls and flipped the main switch.

The monitors blinked on. From an angle within the wall, the big clown head stared back at her stupidly. In the parking lot, most of the cars were gone, but Annie's parents' Audi was still there. Another monitor showed the hall outside the costume room, just below her. She could see the Policeman there, leaning against the railing and staring down at the lit end of a cigarette. Three others showed angles on empty rooms in depthless black-and-white: the dance floor, the costume room, and a large round room filled with steel bunk beds. Everything was still, each monitor like a photograph. Then Lee saw a lump on the dance floor shift. She noticed others sprawled across the floor, then, on another monitor, a few kids on bunk beds in the round room sleeping off the excesses of the night. None of them looked like Annie.

Lee scanned the walls along the ceiling, looking for ducts. Nothing. Then she spotted something on the other side of the room: a steel floor vent set into the carpet. A heating duct? She went to inspect it. It was attached to the floor with four screws. She rifled around in the kitchen drawers until she found a bread knife, which she used to remove the screws, then pry the grate loose. Lee eased herself down the shaft as slowly as she could.

It shot straight down a good ways, Lee had no idea where. To a burning furnace, for all she knew. But there was no turning back now. Every five feet or so was a small lip where the sections joined, and she used these to brace herself, pushing her feet against each lip and resting before lowering herself again until she reached an L that sent the shaft running horizontally.

Lee scrunched herself into a squatting position and made her way forward. She could hear the hum of air running through the vents. The tight shaft continued in total darkness, then she saw a faint glow at the far end. As she crawled toward it, the swell of her belly became truly noticeable for the first time. Not because she was so much bigger but because her body wanted to protect what was inside her. It made crawling difficult. The glow resolved itself into light from a vent, and when Lee got to it she peered through the slats. She was above the dance floor. Lee kicked the vent off and dropped down. The stark fluorescent lights made the room look like a bus station in the middle of the night. The floor was made from thick black rubber mats like one might find on a playground, sticky and streaked with grime. The whole place smelled of old sweat. Plastic bottles and cigarette butts and bits of trash littered the room, and as at a bus station, there were several sleepers along the couches on the perimeter, one up on the empty DJ platform. Each of the sleepers wore a costume that looked shoddy in the light, like a stage prop from a children's play. The whole place looked sordid and cheap.

Lee went to a boy lying on the floor beside a couch and shook him by the shoulder. He sputtered in response, tried to turn away, and finally shot up, rubbing his eyes. His face had a postcoital serenity that turned to panic when she told him that the police were on their way.

"Get up." She handed him a shoe, which had come off somehow as he slept. "Wake up everyone you can find, get them out of here. You only have a few minutes."

The boy sat staring down at his feet, one shoe on, one off, before seeming to decide that the easiest solution was to take off the shoe that was on. He left without waking any of the others, shuffling in the wrong direction at first before finding the door to the exit tunnel. Lee woke the others in turn, each of whom left quickly.

From the middle of the room, Lee spotted the surveillance camera perched like a bird of prey just above the DJ station. The circular walls were concrete covered in thick, dark, velvety curtains. Two large vertical ventilation shafts ran floor to ceiling, one on each side of the room. One was an inlet vent for air from the surface. Another must have been the heating vent, and it broke off near the ceiling and sent off a horizontal shaft lined with outlet vents.

Then Lee noticed something she hadn't before: near the center of the room, one of the big rubber mats was torn and broken around the edges. When she got closer, she saw a handle embedded in the floor. She reached down and lifted. The panel pulled up easily. A circular stairwell, encased in a gray steel tube, led down. There was no handrail, so Lee stuck close to the wall as she made her descent. About twenty feet down she hit a landing and a steel door. The stairs continued down.

Lee listened at the door, but there was nothing to hear. She eased down on the handle, and it slowly opened into another round room with the same dimensions as the dance floor above. Rows of steel-framed bunk beds lined either side, and the floor was strewn with old books and magazines, leftover food containers, and dirty clothes. The beds were messy with blankets and sleeping bags, and breathing lumps slept on several of them. Lee went from bed to bed looking for Annie, nudging the lumps awake and telling the groggy, confused teenagers to get the hell out. Then she recognized a pair of feet with green toenail polish Lee had applied herself. They were sticking out from under a pile of plush blankets. Lee nudged her awake.

Annie moaned languidly and turned onto her back, blinking up at Lee and smiling. "Lee! Hey, Babylove . . . come in with us." She shifted to make room, and Lee saw the other form in the bed, beneath a leopard-spot blanket.

It was just a boy, no older than Annie, rawboned, in a gauzy wifebeater and loose tighty-whities. He had a buzz cut like the jocks in her school used to wear, but he was too skinny to be a jock. Plus, he had an earring. He gaped around the room, disoriented, until the sight of Lee sent him fumbling for his pants.

"Who are you?" The boy's voice was low and scratchy, like he'd already inhaled a lifetime of cigarettes.

Lee turned to Annie. "Get dressed. Now. You need to get out of here. It isn't safe, you understand?"

"What time is it? Where's my phone?" Annie asked the air. "I need to get home before my parents wake up."

The boy had gotten his shirt on and was one leg into his pants when Lee grabbed him by the arm and dragged him to the other side of the room. She turned back to Annie, who was rummaging for something in the bedding. When she'd gotten the boy out of earshot, she pushed him up against the sink and hissed into his face. "Where is he?"

"Who?"

"The Undertaker. Where is he? Where are the rest of them?"

The kid raised his hands. "Hey, I don't know anything about anything. I met your friend last night and we . . . Wait—are you her girlfriend? I'm sorry, I—"

"You're not part of any of this?"

"Of what?"

The boy seemed genuinely confused, but Lee didn't know if she could believe him. She didn't really have a choice. A plan was beginning to form in her head. "What's your name?"

"Teddy."

"Are you okay to drive, Teddy?"

"Of course. I don't do any of that shit, I'm straight edge."

"Let me see your license."

Teddy just stared at Lee, and Lee saw a bit of defiance begin to dawn in the boy's eyes.

"Give. Me. Your. Fucking. License. Teddy." Lee reached around the back of his pants until she found his wallet, dangling from a chain. He didn't resist. Lee opened it. She pulled out his driver's license. In the picture he was a girl, with long straight brown hair and the collar of a prairie dress framing her neck. Elizabeth Pinter. She was seventeen years old.

"Elizabeth?"

"Fuck off. I get enough bullshit in my high school."

Lee handed the wallet back. "I'm sorry about that. But I really don't care about it, either. You know the way out of here?"

"Sure."

"Annie's got her parents' car outside. The blue Audi. I want you to drive." Lee remembered the madness in the Undertaker's eyes, his talk of retribution, and it occurred to her that if she did what she was planning to do, they might come after Annie. "Ask her if she has a relative she can go to. Just for a few days. I want you to drive her there. *Not* her home, you got that?"

"What if she doesn't have any relatives around?"

"Then drive her to *your* home."

"I don't think my parents—"

"Fuck your parents, Teddy. You will drive her somewhere safe that is not her home, and then you tell her to call her parents and get them out of there, too. Do you understand me?"

Teddy just nodded.

"Good. And Teddy?"

"Yeah."

Lee got close up in his face. "You live at 4826 Sansom Street. If anything happens to Annie, if you let any harm come to her, I will hunt you down and hurt you. You understand?"

Teddy nodded, very quickly, looking not at Lee but at some point beyond her.

Lee left him there and went back to Annie, who had managed to pull half her clothes on before falling back asleep. Lee woke her and got her standing. She took Annie's head in her hands and kissed her, once on each eye. "I'm sorry," she said.

Annie just teetered there, confused and a little giddy from the kisses.

"Go with your friend, okay? He knows what to do." Lee pulled Annie out of the bed and nodded to Teddy, who took Annie around the waist and left the room.

The room smelled of mildew and ammonia. Lee sat on a bed and stared up at the surveillance camera. If someone was still here, he or she was watching her now. Lee got up, gave the finger to the camera, and opened the door. She went down.

NINETEEN

THE level below let her out onto a narrow circular floor surrounding the tube of the stairwell, which was in turn surrounded by a circle of doors. Lee walked around the corridor twice, looking up at the small, rust-colored figures riveted into the wall above each door. She recognized them by now, though she couldn't tell which was which. Duchamp's nine Bachelors: Delivery Boy, Gendarme, Cavalryman, Undertaker, Flunky, Busboy, Policeman, Station Master, Priest.

Several of the doors were cracked open, the rooms unoccupied. Lee poked her head into a wedge-shaped room the size of a cruise ship cabin. It had a neatly made bed in a metal frame bolted to the wall; a desk at the far end held a computer and several books. She edged into the room and opened an old armoire. Hanging inside were three antique policeman's uniforms, their thick blue wool moth-gnawed and faded. They were quite old, she supposed, but in the fluorescent lighting they looked like one of the moth-eaten uniforms her uncle the reenactor wore. He'd died young and was buried in one of those suits.

She looked into another open room, almost identical but emptied. Except for an open file box. Lee could see a stack of paper inside. She came into the room and picked one up off the top: Edie's MISSING poster. There must have been hundreds of them, maybe a thousand. Lee stared down at the paper dumbly until she understood: Edie had never disappeared at all. It had been a ruse to get Lee to the silo—they had bet on the fact that she'd go looking for her here. They'd been in control the whole time. They were still in control, running her through this underground maze.

The stairwell went down to another landing, this one with a door on the landing and a steel gate on the floor to more stairs. The gate was locked. She heard footsteps coming down. She tried the door.

Lee came into a round room much larger than the Bachelors' rooms; it took up the entire level. There was something off about the space; it felt smaller than it should, judging by the levels above. Maybe it was just that the room was so crammed with stuff. Where the walls upstairs were beige-painted concrete, these were paneled in dark-stained wood and hung with old oil paintings. A bed on an elaborate iron frame stood at one end. Lee might have been standing in a preserved bedroom of some old European château. In a dark wood armoire hung four identical black suits that she recognized as the Undertaker's.

Lee searched the room for another vent cover. She knew there had to be one here somewhere, but it was hard to spot through all the clutter. One wall was covered in African tribal art: masks, totems, fertility figures with huge erect penises, and a long wooden spear with a polished steel head. A hand-crank Victrola stood in one corner, and on the large oak bookshelf was an antique grinding machine on a three-legged base. The books were all leather-bound. A marble chess set stood on a table by the bed. The wall opposite was taken up by a full-sized reproduction of *The Large Glass*. Like the one beneath the museum, it had the missing elements intact.

There was no television, no stereo equipment, no computer, no laptop or cell phone charger coming from a wall outlet. Nothing at all that could be placed as part of the past thirty, fifty, maybe a hundred years. Something about the freakish obsessiveness of it all—the idea that all this death and destruction was somehow connected to some old goon's fetish for the past—made Lee sick.

A door opened into a small bathroom, its porcelain sink lined with antique shaving instruments—a fur brush, a straight razor—as well as a cake of shaving soap and an old cologne bottle. On its label was a small photo of a homely woman in a black feathery hat. There was a claw-foot tub with rust stains like dried blood running along the water line and around the drain. Lee uncorked the bottle and sniffed, recognizing his sandalwood cologne, like forest loam. When she put it back, she saw the vent in the wall above the mirror. She knew they could see her as long as she was in any of the main rooms, but she might be able to get to where she wanted to go if she could make it back into the ventilation system.

Lee climbed on top of the sink, grabbed the razor, and set to the screws. She was working on the last one when she heard the door to the bedroom open. She dropped the vent cover into the tub, not caring about the noise as she pulled herself up and into the shaft.

Lee fell straight down and nearly crashed through to the bottom of the shaft, but the steel bowed and held. Pain shot up both legs, and she squatted gingerly to make sure that she could stand. She thought of the baby, and her body tensed involuntarily. She'd known a girl from school who had gotten pregnant and then miscarried eight weeks in during track practice. The girl had acted relieved, telling the story with a "whew" and an exaggerated wiping of her brow, but Lee could see the sorrow in her eyes. The thought of miscarrying here, of bleeding out the baby here in the darkness, made her more afraid of anything the Undertaker might do to her. Lee craned her neck up. Not much light came through from the room above, but she thought she saw a shadow move.

Dim shafts of light bled through a series of vent covers ahead, and she crawled toward them. An acrid, chemical smell tickled her nose, then feathered her lungs. She reached a vent cover and peered through. The room was the size of the room with the bunk beds, except it was filled with lab equipment: long-necked beakers and coils of tubing and large square machines and bottles of chemicals. At the end of the vent shaft she could see a huge fan enclosure leading to an outlet shaft. And just to the right of it, stacked against the wall, a tower of huge plastic chemical drums. Here was the room she'd been looking for. The drums would be full of combustible solvents. If she could set a fire down here in the lab, she thought she could make it up and back out before the whole place went up.

Lee was about to kick out the vent cover when she heard a door close, then footsteps. Something metal scraping against a wall. She could sense him below, pacing the length of the shaft, trying to figure out where she was. She felt a light tapping against the steel, then a blow hard enough for the metal beneath her to buckle. She stopped breathing. Then a third blow came, and something nearly pierced her arm. He pulled it back, and a shaft of light came up through a three-inch gash in the metal. Another blow, and another gash opened up just behind her. Lee scrambled forward as fast as she could, a mouse in the walls. He tracked her as she went, sending the spear blade through the thin steel of the duct at intervals, missing her each time by inches.

With the light coming through the gashes in the steel, Lee could see, maybe fifteen feet ahead, the vertical access shaft that she knew must lead directly to the surface. He sent the spear up just ahead of her and left it in this time, thrashing back and forth in front of her, and Lee leapt back instinctively. He must have heard exactly where she was, because he yanked it out and Lee surged forward just as the spear emerged through the metal behind her. She found the vertical outlet shaft and pushed her way up.

He was still down below, she could hear him pacing, then thrusting the spear up through the duct with a grunt. Lee kept her feet braced against the puckered seem of the shaft and held herself there, her muscles beginning to collapse under the strain. Even after she heard his footsteps leave the room, she held herself, working it out in her head. He might be faking an exit, waiting for her to return. She had no choice; she'd have to abandon her plan.

Bracing against the sides of the shaft with her feet and arms, she made her way up a few inches at a time. It was slow and punishing on her legs, tiring her quickly. She passed a horizontal shaft with a fan enclosure blocking her way forward. Lee knew where she was now, and knew from before how long it would take to get to the top. By the time she got there, he would be waiting.

She crawled forward instead, squeezing between the blades of the fan until she got to an open vent, then dropped into a maintenance room. She popped open one of the large metal fuse boxes and began flicking switches, two at a time, sensing the power go out in the complex level by level. When the lights in the maintenance room went out, she felt for the rest of the switches in the dark.

When they were all off, she sat and let the darkness in, breathed it in and let it fill her lungs. As she gave Tomi a silent thank-you for everything he'd taught her on their creeps, she felt her internal radar begin to realign itself. Soon she could almost see the room through the blackness: the propane pipes and huge valve handles that circled the room, the clunky old industrial furnace, the coils of fat wires running from the walls.

Lee let herself out of the maintenance room and into the spiral staircase. She felt her way up the winding steps, past one landing, then another, until she reached the hatch. She heaved up on it with her shoulder. She could feel the blackness open up around her, the space expanding, as she climbed up onto the rubber mat of the dance floor. She made her way across the room in the direction of the entrance corridor. The door to the stairwell up would be at the other end.

Lee was halfway down the corridor, moving quickly, when she heard a grunt, followed by labored breathing, and something clanging around in the dark space ahead of her. She couldn't see the Undertaker, but in her imagination he was enraged and sightless, stumbling at her with the spear, assaulting the air in front of him like some lunatic threshing machine.

She moved backward through the dark, using the walls for guidance. She heard him swear, then the sound of metal scraping down the wall. Unbalanced footsteps coming toward her. Lee pressed herself against the wall, but he was confused, stumbling in the dark, and she could hear him bouncing off both walls as he approached. Then a moan began to rise from somewhere in the darkness. He lumbered toward her, and Lee moved silently from one wall to the other, trying to anticipate his careening advance.

Her heart was thumping in her ears, playing havoc with her senses. The smell of sandalwood was everywhere now; she was swimming in it. She lost track of which way the stairwell was, and she nearly lost her balance as his hot grunts grew close enough to feel against her cheek. He was right there, in front of her. He'd stopped moving, too, though she could hear him breathing, heavy and labored, as panicked as she, and she knew that he sensed her as well. He had stopped to listen.

Her heart was so loud within her she was sure he could hear it, and the more she tried not to breathe, the louder it got. Still, she stayed motionless. She could hear him move forward again, just a step, testing the space between them, and Lee squatted low, moving toward him, guessing by what was left of her instinct which side of the corridor he was on and moving as silently as she could to the other.

She felt a movement of air in front of her face and heard the spear clank against the wall. Lee crouched lower and eased forward. He was in front of her now and a little to her left. The darkness gave nothing away, but it amplified his presence and his shallow panting breaths. Lee inched forward a bit more; when he grunted she dropped to the ground. She felt the spear pass over her head and heard the crack of metal against concrete and the splintering of wood and felt the broken spear tip hit her shoulder. Lee gasped involuntarily, and that was all it took. She tried to spring up, but he had ahold of her hoodie. He heaved her up, then slammed her hard against the wall. The blow sucked the air out of her even as she kicked out helplessly against the dark weight of him.

"I did not want it to come to this," he whispered. "Know that." He had her pinned against the wall with his shoulder, and she could feel him reaching for something in his pocket. As he brought his hand out, Lee felt the measure of his breath once more and slammed her head forward as hard as she could. She felt his nose crumple against her forehead, and he rocked back, just enough for her to drop and roll to the ground. She felt the air shift, felt something slash through her sleeve and across the skin of her arm. But then she was on her feet and sprinting forward.

Lee stopped just short of the stairwell. He was stumbling in the dark behind her. She ascended steps three at a time, skidding awkwardly through the first landing, allowing herself one hand along the wall, until the wall ended at the large steel door to the outside.

Lee grabbed the handle and shouldered into it. It didn't move. She paused, tried to breathe, felt panic taking over again. She took one breath, two, three, four, until she found a rhythm. She reached into her jeans and pulled out the lockpick set. It was a military-grade steel door, but it was also antiquated, probably fifty years old or more.

Lee felt through the picks until her fingers landed on the rake. She pulled it out and then a tension wrench. She found the lock with her thumb and inserted the wrench, twisting it until she found the direction of the mechanism, then held the torque. She pushed the rake into the lock, but her fingers were slick with blood, and it dropped to the ground. Holding the tension wrench in the lock with one hand, she felt around with the other on the ground. It wasn't there. She felt against the wall and everywhere in the vicinity. Nothing. Lee pulled the wrench back out and crawled around the landing on all fours, feeling for the thin pick. Finally, on the top step, she found it. She wiped the blood off her hands and picked it up. She heard a door slam shut downstairs.

Scrambling back to the door on her knees, Lee inserted the wrench again, then the rake. She jiggled along the tumblers until she heard the clicks she was looking for. She turned the wrench and shouldered open the door, which emptied her out into a morning light so blinding she nearly stumbled back. Lee let the door close behind her. The outside world blurred into focus, and she stared down at herself. Blood from her cheek ran down her chest, and the sleeve of her sweatshirt was heavy with blood from her arm. She allowed herself a look at the gash: a red six-inch channel that ran the length of her tricep.

She was cutting through the weeds and underbrush to get to her egress point at the rear wall when she passed the little utility shed and saw what was inside. She could hop the fence and be gone in thirty seconds, but she stopped.

The rotted door of the shed broke open on the second kick, and Lee moved around the generator to the three gas cans lining the back. Two were empty, but the third was full. It was as tall as her thigh, and Lee had to drag it two-handed out of the shed. Her arm spasmed in pain. The rusty outlet vent was at the base of the clown's head, half covered in weeds and dried brush. Lee cleared it, exposing the dark shaft. At the bottom would be the lab.

Lee unscrewed the cap. She took off her sweatshirt and stepped on it, then grabbed hold of one sleeve and pulled as hard as she could. It tore off at the shoulder. Lee stuffed it into the can. She maneuvered the can up onto the lip of the shaft and pulled out the old brass lighter. As she flicked the cap and struck it lit, Lee thought of Mr. Velasquez. She touched the flame to the fabric, and it coughed alight, burning the hair on her arm. She stepped back and tipped the can forward with her foot. It fell, tumbling, a ball of orange flame lighting the black walls of the shaft. There was a pop followed by a bright yellow flash from down below. Then nothing. It must have extinguished on the way down. Fuck. But there was nothing more to be done.

Lee turned away and was heading toward the rear wall when she heard a muffled boom from somewhere deep below. She turned to see a sudden burst of flame erupt from the shaft. A lazy cloud of dark smoke followed.

The flame was gone in an instant, but it had licked one ear of the great plastic clown's head, which caught fire quickly, spreading to the clown's painted curls and its enormous bowler hat. The fire was pluming black smoke, and great globs of burning plastic dropped to the ground, bubbling near Lee's feet. She stepped back. The fire had wrapped around to the clown's nose when the door of the Silo opened, spilling out the Undertaker, followed by a thick cloud of gray smoke. He fell to the ground coughing, and then the nose of the clown collapsed and dropped in one bubbling red mass of burning plastic onto his shoulders. He screamed and flipped over, tried to tear his jacket from his body, when another mass fell onto his chest and neck. The man arched his head back with a horrible gurgle, and his eyes rolled back and met Lee's for only a moment before she saw the life leave them.

She stood over him, looking down, the clown's head only a black mound of burning plastic behind him. In one hand he held a green neon glow stick, what he must have found to light his way back to the surface. She reached into his coat pocket and took back the little ball.

· BOOK VIII ·

In Advance of
the Broken Arm

TWENTY

THE keys to Steve's car were in her bag, probably melting somewhere down below, so she took a bicycle someone had left against the gate. The ride back opened wide the wound on her arm, and by the time she rolled into the city outskirts and passed the old paper mill that had been one of her first creeps with Tomi, Lee had dark branches of blood running down her whole left side, soaking big ruddy blooms into her jeans. She was dizzy with fatigue as she dropped the bike in the alley and stumbled through the backyard.

Mrs. Velasquez opened the door without expression, though Lee knew she recognized her, and Lee broke down there in the doorway, stuttering, "I'm sorry," before the tears came so heavy she could not get another word out. The woman took Lee's hand and led her into her home without a word. She sat Lee on a chair in the kitchen and examined the gashes on her cheek and arm, then handed Lee a glass of water and disappeared. From her seat in the kitchen, Lee could see into the living room, where the twins were watching television.

Mrs. Velasquez returned with a small box, a woven drawstring pouch, and a plastic bottle of rubbing alcohol. She took a clean rag from the kitchen and soaked it beneath the faucet, then wiped the blood from Lee's face and neck, her arm. She helped her out of her shirt and wiped the blood from her breasts and stomach. Then she took the bottle of alcohol and poured it over the wounds, not caring when Lee clenched her jaw and hissed with pain. She soaked a new rag with alcohol and wiped the wounds down. Lee watched as the woman removed a needle and thread from the pouch and began to thread the needle. The woman spoke English, Lee knew, but never said a word.

As much time as she'd spent with Mr. Velasquez, as close as she'd grown to him, she had never been in his home. It felt strange to be here now; how normal everything looked, how much smaller than the man she'd grown to revere. She heard something behind her and turned to see Angela, the daughter, staring at her from the doorway. Vasco Jr. and Tino had left the TV and stood behind her. When Lee met their eyes, they turned away and returned to the living room. Lee had held the boys in her lap not so long ago, reading with them and playing games. They were shy now, like strangers again.

Angela came into the kitchen and sat across from Lee and watched as her mother took the needle and pulled it through the gash on Lee's arm, then circled it through and did it again, and again. Lee closed her eyes and tried not to scream, or cry, or emit anything more than a low hum, which came through her clamped teeth no matter how hard she tried to keep silent. Halfway through, Mrs. Velasquez offered Lee a bottle of whiskey to drink, but Lee refused, smiling thinly her gratitude. Mrs. Velasquez returned to her task without smiling back. The woman had done this before, Lee could tell. Maybe she was a nurse, like Lee's mom, or maybe this was simply a task she'd had to do before. Lee wondered how much the woman knew about Lee's role in her husband's death, whether she blamed her.

"Where is the father?" the woman asked.

Lee stared down at her belly. "Dead," she said. She felt the woman's eyes on hers and looked up. "He was just a boy, not much older than me."

"You loved him?"

Lee nodded. She knew that was true, whoever Tomi was.

The woman didn't say anything more. When she was finished, Mrs. Velasquez put away her needle and thread and capped the alcohol bottle and wrapped Lee's arm in clean white gauze and over that a brown elastic bandage that she fastened with two clasps. She examined her work, testing the bandage and running a finger along the stitches of Lee's cheek. Satisfied, she indicated for Lee to stand and follow her. Lee did, into the bathroom, where the woman had already had the bath full. A folded striped towel was on the toilet seat. She shut the door behind her and left Lee in the room, and Lee took off her shoes with some difficulty, her arm already stiffening, then stripped off her remaining clothes and stepped into the bath. She lay soaking there, her bandaged arm hanging off the side, until the water grew lukewarm, falling asleep briefly, then jolting back awake.

Lee got out of the water and dried herself carefully. The woman had put a clean shirt beneath the towel, a white, short-sleeved man's shirt. She recognized it as one of Mr. Velasquez's. She pulled it on. There was also an improvised sling made from a torn T-shirt, and Lee put this on as well. The throbbing in her arm had subsided a bit. She went to the mirror to take herself in. A bit of fullness had come back into her face and arms, and her hips had even widened a bit. The light rise of her belly pushed her back forward, giving her body the curve of an ocean swell. She gave her eyes one more long look, examining the cracked green icicles of her irises. The whites were bloodshot, but otherwise her eyes looked okay. Lee thought about the drug she had ingested, and her mind went to her baby, and for the first time it came to her not as a flapping tendriled parasite but as a perfect little human form.

When she returned to the kitchen, she found that Mrs. Velasquez had left a plate of food for her on the table, beans and tortillas and pulled pork, and Lee ate gingerly, balancing her hunger with the pain in her cheek. When she was done, she put the dishes in the sink and came into the living room. The woman was gone and the children were gone and the house was silent. Mrs. Velasquez had left a pile of blankets on the arm of the couch, and Lee knew it was an invitation to stay the night at least, and a small part of her broke inside at the kindness of it. But she'd allowed others to take care of her for too long.

The streets were quiet but beginning to populate in the early New Year's morning. Lee kept her face down as she pedaled. When she got to the museum, she circled around, then left the bike against a tree and walked to the back. It took all her strength to pull the grate up with just one arm. Once she had lowered herself down, Lee didn't have the strength to pull it back, so she left it there and descended. Moving through the bowels of the museum again was slower with her arm in a sling, but she pulled herself through the dark tunnel an inch at a time, allowing herself to rest when she needed to. Every time she did, it became more difficult to get moving again. She wanted so much to sleep, to drop right there and let the blackness take her. She'd formulated the plan on the ride from the Silo. Life meant so little to these men. But what did mean something—everything—to them was Duchamp's last work. Destroying the thing would erase everything they believed in. And every time she stopped and felt her fatigue begin to drag her down, her rage would flow in and take over.

In this way she finally made it through the maze of drainage tunnels and up the ladder into the subbasement of the museum. Again she stood amid the centuries-old sculptures and paintings and artifacts. She walked through a gauntlet of statues, looking up to the faces of men whose memories had been idealized in stone, whose histories had been turned into *aura*. It was nothing; Lee felt nothing. Their eyes were dead; they stared unblinking.

The ladder was still where she and Tomi had left it. Lee climbed it awkwardly, then with some difficulty managed to pull herself into the ventilation shaft. At the end, where the shaft opened up into the next room, she grabbed hold of the water pipe running along the ceiling and hung there a moment before dropping to the floor. She landed awkwardly, favoring one leg and biting into her cheek.

Lee let the coppery taste of blood slew around in her mouth before pushing to her feet. She felt around until she located the light switch. It all looked so commonplace now, like just another storage room. The big desk full of papers and open books, an old black vinyl typewriter cover lying flat like a deflated balloon. The stuffed bookshelves, the dusty old machines and lab equipment. Lee heard something from the other side of the door and moved close to listen. It was a single voice, too low and papery for her to make out the words.

She had nothing to use as a weapon. What had she been planning to do, barge in and hope they would just stand by and let her destroy everything they'd worked for? She might be able to get to the door of the room before they heard her, but what if she couldn't? Lee picked up an antique beaker and hefted its weight in her hand, but then she put it back.

On the other side of the room was *The Large Glass* replica, hanging by hinges on the wall. All the parts that Duchamp had planned to put in but hadn't were here, in place: The Spiral. The Boxing Match. The Juggler of Gravity. Lee tried to imagine the whole system in motion, the Bride all hopped up on love gasoline, dreaming her erotic dreams and calling down to her Bachelors in her singular, inscrutable language. The Bachelors below, that band of slapstick buffoons, bunch of cartoon wolves with lusty pop-out eyes farting out their gases and shooting their jiz up at the Bride in futile hope of winning her attention. Of undressing her.

Lee mapped out the lattice of cracks on the glass until she saw a piece that approximated what she wanted. She took out her lockpick set and began scraping one of the finest picks back and forth along the crack, trying to wedge the pick in and pry the piece out. But she couldn't get the pick in at all. She put the set away. Fuck it. She grabbed one end of *The Large Glass* panel and swung it carefully until it was flush with the wall. She hefted its weight in her arm and gave a few practice swings before heaving it forward with all her strength. The panel swung in a broad arc, then hit the wall with a crash and exploded in shards of glass that came raining across the room. The voice from the other room stopped. Lee scanned the space until she spotted it lying on the table: a thin, evil-looking shard about a foot long, a bit of the Bride still attached. She picked it up and slipped it into her sleeve, turning just as a man stumbled into the room.

He stopped just inside the doorway, stood gaping at her. Lee recognized him immediately. He was dressed in the same old butler's uniform he'd worn the day he had followed her and taken her picture, almost a year and a half ago.

He came up to her, more curiosity in his face than malice, and put his hand out. She resisted the impulse to slice it open and let him take her down the hallway. More of the nine would be here, though Lee didn't know how many. As they passed the door in the middle of the hall, the one she'd peeked into before, Lee eased the shard into her palm. If she could stab the man through the neck, she might have enough time to get into that room and destroy the thing inside. But then the man slowed and put an arm around her, gently easing her in front of him. Lee slipped the shard back. Through the open doorway at the end of the hallway, she could see a figure in a chair, sitting at a table in the room beyond.

As she got closer, Lee could see that he was in a wheelchair, antique and made of lacquered wood gone golden with age. The wheels were cracked red rubber. He looked a thousand years old, his withered skin covered in spots.

"Come in, my girl." He wore a dark vestment of thick wool, with a line of buttons that ran up to the collar, tight around the fold of his neck. He was thin, his skin stretched across his bones. He held a brown cigarette in a short lacquer holder between two fingers. "My name is Richard Corless," he said. "I've waited to meet you for a long time."

The room had a long wooden table at its center and eight chairs around it. Dark wood molding ran along the baseboards, and the walls not covered in tapestries had high shelves filled with books.

The Priest offered Lee a seat. She remained standing. "We were just discussing your whereabouts," he said. "You've left quite a mess behind. But now here you are, without either of us lifting a finger. Are we just so lucky?"

The other man stood about awkwardly, not really knowing what to do with himself.

"Does he always stare like that?" she said.

"You'll have to forgive Jonathan. It isn't every day he comes face to face with . . . well. Your presence is electric for him."

"He's dead, you know. Your Undertaker. I killed him." Lee looked for a reaction but got none.

"We had our differences, he and I. And he became a mad dog in the end. Someone had to put him down; I find it fitting that it was you. But I am truly sorry he won't be here to witness the fruition of our efforts together."

Lee visualized slicing the glass shard across the wattle of his neck. "What differences?"

"Philosophical, mainly. But in this case philosophical differences are everything."

The Priest was on the other side of the table now, his man standing just behind him. She thought of driving the shard through his larynx, imagined how his dying coughs would sound. She looked past him to a framed photo on the wall, a mannish-looking middle-aged woman holding a stole delicately around her neck, her head covered by an elaborately decorated hat, her mascaraed eyes staring obscurely back at Lee. She looked like someone Lee recognized, though Lee couldn't place her.

"Sit, please. We have much to talk about. I'm sure there is a lot you want to know."

Lee took a seat at the table across from him.

"It's important that you understand everything, so allow me to begin with a bit of context.

"History is full of visionaries. Some were engineers, others scientists. Some were artists, others simply great thinkers. A very select few were all of these. We see Leonardo da Vinci as one of these few. Da Vinci was not only an artist but a great inventor. He made detailed designs of devices that he knew could not be realized with the technologies of his time—the airplane, the machine gun, the diving suit, the armored tank, the automobile. He was so far ahead of his time that his visions would not be fulfilled for hundreds of years after his death. Duchamp was such a visionary. But his visions were conceptual, theoretical—we barely have the vocabulary to conceive of them, even now, much less the technology to realize them.

"Duchamp was not fully recognized until long after the world had thought he'd stopped making art, ostensibly to dedicate his life to chess, a constantly moving system of complex hypothetical geometries. But to think that he stopped his investigations to pursue what is ultimately little more than a game is absurd. He published a weekly chess column, competed in tournaments around the world. But this was only cover and diversion. Chess appealed to his nature. He was a player who always preferred the beautiful play to the winning one. But it was not his real interest.

"No, what he had been doing this entire time was research. For twenty years he dedicated himself to research for his final work."

As the Priest went on, nearly lost in himself, Lee wondered if she could bridge the distance between them before the other man could stop her.

"Duchamp made a blueprint of his vision early on. He called it *The Bride Stripped Bare by Her Bachelors, Even*. But he understood he simply did not have the knowledge to realize the promise of that blueprint. And so he decided to teach himself. He spent a lot of time in libraries in New York and in Washington, D.C. And he kept up correspondence with certain luminaries in their fields—Heisenberg,

Max Born, Max Planck in physics, but mystics, too: Gurdjieff and Ouspensky. Even Aleister Crowley for a brief period, until he decided that Crowley was only a flimflam man.

"Around 1945 he felt that he was nearly ready to begin. So he sent his great friend Walter Arensberg, the man who had most of Duchamp's major works in his collection and the only man Duchamp trusted, into negotiations with the directors of the major art museums around the country. The Chicago Art Institute, the University of California, the Museum of Modern Art in New York, and many others were vying to house Duchamp's oeuvre. But it was the Philadelphia Museum of Art that intrigued Duchamp the most. Because what Duchamp was after was not simply a space to house his works."

The Priest smiled, and it was like watching a fish twitch. "In 1947 I was an assistant to Fiske Kimball, the director of the PMA. I was just out of college. An internship, you would call it today, though I received a small stipend. As a very young man I was essentially invisible, helping Mr. Kimball with such duties as cataloguing exhibitions and seeking out the locations of various works. And I remember meeting Mr. Duchamp briefly on several occasions."

Lee couldn't help herself. "What was he like?"

"The best way to describe him is to say he had a quiet luminosity. Duchamp was a gracious man, unfailingly polite, and he had a way about him that would put you at ease immediately. Even a young man of no consequence, such as myself. I was not allowed to be present during the negotiations, though I was once called in to bring Mr. Duchamp coffee, and I remember he stopped what he was saying to look me in the eye and thank me."

The man paused, as though in reverie, and Lee pitied him for a moment—how lost he looked in his devotion. Then she wondered what it would feel like to stab his eyes out.

"Needless to say, Mr. Kimball acquired the collection, and many of my duties over the next few years involved cataloguing it and maintaining a correspondence with Mr. Arensberg. I always wondered how Mr. Kimball had been able to beat those other museums out. Initially I thought it had to do with his personality. Mr. Kimball was a quiet man, but his reputation was so solid that I watched people hand over priceless collections with the ease of someone loaning out their car. But in 1955, after Mr. Kimball had passed, I was going through his papers, and I discovered something that told a different story."

The other man kept his place beside the Priest, staring across the table down at Lee. He didn't look too quick, but he was big, and Lee stood no chance against him.

"Fiske Kimball was the director of the museum, but he was an architect by trade, and I happened to find some blueprints he had drawn of the subbasement of the museum. As his assistant I knew the museum well, very well. And here I saw that sometime in the late '40s, sometime after his discussions with Duchamp, he'd had a series of rooms excavated. Rooms I never even knew existed."

A kettle whistled behind her, and Lee jumped. The other man moved to a small kitchen area to turn it off.

"We are sitting in one of those rooms, of course. You see, this is what Mr. Duchamp stipulated as part of the agreement: that he be allowed a space within the museum itself, a space that none but a tiny handful of people could know about, in which he could work undisturbed. He still had his studio in New York, and he continued to work there as well, on *Étant donnés,* but he wanted to keep work on his other project separate from that. And so he commuted between the two cities a few times a week by train, though more and more he stayed here. They did a very nice job on the space. A small bedroom, running water, a toilet, even a kitchen and a bathtub."

She felt the man behind her again and tensed up as he reached around and placed a cup of tea in front of her. He moved around the table and placed one in front of the Priest as well. The old man blew on his cup, then took a sip. Lee didn't touch hers.

"Look around. It's almost exactly as Duchamp left it. I've been living here for over forty years, and I haven't changed a thing. His biographers all wrote about his Spartan existence. And it was. His New York studio was nearly bare. But down here was another story. He simply had too much material to live so sparely.

"One night after the museum had closed its doors, I let myself in. *Étant donnés* wouldn't be in place for over a decade, but the room that had been built to house it had a secret door. I believe you know the way. Mr. Duchamp was here when I came down, sitting at this very table. If he was surprised by my sudden intrusion, he didn't show it. He just looked up, inhaled from his pipe, and exhaled very slowly. He gestured to his chess table, the very one you see here, then asked me if I played.

"To this day I wonder if it had all been set up. If he and Mr. Kimball had somehow laid this trail of bread crumbs for me, knowing that I would follow it, knowing that I would agree to become Mr. Duchamp's assistant. Mr. Kimball knew how loyal I was. He knew I could be trusted with such a secret." The old man stared at something behind Lee, absorbed in the memory.

"But he never did trust you with it, did he?" she asked.

His eyes refocused on her. "What was that?"

"His secret. If he had trusted you with it, you would have figured out his machine or whatever it is a long time ago," she said. "What did he need you for? To get Chinese takeout for him? Return his library books?"

He didn't answer, and she knew she had touched a nerve. If she could just get a big enough rise out of him, she might get him over to her side of the table. She pulled her hand beneath her sleeve and gripped the shard.

He stared at her for a long time, the other man looking nervous. But then the Priest laughed. "It is true. Duchamp took his secret with him to his grave. For over thirty years I tried to unravel it. I had at my disposal all his books. I had all his notes. His private journals. His correspondence. But Duchamp was nothing if not cryptic. A single line could carry layers of enfolded meaning, oftentimes contradictory meanings. A word could have three or four different interpretations: one a red herring, one a clever little private joke, one a path to illumination.

"Still, over the years I made progress, began to piece things together. Duchamp was a man of astounding intellect and vision. To his death he could grasp the most complex and abstract scientific thinking of the day, as well as understand the layered metaphors behind the esoteric arts of the past. Duchamp was a kind of scientist as well as an artist, but he was an alchemist, too. When asked for an adjective to describe his work, he once said: 'Metaphysical, if any.' His true talent lay in his ability to bridge these seemingly incompatible disciplines. For him, the artist is 'a mediumistic being who, from the labyrinth beyond time and space, seeks his way out to a clearing.' Duchamp said that himself. And I think the same could be said about you, don't you agree? Have you not found your own way, out of a maze and into this clearing? Have you not relied on some power, external to yourself and yet of yourself, to do so?"

"You led me here. You've wanted me here this whole time. Why? Who am I?"

"You are no one. And yet I can't wait to tell you who you are, because you are at the center of all of it."

"All of what?"

"Duchamp's life's work, of course. His work has influenced the landscape of art for the entire twentieth century, but what people do not understand is this: what Duchamp was working on has the potential to change the entire course of human consciousness, change our understanding of the universe in such a way as to make Einstein's theory of relativity look like simple arithmetic."

"But you aren't smart enough to figure it out. Even after decades of trying."

He laughed again, but it came out forced. She moved her arm, and the glass cut into her hand. Lee tried not to alter her expression, though she could feel herself wince.

"No. Not the science of it, anyway. I was forced to seek outside assistance. In 1999 I began trawling scientific journals, looking for a physicist with vision and promise. I put a few of Duchamp's findings into a dossier, enough to hint at the enormity of its implications but not enough to give too much away, and mailed copies out. I only got one bite." He smiled. "The man, a recent graduate of MIT named Lajos Bakó, was intrigued enough to write me back. We agreed to meet.

"I brought a sheaf of transcribed notes designed to whet his curiosity. Again, they were carefully assembled, with the intent to give him a hint of the puzzle while leaving him wanting more. I even threw in a few of the more . . . esoteric, hermetic implications, to test his openness to such data within the system. He didn't even blink. Lajos was on board immediately. I fed him notes bit by bit and watched his comprehension of the project swell to meet my own. His understanding of the science behind it was such that it took him a year to work out what it had taken me ten to realize. After that year I trusted him enough to allow him entrance into these rooms.

"We spent another year in large part holed up together down here as we went over and over Duchamp's archives. And we understood that even with the two of us together we could never achieve what Duchamp was attempting to do alone. And so was born the Société Anonyme. We recruited by word of mouth. Lajos brought in two other scientists he knew would understand the vision behind the project. I was curator of the modern wing by this time and recruited from the few people I knew who I thought could appreciate the work of a true visionary. And a few of them brought in people. In the end we had nine."

"Is that when you started playing dress-up?"

"We hadn't planned it that way. I was already in my sixties, but there was a lot of youth in our group. We had a Société; they wanted to throw parties, exhibitions. And there were nine of us, after all. It was just a coincidence, but one of them, I don't remember who, made the connection—Nine Bachelors. We were setting up an exhibition in which we were going to perform Duchamp's *Erratum Musical*, and someone said, 'Why not take on the roles?'"

"So you appointed yourself the Priest."

"We each naturally gravitated toward our true role, I suppose. I can only say that now, of course, with the benefit of hindsight."

Lee looked directly at the man beside the Priest. "Who'd want to be the Flunky?"

"Yes, well, Jonathan was the most . . . *agreeable* among us, he didn't seem to mind." He turned and gave the man an avuncular look. The Flunky looked down at the table.

"Jonathan doesn't talk?"

"Not anymore. He used to be quite articulate. A rather ingenious electrical engineer."

"What happened to him?"

The Priest shook his head sadly. "An early casualty of some unfortunate experiments in consciousness expansion. Jonathan took the drug quite willingly, but still, I always disapproved. I blame Lajos for it."

"Lajos was the Undertaker?"

"Lajos became the Undertaker, yes. It was all in good fun, of course. The sense of play in our little group was something that Duchamp would have appreciated. It was in 2004 that things began to turn in a different direction. An unsavory direction, if you ask me, but then I am an old man and my ways are set. By then technology was catching up to Duchamp's imagination, but the equipment was expensive, and we needed money to afford it. It was Josef, the Station Master, who put forth the idea. He was a friend and colleague of Lajos's from graduate school. A chemist. He showed us how we could manufacture drugs from this very location, then sell them at the events we threw. I was against it, as were several others, but we were outvoted."

"The drugs are made at the Silo. I saw the lab."

"The Silo came later, after an explosion in our lab down here—an explosion that could easily have been avoided—left me without the use of my legs. I have not always been like this. Only the past eight years."

"You lost your legs down here?"

"I lost the use of my legs, and we lost one of our own. We lost our Busboy."

"I thought DreamClown was your Busboy."

"You know more than I had given you credit for. Roland was our original. Kyle—DreamClown, as you call him—is the boy who replaced him."

"So one of you dies and you replace him. It's that easy?"

His face changed, and again Lee thought she had gotten to him. But then his expression softened, which scared her more than if he had become angry. "It is never that easy. How easy will it be to replace the father of the child inside you?"

Lee bit down on her cheek so hard she could taste her own blood once more. It took everything she had not to jump over the table.

"I'm sorry, that struck a nerve. It was uncalled for. You lash out at me, I lash back out at you. You see where it gets us? Only a wake of dead bodies. I was not behind any of that, I want you to understand. And your boyfriend, he was one of us, you know. We all grieve his loss."

"You're lying."

"Tomas was one of the original nine. He was just a lad, maybe sixteen at the time he took the role of Delivery Boy. Perhaps not the most glamorous title, but his role was integral."

"I don't believe you."

The Priest smiled tenderly at her, with pity, as he wheeled back and pulled a photograph from the wall. He slid it across the table. The photo was black-and-white: nine men costumed in the old suits and uniforms she recognized by now, arrayed on the steps of the museum. The Undertaker and the Priest stood in the front, the Undertaker looking exactly the same, as though he were ageless; but the

Priest looked much younger, though the photo couldn't have been more than ten years old. And there, in the second row, Lee recognized Tomi. He wore a too-big jacket with stripes on the sleeves and epaulets and brass buttons running up the front, and a pillbox cap. He had a leather messenger bag slung over one shoulder, and he looked like just a boy, his big brown eyes and his puffy face expansive with glee. He was the only one smiling, like he just couldn't help himself. Hermes, messenger of the gods, Lee thought to herself. The Delivery Boy. She should have known.

"He was so sincere, so naked in his intentions . . . it was hard not to believe in him. And he was nothing if not persistent, as I'm sure you are aware."

"The night we met, at the Silo, that wasn't a coincidence, was it?"

The Priest shook his head. "I sent him there. To rescue you."

Lee's mind was stumbling. She tried to recall all her interactions with Tomi in this new light, but it didn't make any sense. "Rescue me? Why?"

"The Société Anonyme had split. We no longer had the same goals, and you were at the center of those goals. In fact, you were the reason for our split. The fissures were there, even before, but it was our discovery of you that broke us completely. I saw your true role, and I feared what would happen if Lajos or Josef got ahold of you. They had both become so unpredictable. The night that Tomi brought you to the museum, he was meant to bring you to me. But then you and he, well . . . he had a moment of libidinal weakness and didn't follow through. Shortly after that we discovered a mole in our midst. We decided you would be safer if he just kept an eye on you himself."

"So he was spying on me for you the whole time."

"If it hurts any less, know that by the end we were no longer sure of his allegiances. I asked him to simply take *With Hidden Noise* from you, but he wouldn't. He dropped contact after that, and we could no longer protect him."

"You didn't protect him. You killed him because you thought he wasn't loyal."

"We did not kill him. Lajos killed him."

"It's the same thing."

"If things had gone as planned, Tomas would have brought you here months ago, and none of this ugliness would have to have happened."

Lee turned the photo over. She didn't want to look at it anymore. "What do you want with me?"

The Priest smiled thinly. "Do you believe in destiny?" he asked.

The question wasn't worth her response.

"I believe you've seen her photo, no? You must admit, the resemblance is remarkable."

"Who was she?"

The Priest held out another photo. It was her. But a different photo than the one she had first seen in the Station Master's room. In this photo she was nude, stretched out in a field of dry reeds and holding a chess piece aloft in one hand.

"Áille Trivett. Duchamp met her in the summer of 1912—one hundred years ago exactly, as it so happens—in Paris, where she was studying painting. She was a beautiful woman, her mother Irish and her father French. She was married, but over about a year they had a quiet but passionate affair. He was determined that she would leave her husband for him. But when the war broke out and her husband joined the Allied cause, she returned home to Normandy to look after the household, as was her duty. Duchamp was heartbroken. I know this because he wrote about her in a journal I found buried among his papers. And in it were two photos of Trivett: this one and the other one you saw.

"Most art historians say that Duchamp left Paris for New York because America was more receptive to his avant-garde ideas. But his journals state otherwise. He was too despondent to remain in Paris; the city had too much heartache for him. But she never left his thoughts.

And years later he tracked her down, living in Switzerland, a widow, her husband having died in the Second World War. Duchamp traveled there in 1946, but he was too late: she had passed away, had in fact taken her own life, only a week before he arrived. He stayed at a hotel and took pictures of the waterfalls nearby. They became the backdrop of *Étant donnés,* which was first conceived there. It is known that Duchamp used his girlfriend at the time as the model for the woman in the work. For the woman's body. What nobody knows is that he used Áille Trivett as the model for the woman's face. She was his Rosebud."

Lee had seen inside the room that was *Étant donnés.* She had seen the figure up close. "She has no face. It's just a headless mannequin in there."

"Yes. That is what ultimately became the work. But the original contained a likeness of her face." The Priest smiled wanly. "Duchamp left it out intentionally, a private joke of sorts. Because she had disappeared. Would you like to see it?"

The Priest turned and opened a drawer behind him. He removed an old box and laid it on the table. When he opened it, Lee saw a plaster cast of her face staring back at her.

"Uncanny, isn't it? So you see? Destiny. Do you think it coincidence that you stole *With Hidden Noise* from us? It was part of your destiny already set into motion."

"Did you know by then that the key was inside it?"

"Ah. This is where it gets interesting. Do you know what a lacuna is? A lacuna is simply a space, a missing piece. It can be a section missing from a manuscript, or a space of silence in a piece of music. Or it can be the missing piece of a puzzle. Duchamp left lacunae in his *Large Glass:* the Juggler of Gravity and the Boxing Match. The Spiral. Their absence upsets the whole composition. For many years we had overlooked *With Hidden Noise* as merely a work of whimsy. But we failed to recognize that all Duchamp's works were linked. Realizing this forced us to reexamine this piece that we had long ignored. Some of us had tried to decipher its cryptogram, to no satisfactory end. But when we took another look, in the light of the lacunae of *The Large Glass*, it suddenly became obvious. No cryptographer could have deciphered the code; in fact, his training would only have gotten in the way. Simply because there was no code to crack."

He unfolded a piece of paper and pushed it across the table. Lee stared at the too-familiar cryptogram, each block of text framed within a square box he had penciled around it.

P . G.	. ECIDES	DÉBARRASSE .
LE .	D . SERT .	F . URNIS . ENT
AS	HOW . V . R	COR . ESPONDS

. IR .	. CAR . É	LONGSEA →
F . NE,	HEA .,	. O . SQUE →
TE . U	S . ARP	BAR AIN →

"Tell me what you see."

Lee looked away. She was so tired. "A bunch of meaningless words."

"Exactly. It is our nature to try to extract meaning from the seemingly meaningless. But sometimes meaning is not found where we expect it to be. The text looks meaningless because it is. There is no sense to be made of it. What there *is* is lacunae: missing letters and missing connecting words that might make sense of the thing. Our impulse is to find the key that will crack the code that will allow us to fill in those lacunae. But what if there were no pattern or code to break? What if the entire point of it were the lacunae? Do you want to know how I figured this out?"

"No."

"Indulge me, please."

Lee said nothing, which was all he needed to go on. "I had never paid much attention to *With Hidden Noise,* until I began to realize that all of Duchamp's works are connected. That they are all pieces of a larger puzzle. And as I was going back over his entire oeuvre, it struck me that each of the two plates of *With Hidden Noise* is a square, just like a chessboard. Now look at this."

The Priest reached back and took from a shelf behind him a small box. When he opened it, there was only a yellowed sheet of paper inside, folded in quarters.

"You recognize it. I see it in your face."

It was the exhibition announcement that Duchamp had designed, with the chess problem and the falling cupid. "Tomi showed it to me."

"Did he? How curious. I hadn't shared any of this with him. I suppose he'd worked it out on his own. Such a smart boy—what a shame." He paused. "Did he explain to you what it shows? The cupid, you see, is meant to point to a pawn on the chessboard. Or at least that is what we are supposed to believe. But look at this." He centered the text from *With Hidden Noise,* then laid the cupid over it and held it up to the light. "Where is he pointing now?"

Lee stared up at it. "One of the periods."

"Exactly." He took the cupid and centered it over the second box, now holding this one up. "And now?"

Again it was pointing at one of the periods. Tomi had thought it might be pointing to some sort of map, but that wasn't really it. "The periods are the lacunae," she said.

"Exactly. And Duchamp was pointing us to them. As soon as I recognized this, I knew where Duchamp had hidden the key. Within the lacuna of *With Hidden Noise* itself: the space at the center of the ball of twine. The problem is that Lajos had embedded a mole with us, and so before I could send Tomi to retrieve *With Hidden Noise* and bring it to me, Lajos got wind of it and sent Kyle, our Busboy, to get to it first. That is how it ended up with the Station Master. But you stepped in and took it back. You tell me: how could this be coincidence? Áille Trivett was Duchamp's own lacuna, and you, her spitting image, happened to fall into possession of the thing. You see? Destiny."

"You said that there were fissures even before you saw me. What happened?"

"After the explosion, I was in the hospital, in and out of consciousness, for a week. And I wasn't released for several more weeks after that. By the time I got out, Lajos had purchased a derelict missile silo with the cash accumulated through that nasty business and moved the entire operation there. Honestly, I was glad to get it out of this space. But I could read the writing on the wall. It was the beginning of the end.

"With me sequestered down here and Lajos taking over the drug operation, running his parties, and Josef running his little bordello, they had lost sight of what was important, the reason we came together in the first place. We had always had our differences, Lajos and I. He saw things from a purely scientific angle, while I understood there is a layer of reality that cannot be explained solely through science. That there is both a physics and a metaphysics behind everything. We complemented each other, but no more. He got caught up in the mania of idolatry, all those young people throwing themselves at him, hanging on his every word. He became nothing more than another cheap cultist."

"So you were jealous because he was fucking teenage girls and you were stuck down here with nothing going on below the waist?"

Again the Priest laughed. Nothing she said was rattling him anymore. "While he spent his time with all that, I kept at it down here, unpacking Duchamp's secret one concept at a time. For over eighty years scientists have attempted to find a unified field theory, to no avail. And yet somehow a single artist, working without the benefit of any scientific equipment, found the solution to this long before it was even known to be a problem. He found the solution in alchemy."

"Duchamp wasn't a mystic," she said. She'd read enough to know that. "He said himself his work had nothing to do with alchemy."

"I'm happy to see you've done your research. But Duchamp said a lot of things, many of which are contradictory. He was always wary of anyone getting too close. Let me share with you what I know, and you tell me that he was not an alchemist at heart. Both science and

alchemy tell us that the universe is made up of a single eternal substance. In alchemy that substance is called ether. In physics it is the
God particle: the smallest, most fundamental building block of the
universe, from which all mass is formed. String theory hypothesizes
that tiny subatomic strings decide through the frequency of their vi-
brations what form that mass will take. Alchemy understands the
substance of the universe as paired opposites: light and dark, yin and
yang, male and female. *The Bride Stripped Bare* is a classic hermetic
tableau: a vertical image bisected into two planes, representing the
paired opposites of the universe. The goal of alchemy, like the goal of
the Bachelors in Duchamp's work, is to achieve a marriage of these
opposites. And the key to this, which all alchemists seek, is the philosopher's stone.

"Traditionally the philosopher's stone was thought to be a substance capable of turning base metals into gold. But I knew that
Duchamp would never have interpreted the Holy Grail of the alchemists in such a pedestrian manner. To him, alchemy was not a means
to wealth and power; it was a way to bring together the physicality of
science with the metaphysicality of human consciousness. And I came
to understand something quite profound. No one considered that
the philosopher's stone might be not of nature but man-made. A device. It was as though a light had turned on within me: perhaps Duchamp was not *looking for* the philosopher's stone at all but *building*
it. Putting it together piece by piece. His life's work, his final work,
which everything he did was working toward. In the end Lajos saw
only gold in it. But it is about much more than money. Duchamp
said: 'Art is an outlet toward regions which are not ruled by time and
space.' I suspect that the realization of his final work might in fact
alter the very fabric of space-time."

Lee remembered when Tomi had given her that same quote.
Later she had looked it up, on her own. Duchamp had been talking
about art being the only expression that allows man to go beyond an
animal state, to be an individual. It had nothing to do with the

theory of relativity. Lee had thought the Undertaker was mad, but at least he believed in something real. She thought about the books in the other room, on cryogenics and neural mapping. Immortality.

"The Undertaker was after money. You're just a frail old man afraid to die."

"This is not about living or dying. This is about transcendence. The entirety of a man's consciousness lives up here," he said, pointing to his head. "Where the body goes, it goes. When he dies, all his memories, his dreams, his hidden desires go, too. Is that fair? If you could find a way to change the laws of that, wouldn't you?"

"Even if Duchamp's machine did prove something, you'll be dead before you can see any of it realized."

"It won't take as long as you think. In any case, I'll wait as long as it takes—there have been great advances in cryonics over the past few years. It took forty years to get from the birth of quantum theory to the first atomic bomb. With the hyperspeed of current technology, who knows how quickly we can pluck the fruits of string theory?"

"You want to make a copy of yourself. But where will you put it? In some hard drive? You'll be as trapped as you are down here."

He smiled at her. "Alchemy is about marriage. The Bride, don't you see? Not coincidence; destiny. You and I will be united in the most beautiful way imaginable."

She understood then. The Thrumm kids. They'd been vacuumed out. They were vessels, emptied of consciousness and waiting to be filled. And he had chosen her as his vessel. They would vacuum her out, too; the Priest would freeze himself, they would map out the neural pathways of his brain, then one day, when it was all ready, they would just pour him into her like water into a jar. "You're worse than any of them," she told him.

"None of them could see as far as I. Lajos, Josef—they never envisioned any of this. All they could see was money. They didn't even know why you had come to us. They only knew that you looked like her and that you must be significant, but they had no idea how."

"Did Tomi know about this?"

"Tomas was too open, too trusting, and thus not to be trusted with certain information. He was always loyal but wasn't privy to all our goals. Tomas was more interested in the art of it, anyway. Now, I believe you have something for me."

Lee tightened her grip on the glass shard, though it cut into the soft flesh of her palm. She got up and came to stand beside him. As she took the little ball from her pocket, his eyes grew wet. When he reached for it, she would grab his wrist with one hand, and with the other she would slice his throat from ear to ear. But he made no move to take it.

"The key was under my nose the entire time," he said. "It pains me to think of how many years I wasted because I simply was not clever enough to figure it out."

Lee held the little ball out. "Take it. I don't want it anymore."

The Priest wouldn't look at it. "Lajos sent an assassin after me, you know. After all these years. His ego simply got the better of him. Would you like to see him?"

The Flunky dragged from the corner a battered leather steamer trunk, its corners tacked with brass plates, sides marked with peeling stickers from old hotels in Paris, Tangiers, Amsterdam, San Sebastián. He clicked open the locks, then opened the trunk and stepped back. She recognized DreamClown by his hair and by his glasses, which were turned around and sat at a grotesque angle on the side of his head. He wore the Busboy uniform and had been folded into the box like some magician's assistant. She couldn't tell how he had been killed.

"I never wanted all this death. But now it's over. We have come to the end. So why don't you give me that blade. Before it cuts you any further."

Lee didn't even try. She had nothing left. She just let the shard drop to the floor, where it broke to pieces. Blood dripped from her sleeve in a constellation of red drops. The Priest removed a handkerchief from his pocket and offered it to her. It was old, brittle, initialed "MD" in plain script. She closed her bloody hand around it. Then she opened her other hand and let the little ball roll across the table.

The Priest watched it come to a stop just in front of him. He stared down at the thing, one hand hovering over it, as though to touch it would make it disappear. Then his hand just dropped down and plucked it up, like a bird snatching something from the ground. He held it to just past the tip of his nose, and turned it in his fingers. "Have you examined it?" he said.

She'd turned it over in her own fingers countless times, following the paths of its ridges with her eyes. They seemed to fold in on themselves endlessly. But she just shrugged her indifference.

"It must be the most complex key known to man: impossible to reproduce, made for a lock impossible to pick. A masterwork of complexity." Then it was gone, disappeared into the man's fist. He pushed himself away from the table.

The Priest offered Lee his hand. She ignored it but followed as the Flunky wheeled the Priest out of the room. When they got to the door in the hallway, the old man removed an old iron key from his neck and handed it to the Flunky. The lock clicked loudly, and the door opened into a darkened space. As she stood outside beside the Priest, the Flunky went in and began lighting candles set around the room's walls, eventually illuminating a large circular room, its chalky walls blackened by smoke. Works she recognized now as Duchamp readymades stood on small pedestals between the candles: a urinal, a bicycle wheel, an old snow shovel, a bottle rack. There were others, too, obscured by the room's centerpiece. A large humidifier hummed in the corner.

At the center-rear, half shrouded in shadow, stood a contraption at once sculptural and mechanical, which Lee recognized and yet did not. The whole thing stood on a steel platform about ten feet on each side.

The Bride and her elements hovered in the air five feet off the ground. Then Lee noticed the filaments, so thin she could hardly see them, attached to the ceiling. The Bride was made from hammered metal, copper maybe, and she looked even more insectoid in three dimensions than she did in *The Large Glass*. She seemed at once indifferent and seductive, innocent and commanding, from her vantage above Lee, above the Priest and the Flunky, above the Nine Bachelors who huddled beneath her in a claustrophobic circle. They, too, were hammered from metal, ruddier than the Bride, and Lee could tell they were hollow inside, empty molds. Beside them and slightly in front was the contraption known as the Glider, a frame of soldered metal strips, and inside that the Water Wheel, made of metal and carved wood. Beside that an enormous Chocolate Grinder squatted on three short legs, the Scissors contraption attached to its top and connected by filaments to the Glider on one side and the Oculist Eyewitnesses on the other, their three circular eye charts hovering in the air like B-movie UFOs. Behind the Chocolate Grinder a series of funneled Sieves arced in the air and ended in a spiral corkscrew that wound its way up, fluke-like, through the Eyewitnesses.

There was even the Boxing Match, a complicated extradimensional geometry of tiny gears and arcing planes placed just above the Eyewitnesses, and above that the Juggler of Gravity, which looked alien and biomechanical, like a blown-up photo of a virus Lee remembered from biology class. And hovering above it all, above the Juggler and above the Bride, so light and ethereal it looked projected instead of real, the cloudlike apparition of the Bride's Cinematic Blossoming.

It all just waited there, inert yet on the brink of living.

"It is something to behold, is it not?" The Priest was right there beside her, and she jumped a little, having imagined herself, for a brief moment, to be alone. She felt his hand touch the elbow of her injured arm, and she didn't move away. "All the years I served him, he never let me enter this room. And I honored that until the day of his death. He passed in France, and I went to his funeral, of course, and it shames me to say that while I was there I found the key among his possessions. I was like you are now, the first time I laid eyes on it: speechless in my awe.

"Duchamp thought of a work of art as a 'delay.' The concept holds within it the idea of time, the fourth dimension. But what you see in front of you has the potential to show us many more dimensions than that, enfolded realities that we have never before had access to."

She couldn't take her eyes off it.

"Duchamp once said that 'the great artist of tomorrow cannot be seen, should not be seen, and should go underground,'" the Priest said.

Tomi had given her that quote when they'd first met. The idea of being underground had appealed to her at the time. It no longer did.

"I had always interpreted that to mean that true art is made outside the influence of fame or ambition. But perhaps it is more than this. Duchamp believed that the observer of a work of art had an influence on it, that the act of observing a work of art forever changes that work. He said, 'The poor *Mona Lisa* is gone, because no matter how wonderful her smile might be, it's been looked at so much that the smile has disappeared.'" Lee could not tell if the man's own smile was meant to emphasize this point, but it was grotesque, all dirty teeth and stretched lips. "Duchamp kept this final work here, quite literally underground, in no small part because he knew that the more people who saw it, the more its essential nature would change. Try to take in the importance of this moment. I know you feel it. I can see it in your eyes."

"Its aura," Lee said, not meaning to. But he was right, she did feel it. Perhaps this was the feeling that Tomi had been trying to get her experience.

He looked at her, surprised. "Aura. Yes, that's it exactly."

She hated that she thought it was beautiful; she hated that she could feel its aura. But she knew that Tomi would have felt its aura, too. The Priest nodded to the Flunky, who left the room and returned a moment later carrying a beaker of viscous red liquid. The man approached the apparatus and poured a measure through a small funnel and into a small opening in one side of the Bride.

"It took Josef years to deduce the chemistry of her love gasoline," the Priest said.

A thick power cord ran from beneath the platform to an outlet. At the far corner of the platform was a single switch. The Flunky bent down, hesitated, and then, with the Priest's silent assent, turned it on.

Nothing happened, not exactly; nothing lit up or whirred or clicked to sudden readiness. But, slowly, something began to hum from inside, gears began to whir and lightly plunk, as though it were gradually awakening.

Lee looked at the Priest, at the Flunky. Their faces carried the naked expectation of children at a puppet show. Everything before this had been anticipation of this moment. Everything after would be determined by it.

The Priest still had his hand on her arm, which she realized only when he took it away. He took her other hand. His fingers felt papery and dry. He placed the little object in her palm. "Please," he said. "Do the honor."

"Do what honor?"

"The key, of course. You're to place it in the lock."

"Me?"

"I think it's only appropriate. Don't you?"

Lee stared down at the humming machine. There was a small slit, widening at the center to an oval hole about the size of a fig, in the steel base of the machine. The welding path that puckered around its edges had been finished to a smooth, swelled ridge. Red drops began to form around the ridge, like bits of dew, fattening until they flowed down the side of the machine. The Priest took her hand in his and guided it toward the hole. He placed her fingers just above it and waited. As she pushed the little ball into the hole, a single drop of red fluid touched it and seeped into its folds. She let go, and the ball disappeared into the machine.

She heard a low whir, followed by a click. Nothing happened for several seconds. Then the Cinematic Blossoming floating above the Bride shimmered in the air, rippling like fronds of kelp underwater. The sounds began as a subterranean pulse, as though Lee were standing inside a tree carrying thousands of insects, but there was something else, an even deeper undercurrent of low moaning that permeated it all. All of it was coming from the Cinematic Blossoming, which was undulating now like some enormous larval thing. Lee felt something happening—millions of tiny strings vibrating inside her, their frequency conforming to that of this strange machine.

She looked at the Priest. He sat staring up at it, his eyes moist and his tongue swishing around against his cheek. His Flunky was breathing hard, nearly hyperventilating in his excitement.

And then, near the base of the machine, the Bachelors began to move. One at a time, they trembled and jerked. Above them, the Bride on her filament thread began to move as well, as though an engine was starting—pistons firing, slowly at first, then faster, her gears and arms rocking her body back and forth in the air. As she got moving, the Bachelors below grew increasingly agitated, popping and bouncing off one another in a twitchy dance.

The insectlike part of the Bride's lower regions uncurled itself, the spindly legs unfolding from the body and opening up a constellation of holes along her underside. And then she was raining down on them, her love gasoline saturating the Bachelors and sending them into paroxysms of desire.

The Bachelors began to heat up, turning bright red and expanding visibly. And as they did, they emitted a gas; glowing neon red and with a chemical odor of synthetic hibiscus, it seeped out and was caught in the network of Capillary Tubes that ran from their heads. The gas traveled up the tubes, slowly, pushed on only by its own delicate expansion, and as it did, the Water Wheel cranked into motion, spinning forward slowly, and then the Glider surrounding it began to rock back and forth, slowly too at first, then faster and faster until it was rocking and shaking the entire machine.

Each time the Glider rocked forward, the Scissors attached to it opened and closed and the great Chocolate Grinder beneath churned. By the time the gas had reached the end of the Capillary Tubes, funneling into a single spout, the machine was shaking so much Lee thought it might fall apart. The Priest and the Flunky were sweating now in their anticipation, the Priest licking from his lips the tears that streamed down his face. He had the look of someone gazing upon the face of God.

As the gas coalesced and exited the Capillary Tubes, it got funneled through the Sieves, which arced above the Chocolate Grinder and transformed the gas into a cloudy, viscous liquid; from there it was pumped through a small, butterfly-like device into the Spiral. Lee watched it rush through the Spiral, up, up, through the three eyes of the Eyewitnesses, past the slicing blades of the Scissors, which cut and dispersed it as drops, through the extradimensional geometry of the Boxing Match, and up into the Bride's domain, to the Juggler of Gravity.

The Juggler, a frantic, rattling contraption on spindly grasshopper legs, took hold of each separate drop of fluid and hurled it up in the air, toward the three open windows inside the cloud of the Cinematic Blossoming. But the undulating cloud seemed to elude each of the shots, as a matador might elude a bull, until the ninth and last shot missed its mark and dissipated into the air. And with that the insect hum of the machine began to diminish and the Bachelors, their frenzy now a dance without a partner, began to slow down, until they just kind of toppled onto one another in a broken heap.

In a minute the machine sat still, steam hissing from its undercarriage, the Bride spasming lightly in the air. And then Lee saw something she wasn't sure she was seeing at first. It seemed like an illusion, like a trick of the air, but gained in clarity until she was certain of it: within each of the Cinematic Blossoming's three windows an image was forming—fuzzy sparks of colored static initially that began to take clearer shape. Three holograms, hovering in the air in three dimensions. Or was it four dimensions, or six? Or eleven? In any case they were there, and Lee recognized them, she had seen them before: they were close-up sections from *Étant donnés:* one the upheld oil lamp, the next a detail between the woman's spread legs, and finally the shimmering blue-gray waterfall. Then, for a brief moment, the last image flickered, and it wasn't the waterfall she was seeing but the Paleolithic Man display at the aquarium, where she'd left Tomi's body. Another flicker, and it was back to the waterfall. It seemed impossible. Lee wondered if the Priest and the Flunky had seen it.

But they were just staring forward, their expressions showing nothing but confusion. And then the great machine cranked to life one more time and burped out, in an antiquarian cranking of gears, a small slip of paper from a thin slit in the base that Lee noticed for the first time. The Flunky stooped and plucked it out. He handed it to the Priest, who read it to himself.

"What is it?" Lee asked. "What does it say?"

The Priest looked flummoxed. *"'Le hasard est une pute qui butine de maquereau en maquereau.'"* He looked as though he was working something out in his head.

"What does that mean?" She couldn't help it, but she needed to know. How could all of it be contained on a slip of paper the size of a fortune cookie?

"It's French. Translated it means . . . something like 'Chance is a whore who flits from pimp to pimp.'"

"What?"

A dark cloud seemed to have settled over the Priest, and his face went from perplexed to angry. "It means chance is a fickle bitch."

Lee heard the words but still couldn't make sense of them. "I don't understand."

"Don't you get it, you little dullard? A joke. He was just having a laugh." His face seemed to collapse under the weight of this realization.

Lee looked at the two men, at their blank, voided faces. They were as shattered as the machine in front of them.

"That's it?" she said. There was nothing at first, beyond what she thought was the dull, waning hum of the machine. Was it all just a gag? Lee thought about what she knew about Duchamp. It would have been equally like him to spend his life encoding the answer to the cosmos behind a cryptic puzzle as it would to do the same with a cheap joke. But she had seen something in there, something they hadn't. Or had she?

Then she realized that the hum was coming not from the machine but from within her, from that hollow center she used to burrow into sometimes. The anger welled up from that spot, slowly at first, then more and more until rage was all there was. "You wanted to know what you have no business knowing, to control what you can't control. And you killed for it. Tomi, Mr. Velasquez, Derrick, DreamClown. Those poor, hollowed-out kids. All in the name of this carnival attraction?" Lee was shaking. "You say you just wanted to know the universe. Well, the universe could give a shit about you. It looks right through you. Was it worth it, now that you know that all of this was just a man amusing himself? Would it have been worth it if you were right? You pathetic old man. Duchamp laughed at people like you, people who see only what they want to see in everything."

The Priest did not take his eyes from the flickering hologram, as though the answers he sought were still to be had there. The Flunky stood beside him, staring down at the ground. They weren't listening to her. Lee saw herself lifting the snow shovel from the wall and slashing it across the wattle of the Priest's neck. But the image gave her no satisfaction.

Lee left them there. They made no move to stop her. She was no longer shaking, and the anger had retreated back to a dull hum. In the lab she climbed to the trapdoor. She came out through the tableau of *Étant donnés,* the same way she and Tomi had climbed out those months before, not bothering to step gingerly this time, and she brushed against one of the mannequin's fingers as she walked past, breaking it. When she came out the door, several people gawked at the petite, bandaged girl exiting the artwork, but no one said a thing; thinking, perhaps, that this was all just another part of the show. She exited the museum into the silver-hued morning and felt the air in her lungs and forced each step, knowing that if she stopped, she would collapse.

· BOOK IX ·

Portrait of a Young Woman

TWENTY-ONE

A notice to vacate had been slipped under the door. She stood for a while, holding it in her hand, knowing that it wouldn't be long before the landlord, or an agent of the landlord, came by again. She wondered whether rooms had aura, whether they contained something of their residents, something that lingered after they were gone. If it wasn't Tomi's aura she was feeling, she didn't know what it was. Lee put a hand to her belly and let herself feel sick. Not drug sick, or revulsion sick, but baby sick. She'd pushed it back and ignored it every time before, but now she let it take her over in waves of nausea. It felt good.

The place was in the same ransacked state they'd left it in, and Lee began cleaning. At some point someone would let themselves in, and Lee wanted them to find a tidy space, the way Tomi liked to keep it. It made no sense, but she couldn't help herself. She righted the dresser and refolded his clothes before putting them back in his drawers. She righted the refrigerator and emptied it of its rotting food, then scrubbed a dried pool of milk from the floor. She watered a desiccated plant on the sill above his sink. She picked up the papers strewn about the room and stacked them in a neat pile, which she put in the drawer of his desk. She returned the slashed cushions to the couch, cut sides down, and she made his bed.

When she was done, she stripped off her clothes and showered for a very long time, turning the water up as hot as she could stand and washing her hair, what there was of it, three times. She put on one of Tomi's T-shirts and pulled on a pair of his boxers and his jeans. The T-shirt wasn't clean, and she could smell him on it. Lee got into the made bed and pulled the covers up over her head.

She woke to the late afternoon sun fading across the room, wondering who would contact his family in the Czech Republic. She thought of his body, abandoned in the old aquarium on Petty Island. Lee searched the place for something with information on his parents— an address book, a letter, anything. She found nothing. There was an old laptop in the back of the closet that whoever tossed the place must have missed, but it had been wiped clean. Maybe on his USB drive?

She inserted the drive and opened it, scrolling through various folders until she found the one where most of Tomi's personal files seemed to be contained—scans of his artwork and essays he'd written for various small art journals. She opened a folder called "Pics" and lost herself for a half hour, scrolling through photos of creeps he'd made when it was all purely solo. And then she saw a folder simply titled "Lee." There was a single photo inside, and Lee hesitated before clicking on it. The photo was of her, sleeping on Tomi's bed, taken from above. She was curled into herself, wearing only her underwear and one of his T-shirts. There was such tenderness in the photo she could almost love the girl there, a stranger in the oblivion of her sleep. Lee let the image sink in, then dragged it into the trash and emptied it.

Then she found a folder labeled "Family." It was full of pictures, very old black-and-white photos of a life on a European-looking farm: a dozen people crowded around a large wood table outdoors, sharing a meal; two sisters dancing in a field; a man with a foot-propelled helicopter contraption attempting to get airborne. It looked like the kind of place Tomi imagined them going in his fantasies. There were later photos, too, in color. There was one of Tomi, he must have been about four, holding in both arms a big floppy house cat. His grin had never changed. She could see in the mirror behind him the reflection of the photographer, a stout man whose face was obscured by the flash. His father, maybe. Another photo showed Tomi outside, a few years later. It must have been Halloween, because he was dressed as a medieval knight, with a shield in one hand and a bag of candy in the other. He was grinning unabashedly and standing in front of a house; it looked like any suburban house in the United States.

There was nothing in the folder that looked like an address. She was about to shut the laptop when she caught herself and did what she should have done from the get-go: open his contacts folder. There, under Černák, she found an address. In Dubuque, Iowa. She stared at the house number, then opened the Halloween photo again. The same number was on the house, behind him. It took a moment for this new information to reconcile itself with what she thought she knew. Tomi hadn't grown up in the Czech Republic at all. He had grown up in Iowa.

Maybe it had all been a lie. Maybe only some of it. Lee realized she didn't care. There had still been truth between them, even if every detail he'd told her had been fabricated. And his parents still deserved to know. Lee dug a piece of paper out from the drawer of his desk and found a pen and sat staring at the blank page for a long time before writing, "Dear Mr. and Mrs. Černák," then sat a while longer. She couldn't imagine how to tell them of Tomi's death, how even to begin. Finally she settled on a short note, saying that Tomi had been killed while trying to protect her. That he was a good man and that they should be proud of the son they raised. She told them where his body was. She used the word "sorry" six times in five lines. She didn't mention the baby. Lee folded the letter, put it in an envelope, and licked it shut.

Something beeped from the computer. In the lower right corner the icon of the Subnet was flashing. Lee sat staring at it for a long moment before moving the mouse to it and clicking.

A chat box came up. Then:

[Teutonik23]: Bride?

Lee paused, then typed:

Who is Bride?

[Teutonik23]: Who is this?

H3rm3s. Who do you think?

[Teutonik23]: That is really you?

Of course. Who else?

[Teutonik23]: We all thought you were dead. We set up a fucking memorial to you.

Lee typed:

Why would you think I was dead?

 [Teutonik23]: Your girlfriend gave us that impression. What is going on?

Lee thought about how to proceed.

She disappeared. When did you hear from her?

[Teutonik23]: Several days ago. Why would she tell me you were dead?

Maybe because I broke up with the bitch. But I need to reach her. Do you have a way for me to contact her?

[Teutonik23]: No. But she is in danger. I need to find her, too.

What do you mean, she's in danger?

[Teutonik23]: We had an infiltrator. He was using her.

Who?

[Teutonik23]: Can we turn video on and talk?

Lee thought for a moment.

I'm not in a place I can do that right now.

There was a long pause, then,

[Teutonik23]: H3rm3s, what is the one thing you told me, that you made me promise never to repeat?

Lee tried to type something, but there was nothing to type.

[Teutonik23]: Who is this?

She thought about all the people she had trusted who had betrayed her. Her mother, Steve, Edie, Derrick, DreamClown. But Tomi? Tomi had lied to her, but he never betrayed her. He'd loved her. She had trusted him because her gut had told her to. What was her gut telling her now?

Lee clicked on the video icon. She saw her face pop up in a window on the monitor. The wound on her cheek was purple and puckered with each hard stitch. Then she saw Teutonik, there at his desk, a fat gray cat on his lap.

"What do you want?" she said.

"I thought that might be you," he said. "I was sure it was not Hermes, in any case. Hermes would never have called you a bitch. I am relieved to see you are okay. But it was not good of you to make me believe that Hermes was still alive."

"His name was Tomi. Tomas Černák."

"Did you see the memorial?"

"No."

"Look for it on the Subnet. It was a proper wake. You were missed."

"How did you find out about DreamClown?"

"That he was S.A.? We figured it out when we were scrubbing some of Hermes's more sensitive presence from the Subnet. We found some documents. I'm sorry I didn't know sooner. I was trying to help and I put you in danger. Don't worry, we will take care of him. The Subnet knows how to take care of those who cross us."

"He's already been taken care of." Lee scanned his face for some reaction.

"May I ask how?" Teutonik didn't look surprised but appeared genuinely sad.

"How do I know you aren't with them, too?"

This seemed to stump the skinny old German, who leaned back in his seat and ran his fingers through his beard. "Come back in two days," he said finally. "You will see. The Subnet takes care of its own." He waited for her to acknowledge this, then the screen went blank.

Lee had to know something for sure, so she rode her bike out to the house she never thought she'd revisit, parked it a block away, then snuck up through the back and to the rear bedroom window.

She could see Edie's sleeping form in the bed, and that was enough; she didn't need more. But as she was turning to go, she knocked over a flowerpot, and Edie sat up and saw her. Edie's eyes widened, then she blinked and kept blinking, as though she'd seen a ghost and was trying to blink it away.

Edie had put on a little weight around her cheeks, and she'd let her hair grow down to her shoulders and go its natural color, which Lee only now realized was brown. Lee thought about just walking away, but then Edie was at the window and the window was open and she was staring into Edie's green eyes. She felt that familiar tug inside, that need, and hated herself for it.

"Lee? Is it really you? Get in here," she whispered, opening the window all the way. "Wow, fuck."

Lee shook her head. "I just came to make sure you were all right."

"Me? What about you? Look at you, I didn't think it was possible but you're even skinnier. Except for your tits, holy shit, what, did you get them done? Can I feel them?"

Edie actually reached out, making Lee shrink back.

"You were the talk of the school all last year, you know. Where have you been? There were rumors flying around that you stabbed a girl in Juvie and then escaped. That is so dope."

Lee said nothing, afraid she might start crying.

"I know, I'm a fat pig, right? It's true what they say about the freshman fifteen. But fuck, college totally rules, you have no idea. You know where I am? University of Fucking Michigan. Can you believe it?"

Edie was the same old Edie, breathless in her excitement. Lee found a smile, but she could feel the sadness in it.

"You poor little bird, look at you. Where have you been staying all this time? What's your situation? Listen, I've got my own apartment in Ann Arbor. You can come live with me. We'll keep you undercover, it will be so sexy. You won't be able to go to school, of course, but other than that it will be exactly like we always talked about. I'm going back in a week. Where will you be until then? Where the hell have you been, Lee?"

Lee leaned in through the window and kissed Edie on the cheek, then she left.

Lee had noted the address weeks before. She had never seen the building, though, and when she arrived, it took a while to locate the pink corner structure, which looked more residence than medical facility. A small sign on the door said simply PHILADELPHIA WOMEN'S CLINIC, with a phone number beneath.

Lee walked around the block. She took in the meat laid out in trays in a butcher's shop, the wreaths of salami lining the wall behind the register. Someone had spray-painted two dots, one red, the other green, onto the window of a drugstore. She stared at the whimsical display of a hardware store, a little circus scene of figures made up of bits of hardware and pipe fittings. She couldn't help but think of Duchamp's Bachelors. She thought about going to a movie—there would still be time in the day when she got out, but she didn't have enough money on her. She was at the docks before she realized where she had been walking and, before she knew it, was at the end of the pier, where the little boat she knew so well was still tied up where she'd left it. Lee undid the rope from the dock and got in. She was halfway across the reach when she turned back around. She'd just make her way back to the clinic, and be done with it. It would be over.

By the time she got to the aquarium, she was muddy from where the boggy ground had sucked on her shoes, making the trip slow and treacherous. She nearly fell three times, righting herself each time with the knowledge that if she fell down into that mud, she might not have the will to drag herself back out. Lee let herself in under the bent door of the loading dock. She stopped at the Cambrian display and stared down at the little plastic seascape from which she'd plucked out the note. This is where it had all begun. Some thirteen weeks ago she had learned of the thing growing in her belly, and since that day her life had crumbled into ruins.

She didn't know how long she'd been standing there, held in the underwater dream, but she knew she was avoiding what was in the next room. If she left now, she could still make it to the clinic before it closed. Lee knew that if she didn't do it today, she wasn't going to do it. The thing would continue to grow, and her life path would fulfill its downward trajectory. She'd be a fugitive, homeless, and pregnant.

As she entered the room, she could make out his dark form on the platform of the Paleolithic Man display, where she'd left him, half covered by the horsehide blanket. She stopped, not wanting to see his face bloated or eaten away by animals and insects. Lee wanted to cry; she could feel the tears building inside her, but nothing came.

"I know you lied to me," she told him. "I know that now. But I don't care. Because I also know that you loved me. And if you want to know, I loved you, too." She paused, wondering what else to say. "I wrote your parents. I don't know what you would have wanted me to say, but I just kept telling them I was sorry. I am sorry. It was all for nothing. I took that thing for nothing, and all those people died for nothing. And you . . . you died for nothing, too. But I can't keep it. I know you wanted to, and maybe if you were around I could, but I can't do it alone. I couldn't bring it up seeing your face in it every day." She thought of the picture of Tomi as a little boy. "Your stupid smile."

Lee took a few steps forward and stopped again. Something wasn't right. His body seemed deflated, hardly a form at all. As she got close to the platform, she could see that what she'd thought was a form was only the folds of the blanket. There was nothing beneath it. Tomi's body wasn't here; it was simply gone. Lee went back to where she had held him, dying, in her arms. There had been blood, a lot of it. There was nothing now; the floor was clean. There was even a layer of dust.

Then her eye landed on a folded piece of paper, tucked beneath the blanket where Tomi's head would have been. She pulled it out and unfolded it, shining her light onto the torn notebook paper. A note written on the inside read: *"D'ailleurs, c'est toujours les autres qui meurent."*

Lee recognized the quote. It was Duchamp's epitaph, translating to something like "Anyway, it's always the others who die." Lee thought again about what the Priest had said, about Duchamp's machine altering space-time somehow. What would that look like—could it change events of the past? Her heart began to pound so hard she could feel it. She looked around for some other sign as to what had happened, but there was nothing else.

Lee looked at the paper again. There was something, a faint image, coming through. Lee shined her light through it, and there it was, a watermark: the little falling cupid she recognized from Duchamp's unsolvable chess problem. And she could see now, the cupid's arrow pointed directly at the center of the word *"D'ailleurs."* Lee stared at it until she saw the name embedded within: Áille.

For a moment she let herself imagine that Tomi was alive. That somehow he had never even died. That he was . . . what? Going about his day-to-day as though none of this had ever happened? Wandering around somewhere in a fugue, wondering who he was? She fantasized about seeking him out, finding him, taking that bus to Detroit together after all. Then she stopped herself before she could dig any deeper into this rabbit hole. The Priest was mad; the Undertaker, too. All of them were. In the end they saw only what they'd wanted to see. And now she was doing the same. This note . . . this wasn't Tomi. This was them, cleaning up after themselves. Still playing games. She looked around the empty aquarium. She was sure she was alone. But she'd been wrong before.

When Lee got back to the dock, it was late afternoon, judging by the height of the sun. She still had time to make it to the clinic. For a long time she stared at the door, until a woman came out and asked Lee if she wanted to come inside. After a moment Lee said, "I'm just waiting for someone."

The woman looked at her like she'd heard that before. She smiled. "You can wait inside, if you like. It's okay. Or if you just want someone to talk to . . ."

Lee shook her head. "That's okay. I'll just come back."

In Fishtown she found a café with Internet access and opened Tomi's laptop. She'd taken it, along with a few items of clothing and anything else she thought she could use; she knew she wouldn't be coming back. Almost immediately the Subnet logo began flashing. Lee went to an isolated corner of the café and plugged in a pair of Tomi's earbuds. She clicked on the flashing logo.

"Good afternoon, Bride," Teutonik said.

"Don't call me that."

"I have something for you. I told you the Subnet takes care of its own, and we have."

"What are you talking about?"

"Forgive me, but we did some digging and we know your situation. On August twelfth you escaped from the Queensbrook Juvenile Detention Center. Currently you are wanted for questioning in the murder of Derrick James."

"I didn't do that. I mean, I escaped that juvenile shitbox, but I didn't kill Derrick."

"The authorities think you did. Can you prove otherwise?"

Lee thought about it. "No."

"No matter. We have already begun the process: Birth certificate, passport, driver's license, social security number. High school diploma— graduated with honors? You're smart enough, why not? Valedictorian? Perhaps that is too much, I don't know. But with a clean slate, why not give it all to yourself?"

Lee didn't know what to say.

"Just come up with a history of the person you want to be— name, birth date, education, jobs . . . a foundation, something to build on. What follows will be up to you. We have some very re- sourceful people in our network. Take your time and give me the details when you're ready; we'll take care of the rest."

Lee told herself not to believe him. Trust had gotten her betrayed too many times. But she didn't regret trusting Tomi. And if the uni- verse was throwing her another betrayal, the universe could fuck itself.

Lee left the café with one more thing she needed to do. Something the Priest had said, combined with something she had seen, that had been worming around in her head, and she couldn't shut it down. She had to see for herself.

It must have been thirty-five degrees out, but she was sweating by the time she got to the Silo. The way was mostly uphill, and riding one- handed had assaulted her shoulders. She parked the bike in the woods before the first hill and made her way by foot around the back. Crime scene tape marked the perimeter, but there were no police cars to be seen. Four days had passed since the fire, and the place was deserted. Lee ducked beneath the tape surrounding the entrance. The fire had spread to the generator shack and to the dry brush, and the ground was all black ash. The brick outlet vent stacks came up through the ground, and Lee peered down one into the darkness below.

The big steel front door had on it a condemned notice from the city, warning of dangerous internal instability. She let herself in, coughing as she descended the stairs. The air smelled of old smoke and something chemical. She turned on her flashlight when she got to the bottom and headed to the central stairwell and into what had been the dance hall. The floor was sticky black tar. She opened the door in the middle of the floor and went down.

The concrete walls of the room where she'd found Annie were scorched black, all the wires and light fixtures melted. Even the steel duct housing was melted and warped and falling in places. The carpeting had melted into a thin black crust that cracked when she stepped on it. She went down two more levels, each one with more soot and more lingering smoke. When she opened the door to the Undertaker's room, she had to pull her shirt up over her face to breathe. Everything that had been wood was burned to charcoal, and shining her light through it was like looking at the wreck of a ship uncovered on the bottom of the ocean after hundreds of years. The brass fixtures were intact, as was the old iron bed frame. The wood paneling had burned away. It was just a concrete-and-rebar bunker again. Marble chess pieces lay scattered about the floor. Lee picked up a knight and blew on it. When her light washed over what used to be his bed, she saw the gun, its melted grip fusing it to the frame. Something was off about the bed, some trick of perspective that made staring at it impossible, and she sat on the ground, suddenly feeling dizzy. The place must be noxious with chemical fumes.

She went down two more floors, stepped over a collapsed vent housing, and entered the lab—or what was left of it. She couldn't imagine the temperatures that must have been reached in this room. What once was a wall of stacked plastic chemical drums had melted into a black mass on the floor, like a frozen tar pit that had half-engulfed bits of steel and glass that had fallen into it while it was still liquid. A few of the steel frames that had housed the larger machines were intact, but otherwise everything had been destroyed. All the glass jars and beakers had melted as well, pooling where they sat into igneous blobs of soot-encrusted crystal. She shined her light over the blackened concrete. The lingering chemical smell was so dense down here Lee could not stand it, but she walked to the wall on the opposite side, behind what had been the massive fan enclosure. Now the fan blades lay in a heap of twisted metal on the floor, and the enclosure itself was pretty much burned to the ground. Lee picked her way through it gingerly until she reached the far wall. She walked back to the other end carefully, measuring her paces.

She went up to the Undertaker's study. Each of the levels should be the same diameter, and yet she'd sensed when she was here before that this one was smaller than it should be. She paced the room and confirmed it. Lee turned to *The Large Glass* replica, still hanging there on the wall. It was singed, the glass warped, but otherwise intact. She ran her fingers along its sides until she found a tiny latch. She pressed and with a click the whole panel swung outward from a hinge on the other side. Lee let it swing past her, then shined her light on the wall. There, behind where the circle of Bachelors would have been, was a safe dial and a latch. Lee ran her light over the whole wall and saw now the steel door laid into the concrete.

Lee spun the dial. Mr. Velasquez had taught her rudimentary safe-cracking skills, but those applied to cheap home safes, and she wasn't sure about this one. It must have been fifty years old at least, but it looked formidable. She reached into her bag and took out the small amp she had from her burgling days. She plugged in the earbuds, then pressed the amp to the steel door and turned the dial slowly, listening for the soft click of a tumbler clicking into place. She turned the dial a full revolution, then another, and another. She heard a whisper of gears, and that was all. She just wasn't skilled enough.

Mr. Velasquez had taught her that, before even attempting to crack a safe, she should try the easier route and look in desk drawers for the combination, which was sometimes taped along the bottom. Or to try to find the birth date of the owner, always a good bet. Lee had no way of finding the birth date of the Undertaker, but maybe . . . She went back upstairs, into the control room. Everything had been blackened and smoke damaged, but the room was set apart from the burned floors below and mostly it was intact. She went to the bookshelf and pulled out a smoke-blackened biography of Duchamp. His birth date took some finding, it was buried in the text, but she finally located it. July 28, 1887. She tore out the page and brought it downstairs.

Lee spun the dial several times clockwise, stopping on the seven. Then counterclockwise, past the seven, to twenty-eight. Clockwise again to eighty-seven. She gingerly took her hand from the dial, placed it on the lever, and pulled. It swung down without a click. Nothing. It had just been a shot in the dark anyway. Then she thought of something. Europeans wrote the date in reverse, didn't they? She tried it again: clockwise to twenty-eight, counterclockwise to seven, clockwise to eighty-seven. The click of the lever was the sweetest sound she'd heard in a long time. She swung open the door and shined her light in. Inside were stacks upon stacks of brick-sized bundles of bills, the columns in back reaching nearly to the ceiling.

She picked one up, flipping through it. It was all twenties. She tore off the rubber band and counted. A thousand dollars, exactly. Then she saw another stack near the door that was all bricks of hundreds. Five thousand a brick. Lee emptied the duffel bag and stuffed bricks in instead: five thousand, then fifteen, twenty, twenty-five, thirty, as she did the math in her head.

Four years of school at forty thousand a year, plus living expenses for her and a kid. Tomi had always imagined it a girl, and that's how Lee saw the child, too. She'd be a little girl by the time Lee graduated. No more shit holes. Seventy a year times four equals two hundred eighty thousand. Lee added a bit extra for emergencies, then doubled what she had—something to leave for Mrs. Velasquez. By the time she had six hundred thousand dollars in her bag, it was bulging and so heavy she had to get under it to get it on her back. Her bad arm screamed at her. Lee took a last look. She had hardly made a dent in it; piles of cash still approached the ceiling.

She was backing out when she saw something wrapped in plastic jutting out behind one of the piles. It leaned to one side of the safe and was pushed to the back. Lee set the bag down and pulled it out. It was large and rectangular and wrapped in duct tape and Hefty bags. She tore it open and could see the edges of half a dozen frames. Lee worked two fingers under the plastic and pulled down along the front, the tear opening onto a painting of two peasants in a wheat field. Lee tore the wrapping off and looked through the paintings. They were the kind she'd seen hanging in the museum: impressionist and cubist and fauvist works that did little for her at the time and still did little for her. They seemed old and drab here under the beam of her flashlight. If they were real they were probably worth more than all the cash in the room, but that knowledge did nothing to raise her appreciation of them. A smaller painting, sandwiched between two larger ones, caught Lee's attention and she pulled it out.

It was a small study in oil of a young woman with a long face, red lips, and large black depthless eyes. They weren't the eyes of a Thrumm kid; they were just sad and inward-looking. She had wild, dark brown hair, a long neck, and skin like churned butter. The work was done in loose, expressive brushstrokes that gave a kind of impenetrable depth to its subject. It was the kind of work, Lee knew, that Duchamp would have dismissed as retinal. But she didn't care; she thought painting was beautiful. It was small enough that it fit in her bag.

Lee retouched the safe door and relatched *The Large Glass* over it. She climbed back up the stairs with difficulty, resting at each flight and trying not to breathe too much of the chemical air but nearly out of breath by the time she got to the top.

It was dusk when she reached the motel. She paid in cash, doubling the rate in lieu of an ID. In the room she dropped the bag on the floor and took a shower. When she climbed out, feeling truly clean for the first time in memory, she pulled her dirty clothes back on and took a blank piece of paper from the desk. She thought about the questions Teutonik had asked her, the new bio she was supposed to come up with. Lee supposed she should start with a name.

ACKNOWLEDGMENTS

THE people to whom I owe gratitude for helping me with this book are legion. Here are a few from the top:

I am deeply indebted to the tenacity and wisdom of my agent Julie Barer, who stuck with me way beyond the point of reason and kept making me go back at it. And to my editor, the wonderful Laura Tisdel, for her sharp eye and unforgiving bullshit detector, and for helping me realize the novel this came to be. I am not too proud to say that this book would still be an inchoate mess without the two of them behind it.

To the whole brilliant team at Viking Penguin, whose unwavering support has meant everything to me.

To Steve Dunn and the Eastern Frontier Foundation in Maine for their enormous support and inspiration. I also want to thank the Hermitage Foundation in Englewood, Florida, which allowed me the time and space to research and write a good chunk of the book.

To my ridiculously generous friends Julia and Shane Stratton for being my Philadelphia tour guides. To Oldřiška Baloušková for her wisdom on alchemy and her translation help into Czech. To Tom Bissell and D. Foy for their encouragement at the right times.

ACKNOWLEDGMENTS

To the generosity of those who slogged through early versions of this book, and whose insight helped to make it better draft by draft: Marco Morrone, Chris Hebert, Samuel Park, Jenn Stroud-Rossmann, Michelle Falkoff, Anderson Berry, Eugene Cross, Shauna Seliy, Brett Stithem, Zayd Dohrn, and Rachel DeWoskin. And to John (Marcello!) Beckman for that and so much more.

To Ellen McClure and Dr. Raquel Cross for their help translating into French and Spanish, respectively.

To Andrew Stafford, for his insights into *The Bride Stripped Bare by Her Bachelors, Even,* generally, and his thoughts on "The Boxing Match," specifically.

To Teri Boyd and Saša Hemon for love and cabbage.

And to my parents, Mitchell and Lucia Rose, for everything.

Most of all, my love and gratitude goes to my wife, Nami Mun, for persevering with me, and to our son, Auggie, for changing the way I see.

Additionally, I'd like to acknowledge the following sources in assisting with research and inspiration:

On Marcel Duchamp: *Duchamp: A Biography* (Calvin Tompkins, 1996) and *Marcel Duchamp: The Afternoon Interviews* (Calvin Tompkins, 2013); *Affectionately, Marcel: The Selected Correspondence of Marcel Duchamp* (Francis M. Naumann and Hector Obalk, eds., 2000); *The Writings of Marcel Duchamp* (Michel Sanouillet and Elmer Peterson, eds., 1989); *Marcel Duchamp, Notes* (Marcel Duchamp, 1983); *Marcel Duchamp, In the Infinitive* (Richard Hamilton and Ecke Bonk, 1999); *Duchamp in Context: Science and Technology in the* Large Glass *and Related Works* (Linda Henderson, 2005); *Alchemist of the Avant-Garde: The Case of Marcel Duchamp* (John F. Moffitt, 2003); *Marcel Duchamp: The Bachelor Stripped Bare* (Alice Goldfarb Marquis, 2002); *The Duchamp Dictionary* (Thomas Girst, 2014); *Three New York Dadas and The Blind Man: Marcel Duchamp, Henri-Pierre Roché, Beatrice Wood* (Chris Allen and Dawn Ades, eds., 2014); *Dialogues with Marcel Duchamp* (Pierre Cabanne, 1987); *Marcel Duchamp: Manual of Instructions:* Étant donnés (Philadelphia Museum of Art, 1987); *Marcel*

Duchamp: Étant donnés (Michael R. Taylor, 2009); and *Marcel Duchamp: The Box in a Valise* (Ecke Bonk, 1989). And to the Philadelphia Museum of Art, the guards at which must have wondered about the suspicious guy spending so many hours in the Duchamp Room.

On physics: *The Elegant Universe* (Brian Green, 2010); *The Holographic Universe* (Michael Talbot, 1991); *Quantum* (Manjit Kumar, 2011); and *Seven Brief Lessons on Physics* (Carlo Rovelli, 2016).

Like much of the book, the defunct Atlas missile silo turned drug lab/rave center has a basis in reality. I first read the story here: www.vice.com/read/life-is-a-cosmic-giggle-803-v18n5.

Even off the Darknet, Duchamp has a large Web presence. I encourage a lot of free exploration, but found the following Web sites especially fruitful:

For the definitive Web site on all things Duchamp, visit the Marcel Duchamp Studies Online Journal Tout-Fait: toutfait.com.

The Marcel Duchamp World Community is also worth checking out: www.marcelduchamp.net.

For a look at the 350K-word treatise on *With Hidden Noise* (yes, this actually exists!) by California State University Sacramento art department professor emeritus Kurt von Meier, "A Ball of Twine: Marcel Duchamp's 'With Hidden Noise,'" visit: www.csus.edu/in div/v/vonmeierk/noise.html.

Because Duchamp's masterpiece *The Bride Stripped Bare by Her Bachelors, Even* is meant to be, in Duchamp's words, a "delay in glass"—that is, a frozen moment in time of a system that is supposed to be imagined in motion—it can be difficult to wrap one's head around. The best and most lucid explanation I have seen of the work is on Andrew Stafford's Web site Making Sense of Marcel Duchamp, which visually demonstrates what the system would look like if viewed in motion. His Web site looks insightfully at most of Duchamp's work, but to get to the animation (and explanation) of *The Bride Stripped Bare by Her Bachelors, Even,* visit the site and scroll horizontally along the time line to 1923: www.understandingduchamp.com.